Three-times Golden Hea
Tina Beckett learned to
almost before she learned to read. Born to a
military family, she has lived in the United States,
Puerto Rico, Portugal and Brazil. In addition to
travelling, Tina loves to cuddle with her pug,
Alex, spend time with her family, and hit the
trails on her horse. Learn more about Tina
from her website, or friend her on Facebook.

Juliette Hyland began crafting heroes and
heroines in high school. She lives in Ohio, USA,
with her Prince Charming, who has patiently
listened to many rants regarding characters failing
to follow their outline. When not working on
fun and flirty happily-ever-afters, Juliette can be
found spending time with her beautiful daughters
and giant dogs, or sewing uneven stitches with her
sewing machine.

Also by Tina Beckett

Mills & Boon Medical

Las Vegas Night with Her Best Friend

Alaska Emergency Docs miniseries

Reunion with the ER Doctor

Sexy Surgeons in the City miniseries

New York Nights with Mr Right

Jet Set Docs miniseries

Second Chance in Santiago

Also by Juliette Hyland

Mills & Boon Medical

Fake Dating the Vet

Hope Hospital Surgeons miniseries

Dating His Irresistible Rival
Her Secret Baby Confession

Alaska Emergency Docs miniseries

One-Night Baby with Her Best Friend

Jet Set Docs miniseries

ER Doc's South Pole Reunion

Discover more at millsandboon.co.uk.

EXPECTING HER BEST FRIEND'S BABY

TINA BECKETT

FORBIDDEN TO THE MILLIONAIRE DOC

JULIETTE HYLAND

MILLS & BOON

All rights reserved including the right of reproduction in whole or in part in any form. This edition is published by arrangement with Harlequin Enterprises ULC.

This is a work of fiction. Names, characters, places, locations and incidents are purely fictional and bear no relationship to any real life individuals, living or dead, or to any actual places, business establishments, locations, events or incidents. Any resemblance is entirely coincidental.

Without limiting the author's and publisher's exclusive rights, any unauthorised use of this publication to train generative artificial intelligence (AI) technologies is expressly prohibited. HarperCollins also exercise their rights under Article 4(3) of the Digital Single Market Directive 2019/790 and expressly reserve this publication from the text and data mining exception.

® and TM are trademarks owned and used by the trademark owner and/or its licensee. Trademarks marked with ® are registered with the United Kingdom Patent Office and/or the Office for Harmonisation in the Internal Market and in other countries.

First published in Great Britain 2025
by Mills & Boon, an imprint of HarperCollins*Publishers* Ltd,
1 London Bridge Street, London, SE1 9GF

www.harpercollins.co.uk

HarperCollins*Publishers* Macken House, 39/40 Mayor Street Upper, Dublin 1, D01 C9W8, Ireland

Expecting Her Best Friend's Baby © 2025 Tina Beckett

Forbidden to the Millionaire Doc © 2025 Juliette Hyland

ISBN: 978-0-263-32517-1

09/25

This book contains FSC™ certified paper and other controlled sources to ensure responsible forest management.

For more information visit www.harpercollins.co.uk/green.

Printed and Bound in the UK using 100% Renewable Electricity at CPI Group (UK) Ltd, Croydon, CR0 4YY

EXPECTING HER BEST FRIEND'S BABY

TINA BECKETT

MILLS & BOON

To my family, as always!

PROLOGUE

SETH GRAHAM SLOUCHED on his couch after a harsh reminder about the fragility of life. Right before leaving the hospital, he'd gotten a call that his five-year-old patient had succumbed to a massive infection, despite multiple surgeries. All from a head-on collision that had already claimed the life of his sister and father. Seth's part of the surgery had been to repair the child's nose and a shattered orbital socket. But there had been other, more life-threatening wounds, such as puncture wounds to the abdomen from the car's metal frame, which is where the infection was thought to have originated.

He'd gone down to relay his condolences to Bradley's mom, who'd been by her son's side day and night, and found her crumpled on the floor beside his bed, two nurses crouched down beside her in an attempt to comfort her. He would never forget that sight as long as he lived. Or the way her brown eyes had stared up at him as if pleading for him to change the outcome. To bring her boy back to life. He couldn't. He'd learned that the hard way.

Switching on the television in an effort to combat the images playing in his head, he tried to shake off the memory. Except the comedy that played across the screen seemed grotesque in the face of what had happened to Bradley and his family.

He froze at a knock at the door, remote still in his hand. He turned off the TV and tossed the remote onto the side table, waiting for a second to see if whoever was at the door would move on his or her way. He hoped so. He really wasn't in the mood to entertain his next-door neighbor, who'd periodically started leaving baked goods outside his apartment. A not-so-subtle hint that she'd like to be more than just neighbors. Seth wasn't interested. He'd had his share of girlfriends over the years, but no one he'd have to see day in and day out if things went south. And they invariably did. He just couldn't commit. And he wasn't sure why.

That wasn't true. He did know why. He just had no interest in trying to dissect those reasons. Bradley's death, though, seemed to hammer home that his current life path held less possibility of heartache than the journey the boy's family was now experiencing. If he was this torn up over a child he barely knew…

The knock sounded again. And this time it was accompanied by a shaky voice. "Seth. Are you home? God, please…*please* be home."

The words had him hauling himself from his couch, not bothering to grab his shirt from the chair next to him. He recognized that voice immediately. But what he didn't recognize was the abject hopelessness he heard in her tone.

Therese was the most optimistic person he'd ever met and had always been the perfect foil for his own melancholic outlook on life.

He yanked open the door and met green eyes that that were awash with tears. And right now, there wasn't an ounce of optimism in them. "Rese, what's wrong?"

She fell against him, and between sobs, he tried to make out what she was saying but only caught bits and pieces of her words.

"…Oh God…trying to surprise him…wasn't alone."

He gripped her shoulders and gently held her at arm's length. "Slow down, honey. Tell me again."

She stared at him for a long time before her next whispered phrase emerged. "W-what's wrong with me?"

This time he understood the individual words, but not what she meant. Was she sick? She'd mentioned trying to surprise someone. Her fiancé, maybe?

"Does this have something to do with Bill?" He wasn't the man's biggest fan and he couldn't pinpoint the reason. The man was wealthy and successful and, on the surface, seemed like an all-around good guy. But there was something just a little bit oily about him. Seth had convinced himself that he was just jealous of Therese's happiness and had damned himself for it. But it was what she'd always wanted. He remembered her talking about wanting a marriage like the one her mom and dad had even when she was much younger. There had been flashes of attraction between them a couple of times, when time had stood still and he'd sensed she might want to move past friendship, but he always reminded himself that the last person he'd ever want to hurt was the woman standing in front of him. The one whose green eyes relayed a pain and devastation that made his chest ache.

She didn't say anything, but the look on her face said it all. Something had brought her to his apartment, a crushed, fragile shadow of the woman he knew. Just like his mom had been. Anger crowded out everything else in his chest. "What did he do?"

"I went to his office... I was so excited about the news that I'd been accepted for the job I'd interviewed for at Sunrise Medical Center. I start the middle of next month. You remember? I know six weeks is still a ways out, but I thought he'd be happy for me, but when I went to his office..."

She'd applied for an open position in the physical therapy department. She had asked to use him as a reference for the position. He started to congratulate her, but the words caught in his throat. That's not why she was here. Or why she was upset.

He used his words to nudge her. "You went to his office..."

"I didn't knock. I never have before. He was there." Tears now flowed down her face in a stream. "He was on his couch...w-with Darla. And they...they..."

He searched his memory banks for the name but came up empty. And it really didn't matter. Because it was clear what she meant. Bill was on his couch with this Darla person and they weren't just having a chat. And now he knew exactly why he'd never liked the man. He wasn't just oily. He was an ass.

Seth touched her face. "I'm so sorry, honey."

Her eyes closed for a long time. "What's wrong with me? Why is this happening again? First Doug, then Troy. A-and now Bill."

He knew why she was asking. Seth had taken Rese to her senior prom—after finding out her date, the drum major of the high school's marching band, had cheated on her with another clarinet player. And then a serious boyfriend she'd had in college had dumped her out of the blue, saying he wasn't ready for a long-term relationship. Except weeks later, Troy had already started dating someone else.

He tipped her chin up. "There is nothing wrong with you. You're beautiful and kind and don't deserve any of this. Don't go home tonight. Stay here. I'll help you go pack your things tomorrow."

"I… I just can't help thinking…"

"No." He leaned closer, shaking his head. "This is on him, not you."

She wrapped her arms around his neck. "Just hold me, Seth. I need to feel okay. Just need to believe that life won't always be like this."

He probably wasn't the best person to restore that belief. But as her face pressed into his neck and the warmth of her skin penetrated the chill he'd been feeling ever since leaving the hospital, his hand came up to cup the back of her head, pressing her closer. And suddenly he felt something soft touch the area just beneath his jawline. It moved a little to the side and repeated.

She was kissing him.

He swallowed hard, but where he should have been pushing her away, he couldn't force himself to. Not because he was afraid of reinforcing her feeling of not being enough, but because a roaring need had just hit him out of nowhere. Hadn't he just been looking for something to take away the heartache of today?

An internal voice warned him that this was not the way. But even as it whispered inside his head, her mouth had reached his and paused there as if waiting to gauge his reaction. Then her fingers touched the bare skin of his chest, and he shuddered, knowing exactly what was going to happen.

He leaned slightly back and stroked her silky hair back from her face. "Nothing is wrong with you, Rese. Nothing at all."

And then he kissed her with everything he had inside him, hauling her against his body and holding her tight. Consequences be damned. Because right now all he wanted was what she seemed to be dead set on offering. All he had to do was say yes.

Except he didn't need to say it, because she said it for him, the words whispered against his mouth. "Oh Seth…yes…yes…"

CHAPTER ONE

Thankfully Therese wasn't due to start at the hospital for a few more weeks. She'd needed to get her stuff out of Bill's apartment, which he'd fought, doing everything from buying her flowers to repeatedly phoning her. But she wasn't going back. She couldn't. Her trust was irrevocably broken. And she would never get the image of that woman straddling him on the couch out of her head. In the end, Seth had gone with her to clear out her things. Fortunately, once her ex heard who was coming with her, he'd thankfully vacated the place during that time frame. She'd left her key on the kitchen counter. And that was that.

Oh, how she wished it were that easy.

But it wasn't. There was what had happened with Seth the night she'd found Bill and his assistant. She'd ended up spending the night at his place, and although they'd made love with an intensity that had taken her breath away, he'd opted to sleep on the sofa afterward. He was right, but it had felt like yet another rejection. But the next morning, Therese was so glad he'd made that decision, since she didn't have to face him right away.

She'd woken up in his bed disoriented for a moment, and then horror set in at what she'd done. At how *she'd* initiated what had happened. She was sure he'd recognized her desperation and had probably felt sorry for her. That thought had cut with a humiliation she couldn't quite shake. She'd be very lucky if she hadn't ruined a lifelong friendship. But when she finally ventured out of the room and found Seth was still home, she'd tried to talk to him about it. He'd interrupted her, saying he understood that emotions had been high and that neither of them had been thinking straight. It wouldn't happen again. And the way he'd said it... it sounded like a promise. Until she could find a new place, he'd offered her the use of his bedroom. And he made it clear he would continue to sleep on the couch.

Unfortunately, after a week's search for someplace that was available immediately and at her price point, she sagged on his sofa, feeling defeated. To continue living with Seth was out of the question. It would be like flirting with fire. What was it they said? Once you broke taboo, it was easier to jump in and do it again. And again. But then she really would lose him as a friend. Because she had already proved that she did not come out a winner when it came to relationships. And she'd known Seth a long time. They'd talked about what they each wanted out of life.

She wanted a happy marriage and a family. Not Seth. He liked women. And they liked him. He'd had so many casual dates that she couldn't keep track of their faces. Including the newest face that had appeared on his doorstep yesterday, wielding a pan of what looked like muffins. She'd taken one look at Therese and turned on her heel with a sniff of disdain, taking the baked goods with her. Seth had grinned and thanked her for taking care of that little problem.

The last thing Therese wanted was to become one of those "little problems." So she would steer clear of the dark waters she'd stirred up and stick to the shallows, where there was little fear of drowning. Or of finding new heartache. Something she seemed to be good at.

Seth came through the door of the apartment and took one look at her face. "No luck?"

"No." She bit her lip. "I'm so sorry. I really am trying."

"I know you are. The housing market in our area is unreal right now." He sat down next to her. "So don't laugh at what I'm about to say."

She'd never felt less like laughing in her life. And if he offered to let her be his roommate, she wasn't sure what she was going to say. Because she couldn't. He only had one bedroom. And even sitting on the couch with him made her hyperaware that his form was stretched along its length every single night. The only alternative was to go home and live with her parents. And as much as she loved them, she wasn't sure she could do that. Her mom would coddle her once she learned what had happened with Bill, and without trying, she would end up making her feel worse than she already did. Her dad would go storming over to Bill's office and do or say something he shouldn't. And she certainly didn't want either of her parents to guess what had happened between her and Seth.

"I can assure you, I won't."

"It's not ideal, but I have a travel trailer parked at a nice RV park. You can stay there until you find a place.

There would be no hurry that way, and you could find something that really suited you."

She'd never thought about looking at something like that. But she could see how it might be ideal. At least for now. She didn't have any furniture to speak of. "Are you sure? Don't you use it?"

"Occasionally when I want to get away for a weekend, but I haven't used it in a month or two, and it would be much better to have someone in it than for it to sit unused."

How to answer without sounding absolutely desperate and relieved. "I would want to pay rent."

He looked like he was going to say no, until she gave him "the look." The one that warned him to take care with whatever was about to come out of his mouth. "We can talk about that once you've seen it. You might want to run in the other direction."

She blinked. Was it some sort of decrepit metal box? Surely not. Seth liked his comfort, and he liked his toys, such as the sailboat that he'd taken her out on a time or two. "I doubt that. How far is it from the hospital?"

If it was a two-hour drive, she didn't see how that would work either.

"About fifteen minutes...unless it's the height of rush hour. Then it can take a half hour or a little longer."

That wasn't too bad. "Will the RV park let you sublet to someone else?"

He nodded. "But I'd rather not write up any kind of formal agreement. You'd just be there as my guest. Otherwise you'd have to get approval from the park owners, which will include a credit check. And all that will take time."

The credit check didn't matter much, but he was right. She didn't see it being a long-term housing solution, so being his "guest" might be the best answer. And it sounded like he was ready to have his apartment to himself again.

To entertain the muffin lady? No, he hadn't seemed interested in pursuing her. Seth only dated women who knew the score.

He pulled out his phone. "I have pictures of it, if you want to look."

"It's okay, Seth. The other choice is to go back home, and I'd rather not do that unless I have to. I've come to value my independence. So if you're sure, I'll take it. Tonight, if possible."

"Tonight it is."

Six weeks later, she woke up in the most comfortable bed she'd ever slept in, still stunned by what he'd called a travel trailer. Well…it was in the sense that it could be moved elsewhere if he ever wanted it to be. But why would he? The place was immaculate and comfortable, and the RV park was just as welcoming, boasting amenities that ranged from a pool to a Laundromat and a clubhouse. It was also just a ten-minute walk to one of the nearby beaches. She found herself there most days, biding her time until she started her new job. Her old hospital had let her use her weeks of accumulated personal days in lieu of working out her notice. So she was at a loose end.

She could see why he liked coming here. If it were her, she would be here every chance she got. Wandering down the hallway to a good-sized bathroom, she stared in the mirror at her reflection, making a face at the dark circles under her eyes. The result of all the changes in her life. But things had to get better from here, right?

Maybe she should consider buying her own travel trailer—something a little more simple than this one—and parking it in a year-round park. Living small seemed to be all the rage right now, and lately she'd been obsessed with watching shows that featured tiny houses.

She hadn't seen Seth since he'd brought her here and had watched as she wandered around the unit marveling over everything from the spacious living room to the bedroom on the other end of the trailer. It hadn't taken her long to agree to live there, relieved that he again insisted that she not be in a hurry to find something else. Because it was proving a lot harder than she'd imagined, and the weeks had rushed by. Another reason to keep her eyes and ears open for something like this.

She was due to start work today. But there was just one situation she needed to clarify before she left for the hospital, and then she would be free of her last worry when it came to Bill and their relationship. She glanced at the small rectangular box she'd purchased yesterday evening and wrinkled her nose. What would she do if she found out she was pregnant? Even though she and Bill had talked about starting a family soon, the thought now made her queasy. She hoped the birth control pills that she'd stopped taking just before her ex had been caught cheating had still been circulating through her system. Especially since she'd had sex twice since that time. Once with Bill.

And once with Seth.

That last one sent a shiver through her. If he thought a woman bearing muffins was a problem, what would he think if...

It was unlikely that she'd have gotten pregnant either time, but not impossible. And the sooner she knew, the better. Especially since her period was overdue. By a little over two weeks.

Just whacked-out hormones, Therese. The result of stress and withdrawal from the Pill. Her doctor had said it might happen.

And if she were pregnant?

You're not. Stop thinking about it!

She wasn't going to worry about that unless she took the test and it verified her worst fears. She grabbed the box from the counter and removed the instructions. She should know in just a few short minutes. What once would've filled her with a sense of anticipation now brought dread.

She'd probably see Seth today, since they were working at the same hospital. It was another thing she dreaded.

She closed her eyes for a few seconds. She could think about that once she took the damned test.

Reading through the package insert, she laid out the items she would need and went to work.

Please, God, let it be negative.

* * *

Seth had just come from a patient's room when the elevator doors opened and out stepped Rese and Beth Gaines, the head of HR. He smiled a greeting at both of them and headed their way, stopping short when Beth was the only one who acknowledged him. Rese was busy looking anywhere but at him.

He thought they'd gotten through all of that, especially with the amount of time that had passed. But evidently not. He'd purposely left her to her own devices over the intervening weeks so they could both get their feet back under them. Was she afraid he might say something to Beth that would give away their secret? Not likely. He'd told her he wanted things to go back to the way they'd been before, and he hadn't been kidding. Getting involved with her in any way except for friendship would bring complications that he didn't want or need. And Rese had already been hurt by more than one man.

Besides, he had colleagues from another department who'd been married to each other for five years—and had three children under the age of four—who were on the verge of splitting up, and the tension between the two of them when they wound up in the same space together was palpable. He could only imagine what things were like at home.

Kids only made things harder on everyone. His dad had made that very clear—with his *this damned kid* comments—and Seth had seen evidence of that for himself. It was another reason he didn't want any of his own. He'd always been pretty careful about making sure of that. Almost always, anyway.

Beth came over and shook his hand while Rese stayed where she was. The woman turned to glance back at her with a tilted head, and she finally ventured forward, but it looked like she was trudging through sludge that kept her from moving normally. And the forced smile she gave him looked…macabre.

What was wrong with her? Was it just the fear of discovery? Or something else. Maybe living in the travel trailer was proving unbearable.

Beth let go of his hand and introduced them. Seth nodded. One thing he didn't want to do was lie when no lie was necessary, so he spoke up. "Therese and I have known each other since elementary school. We're pretty good friends, right, Rese?"

She nodded, but again the movement looked stilted and awkward. "Yes. Yes, we are."

There was a shakiness in her voice he could only assume meant she was trying to keep their night together under wraps. Well, so was he, but at least *he* was doing his damnedest to make it look like he actually liked her. Which he did. Rese, on the other hand…well, he couldn't say the same about her.

"Oh, that's right, Seth was listed on your résumé, right?" She turned to him. "Maybe you could finish showing her around the department if you have a few moments? I'm due back for another interview."

"I'd be happy to." Yeah, right. He should be. But something—rather *someone*—was making this whole encounter feel incredibly awkward.

"Great, thanks." She smiled at Therese. "See you later. Thanks again for joining the team here at Sunrise."

"You're welcome." The smile she offered to Beth was real enough. Until she looked back at Seth and that smile morphed into something else entirely. Or maybe it was active dislike. He'd thought they'd parted on good terms, even if there were some residual feelings of awkwardness. But this felt like more than that.

He waited until the elevator doors had closed behind Beth before turning back to Rese. "Is the travel trailer okay?"

"What? Oh yes, it's fine."

"Then what is with you today? Is it Bill? Is he still harassing you?" Her ex had given her a hard time about ending things.

"No, he's not. And I'm fine."

Wasn't the joke that *fine* was a code word for not so fine? And she'd used that term twice now. He probably wasn't going to force whatever it was out of her. But he did want to give her a chance to say so if something was bothering her.

"Are you sure?"

"Yep."

Well, he'd tried. "Okay then. Are you ready?"

"Ready?" She met his eyes for a brief second before looking off in the distance. "Oh, for the tour. Yes."

What else would he have meant?

There was no way he was touching that. Especially when her teeth came down on that luscious lower lip. One he had no business noticing. "Then let's go."

The tour took exactly ten minutes, including introducing her to the staff who were on her floor that morning.

"Thanks," she said when they were done. She acted like she was going to move away, and so he touched her hand. "Rese, let's grab some coffee, okay?"

He didn't want all of their dealings to be like this one. He truly valued her friendship, even if they didn't always talk every single day anymore. But she'd always been his sounding board and the person he'd confided in when something happened with one of his patients.

Like Bradley?

Exactly like that. If he hadn't been in such turmoil about that, their night together would never have happened. He'd have been able to keep his head, like he had the other times they had gotten too close to that line that would take them beyond friendship. Maybe she was worried that he was falling for her. It would explain a lot. He could start by telling her what had happened on his side. And maybe it would put her more at ease.

"Why?"

"I want to talk to you about that night." He realized he'd been wrong in not letting her have her say after things had gotten out of control. Maybe if he had, this wouldn't be so hard now.

Something shifted in her face. If anything, the clouds he'd seen in her eyes got even darker. "I really don't think—"

"Please, Rese. Just have coffee with me."

Her shoulders slumped. "Okay."

He should be relieved that she seemed so loath to

spend time with him, but he wasn't. And he couldn't help feeling like there was more to this than what had happened between them. But at least she'd agreed to go with him.

They made their way down to the Sunrise to Sunset café, which was separate from the main cafeteria and only offered coffee, tea and small pastries. He ordered a large black coffee for himself and was mildly surprised when she ordered an iced decaf chai. She just shrugged at the look he gave her.

"Too much coffee makes me jittery."

He did remember that about her. If she went beyond two cups, she got shaky and didn't feel well. Maybe she'd already had her quota this morning. "I know it does."

They found a table outside that boasted a concrete bench and was shaded from the sun. It was also some distance away from anyone else who was also enjoying their break. She took a sip of her drink and then immediately started in. "I thought we'd settled everything about that…er…night."

"We did, but I wanted to explain why I was so quick to jump in with both feet. I had just lost a five-year-old patient. And it hit me hard. Harder than maybe I realized at the time. And so when everything…happened, I think I saw it as a means of escaping the movie that was playing in my head. I just wanted to forget, you know?"

"I get it. I wanted to do the same." She grabbed his hand. "But I'm so sorry about your patient, Seth."

"Thanks." He let the warmth of her fingers linger for a second or two, then squeezed them and released his grip. "I thought maybe if you knew the context things wouldn't feel so awkward between us. Or am I wrong?"

"No. Not at all. Thanks for telling me."

This time the smile she gave him had a hint of real warmth to it, although there was still a wariness in her face that he didn't completely understand. All he could do, though, was take her at her word. "Is there anything else you want to tell me?"

"Tell you?" She reared back in her chair and stared at him before blinking several times. "Um…no. Nothing."

And just like that, things went right back to stilted and uneasy. He didn't understand it. She'd been fine until he'd asked that question. Maybe he had it wrong. Maybe she wasn't afraid he was falling for her. Maybe she was afraid of doing just that with him. Oh hell, he hoped not. Because it probably wouldn't end any better than his colleagues' relationship had. Or his parents'. She'd just gotten out of a bad relationship, so maybe she was rebounding. Or maybe he needed to take her at her word when she said she'd been trying to forget, the same as him.

"Okay, then." A thought came to him. "Are you still doing physical therapy that deals with facial muscles?"

"I am. I worked with the plastic surgeons at my previous hospital and did some specialized training in that area. Why, do you have someone you want me to look at?"

"No, not at the moment, but I'm sure I will at some point. Not every PT wants or likes working with those patients. Or with children in general."

"You make it sound like a real problem."

He shrugged. "It can be more difficult than a lot of people realize, and especially with cleft lips and palates there's some overlap with speech therapy."

"I can't imagine someone refusing to work with a child who needs help."

He hadn't meant it to sound like that. "They don't refuse to work with them. It's just not everyone's cup of tea." He smiled at her drink. "No pun intended. I can see how it might be boring to some people. Doing PT on a broken back or a sports injury probably seems more exciting. And rewarding."

"Not to me."

"I'm glad." He took the last swig of his coffee. "Are you starting actual work today? Or is this just orientation and acquainting yourself with the hospital?"

"Bingo. I assumed I was actually going to see patients today, but they're reworking my cubicle, so evidently my actual first day is tomorrow. I've finished all my paperwork, so I guess I'll head back to the RV park."

"So you're free the rest of the day?"

"Not exactly. My mom is dropping by to see where I'm living."

She made a face, which made Seth laugh. Barbara Cameron was the sweetest lady you would ever meet, but she was also a worrier. "Do your parents know about Bill?"

"Yes. I figured it was better just to rip off the Band-Aid. Plus, it would have been hard to explain why I was moving out of our shared apartment. I didn't tell her everything, though. She doesn't know he cheated on me. Or about…what happened later that night."

"There's no reason for her to know about that at all, is there?"

"No." But the way she drew the word out made him tilt his head at her. "But I think she's going to start wondering why I'm staying in your trailer. The way her mind works, she might figure it out."

"Does that mean you'll tell her?" Seth honestly didn't see how that would help at all. And it might even make Barbara think that things between them could become romantic when nothing was further from the truth.

"Not unless I have to."

Again, he wasn't sure what to do with that. He couldn't think of any reason they would need to tell Barbara anything. But he didn't feel like pressing the matter. Besides, it might make things worse between them when Seth had been trying to make them better. So he just nodded in agreement.

"I hope your visit goes well. Tell her I said hi."

"I will. Thanks." She paused and then added, "I'm sorry if I end up making things awkward for you here at the hospital."

He frowned. "In what way?"

"I… I just never thought things would end like they did between me and Bill. It made me realize you can't control every aspect of your life. But actions have consequences even if you don't mean for them to."

Ah, she was talking about their night together. The only consequence he could think of was that people at the hospital might find out that she'd spent the whole night at his apartment. And since there was little chance of that…

"It'll be okay, Rese. You'll see. Just give it some time. Things normally work out the way they were meant to."

"Do they?" She stared at him for a second before reaching out and gripping his hand again as if it were her lifeline. This time he let her fingers stay where they were. "I really hope you're right."

A shiver of foreboding went over him. Had he tempted fate by saying that out loud? And when he thought about cases like Bradley's, he couldn't see how that had turned out the way it was meant to. He'd only said it to try to make Rese feel better about everything. And when it came to them, he didn't believe one night together could irrevocably change things between them, unless they let it.

And Seth had no intention of letting a moment of weakness destroy a lifelong friendship. So they would get through this. Whatever it took.

She took the next couple of days and the weekend to think about the consequences of that pregnancy test. Really think about them—about how she was going to handle them. Seth's words about things working out as they should had struck deep.

When she and Bill had decided to start trying to have a baby, she'd known she was more excited about the prospect than he was, but she'd chalked that up to nerves. But now she had to wonder if that was entirely true. Had she pushed for this and driven him away?

He should have just broken off the engagement if that were the case. Then he could have done whatever he wanted to. And not wrecked her faith in relationships.

At thirty-eight, time was running out for her to have a biological child. So she would choose to look at this pregnancy as a blessing and go it alone. The problem was what to do about the paternity aspect. If Bill was the father, it was better that he know now than to find out later and have him turn it into a court battle that had nothing to do with the baby. He had not wanted to end their relationship over the affair. Or maybe, being a lawyer, he just didn't like coming out on the losing side. And as she was finding out, Bill didn't forgive easily.

Neither did she. Well, she did, but it didn't mean she would be anxious to go back and repeat her mistakes. She wanted this baby. But it wasn't going to change the fact that she and Bill were through.

And if Seth was the father?

She sat in her cubicle and groaned inwardly, even as she fished out noodles with her chopsticks and took a bite. She'd added a little bit of ginger to hers just in case she got queasy. But so far, her stomach had held steady, for which she was thankful. Maybe she'd bypass morning sickness altogether. It would be one small blessing amid all the other uncertainty.

Her mom and dad already knew. She'd told her mom the day she came to visit her at the camper. And the questions Rese had fretted over were never voiced. Nor was there any dismay over the news of her pregnancy. They were both thrilled. And Therese knew they would give her any support needed.

And Bill? Or Seth? Would either of them lend emotional support, whichever one of them was the father?

Frankly, she could do without Bill's interference.

Nowadays there was a way to determine paternity without an invasive amniocentesis. All it took was a blood draw, which could be done as early as eight weeks. For that she was grateful. But that was still a couple of weeks away, and she would need a DNA sample to match it against. And that's where the problem was. She could ask Bill for the sample. But to do that would be akin to admitting that there was a question as to the baby's parentage. Which meant he would know she'd slept with someone else close to the time of his affair. And he would want to know who. Then the accusations would fly, since he'd always been jealous of her and Seth's friendship.

And if she asked Seth for the sample, there would be no such questions. He would already know the entire story and the whys behind it. And if it were his baby, she wouldn't need to tell Bill anything.

And if it wasn't, she could simply go to Bill and tell him about the pregnancy without the messiness of a confession.

Messiness? There would be that even without a tell-all explanation. She would be happy to simply have this child and parent it herself. In fact, that would probably be the easiest solution. But was it fair to whoever the biological dad was?

She didn't know. And despite all of the thinking she'd done, she still hadn't come up with an answer, other than the fact that she was going to have this baby. And once she got past this step, she would allow herself to be happy. Really, really happy.

Even that thought made her smile as she took another bite of her noodles. It had been a busy morning, and she had been glad for that as it had provided a distraction from her musings.

She had two cases that looked to last several weeks. One was a complicated orthopedic case that had involved rebuilding a shattered femur, and the other had come from Seth's department and involved a neck and face injury resulting from a bicycle accident. Thankfully the girl had been wearing a helmet, or it could have been worse. Much worse. But she'd crashed through a wooden fence and had severed some muscles and tendons on the left side of her face, and there'd been an in-depth surgery to rebuild some of the damaged tissue. They'd had to harvest muscle from another part of her body and put it in her cheek. It had left her with some weakness on that side, making it hard for her to smile or enunciate some of her letters. Jotting down notes on the latter, she glanced up when she sensed someone standing over her.

It was Seth. And he did not look happy.

She swallowed. Surely he didn't know. Not yet. "Hi. If you're looking for Marinda and her mom, they just left."

Rese could only hope he wanted an update on his patient. But somehow it didn't feel like that.

"I'm not looking for them. I'm looking for you."

CHAPTER TWO

"You're looking for me?"

Seth wasn't sure coming down here was the right thing to do, but it had been almost a week since he'd seen her. And someone had posted the May festival dates online, and they'd been a vivid reminder that things were not as they were last year at this time. Still, he wasn't sure he should broach the subject, and yet if he didn't, would she wonder why?

"Cajun Fest is just a week from now."

Her eyes widened, and then relief seemed to sweep over her. "I'd totally forgotten about the festival."

"Yeah, me, too. I just saw someone post about it. Do you want to go? Although I'll understand if this year you decide you don't want to go. With me, at least."

He and Rese and a group of friends had always gone to the four-day event together ever since their high school days. She loved the Louisiana-inspired festival and everything that went with it, including the dancing and music. One by one those other friends had dropped out as they moved on to other seasons in their lives, like families and kids. So for the last few years it had been just the two of them. She'd tried to invite Bill to join them the past two years, but he said his stomach couldn't handle the spices, and he had no interest in spending even one day outside in the heat. Seth had always wondered if Bill disliked their friendship, but he hadn't wanted to let go of the tradition, and Rese insisted that her fiancé would come around. He never had, and now he was out of the picture. And he was surprised to find that he wasn't unhappy about that fact.

Before he could digest what that meant, Rese looked up at him with surprise. "We *always* go. Of course I want to. It'll take my mind off things. When is it exactly?"

Was she talking about Bill's cheating? Or the night he and she had spent together? He gave her the dates.

Rese pulled something up on her phone. "Okay, it looks like I only have Saturday and Sunday off. Would that work? With everything that happened, I forgot to keep track of the festival. I normally ask for all those dates off."

"I can't do all four days either this year. But Saturday and Sunday work. I'm on call Sunday, but it's rare that I ever get paged."

She nodded. "Sounds like a plan. Do you want to meet at the venue? Spanish Landing Park is only a thirty-minute drive to the RV site, so you could always stay overnight if you didn't want to make the hour-long trek home Saturday night." She grinned. "You do realize your camper has more bedrooms than your apartment does? You wouldn't have to sleep on the couch this time."

She immediately turned pink, and he figured it was over the reference to the night they'd spent together and not the fact that his travel trailer had a small second bedroom.

He refused to think about the implications of spending another night alone with her and did his best to banish the explicit images that worked their way into his brain. Because none of that was happening again. This time he'd be prepared and would go straight to the bedroom the second they got back from the festival. The *guest* bedroom, he reminded himself.

"That will work." He sat in the seat that was next to the desk. "So how did Marinda do with her therapy?"

They spent the next twenty minutes or so discussing the case, and Rese had some insights that he'd missed while talking to the girl's mother. "You think she's going to keep Marinda from working hard?"

Rese shrugged. "I don't know that for a fact. But she was present for therapy, and any time the girl gave the slightest hint of discomfort, her mom was right there, advocating for a 'slow and gentle' approach. But if we go that slow, it's going to allow scar tissue to move in and inhibit movement even more, if we're not careful."

"Hmmm... I agree. When is her next session? I have a recheck scheduled for two weeks out, but I'd rather get this settled sooner rather than later."

"Me, too." Rese checked the tablet on her desk. "Let me see how the next couple of sessions go, though. If progress stalls, I'll let you know."

"Are you sure? Unless I have a surgery scheduled, I can normally move things around if need be. Promise you'll let me know if things don't improve."

"Don't worry, I will. I'd rather you play the bad guy, so that I'm able to maintain some rapport in my dealings with her mom. If things turn antagonistic..."

He got it. "She might try to move her daughter to another PT center and not get optimal results. Especially if the new center allows Mom to push them around."

"Exactly." Rese swiveled her chair to look at him. "I really do want what's best for her. And that means not coddling her. I won't push her harder than necessary."

"I know you won't."

He wasn't sure how he knew that, since he'd never directly worked with her before. But he'd known her a long time and had never known her to be mean or unkind. Even her split from Bill had been done in a civil manner. At least on her side. She could have ranted and raved at him for what he'd done to her—and she'd have been well within her rights—but she hadn't. She'd simply been matter-of-fact that their relationship was done, and she would not go back on that. Her therapy style would be the same. She would do what was right with a strength and determination that was tempered with reason.

"Thanks for that. Marinda's mom made me feel like I was being mean just to be mean. I even tried laying out my plan for therapy and asked what her goals for her daughter were. Of course her goals were spot-on, but the road to get there wasn't realistic. She definitely doesn't subscribe to the 'no pain, no gain' camp. And while I don't prescribe pain just for pain's sake, PT often involves some discomfort."

"Yes. Or the body tries to protect itself at the expense of healing."

"Exactly." She looked at him as if surprised.

He smiled. "Reconstructive surgery almost always

involves discomfort. There's no getting around reality. I wish there were a magic pill that would just dissolve all of our problems, but there's not."

Rese's teeth came down on her lip, and her eyes filled with tears.

He scooted his chair closer. "Hey. What's wrong?"

There was a long pause before she shook her head and dashed moisture from her cheeks. "I just didn't expect anything that has happened. I don't mean professionally, but personally. I'll be okay, though. I just have to work through things in my own time."

"I get it. This sounds hard, but I'm glad you found out what he's capable of before the wedding." He wished he could say the same about his mom. But then again, if they hadn't gotten together, Seth wouldn't be here.

"Me too." She sucked down a visible breath. "Now let's talk about something a little bit lighter. Like the festival. Any idea which bands are playing this year?"

The minute Seth left her area, she sank into her chair and knew in her heart of hearts she was going to have to tell him. And soon. His "magic pill" comment reminded her that she could have simply taken medication to terminate her pregnancy, and no one would have known it ever existed. She hadn't wanted to do that. But her reaction to his words had shocked her. She'd almost broken down completely and had only just managed to pull herself together. He'd taken her words to be about Bill, and that was fine. For now. But since she'd decided to have this baby, she didn't want there to be any secrets. For her sake, for the baby's sake, and ultimately, she needed to come clean for the father's sake, whoever that turned out to be.

She and Bill might not have worked out, but she would not keep him from his child if he wanted to be a part of their lives. And if it were Seth? Well...if she'd worried about their night together affecting their friendship, what about finding out he was going to be a father? He had always told her he wasn't cut out to be the happy husband type. It was why they'd been able to maintain their friendship all these years. She knew they wanted different things out of life. So although he was gorgeous, she'd been able to steer clear of any kind of romantic attachment to him other than the occasional twinges of awareness that she'd always been able to manage. At least until the night she'd found Bill with another woman.

Seth was a great and loyal friend. But it was also a role that he could walk away from if things didn't work out. But fatherhood? Well, you couldn't erase DNA. Oh, he could walk away, but she'd rather him decide that sooner rather than later, and break not only her heart, but that of an innocent child.

So yes. He needed to know.

And if he refused to have his DNA tested?

Damn. She hadn't thought about that option. Then she would have to do what she'd been hoping to avoid and go to Bill and tell him the truth.

Maybe neither of them would want to know. And if that were the case, it would be the easiest scenario of all. Because then she really would be on her own to raise this child. Just as if she'd gone to a sperm bank somewhere and opted for an anonymous donor.

She'd thought she might wait for the eight-week mark to tell anyone—at which time she could go for the blood draw to determine paternity—but the more she mulled that over in her head, the more it seemed better to do it now. If she waited much longer, Seth would be angry that she'd kept this from him, especially since she was using his travel trailer for housing at the moment. And then there was Cajun Fest. If she went with him as planned, all the while knowing she was carrying what might be his child...

So yes. Better now than later.

As in right now?

Oh baby... The thought made her laugh and put her hand over her abdomen, glancing down. "I wasn't talking to you."

"Sorry?" The question made her jerk her head up. A man passing by had heard her remark.

Her teeth clamped down on her lip. "Oh. I'm just talking to myself."

The lanyard around the man's neck made her realize she still didn't know everyone who worked in the huge department. So she stood. "I'm Therese Cameron, new physical therapist specializing in pediatric cases. I'm evidently slightly eccentric as well."

He shook her proffered hand but quickly released it. "Luca McDonnell. I've been here for a while...and hopefully not eccentric."

The man said it with a straight face, and Rese couldn't tell if he was joking or completely serious. But whichever it was, Luca Last-Name-Not-Remembered could probably make even her dead grandmother swoon with those low mellow tones. Except there was something in his demeanor that seemed to say "keep your distance." Not a problem, since she had no interest in getting close to anyone right now. Especially not men.

"Good to know." She tried to think of something casual to add. But there was nothing. *Nada*. So she settled for a lame, "See you around the department."

"Yep." And with that he continued on his way.

Okay, well not everyone liked being chummy, except maybe her. And that was okay.

"And if you didn't talk to yourself so much, Rese, maybe you wouldn't come off as such an oddball."

Realizing she'd muttered that warning out loud, she shut her eyes with a grimace before looking at her smartwatch. Just after five. Was it too late to check and see if Seth was still in his office?

She picked up her phone and found his number, then texted him.

Are you still here?

While she waited for his reply, she scrolled through her social media account since she was officially off duty for the day. He could be with a patient. Or he might have been on his way home when he came down her to see her. If she didn't hear from him in the next ten minutes or so, she'd head out and tackle the problem of telling him the news tomorrow.

Still here. What's up?

Eeek! She hadn't expected him to reply so quickly. And now she couldn't think of a way to ask to talk to him without it sounding weird.

Do you have a few minutes?

Yep. Want me to come down there?

Oh no. There was no way she wanted to talk about this in this bustling place where Luca or almost anyone could hear. She didn't really have an office space like he did.

Would you mind if I came up there? Are you in your office?

This time he didn't respond right away. The more minutes that ticked by, the more nervous she got. Finally, after an agonizing five minutes her phone pinged.

Yep. See you in a few.

The words contained a terseness that would have done Luca—her new colleague—proud.
Not fair, Rese. You don't even know the man.
Gathering her things together, she got up from her seat and headed for the exit that led to the main hospital. Her thoughts and fears were steadily gathering in her throat, making it hard to swallow, not to mention breathe. The sooner she got this over with, the better. That assurance did little to help her prepare for what was to come.

* * *

He was pretty sure she didn't want to talk about Cajun Fest. But whatever it was, he didn't think he was going to like it.

You got all of that from a few texted words, did you?

Less than five minutes later, there was a knock at his office door. "Come in."

Rese peeked her head around the corner, and he motioned her to come in.

He forced a smile. "Not backing out of Cajun Fest already?" Even though he'd already figured it wasn't about that, he'd needed to say something besides telling her to spit out whatever it was.

"No." She dropped in one of the two chairs in front of his desk as if she needed to get whatever this was over and done with. "But you might want me to after I've said what I need to say."

Oh hell. She wasn't going to tell him she was in love with him, was she?

He looked in her face. No, there was no sign of any kind of wishy-washy emotions. Her eyes held a steely determination that made him tense.

"I don't understand."

"I know." She got up and paced around his office, picking up a framed photo of what looked to be colleagues. Probably one of those work gatherings that had been captured digitally and then framed for everyone involved.

Rese set down the picture and turned back to him. "Remember how we said we wouldn't let that night change our friendship?"

The tension in him grew in steady increments until even his jaw felt stiff when he tried to talk. "I do. Are you here to tell me that it *has* affected it?"

"Not on my side, but you're probably not going to be happy about it."

This time he stood up and faced her. "Just tell me, Rese. Whatever it is, it can't be that bad." But even as he said the words, he didn't believe them. Whatever it was, it was probably going to have an effect on both of them. How he knew that he wasn't sure.

"Okay." She sucked down a deep breath. "I'm pregnant."

The word sat in his head for several seconds while he tried to make sense of it. "Pregnant."

Ah hell. Poor Rese. This was probably the last thing she wanted to happen after breaking it off with Bill.

"Does he know?"

She blinked. "He?"

Why did she act so shocked? Why else would she come here and tell him she was carrying her ex-fiancé's baby. Except she hadn't said it was Bill's.

Then, like a line of dominoes that had been carefully placed for destruction, the first one fell and started a chain reaction.

Hell no. There was no way it could be.

Even as he thought it, he knew it very well could be. His memory of the initial moments of that kiss might be hazy, but one thing he knew for a fact was that he hadn't used protection during what had happened afterward. Somewhere in his head he'd just assumed...

Not an excuse, Seth.

He took a deep breath. "Whose baby is it, Rese?"

What if she hadn't slept with Bill in the last six months?

She came slowly back to the desk and stood in front of it with the most miserable gaze he had ever seen. "I don't know."

The whispered words slid inside his chest with an accuracy that was both silent and deadly.

"What does that mean?"

"Bill and I discussed starting a family, and so I stopped taking the Pill a couple of days before... I found him with someone else."

And that night, Seth had made love to her. And because they were so familiar with each other, he'd known she was taking birth control pills. But she hadn't gotten around to telling him that she was no longer on them. Then again, why would she?

He sat down and tried to process what she was telling him. No, that wasn't quite true. He'd already processed her words far too well. He just didn't want to accept that they might be true.

"Did you sleep with him after you stopped taking the Pill?"

"I did."

"And you haven't told him about the pregnancy."

"No." She sat back down as well. "I didn't want this to happen. But it has, and I-I...well, I want to keep the baby. Actually, that's not accurate. I *am* keeping this baby."

He scrubbed his palm over the scruff on his face and tried to think. Was he angry she was keeping it? No. Was he happy?

Dammit, he had no idea. Fatherhood had never been on his radar. And he'd never wanted it to be.

"What is it you want me to say?"

The second the words were out, he realized they were completely selfish. Rese was his closest friend. It wasn't like she'd set out to trap him with a pregnancy. He knew her, and that was not her style. It was an accident.

"You don't have to say anything." She closed her eyes for a minute. "But I do want to ask something."

Was she going to ask that the baby take his last name? That he be involved with every aspect of its life? His insides curdled at the thought. He didn't say anything, though, just nodded for her to go ahead with her question.

"I came to you first, because…well, if it's not Bill's child, I'd rather he not know. I mean If I run into him six months from now, he'll realize I'm pregnant, but I won't have to approach him about it."

"So you're hoping it's mine?" This time he didn't try to hide his shock. And he sure as hell didn't know what to think about it, if that's what she was saying.

"That's not what I mean. But if you could agree to…" She paused for a long second before continuing, "If you could agree to a cheek swab to compare to the blood draw that I'll do at the eight-week mark, it would help me know whether or not I need to inform him. If the baby is not yours, then it's his. If that's the case, I'll tell him. But if not…"

"If not, it has to be my child."

"Yes." The word was simple and unadorned. And

that gave it even more impact than if it had been accompanied by a long explanation.

"I see."

"Seth, I'm so sorry. I never meant for any of this to happen."

As horrified as he felt right now, there was no way he was going to let her carry the blame for something they'd both caused. And maybe *horrified* wasn't the right word. But he wasn't sure there existed a word that encompassed the tangle of emotions that was twisting and turning inside him right now.

"It's not your fault. At all." He came around the desk and put his arm around her. This was still Rese. His best friend. "I should have used a condom. I just didn't think—"

"Neither of us did. If we had…well, if we had, we probably wouldn't have done what we did. I'm just sorry to have put you in this position. If you don't want to take the test, it'll be okay. I'll ask Bill to."

If he didn't, she'd be forced to do the very thing she was hoping not to do. And how would he live with himself if he let her have a baby that might be his and refused to acknowledge the fact? Refused to try to find out the truth. If this was his child, he wasn't going to turn his back on his responsibility. He wasn't wired that way.

He kissed her on the cheek and shook his head. "I'll take the test. I want to know."

"Thank you." She leaned her head against his shoulder for a minute before stepping away from him. "I don't expect anything from you. I just need to know if Bill has to be notified. In fact, it would be easier if I could just raise the baby on my own."

"Meaning you don't want me involved?"

She nodded.

That affirmation struck him the wrong way. "I'm not sure I'm okay with that."

Her head tilted. "What does that mean?"

"It means I need some time to digest everything. But if this baby is mine, I think I want to be involved in its life."

"You think?"

"Hell, Rese, I'm trying to do the right thing here. Help me out a little."

She made a face. "I know. I just need you to be very sure before making any promises. I want to do right by this child, and that means not letting someone be a presence in his or her life who later decides to back away."

He got that. And that hadn't been what he'd meant to imply. If anything, they were on the same page. "I understand. Let's get past this hurdle first. You said your blood draw would be at eight weeks, right?"

"Right. I'm just over six weeks right now. So two to go."

"How long will it take for my cheek swab to tell us anything?"

Her eyes widened. "Actually I'm not sure. I'll have to look."

"I can look. But I'll do the test, preferably not at Sunrise. I'll go to an independent lab."

"I was thinking the same thing. I'd rather no one at

the hospital know anything until we know for sure. Then if you are a match, we can decide together what to tell everyone and when."

"Agreed. I'll do some checking and see what I can find out." A thought struck him. "You already knew about this when we had coffee together, didn't you? Hence the decaffeinated drink."

"I did. I just hadn't decided what to do about it at that point. I was still freaked out."

So she'd had a little more time to figure this out than he had. "Of course you were. Were you thinking of terminating?"

"Honestly, the thought crossed my mind, but as soon as it did, I rejected it. I'm thirty-eight and I've been ready to have a child for a while now. It's why I'd asked Bill if we could start trying. If I abort it, I'm not sure how easy it would be for me to get pregnant again. So this might be the one and only for me. I couldn't see wasting the chance I'd been given." She looked at him. "But just to be clear, I did not use you to try to get pregnant."

"I know that. It's not who you are. But I'm happy for you, if this is really what you want."

"It is. I know that for sure now."

"Then let's do what we need to do to make you feel good about it. Are you going to see an ob-gyn here at the hospital?"

"No. For the same reasons we both want testing done elsewhere. I'll go to another hospital, preferably one using a different recordkeeping portal so that it can't be seen by anyone at Sunrise Medical."

He nodded in agreement. "You'll let me know when your appointment is?"

"If you want me to."

"I do." He reached over and squeezed her hand. "And Rese, we'll get through this just like we've done with everything else over the years. You mean too much to me to lose you over this."

"Thank you. And that goes for you as well. And whether or not you decide to be a part of the baby's life, I'd still like to know you're around if I need someone to talk to."

He wasn't sure how realistic that was. He was pretty sure if he decided to opt out of fatherhood, she wasn't going to want him around their child. And that was only natural. So in that lay the question. How much could their friendship handle?

Something he didn't want to examine right now. Not until he'd had time to think through the repercussions and analyze things from every angle. Just like he approached patient care. Hopefully that would work just as well in his personal life.

Could he accept responsibility for a child's upbringing? He wasn't sure he could with his familial background and how much he detested his own father. Hell, he couldn't even fathom making real emotional connections with the women he went out with. And if he decided this was too much to deal with?

Then he was going to have some hard decisions to make.

CHAPTER THREE

A WEEK LATER, Seth texted her to tell her he'd found a lab and they were sending him a testing kit. Which was good, because she'd found an ob-gyn at a hospital on the far side of San Diego and had made an appointment of her own.

So things were moving in the right direction. She hoped.

She wished she could say the same for Marinda's PT sessions. Today would mark their fifth session since her surgery a week and a half ago, and mom was still interfering. Seth had told her that if it continued to let him know and he would move up their two-week recheck appointment. That was coming up soon, so maybe she should hold off on saying anything. He had enough on his plate right now with the pregnancy.

But she also wanted to keep her word. So she texted him again and let him know what time Marinda's appointment was and that things were still difficult with the girl's mother.

Then she tossed her phone into her desk drawer so that she could get ready for her first appointment of the day—which wasn't Marinda's. And which was a much easier case in terms of patient cooperation.

Larissa West was a fourteen-year-old girl who'd suffered a sports injury during basketball practice. A jump shot had gone wrong and Lara had landed badly on her leg, fracturing her ankle. The break had been displaced, so she'd needed surgery that necessitated the use of pins in order to hold things in place. And physical therapy had been a must to regain range of motion. She was out of her cast now, but the joint was stiff and painful.

But Lara's motivation was to get back on the team as quickly as possible, so she'd done everything asked and more. So much more that Rese had needed to apply the brakes and tell the girl that she needed to be patient, because her body was still healing and would be for a little longer.

"It's hard. I want to get back to playing."

"I know you do. But working until you fatigue your muscles and putting excess stress on that ankle won't help anyone. Least of all yourself."

She could only hope she'd gotten through to the girl.

Lara came in on time, and Rese greeted her at the door, smiling and discreetly monitoring her walk as the girl and her mom made their way back to her cubicle. Her movements seemed more fluid than they had been, and she wasn't favoring the foot as much. All good signs.

They sat down. "So how's it been going since your last appointment?"

The girl's eyes unexpectedly watered, and her mom put her arm around her. "Lara's been benched for the rest of the season. Her doctor did some additional Xrays yesterday and feels it'll take three more months to get the joint stable enough for that kind of a stress load."

Rese took a moment to digest the news and to formulate a response. Especially since she agreed with the doctor. With how hard Lara had been working through rehab, she could see that she might also want to rush through and return to playing before she was ready,

"I know how disappointing that must be. And how much you love what you do. But think of it this way. Next season you'll be stronger than ever because you'll have been working hard to stay in shape. And your teammates won't have to worry about you getting hurt again. You'll all be able to concentrate on the game." She paused and worded the next part carefully. "I know how much concentration those plays take, and you don't want your ankle to be a distraction to you or anyone else, right?"

"No." The girl's answer was shaky, but she was sitting straight again. "Do you think you can give me some exercises that will keep me strong so I'm ready to get back in the game as soon as my ankle is healed?"

"Absolutely. I would love to help you with that. Now let's get to work."

The session went smoothly and despite how sad Lara seemed when she'd come in, the girl seemed more relaxed, somehow, and she was able to settle in and do the exercises without pushing as hard as she'd been. Maybe because she knew now that she didn't have to rush to try to actively rejoin the game before the end of basketball season. Rese was probably partly to blame for the doctor's proclamation, since she'd put in her notes that Lara was an overachiever and eager to return to her daily routine. But she agreed with him. If she didn't, then Rese would be the first one to pick up her phone and call the surgeon.

True to her word, she went through the files left for her by the person who'd previously occupied her cubicle and found some strength training that used yoga for flexibility and resistance bands for muscle tone. She handed them to Lara. "Remember, slow and steady wins the race."

The girl crinkled her nose. "Slow and steady loses the game in basketball."

"Touché. But in physical therapy, we want a steady push and pull to get you to where you want to be. See you on Friday?"

Lara's mom nodded. "We'll be here. And thanks for being such an encouragement to her. You always seem to have just the right words."

"I wish all my patients put in the work that Lara does." She smiled at the girl. "Let me know if you have any concerns, okay? I'm just a phone call away."

"Thank you."

Luca McDonnell walked by at just that moment and Lara's eyes widened. "Oh wow, who is that?"

Rese crinkled her nose at the question, while Lara's mom admonished the girl. "He's a physical therapist." She didn't offer any more information. Not that she had any more insights into the man. He still seemed to keep to himself, although she did hear one of the nurses refer to him as Dr. McSteamy. And although

Lara's wide-eyed admiration matched the moniker, when she'd asked who they were talking about, they'd told her it was Luca. But it wasn't just about his looks, they'd said. It was more akin to opening the lid of a steaming pot and getting scalded in the process.

Lara's mom stood up. "On that note and before my daughter decides to make any other comments, I think we'll go."

"Mom!" The girl's drawn-out rendering of the title made Rese laugh.

"It's okay." She met the girl's gaze. "But seriously, take it easy on that ankle, okay?"

"I will."

With that, Lara climbed to her feet, and the pair walked off and down the hallway.

Rese gave an audible sigh. Miranda was her next patient and honestly, she was dreading it. It tended to be the polar opposite of what this last session had been. If today was no better, she would let Seth know.

As if thinking about him had conjured the man up, he appeared in the doorway and was now headed for her area. When he got there, he sat down in the chair Lara had just vacated. "Hi."

The greeting was so typical of their friendship that relief washed over her. She smiled, tilting her head. "Hi yourself. Did you want something?"

There was a slight pause, and he shifted in his seat before responding. "I actually wanted to check in on Marinda. You gave me her schedule, and I have a break between patients right now so thought I'd come down and see for myself how she's doing."

"Thanks. I was going to call you if today didn't go any better." She thought for a minute. "Do you think you could take Mom aside on the pretext of discussing other testing Marinda might need? Then I can work with my patient and see if things go better with just the two of us. Or maybe you could talk to her about the importance of therapy and letting her know that some discomfort is normal and that it's how muscles rebuild themselves."

"I can do that. How long do you need?"

"Her session is forty-five minutes, so maybe the first twenty of those, if you have that much time."

"I do."

"Speaking of which, here they come." Despite her pep talk to maintain a neutral but friendly affect, Rese could feel the tension start to build in her head and neck. She'd dealt with difficult patients before, but for some reason this case was harder. Maybe because she wanted so badly for Marinda to regain function, and there was a possibility that she might not be able to achieve as much as she could.

Seth got up from his seat and greeted them both with a smile, asking the girl how things were going. Peggy, the girl's mom, shifted a glance toward her. "Honestly? Is there somewhere we could talk?"

Oh Lord. She was going to ask for a new PT, Rese could sense it. The muscles in her neck cramped, and the urge to lift a hand to massage them swept over her, but she didn't want Peggy to see how much her distrust bothered her. Maybe because it might make Seth doubt her as well.

"Of course. Why don't we let Ms. Cameron and Marinda start working, and we'll sit here and chat."

"Oh, but…" She kind of flailed her hands around, but Seth didn't back down. And Rese appreciated that. If Peggy really had a problem with her, she sensed they would hash it out together, the three of them.

He said, "I want to be able to watch how Marinda copes with movements that are difficult while we talk. Does that sound reasonable?"

Of course it did, so Peggy couldn't really argue there. She just nodded.

"Okay, Marinda, why don't we go over to the smart board and review some of the tasks we tried last week."

"Okay." She expected her patient to put up a fuss, but she just smiled—the effort a little weak on the left side of her face. If anything, she seemed happy to be moving away from where her mom and Seth were.

They made it to the table that was about fifty feet away, and they both sat down, facing each other while Rese picked up the remote for the screen and turned it on. Then she found the set of speech exercises that would help strengthen the repaired muscles on the left side of her face. A catchy tune soon came across the screen with a young man in a crazy costume leaning in and explaining that they were going to pretend to be pirates. "First we say 'Arrrr' with the right side and 'Arrrr' with the left side. With the right side. With the left side." The television pirate moved each side of his mouth separately to make the sound.

Rese joined Marinda in doing the exercises, watching how her face moved. The girl grimaced as she worked the left side, which was where Peggy would have intervened before. But her patient didn't ask to stop as they repeated the game.

"Then we add some head movement. First we say 'Arrrr' with the right side and 'Arrrr' with the left side…" The man turned his head and leaned in as if addressing an imaginary audience on each side of him.

It might have been her imagination or just the fact that she wasn't having to deal with Peggy at the same time as her patient, but Marinda seemed to be really trying for once.

The actor added a pirate's sweeping arm movements to the mouth and head action and repeated the same line. Marinda actually laughed this time, and Rese smiled in encouragement, really trying to ham it up as she did the movements.

She glanced over at Peggy and saw her watching them, her mouth open as if shocked at what her daughter was doing. No longer dull and listless, the girl's face was animated as she, too, leaned each way and made the sound out loud.

Then the song came to an end, and the pirate again praised his audience and asked them to subscribe to his channel.

"I like him."

"Me, too! Do you want to do this at home?"

Marinda nodded. "Can you tell my mom about him?"

She glanced again over at the pair and saw that Peggy was writing something down. Maybe already making a note of this exercise.

Rese's tension slid away, and she suddenly knew

things were going to be okay. At least with Marinda, and maybe even her mom. The jury was still out on whether things would continue to be okay with her and Seth.

"I will. He has a lot of other cool exercises to do that I think you'll like." She then pulled a mirror out of a drawer on the table that sat in front of the smart board, swiveling it so that Marinda could see her face. Then she went through some exercises that, while not as much fun as the pirate video had been, still kept Marinda's attention, and Rese saw her really trying to imitate the movements enough for her to see real progress. If her mom would let her do these at home, they might just turn a corner.

Seth appeared next to her carrying two chairs. "Can we join you?"

"Of course."

Marinda looked at her mom, and her smile faltered. Peggy must have noted it, too, because she leaned forward to hug her. "I'm sorry, honey. Do you want me to sit back over there?"

The girl shook her head. "It's okay."

But things were different this time. Marinda's mom actually nodded to encourage the girl rather than ask Rese to soften her approach. But would that attitude continue once Seth was no longer in the room? She hoped so. She needed to be able to encourage her patients without him having to advocate for her. And she'd been able to do that with her other patients. It was just this one.

When she glanced at Seth, he raised a brow as if

asking a question. She gave a nod to let him know that whatever he'd said had worked. Or maybe it had just been Peggy realizing that Rese really did know what she was doing.

The last twenty minutes flew by, and then the session was over. She turned to Marinda's mom. "I have photocopies of the exercises we did today on my desk. Do you want the name of the video we did? The channel has a lot of other really good routines that are in a kid-friendly format, if you're interested."

"I would love it. I did write down 'pirate man' but it might be easier to find it if I had the actual name." Peggy actually smiled at her.

Wow, she really was going to ask Seth what his secret was. Or maybe he was just good with women in general.

She gave an internal snort. Of course he was. She'd seen him in action. An image flashed through her mind of another kind of action that she'd witnessed up close and her face heated, along with other parts of her body. Okay. Not the place or the time.

She realized for the first time in a couple of weeks that she hadn't really thought much about Bill or the devastating blow he'd dealt to her self-confidence.

Hmm…that was a weird way to describe it. How about grief of a destroyed relationship? She searched herself. That was there, but it wasn't nearly as strong as she'd expected it to be.

She swallowed. And if the baby were his? It might be easier if she didn't have to deal with Bill ever again, but was it fair to Seth to hope he was the father? She didn't know and didn't want to think about it right now.

She brought her attention back to Marinda and her mom, who were listening to something the plastic surgeon was saying. She tuned in. Okay, he was confirming their appointment time.

Rese stood, and the rest of them followed suit and followed her back to her cubicle, where she set up the time for their next session. She peered into Marinda's face. "Really good work today, kiddo. You'll try to do the exercises at home?"

"Yes."

Peggy put her arm around her daughter. "She will. And I'll help her with them this time. Thank you for everything."

What a surprising turn of events. But Rese wasn't about to complain. "You're more than welcome. We want to get Marinda back to the place she was before her accident."

"Do you really think that's possible?"

That was a question she didn't know the answer to, so she glanced at Seth for his input.

"It's not only possible, it's probable. With time and effort. The key is to make sure we help the muscles become strong and supple and not let them atrophy." He repeated what they'd talked about as far as scar tissue went and how it could inhibit movement.

"We don't want to have to go back in to release tissue unless we have no other choice. You can help prevent that from happening."

It wasn't anything that Rese hadn't already said, but it looked like Peggy was finally ready to "hear" the words rather than just brushing them away.

They ended the session on a good note, and the pair headed back toward the exit.

"What on earth did you do?" she asked Seth once her patient was out of sight.

"I really just directed her attention to what you guys were doing, and she was able to see that Marinda wanted to work, especially when no one handed her a pass to get out of it. And I did all the normal talking about the importance of therapy."

She nodded. "Well, it worked. Thanks for coming down. I thought she was going to ask for another physical therapist when she first asked to speak to you alone."

"I didn't even hint that that was an option. Because anyone worth their weight would expect the same things out of Marinda that you do."

"True."

He sat back down in the chair, and the tension that had slid away came creeping back. That evidently wasn't all he wanted to say to her. "I got the DNA kit today in the mail. I'm supposed to swab my cheek and send it back. The instructions say that it'll take anywhere from a few days to a week to get the results back."

"I can't do mine until I'm eight weeks along." She sighed. "I'm so sorry to drag you into all of this, Seth."

"I don't think you dragged me into anything. I was a willing participant, if you remember right." One side of his mouth quirked up.

Since she'd just gotten done thinking about exactly how willing he'd been, she couldn't stop her own smile. "Neither one of us really thought things through or considered the consequences."

"Isn't that how these things normally happen?"

She laughed. "True. I'm not sure what I'm trying to say. Just that I'm sorry that you're having to pay the price of what we did."

"*Maybe* having to pay the price. And regardless of how the paternity test comes out, I'll still be involved in the baby's life. We're friends. And that's what friends do. I can be the benevolent uncle."

Something squelched in her belly. He'd spoken the truth, so she wasn't sure what made her unhappy about that idea. Or his emphasis on the word *friends*. But just because that night together had trampled all over the boundaries of friendship didn't mean that anything else would or even *could* come of it.

And she didn't want anything to come from it. Right? Right.

"Yes," she said, "that's what friends do. But still. I don't expect you to do any more than that no matter what the results are." She wanted to make sure he knew that she wouldn't demand anything from him that he didn't want to give.

The fact that the paternity test had actually arrived suddenly made things seem very real. In a few short days she would know one way or the other who the father was. And would probably have decided what to do about it, if the test indicated Seth wasn't a match. Then she would have to get back in touch with Bill and between the two of them try to figure out what to do.

And the thought of that left a bitter taste in her mouth. She'd much rather just move on with her life and leave him out of the equation completely.

Was he still seeing his assistant? It didn't matter, because she didn't want him back. She'd made that quite clear. Even if the baby were his, they weren't getting back together as a couple. Love wasn't always strong enough to withstand that kind of betrayal of trust. At least whatever she'd felt for Bill hadn't been.

"I know you don't expect me to, but I've had some time to think. And I want to be involved. No matter who the father is. Just let me know what you need."

The problem was, she didn't know what she needed or even wanted for that matter. And if what she wanted was something he couldn't give? That was something she wasn't going to think about. Not now.

"Thank you, Seth. As soon as I figure that out, you'll be the first to know."

CHAPTER FOUR

JUST LET HIM know what she needed?

Why on earth had he said that? What if Rese wanted a commitment that went far beyond being an active part in the baby's life? Like a romantic one.

She didn't say that, Seth.

But what if he'd planted that idea in her brain? Or what if she thought he wanted more than friendship? It was crazy how he could talk to patients and use reason to convince them of a needed surgery. Or even Marinda's mom. He hadn't even had to say much. All he'd needed to do was ask her to take a step back and see her daughter through different eyes. Through eyes that could see that Marinda was stronger than she'd given her credit for. That, in this case, she hadn't needed protecting, she'd needed her mom to encourage her to try her hardest.

He could do things like that, but when it came to romance, he'd found himself in situations that he neither needed nor wanted more often than he'd liked. Like his neighbor, who, thanks to Rese's presence had finally gotten the message that he didn't want to deepen their acquaintance.

If someone else he'd spent the night with had come

to him and said they'd somehow gotten pregnant, what would his reaction have been? Horror. Much the same as it had been when Rese came to his office and told him she was pregnant. The difference was, he trusted Rese.

He would have tried to do the right thing no matter who the person was...not marriage, but support, both financial and hopefully emotional. He just couldn't do commitment.

Not that he was against it. He'd just never met anyone he cared about enough to dive deeper than a night or two. Most of the time the woman hadn't wanted more than that, either.

Because things didn't always work out. Like his folks. Or his colleagues. Or Rese and Bill. Except in the case of his folks, by the end, his mom hadn't wanted it to work out. She'd just wanted the man out.

He leaned back in his chair. Rese hadn't asked for more. He'd just found himself in a situation he'd had no training for. And he much preferred knowing what was likely to happen. Like he did in the operating room, although even there he'd been surprised a time or two. But at least there he could study things from every possible angle and make a plan of attack. But relationships? Not so much.

His friendship with Rese was the closest he'd ever gotten. But even they didn't see each other every day or even every week anymore, so he didn't have time to get on her nerves.

And she didn't have time to get on his, either. Although that's not what he was worried about. Not anymore. It was more the phantom sensations that crept over him whenever she was around. Even today as he'd watched her work with Miranda. There'd been a sense of pride…and something else that he hadn't been able to put his finger on. But whatever it was, he hadn't been able to take his eyes off of her.

Glancing at the DNA kit on his desk, he reached over to at least get that done. Putting it off would help no one. Not even him. Knowledge was power, right? So he opened the box and pulled one of the long cotton swabs out of its package and carefully twirled it against the inside of his cheek. Then he placed it, cotton side up, in his coffee mug to dry. He repeated it with each of the other provided swabs, letting them dry as well. When the prescribed time had passed, he slid each of them back inside its original sleeve and packaged them for shipping. Then he stared at it for a long time. He wasn't sure why, but he had a feeling this baby was his. And if the test confirmed that, it was going to change his life forever.

And Seth wasn't sure he was ready for that. He didn't like change. He liked his life the way it was, orderly and predictable. Right now, though, it was more like a roller coaster. One that didn't give him time to recover from the first drop before adding hairpin turns and climbs that left him feeling upended and shell-shocked by the time the ride ended. Except this one wouldn't end. This was a human life that would be forever linked to him. But it also meant that Rese was forever linked to him, too.

A warmth settled in his chest and he blinked, trying to analyze the feeling. He wasn't happy about this, was he?

He wasn't sure, but before he let any emotions foment and get set in concrete, he'd better find out for sure what he was dealing with.

He'd personally go deliver the package to the post office rather than use the hospital mail. Not because he didn't trust it, but he wanted to keep this process as quiet and confidential as he could. At least until he knew the results.

So after clearing off his desk and making sure he'd completed all of the tasks on his list for the day, he scooped up his keys from inside the top drawer of his desk and headed out, the packet in his hand and a lump in his throat over what it meant to both his future and to Rese's.

"How are you feeling?"

The question came out of nowhere as she and Seth walked into the venue and paid the entry fee that granted access to all of the music and attractions that Cajun Fest had to offer. The only thing it didn't cover was food.

She glanced at him. Why had he asked that now? So far he'd been fairly quiet about her things other than telling her he would be involved no matter whose baby it was. It had surprised her to realize that she'd wanted to know more than that. She'd wanted to know that he'd be involved in her life as well, with or without the baby.

In a friendship sort of way, of course.

"I'm actually feeling pretty good." It was true. Other

than feeling like she had to pee more often than usual, she hadn't experienced many of the unpleasant side effects that a lot of other women dealt with.

She hadn't seen him in a couple of days and until his text arrived last night asking if she still wanted to go to the festival with him, she hadn't actually been sure he was still planning to come. But they'd done this every year and to not do it this year would have made her more anxious about things than she already was. She'd taken his original question to mean her physical health, which was fine. But her emotional? She was too afraid to examine that right now. So she kept pushing that part of her being just out of reach, hoping to put off those worries until she knew for sure whether this baby was Seth's or Bill's.

Speaking of which. "Were you able to get the DNA test done?"

The place was packed, and she had to watch where she was walking to make sure she didn't careen into anyone, but that was a good thing. It meant she didn't have to look into his face as she asked that question. Didn't have to witness dread or any other negative emotion that might appear. Because she didn't want to know. She was already coming to love this little being that was only weeks old, but knew how unrealistic it was to expect Seth to mirror those feelings.

He didn't even know if it was his or not—and in all honesty, she couldn't blame him if he was hoping the baby wasn't. He'd told her he would be involved in its life whether or not it was his, but if it was Bill's, his words about being like the benevolent uncle had shaken her up a little. Because that kind of uncle only showed up for special occasions with a hug or a birthday gift, but didn't feel the need to attend school plays or ask about report cards. Or to take her to Cajun Fest every year.

"I did. Day before yesterday. It's already been sent, so the results should be in by the time you get that blood draw."

Although she wasn't looking directly at him, her peripheral vision was actively aware of what he was doing. And what he wasn't doing was anything other than looking straight ahead. Just like she was.

They made a great pair. Both talking about the issue, but not really dealing with it other than giving it the side-eye from time to time.

A heavenly scent interrupted her musings, and she turned to the left in time to see a large wok-like pan flip tiny crustaceans into the air. They sizzled when they came back down. She'd halfway expected a slight wave of nausea to come over her like it had with the scent of her shampoo, which she'd switched out for another brand.

But it didn't. This smelled divine, and her stomach rumbled. She started to say something to the being housed in her belly but stopped herself just in time. It seemed too personal to do that right now. Even though it was Seth beside her and not some random person, like when Luca had walked by and heard her talking to the baby. At least he'd seemed amused by what he'd thought was her talking to herself.

But since she didn't know how Seth really and truly

felt about everything, she was going to do her best not to have conversations with her baby in public.

"Can I say that I'm already looking forward to lunch?" This time she did let herself look up at him. "Those crawfish are calling my name."

He looked back at her and studied her face. "Are you sure you should be eating spicy food?"

No. But then again, that hadn't stopped her from doing spicy things with Seth. Things that had maybe created this tiny being. Even the memory of that made a wave of heat sweep through her. She actually fanned herself before she realized what she was doing and tried to make it about the festival.

"Um, we're at a spicy event. Of course I want hot things."

Oh Lord. That hadn't come out right.

Maybe he hadn't noticed. Except he didn't say anything immediately.

Dammit, she'd promised herself that she wasn't going to say anything that would put a damper on their trip here today. Especially not remind him about that night they'd spent together. She wanted this to be a good memory, especially for Seth. Not one that he was going to have to excise with a scalpel.

"I just don't want you to regret it later."

Were they still talking about food?

It would be so much easier if she could treat this like a trip to the sperm bank. Only in her case, if Seth was the donor, she knew exactly what she was getting in terms of character—if that was even an inherited trait—and he was a man of integrity. He was kind. He cared deeply about his work and his patients. And until recently, she'd never doubted that his friendship would be there no matter what.

She stopped and faced him, waiting until he slowed his steps and came back to rejoin her. "Seth, you don't have to do this. I know we talked about things in a roundabout way, but please don't feel like you have to be a part of the baby's life. The DNA test was more to let me know whether or not I need to inform Bill of the pregnancy or not."

Oh Lord. Why was her voice so shaky? Fear. Fear of losing him completely. So before he could say anything, she added, "I don't want to lose your friendship. Please don't agree to anything you don't want. I'm having this baby for me…not for anyone else."

He took a step closer and tilted her face up, his touch a welcomed reassurance. "I couldn't live with myself if this baby didn't have a village around to support it… and you. You're important to me. And this baby is important to me. I'm sorry if I've made you doubt that."

A wave of emotion came over her, and she shook her head, trying to swoosh it away. She hadn't realized how scared she'd been until this very moment. But hearing that he still cared about her made her weepy in a way that she hadn't been in a long time. He gently wiped under her eye with the pad of his thumb, and she realized her tears had been very real.

His gaze landed on her face and stuck there for a long moment. So long that she thought he might kiss her, but instead he put his arms around her and held her close to his chest. She could feel the beat of his heart through the light T-shirt he had on, and the slight scent of pine and loamy earth tickled her nose. It was Seth's scent. A warm and familiar fragrance that she knew by heart.

But how?

Did it even matter? She felt safe and cared for, and she allowed herself to hook her arms around his waist and hug him back. They stood there like that for what seemed like an eternity, although in reality it was probably less than a minute. But although his words had been sweet, this felt more like a promise than pretty phrases ever could.

Before it could get awkward, though, she pulled back and smiled at him. "Thank you for that. I'm not sure what's wrong with me."

He dropped a kiss on top of her head. And it was the sweetest punctuation mark on a conversation that could have been fraught with emotional peril. "Nothing is wrong with you. Except the fact that you're craving spicy food. Don't come crying to me when he or she complains about it later."

It was the first time he'd really talked about the baby in real terms, and while the physical hug may have ended, the emotional one was still there. And she had no doubt that he would follow through with what he'd said.

She just hoped he wouldn't regret it later.

Wasn't that what he'd said moments earlier that had started this whole emotional meltdown of hers?

Well, no more of those. Right now, things were right with the world, and she was going to make sure they stayed that way.

* * *

Seth couldn't remember laughing this much in their past visits to the outdoor celebration. From comedy acts about the bayou to butter running down Rese's chin that he'd dabbed away with a napkin, he'd had fun. She'd consumed more crawdads than any one person should eat at one sitting. And he hadn't been able to stop staring at her. At the way her eyes sparkled and her lips smiled as they went from one booth to the next, sampling food and looking at handcrafted items.

"Look at this!" She motioned him over to a booth where there was a cradle on a wooden frame that lifted it up to bassinet height. "It can be locked in place or left so that it can rock freely. It even has a little motor that will rock it for you."

To demonstrate, she turned it on, and the cradle began gently swinging back and forth. She glanced up at him. "I think I'm going to get it. We can come back for it and take it with us when we're ready to leave."

"Let me."

"No, Seth, I wasn't trying to get you to buy it."

"I want to. Consider this my first contribution."

There was a crazy mix of emotions that he saw flash through her eyes, and he wondered if he'd said the wrong thing. But then she nodded.

"If you're sure."

"I am." He took out his wallet and handed the vendor some money. The man put a sold sign on the item and just like that, the fact that he was going to have a child became real. And scary. But also…maybe even good. At least for a fleeting moment.

They walked out of the booth, and he consulted the list of events for the day. "I'm ready to sit in the shade. You?"

"Oh yes, that sounds wonderful."

They chose to go to one of the stages that had huge sailcloths stretched across steel poles to provide shade, while allowing the slight breeze of the day to drift through and cool things off. They sat on the grass, and he stretched his legs out in front of him, while she sat cross-legged. The band was playing bluegrass and it was an energetic and uplifting rendition of a familiar children's tune. Something they might one day play for their child.

They?

If he did turn out to be her baby's father, then Rese would do the bulk of the parenting, while he contributed from a distance. That was the only way it could be, since they wouldn't be living together. And who knew where she would eventually be residing. It was doubtful she'd want to remain in his travel trailer forever. And that stuck in his belly in a way that he didn't understand. And honestly, he didn't want to understand it. Because that might bring with it some thoughts that weren't sustainable. At least not for him.

So it was best just to go with the flow and see what happened. And Rese was going to make the decisions about when and where she was going to move, and he was going to let her. And if she decided to move out of state?

Something about that made him look to the side at her. She was staring at the stage in what looked like rapt wonder. She had liked any kind of music with a country-and-western flavor, which was probably why she loved this festival so much. It made him smile. At that moment she chose to look over at him, and she smiled back, her head tilting as if she didn't understand.

His fingertip tapped the end of her nose. "You and your country music."

Rese played the banjo, so he could see why she liked this particular group. There were three banjo players in this band.

"You like it, too. Admit it."

"I do. But I think I like watching you enjoy it more than I like the music itself."

The second the words were out of his mouth he regretted it, because despite the cheerful music on stage, the atmosphere between the two of them suddenly got heavy. Their eyes held each other's gaze for several long seconds before she looked away. "I didn't know that."

She almost sounded regretful. And he didn't want that, so he tried to modify what he'd said.

"Rese…"

He waited for her attention to return before he continued. "I do like it. I wouldn't be here if I didn't. It's just fun to see you so wrapped up in it."

"I love music in general."

He named off several of her favorite bands without having to think about it very hard. And that surprised him.

"Wow. I'm impressed. How about this…" She named several classic rock groups. "How'd I do?"

"Now I'm impressed."

She nodded. "We've known each other a long time, haven't we?"

"We have. Thank you for including me in this journey."

She blinked as if not sure what he meant, so he added, "Your pregnancy. You didn't have to, you know. You could have simply told me the baby was Bill's and I would have been none the wiser."

"But that would have been a lie, because I don't know that. At least not yet. And one thing I've never done is lie to you. Not knowingly, anyway."

The band started up again, and this number was a loud one. Loud enough that normal conversation would have been difficult, and Seth was glad. He didn't want to delve any deeper into their history or into where they found themselves now. A year ago, her being pregnant with his child would have been so far out of the realm of possibility as to be ludicrous. Sure he'd fantasized about her before—like the day he'd taken her to her prom and she'd come down those stairs in that green silk dress—but he was pretty sure friends did that from time to time. At least he hoped so, or he was in deep trouble.

This time, he didn't look at her, just let himself enjoy the music for what it was. The lead banjo player walked out onto the short catwalk to showcase his playing skills, leaning over to nod at some folks who were standing close to the stage, his fingers never losing their place. He really was incredible and with his long beard, he looked the part. But when the musician moved to the other side to do the same, the stage wobbled for a second and the man stumbled. But he quickly recovered and went back to playing. But when a second player joined him to do a session of dueling banjos, the wobble reoccurred but this time it progressed, and the whole end of the stage sagged dangerously low, people lurching away from it to avoid being crushed by the supports. The music turned into a terrible cacophony of disjointed notes before stopping entirely.

Seth could no longer see the two musicians, but there were screams that said someone might be hurt. He leaped to his feet to find that Rese was already up. His first concern was for her, if things got out of hand and there was a stampede of folks trying to get away. "Try moving out of the venue."

"What?" she shouted above the crowd.

"Get away from here and call 911. I'm going to see if I can help."

"The person next to me already called. I'm coming with you."

He took her by the shoulders and looked into her pale face. "Rese, no."

Up came her chin, and he knew exactly what that meant. She wasn't going to listen to him. He rolled his eyes. "Okay. But stay close."

He took her hand and towed her through the crush, repeating that he was a doctor and to let him through. The crowds magically squeezed back to open a narrow path for them. Seth was painfully aware of how warm Rese's hand was and how it fit so well into his. Kind of the way his...

Not the time for this!

He kept moving until he reached where the stage had been. One of the band members was standing with his arms out trying to barricade something. Or someone.

"I'm a doctor. Is someone hurt?"

"My mate. He's hurt."

The Aussie accent startled him for a second, but his eyes went to where the man was pointing. One of the banjo players was lying on the ground unconscious, a nasty gash on his head that streamed blood.

He glanced back. "Anyone else that you know of?"

"No. At least I don't think so."

He looked at Rese, and she nodded, so he let go of her hand and moved forward to kneel beside the injured man. Feeling for a pulse, he was relieved to find it strong and steady and remarkably within normal limits. He hoped that was a good sign, although with head injuries, sometimes swelling didn't manifest for a while, and things could go south quickly if there was a brain bleed.

"I need a cloth of some kind. Preferably something clean."

"Coming up." The man with the accent made his way back to the stage and hopped up on it, going to scoop up a towel that was lying next to a microphone. Then he tapped it to see if it was on. "We have a doctor here, but he needs some room to work. We need you all to back away from the stage so no one else gets hurt."

It worked. Light made its way back through the tangled mass of bodies, and Seth saw that Rese was busy placing people to form a human shield around the shattered metal platform.

The police were first on the scene and took over bringing in actual barricades that had evidently been here at the venue.

Soon the physical worry of having his patient stepped on or fallen onto was out of the way and he could do his job. Rese was now beside him and grabbed the towel from the band member. "Hold it on his head to stanch bleeding, while I check the rest of him."

Using his phone's flashlight, he checked the pupillary reflex of each eye. Normal so far. Then he palpated arms and legs and found no obvious breaks, although hairline fractures or broken ribs were always a possibility.

"Was the other guy who was on the collapsed section of the stage injured?"

"Barry?" she asked. "No, he's the one you were talking to who was busy keeping people back. The other band members were spread out doing the same. They've evidently had drills for this kind of thing."

His head swiveled to look at her. "You know this how?"

"I saw an interview with them. This isn't the first time a venue has had problems with stage material."

He glanced back down to see the man's eyes flicker, just as a pair of EMTs came through with a gurney. The man tried to lift his head, but Rese pushed his shoulder to keep him in place.

"Terrance, you've been hurt. You need to stay still until we can get you to the hospital."

Terrance? Did she know them *all* by name? He had no idea what the band members' names were for most of his favorite rock groups. But then when they sat down on the grass to listen, Rese had mentioned that the banjo players in this particular group were outstanding.

The man made eye contact with her and nodded, his hand reaching up to where she was still putting pressure on his wound. "Will I still be able to play?"

The words were low and gruff, but there was a fear in them that pierced his soul. He understood that completely. His hands and his brain were key to doing what he did in the operating room. Without either one of those...

Seth leaned closer. "I think you're going to be just fine. We just want to get you to a hospital and have you checked out to be sure there's nothing else that needs fixing."

One of the EMTs squatted next to him. "You guys are doctors?"

"Yep. Sunrise Medical. Rese is a physical therapist there."

"Okay, what have we got?"

Seth gave him the rundown with the caveat that he'd fallen from about six feet, so there could be a spinal cord injury that he couldn't see.

"Got it." He motioned to the other paramedic, and together they smoothly slid a backboard beneath the man, and then they lifted him onto the gurney. Rese kept pressure on the wound throughout the process.

One of the EMTs thanked her, his look lingering just a second longer than necessary. She smiled at him and then let him take over.

Something squelched in his chest. He hadn't thought that far ahead. Rese would almost certainly meet someone and fall in love again. Maybe not today or tomorrow, but someday. And when she did, what did that mean for their relationship? It had survived Bill, but that didn't mean that the next guy wouldn't take her completely away.

Why was he even thinking about that? It had to be because of the baby.

Even as that went through his head, he wondered if that's all that it was.

So he wouldn't wish her well if she found love again?

Of course he would. He just would feel…

Hell, he had no idea what he would feel. What he did know was he hadn't been Bill's biggest fan in the first place. He'd just seemed a little…well, self-absorbed. Like his dad had always been.

And him sitting here thinking of how Rese's future husband would affect *him* wasn't? Hell, yes it was. Especially since there had just been people injured at a concert.

He shook himself back to the present. "Anyone else injured that you know of?"

The paramedic who had interacted with Rese shook his head. "The police have backed people away from the stage and other than a couple of minor cuts and bruises, mostly from pushing and shoving, it looks like we're good." He looked again at Rese. "I hear you held the crowds back."

She colored and shook her head. "I didn't. Just got people to help block anyone from getting through."

"Good thinking." He glanced at his partner, who flicked his thumb in the other direction signaling they were okay to leave as the police had made a path for them with more barricades. "Well, thanks for your help."

Then they were moving the wheels, bumping over the grassy terrain. Just beyond the area, there were several sets of lights from the first responders' vehicles.

Seth had no doubt that the one EMT guy would be looking up who Rese was, since he'd mentioned the name of their hospital. But it didn't matter. It was Rese's life and up to her how she decided to live it. He needed to remember that.

He went over to her. "Are you okay?"

"Yes, why wouldn't I be?"

He didn't know why, but her frowned response seemed to double down on the fact that she didn't need him to protect her or make her decisions for her. Maybe it was the physician in him that was used to telling people what needed to happen and when it needed to happen. But letting that bleed over into his personal life was neither good nor necessary, and he needed to remember that so he didn't get himself into trouble.

But navigating these waters was new to him. He had some casual friends, but none as close as Rese was, so there was never a temptation to give advice where it wasn't needed. Well, it wasn't needed here, either.

"No reason. Just asking."

She moved closer and bumped his shoulder. "Sorry. I don't know what's wrong with me. I would blame hormones, but that doesn't give me an excuse to bark at you."

"You weren't barking. Just making a few things clear."

"What things?"

This time, he bumped her and reached down to hold her hand the way he had when he'd pulled her through the crowds. "Nothing important." He looked into her face. "I'm glad we came. And not just because we were here to help. It's been like old times."

"Yes, it has." She squeezed his hand but didn't let go. "It's helped me forget what happened with Bill and what the future might hold for me and the baby."

That's right. It had been less than two months since she'd been betrayed and had broken off her engagement. It had to be on her mind a lot. And she may even be wondering if she should go back to him and try again.

"You would never let Bill back in your life, would you?"

"No. I mean I won't lie when I say it hasn't crossed my mind. But when I really sit and think about it, I don't think our feelings for each other were as strong as either of us thought they were. I don't love him. At least not anymore. He's handsome and knows how to say the right things, but I think he's probably relieved, too. Maybe he's like you and never wanted to commit in the first place."

He was nothing like Bill, and he wanted to make sure she knew that. "I never would have cheated on you. Ever."

She swiveled to face him, taking his other hand. "I didn't mean to imply that, Seth. Honestly. I've just never seen you with anyone who made you want to settle down. And there's nothing wrong with that."

"I'm not against marriage per se. I guess I've just never met anyone I can picture spending an entire lifetime with. And the more years that pass it's just easy to keep on going the way I have been."

"I get that." She tilted her head to study him. "Me... I've always dreamed of the day when I would have a husband and a family. But I think I jumped too soon with Bill. He was charming and funny and seemed like every woman's dream man, only now I think I was more in love with the dream than with him. Maybe agreeing to have a baby put him over the edge. But it doesn't erase the agony of finding him..."

She blinked hard for a couple of seconds, and he had the impression she was battling tears. He disliked Bill right now more than he'd disliked anyone. Maybe even more than his father, who could also be charming and funny. Until it no longer suited him to be. Then he and his mom saw the man who hid behind that carefully crafted facade.

"I'm so sorry, Resic."

He pulled her into a hug again, wishing he could somehow erase what had happened to her. But he couldn't. If he thought marrying her would give her a soft place to land, he would offer in a heartbeat. But it wouldn't. And to marry her without it being based on love would do her as much of a disservice as Bill had. Without the cheating part.

"It's not your fault." Her arms looped around his

waist, and she laid her head on his chest. "Thank you for always being there for me."

"I always will be. Don't doubt that." He raised a hand to stroke her hair. It felt so right to hold her like this.

It's because you're friends, and she's hurting.

Exactly. So why would marrying her be so bad? They were friends. And they'd proved they got along well. They were compatible in so many ways. Soooo many ways.

But Seth didn't love her, not in that way. And she didn't love him. She'd loved Bill.

Except she burrowed closer into his chest, and the snuggling awakened things in him that had no business coming to life. He rested his chin against her head, jamming his eyes closed to try to banish the sensation. But her soft hair tickled his skin and sent up a vanilla fragrance that was intoxicating.

"Seth…" His name breathed out on a long sigh, and he could picture how she looked right now. Her eyes were probably closed, long dark lashes fanning across soft, pale skin. And the cheek pressed to the middle of his chest would be pink from the heat of the day. He'd not been oblivious to the envious glances that other men had cast his way. Little did they know she wasn't his. And never would be. She was brilliant and capable and beautiful, and Bill should have been thanking his lucky stars.

Her arms curled up, her palms cupping his shoulders, derailing those thoughts as other—more dangerous—sensations took the wheel and veered down a dirt road, kicking up dust. A road filled with memories of a certain night spent in her arms. The night they'd very possibly created the tiny being she carried in her belly.

I hope it's mine.

The thought speared through him, shocking him with the intensity of longing that came with it. He'd never longed for anything in his life. If he wanted something, he went out and worked for it. And yet this...

Her head came back, eyes meeting his for a long time before dropping to his mouth.

Oh hell. He wished he was strong enough to pull away with a laugh and some offhand remark about being glad the injured band member was okay. But he found nothing offhand in the situation. Because he very much wanted his hands on her—didn't want to break whatever this spell was. Talk about longing. What he wanted most of all was to lower his head and see what her reaction would be. If she wanted the press of his mouth against hers as much as he did. If she wanted to hold him even tighter.

Before he could test that theory, though, Rese went up on tiptoe and did the very thing he was dying to do. She kissed him.

CHAPTER FIVE

HE WAS KISSING her back.

Rese wasn't sure why she'd needed this so much. Maybe it was the rush of adrenaline from what had happened when the stage collapsed. Or maybe pregnancy hormones were driving this bus. But as long as it stayed on the road and didn't crash into anything along the way, they'd be fine, right?

Right.

To think otherwise was to stop what they were doing, and she didn't want to do that. At all.

His fingers slid into her hair, the gentle tug on the strands was heavenly; lifting goosebumps on her arms and making her want him with a strength she hadn't thought she possessed.

It had never been this good before.

Oh wait. Yes, it had. Once. The last time she was with him.

Things with Bill had been okay, but kissing him never had this sharp quality of almost desperate need.

Bill, schmill. She kicked him out her head and concentrated on Seth and what he was making her feel.

She was vaguely aware that life was continuing

to move around them, but when he splayed his legs slightly so that she didn't have to be up on tiptoes anymore, it had another—maybe unintended—effect. It made her very aware of that firm something that was pressed tight against her.

Someone laughed as they passed by them, and the sound shook a little bit of sense into her. But not enough to want this to stop. Just to make her want to continue it in a different venue. One that had a little more privacy. No, not a little. A lot. She wanted it to be just her and Seth with nothing between them. She eased back until her lips just barely touched his and pulled in a deep breath. "Can we...?"

"Yes. Let's get out of here."

They somehow untangled themselves, and then he was towing her down the path that led out of Spanish Landing. The name suddenly made her giggle. Maybe it was just the headiness of knowing what was coming.

He glanced down at her, his expression serious. "What?"

"Nothing. It just struck me as funny that they're having Cajun Fest at a park with the word *Spanish* in it."

If anything, his frown grew. "That's what you're thinking about right now?"

She smiled up at him, hoping it was filled with sensuality and not a cartoon caricature. "Oh, I'm thinking a lot more than that. But it was the only thing that could be said in front of other people."

He stopped and curved his hand around her nape and leaned down for another kiss. Not as long as the previous one, but still, it was filled with a promise that made her shiver. "Good. You can tell me in private. I want to hear everything."

She doubted that. Because not all of it was about sex. Some of it was about things that confused her. Vague swirlings in her brain that whispered of possibilities that had seemed impossible the day that she'd fled Bill's office.

She put all of that out of her mind as they started moving again, and this time, he draped his arm around her shoulders, his fingers sliding along the bare skin of her upper arm and setting up a waterfall of sensations that were making it hard to put one foot in front of the other without stumbling. But she leaned against Seth's strength and hoped it would be enough to carry her. At least for now.

Wait. "We drove separate cars."

"We'll come back for yours."

She blinked. How were they going to do that? The park closed, and she didn't really want to leave it there overnight.

A crack of reality poured its unwelcomed light onto daydream scenarios of lovemaking positions and whispered words in the dark. She stopped. "When?"

He cupped her cheeks. "I'm not planning on going far."

"Oh!" Her dream factory started back up and increased its repertoire, switching to the idea of motel rooms or even…his car.

Would he really do that?

Would she?

Her mouth watered. Oh yes. She definitely would.

They somehow made it to Seth's vehicle, and he opened the door for her and waited until she slid inside. Once he was in the car, he cupped her chin and came in for another kiss. This one was crazy hot, his tongue sliding into her mouth. She wrapped her arms around his neck to hold him there, a sound emerging from deep in her throat. A kind of humming sound that begged him to keep doing what he was doing.

He pulled back. "God, Rese. What have you done to me?"

What had she done to *him*? She could ask him that very same question. But she was glad she wasn't the only one feeling the ground shift under her feet.

He started the car and drove a short distance, pulling into a small marina. And suddenly she knew where he was going. His sailboat was moored here. And although she'd been on it more than once, it had never been for this reason.

The thought of doing unthinkable things on that boat put her heartbeat on overdrive. She wanted this. Not because she'd never made love on a boat before, but because it involved making love with *Seth* on that boat. Another thought that she didn't want to examine too closely. At least not yet. Later, when she was alone, she could dissect things and try to make sense of them.

He parked in a numbered spot, and they got out and made their way down a dock until they got to the very end. The sun was beating down on them, and she wondered how hot it was going to be in the small bedroom he had below deck. Plenty hot. And not just from the sun.

Seth leaped the short distance from the dock to the boat and held out his hands to her. She took them and was able to step across the space onto the deck. The water was smooth as glass with just a hint of movement, the boat rocking beneath her feet. He placed his hands on her shoulders and looked into her eyes. "You're sure about this?"

She laughed. "No, but that doesn't mean I don't want it to happen. Because I do. Very, very much."

His palms slid up her neck, thumbs tracing the line of her jaw. "Same. My next question is: here or out on the water where it's more private?"

"We're already on the water, aren't we? And below deck is plenty private. Besides no one else is around."

"Good." He grinned down at her and let her go long enough to flick a switch. She felt a small vibration under her feet and tilted her head in question.

"The air conditioner. It should cool things off in just a few minutes."

She crinkled her nose. "And if I don't want 'things' cooled off?"

He kissed her again, and this time they were just short bursts that played with her senses and made her want so much more. "Don't worry. I'll heat them back up again."

She had no doubt of that. Memories of their night together played in her head, and she had trouble fathoming the fact that she was going to get to experience him twice in one lifetime. How lucky was she?

Her hands tunneled beneath his T-shirt, enjoying the play of muscles beneath the skin of his back. She traced his spine, the blade of one of his shoulders, and then trailed her fingertips all the way back down, until she reached where his hip bone met the waistband of his jeans.

Before she could venture any lower, he suddenly scooped her up and walked the short distance to the stairs leading below, his steps as sure-footed as they were on dry land. He went down, turning sideways as he reached the narrow door so they could both fit through.

Then they were in the small berth area. Directly in front of them was a bed that took up almost the entire space with a small nightstand on one side. The navy covers were rumpled as if he had slept here recently, and a tiny voice in her head wondered if he'd been in here with another woman.

As if reading her thoughts, he set her gently on the mattress and followed her down, bracing his forearms on either side of her. He nuzzled her neck. "If I'd known I was bringing you here, I would have made the bed. I sleep here sometimes when I need a break from the hospital and my normal life."

A wave of relief went through her. "I thought that's what the camper was for."

He smiled, a sexy dimple appearing in his left cheek. "It is." Then he went back to kissing her neck, her jaw, the corner of her eye.

She didn't have a response for that and was having trouble thinking anyway as his warm lips continued their assault on her senses, before he wrapped his arms around her and rolled over with a suddenness that left her breathless. She was sprawled on top of him and once she sorted out which end was up, she saw some benefits of their current configuration.

Now it was her turn to kiss him, relishing the way his palms curved over her ass and pulled her in closer. A cool stream of air filtered over her skin, a testament to the fact that the air conditioner was doing its job. And so was Seth, judging from the way her whole body seemed to soften and melt as sensitive parts of her came in contact with the rigid strength of his.

The same rigid strength that had brought her to incredible heights before.

Like her hands had done earlier, he slid beneath her shirt, but unlike her, he bunched the garment up her sides, sending a silent invitation for her to lean up a little so that he could get it off, which she quickly answered by doing just that. Then the shirt was tossed to the side while his fingers splayed across her back, one hand going to her head and pulling it down for another kiss.

This time the kiss was long and steamy, the play of his tongue and teeth adding a delicious element to their love play. She couldn't stop the moan that came when he somehow one-handedly undid her bra clasp and she felt it give way. His palms traveled in a smooth line from her nape to the small of her back before stopping.

"Rese, sit up for me."

When she started to scramble off, thinking she was hurting him, he gripped her hips. "No. Sit *on* me."

The sensuality behind those words was incredible, and with her knees braced on either side of his hips, she slowly sank down on him, wishing like anything that they were both naked. Because the feel of him against her made her squirm.

"Yes," he murmured. "Oh hell, yes. Just like that."

He slid the bra the rest of the way down her arms and it was sent somewhere behind her.

Then his hands were on her breasts, kneading, lifting, stroking. Her eyes closed as crazy bits of thought flowed through her, like spending multiple days on this bed while time blurred reality into a stream of sensation and need.

"So beautiful, Resie. So damned beautiful."

He sat up, arms going around her back and holding her in place as his mouth replaced his hands, and he sucked and nibbled and licked the nipple that had gone as tight and rigid as the flesh beneath her. She squirmed again with each nip and realized that's what he wanted. Wanted her moving against him, and so she obliged, shifting her hips back and forth in a rhythm that made his mouth stop for a second. And when he groaned, she felt it in her very being.

God, she wanted this so badly, and yet she was terrified it would be over too quickly. Before she was ready for it to be.

Would she ever be? Ready for it to be over?

His lips reached for her other breast and things went back to the beginning. The slow arousal of the nipple that had already had a taste of what its twin had gotten.

"Oh, Seth…don't stop."

His mouth came up to her ear. "I love the sound of my name on your lips. Love it when you're aroused. Needy. Aching."

She was. All of that. There was no denying it, nor did she want to try. Only one thing would satisfy her now. She grabbed his shirt and tried to get it off of him, but somehow didn't quite have the coordination to get the job done so he helped her, holding her gaze as he stripped the garment off, baring his chest. "I can already feel it. In my head. That slow, wet slide…"

So could she.

She couldn't stop herself from touching him, brushing her palms over his skin and playing with masculine nipples that were ringed with just a sprinkling of hair. She wondered if they were just as sensitive as hers. To test it, she lightly pinched them between her thumb and forefinger, and his muttered oath followed by hands sliding into her pants and cupping her backside seemed to confirm her theory. He liked it. A lot.

He angled her against him in a way that was perfection. Especially when he started pushing against her in rhythmic strokes that was a precursor to the movements that would soon be inside her. Filling her.

She panted something but wasn't even sure what she said. Just knew that she needed more. Whispering his name again, she added, "Please."

"Stand up, Resie."

She slid off the bed, trying to keep herself upright on legs that had turned to rubber; she watched as he sat on the side of the bed, pulling her between his thighs before unbuttoning his jeans and sliding down the fly.

Her teeth came down on her lower lip as he pushed his clothing down his hips, revealing that he, too, was ready for this to happen. So ready.

She did better at removing her shorts and panties than she had when she'd tried to remove his shirt, and she soon had them off. Then they were on the bed again and this time, Seth was on top, kissing her and nudging her legs apart. When they came together this time, there was nothing between them, and he slid home with a smooth thrust that made her see stars. Very good stars. Stars that had her arching into him to take all that he could give. And just like before, he filled her completely, made her want to stay just like this…in suspended animation.

But they couldn't. And as soon as he started moving, she was glad for that. Because as good as that initial entry had been, this was a thousand times better, because she got to experience it over and over again, like the repeated chorus of a favorite song.

Before she was ready, his rhythm picked up and she found that—like it or not—her body kept up with his, hips jerking closer with each pump. It was crazy how good animal instinct could feel.

Animal instinct? Oh no. This went way beyond that. This went all the way to…

He changed his angle, interrupting her thoughts. Or maybe he'd sensed a change in the way she was moving. Whatever it was, it quickly filled her senses as his length slid over her most sensitive spot with each pump of his body, sending her into the stratosphere where things started moving very fast. So fast she could barely keep up with them. She was being lifted higher. Higher. Her body tightening in anticipation, like the crank of a music box whose dancer was about to be set free.

The snapshot of a thousand things burst through her mind. The feel of his stubble against her cheek. The ragged sound of their breathing. The slick moisture of her body against his.

One more thrust and she was gone, her body convulsing around him as wave after wave of pleasure washed over her, seeming to go on forever. And his own groaned release sent another breaker crashing through her before the water slowly receded as if being pulled back to sea, and she could finally breathe again. She pulled the air into her lungs and let it hiss back out. Over and over until she could collect thoughts that had been scattered to the winds.

Except when she gathered them home, they weren't what she expected. They were more like bemused shock. The slight sinking feeling of letting herself go down a path that led away from something good. Like their friendship.

Would this be it? Would the easy companionship they'd shared at the beginning of the festival now morph into more awkward silences and avoidance? God. He might be the father of her child. What would having sex with him again do to his promise to be a part of the baby's life?

Seth rolled off of her and lay on his back, one hand over his abdomen, still breathing hard. The quick separation was raw and unexpected and didn't bode well for where they were at now. His eyes were closed, so she couldn't even attempt to read his thoughts.

She sat up and looked down at him, praying that she hadn't ruined everything even as she chided herself that it took two to do what they'd done, and he'd seemed every bit as invested in this as she'd been.

Damn. She was overthinking, just like she always did. Maybe he was still lost in a sensual haze and having problems processing anything right now. But she didn't think so.

"I can feel you looking at me."

She blinked, not sure of what she was supposed to say to that. Because although his body was magnificent, she wasn't ogling him. But maybe that wasn't what he'd meant.

"This room is kind of small. There's not much else to look at."

He barked out a laugh and then opened his eyes. "You sure know how to make a man feel good."

That made her smile. Because it was something the old Seth would have said. The pre-sex Seth.

"Are you saying I *didn't* make you feel good?" Her brows went up.

His grin faded. "No. I'm not saying that at all. It did feel good." He reached out his hand, letting his fingertips slide across her collarbone and making her nerve endings sizzle. Then he dropped his arm and took a deep breath, eyes turning serious. "I'm just not sure how this started or why."

She searched her brain for an answer to that question and came up blank. "Yeah. Me either." She hesitated, but knew it needed to be said out loud. "But do we even need to know? Or need to overanalyze it? I'm so tired of doing that. Especially after everything that happened with Bill."

The second she said her ex's name, she knew it was a mistake. She wasn't sure why exactly, but Seth was on his feet gathering his clothing. "I need a shower. Do you want to go first?"

"No. Go ahead." She sat there feeling empty as he disappeared through a small door to their left.

He didn't invite her to join him, but then again did she really expect him to? Maybe he'd taken her comment about not overanalyzing what had happened to mean that she wanted more. Even though she hadn't said it, could she have subconsciously meant it, and he'd heard some subtext?

And she couldn't say with any degree of certainty that what had happened wasn't some kind of reaction to her broken engagement and the need to feel attractive and desirable to a man. That first time had definitely been for those reasons.

And this time? Couldn't she have picked up any man and expected it to feel the same?

No. She trusted Seth, and that played a huge part in this fiasco. But it wasn't fair to use him to validate her own self-worth, either.

Or was that even it?

She had no idea, and right now she was glad that Seth had gone into the bathroom. Because that gave her a chance to quickly get dressed and shove her feet back into her sandals. There was a taxi stand not far from here that would take her back to the park to get her car. So she did what she seemed to do best. She fled the scene of the crime before anyone could say or do anything.

Because she was pretty sure that anything she might say right now was just going to make things worse for them both.

Seth left the results of the DNA test on her desk. A week had passed since he'd come out of the small facilities on his boat and found her gone, her note that she'd needed to get back to handle an emergency somehow ringing hollow. Despite a few unanswered texts asking to talk to her, things had been radio silent between the two of them. He did some quick calculations. They should be getting close to the eight-week mark and he had no idea where they stood. Or where he did in regards to what had happened.

Having sex with her had been a huge mistake. He'd known it at the time, and yet he'd let his libido overrule common sense and had taken her back to his boat. The experience had been…well…more than he'd imagined possible. But that's what had gotten them into this mess in the first place, wasn't it? The fact that sex with her was like an out-of-body experience. Once they kissed, he couldn't seem to stop. Hadn't he learned anything about consequences after that first time in his apartment?

Evidently not, because he'd dived right back into the deep end and hung out there for far too long. And this time getting out of the water had taken more effort than it had the last time, and he wasn't sure why.

All he knew was that when she had mentioned Bill's name, it was a reminder that she had been in love with the man…might even still be in love with him, despite her musings to the contrary. You couldn't just shut something like that off with a snap of your fingers.

And how did he know that, when he'd never even been in love before?

The man's name had also brought the sting of what could only be jealousy. And it wasn't a good look. For anyone. So he'd gone into the bathroom with the excuse of needing to get hosed off. And it had been true. But he'd needed to wash away more than the evidence of their lovemaking. He'd needed to clear his head and had hoped that the shock of icy water would snap him back to the present. It had shocked his senses all right, but it hadn't done anything to untangle the knot of dissatisfaction he felt in the aftermath of something that had felt so damned good.

It just felt…incomplete, somehow.

Realizing that he was still standing near her little cubicle like some kind of lost puppy, he gave a frustrated sigh and turned to go but then spotted Luca, who was just coming through the door. The man changed his trajectory, coming toward him. Great.

Luca glanced behind him at the empty area. "Are you looking for Therese?"

"What?" The sense of shock wore off, and he realized he'd left the envelope with the test results in plain sight on her desk, the return address a clear indicator as to what was inside. But there was no going back to try to fix that. And if he denied being there to see her, then Luca might ask him what he actually did want. And that was something Seth wasn't ready to examine. So he said, "I was, but it isn't urgent. I'll give her a call later."

"Sounds good."

They parted after another few seconds of small talk and Seth went on his way. While he and Luca were on friendly terms and had discussed patients from time to time, he didn't know much about the man. Even if they'd been good friends, he wasn't ready to confide in anyone. Especially not when it came to Rese, the sex they'd shared or the pregnancy. He doubted he would ever be ready. But someday the news would get out. Especially if the results were what he now thought they might be.

He was halfway down the main corridor of the hospital when he spotted Rese talking to someone. The conversation was definitely animated, since she was emphasizing her words with staccato movements of her hands the way she tended to do when excited. The recipient of that excitement came into view and he stopped dead in his tracks.

Bill.

A wave of anger came over him. He should be relieved, but he wasn't. What if she and her ex patched things up for the sake of the baby? And what if the baby turned out not to be Bill's and was his, instead? How did he feel about his child living under the same roof as a man who had no qualms about hurting his or her mother or about hounding her to take him back?

Seth should just turn around and go down a nearby hallway that led to the staff lounge, but instead he angled toward the pair. Now that he could get a glimpse of Rese's face, he saw that she was pink, but not with excitement. That fierce frown indicated she was angry. Very angry.

Bill just stood there with his arms across his chest not saying anything. But he had this weird smugness pasted on his face. Then he opened his mouth. "You know it's not over, Therese. It'll never be over."

Rese took a step closer. "Oh yes it will. It's over because I *say* it's over, and you should know me well enough to know I won't change my mind. Not this time. We. Are. Through."

When Bill reached for her, though, Seth closed the gap. "I wouldn't do that if I were you."

Bill turned and then glared at him. Then he looked from one to the other before glancing back at Rese. "Ah, so is this the reason you won't take me back? I already told you, that woman threw herself at me and… I'm only human. I fired her, so she's no longer in the picture."

If Seth was angry before, he was now livid, the pulse in his neck throbbing in a way that spelled trouble. As if sensing that, Rese touched his arm. "Don't. I can handle it." Her words carried a soft determination that he recognized.

She turned back to her ex. "I don't believe you for a minute, and even if I did, it wouldn't matter. The fact that you fired her for something *you* are guilty of is deplorable. And it won't change my mind. Nothing will. So please go."

He looked like he might say something else, but then glanced at Seth and sneered. "I see how it is. You were probably in bed with him the whole time, all the while pointing the finger at me."

"Oh, believe me, Bill, I'd like to point a finger at you, but it wouldn't be my index one."

Seth's lips twitched, unable to hide his smile despite Bill's ugly accusation. Rese had no trouble confronting someone when the need arose. She was right. She could handle it. He'd already known that, but wanted to at least be here to lend support just in case. But instead, he might have made things worse. Or maybe the man just wanted to justify his own moral failings by projecting his guilt onto her. Something his dad would have done.

Had she told Bill about the pregnancy?

He didn't think so, or he was pretty sure Bill would have found a way to weaponize that information as well. For the second time, he hoped the baby was his. That Bill would never have any access to Rese's child. Because he had no doubt he would use the infant as a pawn to hurt his ex in any way he could.

"Fine. I'm leaving. But if you change your mind…"

"She won't." Seth wasn't sure why he said it when it was plain that Rese didn't want his interference, but the words came out of their own volition. What also seemed to have a mind of his own was the sense of relief that she didn't seem to love Bill. She'd said that to him, but he hadn't been sure she'd meant it. He should have known she didn't say things she didn't mean. Nor would she put up with betrayal. He'd seen that back in high school when her prom date had come crawling back out of the woodwork to try to make up with her. She'd turned him down flat as well.

They both stood there and watched as the man walked away. "God, I hope it's not his."

He chuckled, his anger fading. "I just got done thinking the very same thing."

She turned toward him. "You did?"

"Yep. There's no way I want that jerk coming anywhere near the baby. He doesn't deserve it."

"I agree. But if it is his..."

He got it. Rese had a strong sense of right and wrong. She would do whatever she felt was in the baby's best interest. And she would think of the long-term repercussions, when Seth was only thinking of the here and now. "He's a narcissist, Rese. He sure put on a different face when you were together. At least from what I saw."

"I don't see how he could have fooled me like he did. He was always so nice and easygoing, it was pretty easy to give him whatever he wanted. He's never spoken to me like he just did. He made me feel like what happened was my fault."

"They do that. And they hide behind that charm and easygoing personality. Until someone puts their foot down and says no more."

Her eyes swung to his face. "Are we still talking about Bill?"

He had shared parts of his childhood with her... how his mom always worked hard to make sure people didn't see the uglier side of his dad. The side that was able to cut someone deeply using only his words. But what Rese didn't know—because she'd never experienced it—was how his charm disappeared completely when he was drinking. His mom did finally put her foot down when Seth was seventeen, but it took a call to the police to get him to finally leave the house. He hadn't heard from the man in over twenty years. For all he knew Carson Graham had started all over with another unsuspecting woman.

Maybe that's why he'd never quite liked Bill. He sensed something in him wasn't quite what it seemed on the surface. But he'd always hoped he was wrong. Evidently not.

"My dad was cut from the same cloth."

"I know. All I remember about your dad was that he smiled a lot and knew how to say the right things. But then when your mom kicked him out and you told me why..." Her head tilted. "Did you see through Bill when I was dating him? After we became engaged?"

That was a tricky question. Because he hadn't really. Just had his suspicions. But if he'd approached Rese with his concerns and been wrong, it might have caused a break in their friendship.

"I didn't. Like I said, they're good at hiding it." He changed the subject. "I left the results for the DNA test on your desk. Do you have a date for testing yet?"

She nodded. "Tomorrow. I'm nervous. I don't want to burden you with anything, but at this point, the alternative—that Bill is the father—is pretty untenable."

"I get it. And I can go with you, if you want."

"You don't have to." But something in her face said otherwise.

"I'll come. The results will be in in a few days, right?"

She nodded. "Yes, the company said three to five business days. Since you already have your results, maybe it'll be sooner. Are you sure you don't mind coming?"

After what had happened on the boat, he was probably a fool to go. But no matter what else happened, he cared about Rese and wanted to support her in whatever way he could.

And if that support required more than he was able to give?

He'd cross that bridge when he came to it.

CHAPTER SIX

THERESE HAD AGREED to Seth coming, but now she wasn't so sure. She was so nervous that she was nauseous. That scene with Bill yesterday, while horrible, could have been so much worse. They could have had to call security, and she could have been surrounded by concerned coworkers who had lots of questions: *Do you have a stalker? You mean that is your ex...what did you ever see in him?* And while she might have appreciated the support, she really didn't want anyone to know she was pregnant. Or that there was a question about the baby's paternity. Unless you knew the situation and what had gone on during that time, there was no way someone could understand why she'd ended up in Seth's arms the same night as finding out Bill had cheated on her.

Honestly, not even she understood why it had happened not once but twice.

Seth pulled up to the curb next to the hospital and stopped to let her in. There were a couple of folks going in and out of the same entrance she'd used and she wondered again if this was a good idea. What if someone on staff spotted them?

And what?

It's not like people didn't know she and Seth were

friends. It wasn't a secret. Even Beth Gaines from Human Resources knew. What was a secret was her pregnancy and the fact that she'd slept with him.

As soon as they turned toward the central part of the city, Rese pulled Seth's envelope from her purse. "They probably already have a copy of this on record since I'm using the same lab for my test, but just in case."

"Is that on purpose?"

"What? Using the same lab?" She gave a half shrug. "Not really. I don't know how many places in San Diego do the testing. But it was the first name that came up when I did an internet search."

"Same here. But maybe this will make things a little less complicated."

Rese didn't see how that was possible. It was already super complicated, and at least one of the prospective fathers knew about the pregnancy. The other one would hopefully never need to know that he was even in the running. And after yesterday, she hoped she never saw Bill again. She hoped he begged his personal assistant to come back and took up where he left off.

No, actually she didn't. There was a small part of her that felt sorry for the woman. She could only imagine what Bill told her about their relationship. She could even picture the rueful smile he'd probably given her as he delivered whatever story he'd concocted. Probably saying that their relationship was on the rocks. That they were separating. Well, that was a done deal. Hopefully his next target would realize what kind of man he was sooner than she had and would give him a wide berth.

"Do you want me to punch the address for the lab on my phone's GPS?" she asked.

"If you don't mind. I kind of know where it is, but just in case…"

She entered the street number into her phone, and it picked up the spot almost immediately, the computerized voice telling them to go a mile and then make a right, getting on the interstate. Meanwhile, she tried to find a safe topic of conversation. One that wasn't full of land mines that would take either of them by surprise.

"Marinda's PT sessions are going so much better than they were in the beginning. I may be able to cut her loose sooner than we thought."

He glanced over at her before turning his attention back to the road. "Well, that's a pretty big change. But I'll admit when she came in for her follow-up appointment, her mother also seemed different. She was animatedly talking about her daughter wanting to be in one of the community plays."

"That's fantastic. I never would have thought it possible. But her smile is strengthening, and the nerves on the left side of her face seem to be waking up and firing more evenly. I can tell she's been working at home on the PT exercises I've given her."

"And our basketball player. How's she doing?"

"Our basketball patient? She's not even one of your patients." She smiled. That case was one of her favorites. Not because the girl tried hard—which she did. But because Lara was optimistic in a way that reminded her of herself. Or at least the way she used to be. Before the end of her engagement. "She took my words to heart about slowing down and giving herself time to heal. She's no longer trying to bulldoze her way to recovery by doing as many exercise reps as possible. It's like both Marinda and Lara have come back to the middle, which is where they both needed to be. It's not good to push yourself too hard or too little. There has to be balance. In everything."

Even as she said the words, she wondered if she believed them. She'd pretty much been in denial ever since that pregnancy test came back positive. Not about the pregnancy itself. But she hadn't thought through the ramifications enough. What if Seth was the father and they both had very different ideas about how the child should be raised?

"I agree."

Before she could stop herself, she asked, "If the baby ends up being yours, do you want him or her to have your last name?" Maybe they should get some of these decisions made before she actually went into labor.

He didn't answer for a minute. "How would you feel if I said I did?"

She wasn't sure, actually. "Can I get back to you on that? I just want to think through the ramifications, if that makes sense."

"Yes."

His simple answer surprised her. If it had been Bill, he would have been pushing for it. Not in a rude way, but he would have flashed that megawatt smile at her and cajoled her into agreeing to see things his way. He'd done that a lot. And most of the time, his words made perfect sense and she gave in. Maybe it was part of being a lawyer. At the time it hadn't seemed odd, because he'd never been overtly pushy. But looking back she could see the subtle signs of manipulation.

Seth didn't play those kinds of games, though. He pretty much told her what he thought of things and let her work her way through his suggestions at her leisure. She appreciated that. And she also appreciated the way he'd come to her defense when Bill had been in that hallway, trying to talk her into getting back together with him. And when his brilliant smile hadn't worked, his demeanor had changed completely, becoming combative and ugly. Even accusing her of unfaithfulness. But she hadn't been. Not until she knew that they were through. And that didn't constitute cheating. At least she hoped it didn't.

"Hey, I never did thank you for coming over when you saw me arguing with Bill. And yet when I asked you to let me handle it, you did."

His brows went up. "It was damned hard. I wanted to pick the man up by the scruff and toss him out on his ass."

"I know. But you didn't." She hesitated, coming to a decision. "If the baby's yours, and if you're serious about wanting it to have your last name, I think I want to go that route."

He sat in silence, and she wondered if he regretted getting into this conversation. Or maybe he was wondering if she was angling to also use the Graham name. So she quickly added, "Just for the baby. Not me. I don't ever want you to think I'm trying to back you into a corner. I don't want to get married. To anyone. Not anymore."

"I didn't think you were."

The words were soft, but there was a firmness to them that said he didn't want to marry her either. And somehow that stung, although it shouldn't have. No one should marry without love.

Before he could say anything else, her eyes caught the name of a street sign. "Hey, I think we just missed our turn."

"Dammit." The GPS was already rerouting them, but Seth pulled into a nearby parking lot and maneuvered his way to the other side, where a side street was actually the one they were supposed to have turned down. He clicked on his left turn signal and pulled out onto the road.

A computerized voice from her phone announced that in one mile their destination would be on the right.

"Almost there."

"Yep. We are."

The way he said it also gave her a feeling of unease. As if they'd already reached another kind of destination. One in which their journey together would be done.

And she didn't want it to be. Despite the horror she'd felt about the abrupt way he'd gotten out of bed the last time they made love, she was happy that they were still able to ride in a car together without completely shutting down. But she was also doing more and more wondering about whether or not they would sleep together again at some point. And she also knew the more times they were intimate, the more possibility there was that they would overtax the strands that bound them together, and the cords would break apart.

They pulled into the parking lot of a large building whose glass facade made it seem open and transparent, rather than a place of secrets and uncertainty. Or maybe she was just projecting her own feelings onto it. It was also bigger than she expected, but the company didn't just do DNA testing for paternity questions. It also did genetic testing and counseling for a lot of other conditions.

As if thinking the same thing, Seth said, "Does it have a floor listed on the envelope?"

Rese pulled it out of her purse and looked. "No. Just the street address. There'll probably be a list of offices in the main lobby, if it's anything like Sunrise Medical."

"You're probably right." He parked the car and sat in his seat for a minute. Then he looked at her. "I shouldn't have taken you back to the boat, Rese. And I'm sorry. I know I've complicated matters—"

"It wasn't just you. I feel like I pushed you toward what happened. And when you couldn't seem to get away from me fast enough, I was too embarrassed to stick around and face you. But I should have been willing to stay and talk to you about it. Instead of running away."

"You didn't answer my texts afterward. And I thought I'd destroyed everything we've built over the years."

"I know. I was just too confused and upset with myself to be able to talk without crying at that point."

"Hell, Rese. That tears me up inside. I don't ever want to make you cry."

She shrugged. "It wasn't you. I was mad at myself and couldn't think of a way to undo what had happened."

"We can't undo it. But maybe we can learn from it. I think it's hard when the lines between friendship and something else are blurred. Maybe we need to redraw that boundary and both agree to stick to it. No matter what."

"No matter what. I agree. So what do we do now?"

He clicked open his door, and the heat of the day quickly chased away any remnants of air-conditioning. "I think the first thing we do is to go inside that building and put the wheels in motion of finding out who the father of this child is. Then we can go from there."

"Let's do it, then."

They made it into the entryway of the main part of the building, which was evidently divided into three wings that were listed as A, B and C. And from the list of offices, the building didn't just look big. It *was* big. Megalithic, almost. One wing housed a research facility and the other two housed offices. Where specialists and testing labs were listed.

"There," she said. "Paternity testing."

The office was on the second floor and listed a Dr. Saheed, which she recognized from the notes she'd taken when she'd made her appointment.

"Looks like the elevators are just around the corner. Do you want coffee or anything?"

There was a small café, similar to the one they had at the hospital. "Coffee equals caffeine. I'm already jittery, and I don't want to add anything to my system that might hurt the baby."

"Sorry. I forgot. I may grab one on the way back out. I have some appointments later this afternoon."

"Seth, you should have told me. I could have come here alone. What if it takes longer than you expected?"

"Then I'll reschedule my first appointment. I don't have any surgeries on the docket until tomorrow. So there's nothing critical."

"Okay. Hopefully it won't take long."

They got on the elevator and took the short trip to the next floor up. When they got off the elevator, the door they wanted was right in front of them. She hesitated outside of it for some reason.

As if sensing her reasons, he took her hand and gave it a squeeze. "It'll be okay, one way or the other. So let's not worry about anything until we get the results."

"I keep telling myself that the baby's DNA is already set in stone. There's nothing I can do to change it and that I just need to accept whatever happens."

What else was set in stone? The way she and Seth would relate to each other from now on? What if re-setting the boundaries didn't work? What if they kept stepping over that line until one or both of them had finally had it with the other one? Because she was already thinking that she might like to relive what had happened on that sailboat. The problem was, she wasn't like one of Seth's other women. She knew herself well enough to know it wouldn't be any easier to walk away from him than it was to let go of the hand that was still holding hers. And that scared her more than anything.

Seth glanced at her. "So you don't think we should war against the hand we were dealt? That what will be will be no matter how hard we might wish differently?"

Somehow she knew they weren't still talking about the paternity issue, especially since his face had hardened slightly and he let go of her hand. Obviously he didn't have any difficulty letting go. But before she could think of a way to respond to what he'd said, the elevator doors opened again. A man and woman got off and looked at them before stepping past and going into the door of the lab. The man stood and held the door for them with a questioning look.

"Thanks. I guess this is it." Rese stepped inside and waited for Seth to follow before letting the door close behind them. She really didn't want him to see just how much she was dreading this moment. Because really, no matter who the father ended up being, her life was going to change more than it would have if she'd had some anonymous donor.

Why on earth had she been so quick to go off the Pill? Because she'd thought Bill had been on board, even if he hadn't been jumping for joy. He'd never been super demonstrative, though, so she just chalked it up to his personality.

He should have been truthful if he'd had reservations.

Sighing, she tried to turn her thoughts somewhere else. Like the fact that she wasn't sorry she was pregnant. She was going to get the baby she'd always wanted, but had never seemed to have time for before. But now she would. And it was probably time to knuckle down and start looking in earnest for a more permanent place to stay. The camper was lovely, and the little community had been nothing but friendly and welcoming. But it was Seth's and eventually he was going to want it back. Like his life?

She finally let herself look around. Wow. The place was packed. Seats lined the walls and even so, it seemed to be standing room only. "I'll be right back," she said, heading for the reception area, which actually didn't have a line in front of it. She went up and gave her name, then hesitated and handed them Seth's envelope. "This is the potential father's results. Would you like them now, or should I hand them to the tech who's drawing the blood?"

The middle-aged woman at the desk smiled at her as if there was nothing odd about her question. "I can take it." She glanced at it. "Oh, it's one of ours. That makes it easier. I'll make sure the data is already in the system and linked to your name so it'll be ready when your test comes back. Is there anyone else who's doing a cheek swab?"

As in another potential father. There was, but she hadn't yet decided what she was going to do about that if the baby wasn't Seth's. "No."

"Okay. You can go right through that door on your right."

She glanced back at the fifteen or so people still waiting. "I don't want to cut in front of anyone."

"You won't. Most of these folks are members of one family who are waiting on some sensitive results."

At that moment, a young couple came through the

door on the left. The woman gave a thumbs-up sign with a wide smile on her face, and the whole room erupted and everyone seemed to talk at once, laced with a couple of cheers. But the loudest thing of all was the sense of profound relief that seemed to be carved into the very walls of the space.

She was happy for them. They'd evidently gotten the answers they wanted. Rese only hoped she could be as lucky. She glanced back at Seth, and he motioned to himself and then pointed at her with raised brows. Did she want him to come?

Yes. She did. Maybe it wasn't the smartest choice, but what was one more dumb decision in what now seemed like a long line of them? She nodded, and he immediately moved away from the wall and came over to meet her.

Rese smiled at the receptionist. "Thank you."

"Absolutely," the woman said. She was smiling, too, and Therese had a feeling she was rejoicing with the young couple who'd just emerged from the back.

The door to the right didn't open to a corridor. It was another small waiting room, but there was no one else in there except for her and Seth. She went up to the desk, which was much smaller than the one she'd just left behind. "I'm here to do a blood draw for a paternity test."

"Okay." She glanced at Seth. "Do you need to be swabbed?"

"No, I already did that."

Rese added to his statement. "I gave the envelope to the lady at the front desk."

"Perfect. Did they tell you that it'll take three to five business days to get the results? Unless you want to expedite them."

"No. Three to five is fine." Maybe she should ask for them to be back sooner, but even though she was anxious to know who the baby's father was, having a small waiting period might do her some good. She could plan her next move and talk to a realtor and see what was available in the area. And she wanted to prepare her mom and dad for the fact that she would soon know who the dad was.

Ding! Ding! Ding! Winner winner chicken dinner.

The singsongy rhyme went through her head, and for some reason she had to stifle a laugh. She hoped she wasn't going to make a fool out of herself. If not now, then later with Seth. He hadn't asked for any of this. But even so, he was willing to step up and possibly help raise a child he hadn't planned for.

Well, neither had she. Actually...she had. She just hadn't planned to have one with him. And yet here she was hoping that it was him.

"Rese?" He touched her arm.

She shook away the thoughts and then realized someone had emerged from a little cubicle and was motioning her back.

"You don't have to come if you don't want to." And then she looked at him. Really looked at him. "I'm so sorry."

"Hey. We've been through this. It wasn't just you. We both played a part in this. And I'll go back with you."

They went back and while Seth stood against a counter that housed lines of collection tubes, the tech checked Rese's veins. "Both arms look good. Do you have a preference?"

"No, whichever is easiest for you."

"Left then." She tied a length of tubing around Rese's upper arm and instructed her to make a fist.

The woman was good at what she did. She expertly located the vein and pierced it, collecting two vials of blood. Then she slid the needle from her arm and put a piece of cotton over the spot. "Hold that for me, would you?"

She did while the tech labeled the samples with the name, date and time. Then she put a piece of tape over the cotton to hold it in place. "You're good to go. Don't stand too quickly."

It was strange to be on this side of the equation. She was normally the one instructing her patients to be careful when doing this or that. She stood up and for the only time in her life, swayed for a second before someone steadied her with an arm around her waist. Seth. His arm was warm and comforting, supporting her. In more ways than one. And as independent as she was, it felt good—too good—to be able to lean on someone other than herself.

The tech looked at her with concern. "Do you want to sit back down for a minute? Pregnancy can make our bodies a little more unpredictable than normal."

"No, I'm okay. Really. Thank you."

Unwilling to shrug his arm away, she walked out of the room with him and went back to the main waiting room, which had almost cleared out. The big family was probably out celebrating somewhere.

As much as she was loath to lose the feeling of her body pressed next to his, she knew she needed to do so before he really got worried. So she turned, looking up at his face with a smile. "I'm good now. Thanks. And thank you for coming with me. It was nice not to have to go through this alone."

"You're not." He let his arm drop back to his side and returned her smile, although it didn't quite reach his eyes. "Alone, that is."

He said the words, but for some reason—and maybe it was because he'd now put a few feet of space between them—she felt more alone than she ever had in her life.

"Are you okay, Rese?" Her mom sat across from her at the large family table as she nursed her tea. "Does it have something to do with the baby?"

Knowing her mom would jump to the worst possible conclusion, she hurried to reassure her that as far as she knew things with the baby were fine. "But I didn't tell you everything when you came by the camper that day."

Her dad was out on a fishing trip, and it was just as well. She didn't want to see the look of disappointment on his face when she told them that she wasn't positive who the father was. And she honestly had never thought she'd find herself in this position. It was like something from an episode of *Whose Baby Is It Anyway?* a talk show that focused on just this kind of thing.

"Okay. Can you tell me now?"

"I went and had a blood draw yesterday."

"For what?" Her mom's eyes widened. "I thought you said the baby was okay."

"He or she is." She licked lips that felt suddenly dry. "The blood draw was for a paternity test."

There was shocked silence for a quick moment. "But Bill was the one who cheated."

"He was. But after I found out, I was a mess. I ran straight to Seth and blubbered all over him and…"

Her mom put two and two together. "And there's a possibility that Seth might be the father."

"Yes. And I feel so guilty. He didn't ask for this."

Her mom picked up her cup of tea and came around the table to sit in the chair next to Rese's. "Neither did you, honey. You didn't ask to find your fiancé with another woman. Does Bill know about the baby? I assume Seth knows."

"He does. And if it ends up being his, I don't think I'll tell Bill. There'll be no reason to. He…well, he came to the hospital the other day and made a scene. It wasn't pretty."

"I'm so sorry, sweetheart. I'm sorry to say it, but I'm glad you're done with him." She paused again. "Was Seth okay with doing testing? I'm assuming they needed something to match your results to."

"He was. He went with me to do mine, actually, and also wants to go to my first prenatal exam, which is later this week. I put off making that appointment because I just wasn't sure how I felt about everything."

"And now?"

She knew what her mom was asking, but she didn't

know quite how to answer. "I'm happy that I'm pregnant. I've wanted children ever since I was a kid myself. But I'm not sure how I feel about everything else. And I am horrified that I've put Seth in this position. He, unlike me, has never wanted the whole wife and kids thing. He's never even dated anyone for longer than a month or two."

Rese had never been able to do that. She always put her heart on the line every time she agreed to go out with someone. It was just the way she was built. And had been crushed more than once because of it. Well, no more. She was not doing that again, if she could help it.

"Maybe there's a reason for Seth's reluctance. You and he have always been close. I used to think you guys would one day look at each other and have a light-bulb moment. But when that didn't happen...well, I was happy for what you seemed to find with Bill."

"So was I. I never had any real doubts about him until that day I found him cheating." She closed her eyes. "It was so awful. I don't think I'll ever get that image out of my mind."

"I'm so sorry, honey. But it's good that you found out before you got married. And maybe now you can replace it with something even better."

Rese tilted her head. "What do you mean?" She had a feeling she might already know what her mom was hinting at, but there was no way she was going to entertain thoughts like that. It was just setting herself up to be hurt all over again. Right?

"Nothing. All I'm going to say is that you'll know it when you find it."

With that obscure comment, her mom went and brought out two slices of her famous carrot cake along with a container that contained what looked like half the cake.

"Oh no, Mom. Are you trying to turn me into a blimp?"

"Of course not. That's the baby's job." She laughed. "But now that I'm going to be a grandmother, I'm going to spoil that baby rotten. Starting now."

"You do know the baby isn't even born yet, right?"

"I know. But I might as well start now. That way the baby will recognize me after he's born."

"He?"

She gave a half shrug. "I'm almost never wrong, so start picking out names."

Her mom was known for her accuracy in that department. She'd guessed the gender of other relatives' babies and had gotten it right every time that Rese could remember. "Have you ever been wrong?"

"I thought I was once. But then found out I was wrong about being wrong."

Rese laughed and suddenly all was right with the world. Thinking of her baby as a little boy made things seem very real. And not quite as scary as it had been before.

Hopefully that feeling would stick around until the baby was born. And afterward.

CHAPTER SEVEN

SETH MET RESE in the staff lounge to wait for the arrival of A Capella Ambush. The singing telegram service made regular appearances in the staff lounge and other professional areas of the hospital. It was pretty much the worst-kept secret at Sunrise Medical. If it was your birthday, odds were that either the hospital or your department would foot the bill for the group to come and sing to you.

This time Beth Gaines, the hospital's beloved human resource director, was the target. She was due to arrive any minute on the pretext of there being a potluck lunch in the lounge. And judging from the number of people who had packed into the room and the extra-large sheet cake, the whole hospital had taken the "whoever can attend, please do" text to heart.

"I hope Beth is ready for this," Rese murmured, her words almost lost in the countless other conversations that were going on.

"I guess we'll find out."

Her shoulder bumped his when someone tried to get past them, and Seth had to fight the urge to slide his arm around her waist to keep from getting separated. He'd had that same instinctual urge at the lab, when he thought she might faint. And once his arm had been around her, it had been damned hard to slide it away again. And he wasn't sure why or how he felt about that.

A Capella Ambush arrived and somehow managed to squeeze into a corner of the room to wait with everyone else. Luca McDonnell from Physical Therapy pushed through the door, then stopped and looked around with a frowned "what the hell..." expression on his face.

But if he was going to turn around and leave, he didn't get the chance, because someone came in right behind him, saying, "Okay, shhhh, she's coming."

Then the lights went out, throwing the room into darkness as all chatter ceased. Seth was painfully aware of Rese's arm still touching his, and he couldn't for the life of him remember what they'd been talking about. Nor could he force himself to put a few inches between them.

The door opened again, and the lights clicked back on with a loud, "Surprise!" from those who were in the room. The singing group made its way forward until it stood before her. Someone blew a note on a pitch pipe, then:

We're here to wish Beth a happy birthday.
You praise her when hired or curse her when fired,
but you know she does her best to help you stay.
So happy birthday, Beth.
And here's a special surprise from your friends at Sunrise.

A round of laughter ensued, then one of the singers lifted his hands like a conductor and started singing, "Happy birthday to you..." and motioning everyone to join in singing the traditional tune.

Seth couldn't remember the telegram message being personalized before, but maybe it was because it was Beth.

Once they finished, someone waved everyone to silence and then motioned to the table. "Help yourselves to cake, and let Beth know how much you appreciate her." With that, the singing group slid from the room with almost no fanfare—probably headed to their next gig.

When he glanced around, there were several faces that he recognized, but no one looked more uncomfortable than Luca—who slipped out almost immediately after A Cappella Ambush did. Everyone else stayed for cake. Even their administrative director had shown up for Beth's birthday wishes.

As for the birthday girl, she was all smiles as she accepted a slice of chocolate cake from someone within her own department, going around and talking to various people as if it were their celebration rather than her own.

And that was how it was done. Beth made people feel special. He glanced down at Rese. So did she. Not so much in what she said, but how she looked you in the eye when you were talking and made you feel like your opinion mattered.

Like when she'd asked if he wanted the baby to use his surname?

She'd genuinely wanted to know and even though she hadn't yet given him an answer, he knew that she would do whatever she thought was in the baby's best interest.

"Do you want a piece of cake?" he asked her.

"Ugh. No. My mom just pawned half a cake off on me yesterday. Want some of that?"

He laughed. "Maybe. What kind?"

"It's one of your favorites." She sang it to the tune of one of the lines A Cappella Ambush had finished singing.

"She's got a lot of good ones, but if it's carrot, I would not turn that down."

"Yes! I was hoping you would say that. Oh, and Mom is thinking boy."

"Boy what?" When she gave him a pointed look, his brows went up as understanding dawned. "Ah, I see. Can I ask what that's based on?"

"You can, but there's no answer for that. No hocus-pocus. No crystals held over my midsection. She just gets a feeling that she can't explain. But I have to say, I've yet to see her be wrong."

A boy? He swallowed hard as a strange emotion settled over him, and he glanced at her midsection before quickly looking away. It hadn't mattered to him whether the baby was a boy or a girl, but somehow hearing it referred to as a living being made things seem real. So very real.

When they'd made love on the boat, he hadn't noticed a vivid difference between the before-pregnancy Rese and the during-pregnancy version, except her belly may have been the slightest bit more convex than it had been. Although once their clothes had come fully off, he hadn't been in any kind of position to think about whether or not she was showing. He'd wanted her, and that was all that had mattered.

Had that changed? The wanting her?

Hell no, since even standing next to her was bringing back vivid memories from their time on the boat. And with cheeks flushed and lips curved in a smile that she'd aimed only at him, he was having trouble thinking about anything else. In fact, he had to grit his teeth to keep from grabbing her hand and tugging her into the hallway to see if she felt the same way. He forced his thoughts back to the pregnancy.

"Well, I guess we shall see what we shall see, right?" he said.

"Right."

He thought of something else. "Did you ever find an…er doctor?"

There was a slight hesitation. "I did. I'll text you the details."

A reminder that she still didn't want to talk about this in front of anyone else. He got it. But he also knew that the time was coming when people were going to know. And the more prepared they both were for that eventuality, the better it would be.

"Can we talk in person about it instead?" He smiled. "Maybe over cake?"

"Mom's cake?"

"What other kind is there?"

She laughed, her voice getting slightly louder since the room still contained a lot of people talking all at once. "Mom will be flattered that you said that."

"Maybe next time, I'll get half a carrot cake of my own."

She grinned up at him, nose crinkling in a way that

made him smile back and sent his thoughts right back to Hot Night on a Sailboat.

"I'll put in a good word for you," she said.

"Thank you. So where do you want to eat this cake? The camper? My office?"

Both of those were dangerous options, but the words had come out before he could stop them.

She seemed to think for a little bit before answering. "How about Spanish Landing? It's big, but has some nice benches that would give us a place to chat."

Without the temptation that either one of the other places would afford. It was as if she'd read his thoughts.

But who was he kidding? No matter where they were, there was temptation. Did she feel it, too, or was this wholly one-sided?

"Spanish Landing sounds great. When?"

"How about this afternoon after work, unless you're on duty tonight?"

He didn't normally work nights unless there was an emergency. "I don't. Do you want to meet me there or do you want to share a ride?"

As soon as the last words left his mouth, he knew how they might sound. He could only blame it on the crazy direction his thoughts seemed to have taken.

She didn't answer right away, and her cheeks flushed. Maybe he wasn't the only one with thoughts that should be shelved.

When she finally did respond, she said, "Let's just meet there, so you don't have to go out of your way to take me back to the trailer."

They'd be coming in from different places and for him

to drop her off, Seth would have to go about ten miles out of his way. And he never had stayed in that second bedroom like they'd planned on him doing after Cajun Fest because of the stage accident and its aftermath.

"How is the band member? Did you ever hear?"

"I actually visited Terrance in the hospital. He was transported to a private clinic just outside of San Diego at his request. I'm surprised that you didn't get an invitation to go see him."

"Did it come by mail?"

"Yes. I'm not even sure how he got my address, but he did."

He didn't check his physical mail all that often, so it was possible that it was in there, but not likely. Rese made an impression on people. Lots of people, both male and female.

Him included.

She continued. "Anyway, his head is better. Slight concussion, but he's doing well. He actually invited me to play with him for a set at his next concert. I declined of course."

"Why? I've heard you play banjo. You could keep up with him."

"I don't think so, but thanks for your vote of confidence. I haven't played regularly in the last couple of years. Bill wasn't fond of…"

She shook her head.

Ah. That bastard. One more mark against him. "I don't think Bill liked you showing him up at anything. It's no reflection on your abilities, because you are good and you know it."

"I was going to say that Bill wasn't fond of banjos in general. He's not the only one who thinks that. I think you either love the sound of the banjo or you hate it. There's not much middle ground."

There were only three or four people left in the room and a glance at the table where the cake was showed it had pretty much been decimated. Only a few ragged pieces were left on the foil-covered surface.

"Maybe it depends on who's playing it."

"Meaning?"

"Meaning, I like the banjo, but more so when you're the one playing it. If it's anyone else, I can take it or leave it."

She shook her head. "Well, that's not much of a compliment. It's kind of like saying the banjo has a sound that only a mother—or a friend—could love."

Somehow hearing her put him firmly in the category of a friend rubbed him the wrong way. They'd potentially made a baby together after all, so surely that made them... Hell. He wasn't even sure. And maybe that was also something that needed to be shelved. At least for a while. Until he was able to sit down and think things through. For now, though, he'd better act like a friend or he might lose her altogether.

"That's not what I meant at all. I like the banjo when it's in someone else's hands, but when it's someone you know... It's just different. Kind of like the happy birthday song they did for Beth. When it's personal, it's special."

"I guess that makes sense." She glanced at her watch. "Okay, I have to get back to work. So we'll meet tonight at Spanish Landing? Want me to bring anything?"

"Since we're talking about banjos, why don't you bring yours? And I'll stop for some takeout on the way there. Anything special?"

She tilted her head. "Chinese? I've had a hankering for lo mein recently. And are you sure about the banjo?"

"Absolutely." He smiled. "As far as the food, I think you always have a hankering for that—and Cajun shrimp—so nothing's changed."

Except he was wrong about that. Everything had changed. And not just for him. And soon enough, everyone would know why.

Rese walked down the path that led to their meeting spot, her banjo case slung over one shoulder and a cake carrier clutched in her other hand. She'd almost left her instrument at home, but she did some practicing before putting it in her car and found her muscle memory hadn't completely abandoned her. She truly loved playing and used to do it for family gatherings all the time, at least until Bill started joining those gatherings. After that, when people asked her to play something, she'd always just shrug and pretend she'd forgotten to bring her banjo. Bill's look of relief had always made her glad she hadn't pushed to continue the tradition.

He never told her he didn't want her to play. But somehow she just knew. His pained expression always took the joy out of her fingers plucking those metal strings and coaxing a tune from them.

Unlike Seth, who'd attended a lot of their family reunions over the years, and who'd always been front and center when she started to play. He hadn't been lying about enjoying it. She could tell by the way his eyes followed her movements, humming along with her when he knew the tune.

And he had a gorgeous singing voice, harmonizing with hers as if they were always meant to be...

She shook her head and walked a little faster. That way she didn't manufacture ideas she had no business thinking about, much less acting on.

A tug on the strap of her instrument case made her falter, for a second thinking someone was going to snatch it and run. She twisted, swinging the plastic cake carrier as she did and striking out at her attacker.

A muffled "oof" as the blow landed and the sight of a plastic bag falling to the ground made her eyes widen and jerk to the man's face. "Oh God, Seth!" He was bent partway over at the waist, holding his stomach. "Are you okay?"

He held up a hand, sucking down a lungful of air before straightening up. "I will be. As soon as I catch the breath you knocked out of me."

"I thought you were a purse snatcher."

He looked pointedly at the handbag strap that lay diagonally across her chest. "Wouldn't that involve someone actually trying to *get* your purse?"

"My banjo could be sold for good money on the black market."

He sucked down another breath, a chuckle sounding more like a gasp. "There's a black-market banjo ring?"

He went to pick up the plastic bag, peering inside. "You're lucky these were well-sealed."

"I'm so sorry. It was instinctual. Self-defense."

"Believe me. Now that I know what you're capable of, I'll never sneak up on you again. I was going to tell you I'm glad you brought your banjo, but now…"

She laughed. "I'll just take it back to the car."

"Um, no. I've already suffered bodily harm because of that thing. I think I deserve a little play time."

"Playtime?" Had she heard him right?

"I mean as in your banjo playing."

Oh God, of course he did. Why had she thought he was referring to something sexual? Because of her earlier thoughts, that's why. And because they'd already had sex twice. And she was certainly not the strongest person when it came to giving in to that part of her nature. Which is why she needed to keep her head on straight. Especially now when she felt more vulnerable than ever, because of the baby.

She had to remember that whatever decisions she made for herself would affect her child as well. Then again, if they hadn't had sex the first time, there might not even be any baby. And she loved the tiny creature with all of her being. She would not wish him away by wishing that event away. Besides, it had been cathartic, helping her get through the overwhelming grief of her relationship crashing and burning. It had accomplished what crying had not. And for that, she would always be grateful.

She forced herself to speak again. "Where do you want to sit? And did you bring paper plates?"

His mouth twisted, and he looked slightly shamefaced. "No. But I brought chopsticks and asked them to put the portions in smaller containers. I thought we could eat right out of them."

She'd done that many times before. "Of course we can. I just didn't know if you'd want to eat after me."

He eyed her. "I think we're long past that worry."

And so they were. They'd shared a lot more than just germs. So they found an area of grass off to one side and sat under some shade trees, the midsummer sun just starting to make its descent. Even so, they still had a couple of hours of daylight left.

They shared the containers of lo mein and happy family as well as a Szechuan selection that made her toes curl from its spiciness. It was so good. But when she made to hand him that container, he shook his head. "You're spice… I'm nice."

"Seriously? You're going to play that card? Sneaking up on me like that?"

He laughed. "Well, mostly nice."

"I'll agree with that." And she did. For all the times that Seth had seemed broody and distant—especially recently—she could normally bring him around with a joke or sometimes even with a look. It's what friends did: bring out the best in each other. Right? A line from a classic romantic comedy came to mind with the hero claiming men and women couldn't be just friends.

Well, she and Seth had proved the guy wrong. Because they could be. Except, hadn't that hero also claimed that sex always came up?

Yes, but in their case, her fantasies had only been sporadic, because she'd always managed to corral them and keep them from breaking through. The actual sex, though? Well, the first time had been brought on by a tragedy—so surely they could be excused for that. And the second time there'd been a *near* tragedy.

So they just had to avoid anything going wrong when they were around each other, was that what she was saying?

Like her walloping him with her mother's cake? The image of him sprawled on the ground and her leaning over him feeding him bits of that cake before moving in for a kiss… She shook that crazy thought away. What was wrong with her?

Hitting him had been an accident. And besides, here they were sitting beside each other without a single mishap. Or a single kiss.

Before she could stop herself, she glanced at his mouth, unable to keep her eyes from lingering there.

"Don't do that." His words were low. "Or my 'mostly nice' might desert me."

"Sorry." She didn't try to pretend she didn't know what he was talking about, because she'd once told him that she never lied to him. And she wanted to be able to abide by that statement. She put down her food to change the direction of the conversation. "On that note, you keep eating while I play."

She reached for her case and unzipped it, pulling out her banjo and adjusting the strap over her left shoulder. Resting the instrument on her crossed legs, she slid two metal picks on, one on her right index finger and the other on her middle one. Then she added a plastic pick to her thumb. Leaning over her banjo, she started strumming with a light touch.

Thankfully their tense exchange a moment earlier

hadn't robbed her of her ability to find the notes and tease them out of the strings. She started the first song with a ballad about love lost, not thinking about the words she was singing until midway through the song. It could be about her and Bill, except the man the lyrics were referring to had never cheated. They'd just both realized that the love they'd felt when young was no longer strong enough to hold them together.

She leaned over the banjo as she picked her way through the bridge, her hair sliding over her cheek in a way that made her feel like she was ensconced in her own world, hidden from those who might want to intrude. But it was just her and Seth, and he'd made it pretty clear that he was good with not letting things go too far. He didn't want them to, in fact as evidenced by him asking her not to look at him like she'd been.

And she should be fine with that.

Singing the chorus one last time, she finished out the song, and immediately picked the intro to another one that was in the same key. This one had a more upbeat message, and she started the first verse, getting halfway through it when a masculine voice joined hers, finding the harmony with little effort. And there was a certainty about his voice that said he did this a lot to tunes that he heard on a daily basis. Rese did, too. They made it through the chorus, and when she reached the next verse, she nodded at Seth like she'd done in the past, telling him to start singing and she would catch up.

His voice was a couple of octaves lower than hers, and the husky baritone timbre had always sent shivers through her. It was no different this time. He sang of memories that surrounded him. A miner's daughter and the taste of moonshine. There was a haunting quality to the lyrics that made a band of emotion tighten around her midsection.

Thankfully they arrived back at the chorus and, this time, she harmonized when he sang the melody. It was so beautiful and moving, even though this song wasn't particularly sad. She was pretty sure it was due to the way their voices melded together and how the song had always spoken to her heart. And for a brief second, she allowed herself to pretend he was singing directly to her.

But he wasn't. And she needed to remember that.

Once they finished, she took her strap off and dropped her picks back into her banjo's case with a laughed, "Let's take an intermission to eat dessert. Hopefully it wasn't completely smashed when I hit you with it."

If that were so, she might really need to feed bits and pieces of it to him.

"It'll taste good, smashed or not." His brows went up, obviously unaware of her thoughts. "But you might not want to tell your mom that you used her cake as a weapon. It might reflect badly on me."

"No, she would blame me for that. But it doesn't matter. You and I are the only ones who are going to know what really happened tonight."

She tossed those words out in a light voice, without really thinking them through. Because he responded, "What exactly *is* going to happen tonight?"

Her brain froze for a few scary seconds, and she was pretty sure she looked like a fish, her mouth opening and closing as she discarded a few highly suggestive ideas. "Oh...er. Not tonight. I mean right now, and it's not actually night, but it's what I meant and I was not trying to imply—" Her rush of words was cut short by a touch to her arm.

"Relax, Rese. I was joking."

Joking. How had she missed that? Maybe because she was getting more and more tangled up in the strings that held their friendship together. If she wasn't careful, she might tear those strings completely apart.

"Oh. I should have realized. I don't know what's wrong with me."

"Nothing is wrong with you." He gripped her hand and then released it. "I think we're still learning how to navigate around what's happened between us. But I do want to reach those clear waters again—where we can talk without worrying about how the other person is going to take things."

"I want that, too. More than you know." If only she could figure out how to stop *herself* from thinking those things.

He nodded. "So do I. So let's work hard to make that happen."

Rese agreed with him, but deep inside she wondered if that was even possible anymore. Or if it was far too late to go back to the world as it had once been. Or if she even wanted to. A world before she'd had sex with Seth.

CHAPTER EIGHT

Rese's doctor's appointment was two days after their trip to Spanish Landing. Thank God nothing else had happened between them. They'd somehow been able to eat her mom's cake and avoid talking about sex. What they did talk about was the baby and her appointment. She hadn't asked, but Seth had offered to go with her. He didn't have surgery that day, and the two appointments that he did have could be pushed back until after lunch. And Rese had Marinda and they would be discussing a date to complete physical therapy. How had they even gotten here after such a rough start? But both Marinda and her mom were vowing to stay in touch and let her know how things were going, and they hoped she would do the same.

They could count on it. By now her schedule was busy with patients cycling in and out of her little area, but both Marinda and Lara, her basketball player, had left their marks on her heart. She hoped to hear that they were doing big things and that Marinda would be as proud of her newfound smile as Lara was of her jump shots.

She waited outside the hospital for Seth to pick her up. By now, she wasn't all that worried about who saw them together. As soon as she got the paternity results, she was going to start letting people know she was pregnant—especially Beth Gaines, since they would want to plan early to cover her position while she was out on maternity leave. At least that was her plan. She hadn't yet broached the subject with Seth. But she hoped to do that today. Because according to what they'd heard at the testing center, the results should be in any day now.

And she was nervous. So very nervous.

Seth's car appeared and stopped along the curb. He leaned over to pop the passenger door open for her. She slid into the vehicle, sending a surreptitious glance toward the hospital entrance.

So much for not caring what people thought.

Seth looked over as she buckled in. "Are you nervous?"

"Super nervous. You?"

He smiled. "I can admit to an overfiring synapse or two."

"I probably should have made this appointment right after I took the home pregnancy test, but I think I was in denial. At least at first. Now I'm more anxious about everything being okay with the baby than anything else."

"I think you'd know by now if something was wrong."

She hesitated. "I don't mean with the pregnancy, but I'm thirty-eight…geriatric in the eyes of most prenatal caregivers. They'll want to do extra testing. And if something happens to this baby…" She shrugged. "I don't know if I could bear to try again."

And she knew with certainty that she wouldn't be trying again with Seth.

"Resie, let's not get there before we get there, if that makes sense. Just take things as they come."

She loved it when Seth added that long *E* sound to the shortened version of her name. It was like a verbal hug and had always made her feel cared for. He didn't do it often, but when he did, it hit her right in the feels.

She smiled. "You're right of course. And so far, things have gone really well. I've had minimal morning sickness, and my jeans are just starting to get snug. I'm having to leave my button undone, just using a hair tie as a closer—it's a hack I saw online."

"A hack."

"I'm serious, look." She lifted her shirt to show him that the button of her jeans had both ends of a hair tie looped over it, having put one end through the buttonhole first.

"Hell, I guess if I ever get too big for my britches, I can use that trick. But for heaven's sake put your shirt down before someone has an accident. Like me."

She gave him a look. "I barely flashed any skin. If you want me to try harder..." She wiggled her eyebrows at him.

"No. Definitely not." But he was smiling, too.

This was the most comfortable she'd felt with him since the day she came to him after Bill's unfaithfulness. And if she didn't know better, she'd say they'd made it completely back to friendship. This back-and-forth banter was something she'd dearly missed—the ability to say something outrageous and have him act like her big brother about it. Like hiking up her shirt an inch or two.

And she liked where they were now. Maybe things would be okay after all. Maybe they would find out he was the father, and he would take his role and embrace it with alacrity.

Or he would at least come to love the baby. "What do you think of the name Alexander?"

He blinked at her. "That's my middle name."

"Yeah. I know. But you don't go by it. Would it bother you?"

"So you didn't choose it because it's part of my name."

A sliver of unease went through her—for the first time since she entered the car. "I did. But if you don't want me to use it, I'll think of something else."

"It's not that." His hands tightened on the wheel, knuckles turning white. "We don't even know if it's my baby yet or not."

"I know." She clenched her hands in her lap. "I'm sorry, Seth, I'm not trying to—"

"Hey, I know you're not." His hand left the stick shift to cover hers for a few seconds, the warmth of his skin penetrating her sudden chill. "I just don't want you to feel you have to cater to me in any way. Whether it's names or the way the nursery will look or anything else."

Was he hinting that he was ready for her to move out of the travel trailer? That was another thing. She'd still had no luck finding another place to live—not on her salary. It's not that they weren't out there, they just got snatched up as fast as they came on the market. And usually by people who heard about the listing before it even appeared on any realty site. And with her work schedule that was just about impossible.

She hesitated. "I-I can't make a nursery until I actually have a place of my own."

This time he took his eyes off the road to really look at her. "There's no hurry, Rese. You can stay in the trailer for as long as you want. Unless you're embarrassed to be living there."

"Um...no. It's everything I could want actually. The location is stunning, and the camper... Well, it feels more like a home than the apartment that..." Her stomach sank because she realized it was true. Her current location felt more like home than her and Bill's place had. And since it was in his name, she had no doubt that he was still living there. She on the other hand couldn't go back there, even if he vacated it. Because that was no longer her life, and she wanted nothing that belonged to it. She was starting on a new journey. And she was going to have a little traveling buddy to go with her.

"Then stay there. We can take care of the details, Rese."

She should be over the moon. And she was happy. Happier than she'd been in quite a while. Because this decision felt like one she'd made on her own. She hadn't been trying to make someone happy or keep the peace. She was doing something for *herself* and she was going to love this baby like no one else could.

Even though she did hope that Seth would be able to make peace with the fact that he was going to be a father, if it turned out to be his. She knew that some of his commitment issues went back to his dad. He'd hinted at that the day he talked about Bill being like him. She did know Seth had never had any contact with his father since the day his mother had kicked him out. And he had no plans to.

Was he afraid of being like that? He'd never said so, and she hoped he knew he wasn't. At all. And she'd known him for a very long time. Bill might have been able to hide who he was for a few years, but she had no doubt that it eventually would have made itself known, even if she hadn't found him with his assistant that day.

She glanced at him. "Hey. You know you're nothing like your father, right?"

His jaw went rigid, a muscle working in his cheek. "I think we're almost there." He gave her a hard look. "And I'd rather we not talk about my dad right now. Okay?"

"Okay." She was not going to ruin this day by getting on Seth's bad side, not that she saw it very often. And the comment about his dad had come out before she'd had a chance to think through how he might take it. Not good, evidently. Which made her think even more that maybe that was at the root of some of his issues. But if he didn't want to talk about him, then she wouldn't. It was up to Seth to make peace—or not—with his childhood.

Then they pulled into the lot of a hospital across town that had its own maternity wing called the Elizabeth Sanders Women's Center. It had great reviews. Even her mom had heard of it. Speaking of that, her mom had offered to be her labor coach, but what if something happened during labor? She didn't want her mom to be traumatized if things started going south. The last thing Rese wanted to happen was for her mom to be afraid, nor did Rese want to worry about her mom when she needed to concentrate on having this baby.

Ask Seth. A little voice in her head whispered his name, and she quickly dismissed it. There was no way he would want to be in that room with her, staring at her…well…

He's already seen it. And liked it. Oh God. This was not going to go well for her. She needed to figure out another friend or anyone, really, who could do it. Maybe she should look into hiring a doula. Once she thought it, the idea stuck. It was ideal.

Seth found a parking place and turned the car off, sitting there for a minute. Then he turned toward her. "Hey, I'm sorry for going off a minute ago. I don't want to go find my dad or have a relationship with him. And do I think I could end up being a bad father? The answer to that is yes, but not because of anything my dad did or didn't do. But just because of my temperament. I'm not sure I have enough love to give anyone. Especially a child who I know deserves so much more than I have inside of me."

Her chest hurt from the emotion that filled it.

The fingers of his right hand were curled into a tight fist, and she reached over and cupped it between her hands, bringing it to her mouth and softly kissing it. "I don't believe that for a minute. Please believe in yourself."

He stared at her for a long moment before opening

his hand and using it to cup her nape and draw her to him. He pressed his forehead against hers and sat there for a long minute.

Her heart pounded as she willed him to open himself up to the idea that he could be a great partn...father. Oh Lord, she'd almost used the word *partner*.

He pulled back and glanced back out the windshield, taking a visible breath. "Let's see how things go."

Hmm...not exactly what she'd hoped for. But there was time for him to work through things. They still had seven months to go and so much could happen in that time. And surely once he saw the baby on the sonogram or saw his name listed as a strong match on a paternity test, things would change. She wasn't going to argue with him or try to get him to change his mind. She was just going to let things ride. See how things went, like he'd said.

"Okay. Let's do this. Unless you want to stay in the car. You don't have to go in, if you don't want."

"I do want to. Maybe more of my nerves are firing off than I realized." He touched her cheek. "Let's go see what the doctor has to say."

Seth was trying to block out the memory of her voice saying he was nothing like his dad as they sat in the waiting room, but he couldn't. And there was no way he was going to admit that he'd suppressed thoughts that said exactly that. That there might be more of his dad in him than he would admit. But when Reese had verbalized that fear—casting it out into the universe—something had clicked in his brain. And then it was stuck there. Taunting him. Was that why he couldn't have relationships like other people seemed to have? Why he didn't seem to *want* them? There wasn't a woman he'd been with yet that he hadn't been able to say goodbye to without more than a quick backward glance. And he didn't see that changing.

Didn't want it to change. Because if a night or two actually became *more,* he might have to turn and face his father and test his theory that bad behavior could be inherited. And whether it was nature or nurture at play, it didn't really matter here, because he'd gotten hit from both sides.

But when Rese had kissed his hand, her touch light, the contact brief, there'd been a sense of healing for his soul. Or was it that…

Dammit, you're not here to psychoanalyze yourself, Seth. You're here for Rese. Now start acting like it.

So he shoved his childhood back in that little compartment in his brain where it resided and turned to her. "Still doing okay?"

"I think so. This whole thing has been surreal, you know? First the breakup of my engagement. Then the pregnancy. Moving residences. New job."

"I know."

She hadn't mentioned the fact that they'd slept together, but the reality hung right up there with the rest of those changes. And try as they might to get things back to normal, there was an awareness between them that reared its head a lot more now than it had in the past. Even at the park, while they'd joked and poked at each other, there'd been something inside gnawing at him. The way her hair slid across her cheek when she played the banjo, how easily they seemed to sing together, picking up on each other's cues. The way they—

"Therese Cameron?" The woman at a side door interrupted his musings. And right now, he welcomed anything that would keep him from sliding back into that murky pool of what-ifs.

She stood, while he hesitated. He wasn't afraid of going back there. He was afraid that she might not really want him there, despite her earlier words.

"Hey," he said. "Are you sure? I can wait here."

"No. I want you."

This time the turn of the phrase didn't immediately make him think of things that happened between the sheets. Instead, it was a simple request that begged for a simple response.

"You've got me, Rese."

Together they went through the door, and he waited as Rese was weighed, purposely looking away in case she didn't want him to know. But she'd never been one to obsess over things like that.

Then they were in a room and while a nurse asked questions, he sat there letting Rese take the lead. This was her show. And he was happy to let her run it the way she saw fit.

And if you do something wrong and she kicks you out of her life? Of the baby's life?

He'd just have to make sure he didn't. How hard could it be?

Pretty damned hard from where he was sitting. He'd never been great at walking on eggshells, not that Rese had ever asked that of him in the entire time they'd known each other. But she would soon be a mom. And from what he knew of her, she would be fiercely protective of this baby. And he liked that. He hadn't always had that during his own childhood.

"Your vitals all look good. How are you feeling?"

"Strangely good."

The nurse looked at him and smiled. "Are you the significant other?"

He noticed she'd been careful not to ask him if he was the baby's father.

Rese looked at him as if waiting for his response, and he couldn't think of one. He hadn't even thought about this part of the appointment.

He threw out the first thing he could think of. "I'm a friend. I'm here to support her."

"Ah… I see." But the woman didn't see, and from the way Rese now wouldn't meet his eyes she was disappointed in his response.

But they hadn't talked about this. About how they were going to approach these kinds of encounters or even how they were going to navigate things at the hospital once news got out about the pregnancy. He wasn't trying to hide the fact that he might be the baby's father, but those eggshells weren't very comfortable to walk across as most of them were already laying in jagged piles. But to go back and correct himself would look even worse.

But one thing he could do.

He touched her hand. "I'd like to be on your emergency contact list, if that's okay."

Then he glanced up at the nurse. "We've been friends a long time. And I've taken a paternity test. I'm here for the long haul."

If she was shocked, she didn't look it at all, she just nodded and then turned to Rese. "Do you want to modify your paperwork to include your...friend?"

Rese nodded. And suddenly he knew that whatever faux pas he'd committed before, he'd just made things right. So Rese took the clipboard and wrote Seth's name in one of the blank spaces, adding his email, address and phone number from memory. And then it was official. He was in. And right now, there was no place he would rather be.

She handed the information back to the nurse.

"Very good, then," she said. "If you'll take everything off and change into the gown. The doctor will be in soon."

The nurse swept out of the room.

Rese turned to him. "Thank you, but you didn't have to do that."

"I did. And we need to talk about how we're going to handle situations like this. Because I don't know what you want. If the test comes back the way I suspect it will, do you want people to know right away?"

"I'm two-thirds of the way through the first trimester. It's going to be pretty apparent soon."

"Yes. I get it. But it's something we should probably figure out *before* it becomes apparent to everyone."

Obviously it would be a lot easier if they were engaged, or even officially a couple, but they weren't.

"Right now, what I need to do is get into a gown."

She went over to the side of the room where there was a pull-around drape that formed a half circle, hiding her from sight. He could see elbows and body parts as she shimmied out of her clothing and put the gown on. It wasn't like he hadn't seen her before. But he understood her reticence. He hadn't given her much reason to trust him with some things, but he hoped she would come to. Maybe it was time for him to make things clearer so that she felt she could.

Rese had had a lot of changes. He'd had some, too, but his life had pretty much gone on like it always had. And he hadn't moved. Or broken off a relationship. Nor was he carrying another life inside of him. But the longer this pregnancy went, the more changes he could see coming. Yes, they needed to talk. And soon.

The drape hissed as she pulled it back into place and stepped out wearing nothing but a gown, tied in the front, carrying a drape to cover herself from the waist down, which she did as soon as she'd hopped onto the table.

"Are you sure you want me in the room for this part, Rese?"

"I want you to do whatever makes you comfortable."

And that was no answer, but he understood that it was the only answer she had right now.

The doctor came in before he could reply and sat on the stool, wheeling it over to the exam table. At least he assumed she was the doctor. Probably the same age as he and Rese were, she'd paired black leggings with a comfortable-looking tunic, something he could see a soccer mom wearing.

"I'm Dr. Rachel. I understand this is your first prenatal appointment at—" she glanced down at the tablet in her hand "—eight weeks."

She didn't look shocked or sound like it was out of the ordinary to wait until now to have her first exam. "I assume you know for certain you're pregnant."

"I do. I did a couple of home pregnancy tests, and we've gone to a genetic counseling center."

This time the woman frowned. "Is there an inherited trait in your family?"

"Oh, not in mine." She reflexively glanced at Seth, although he knew she wasn't trying to put him on the spot.

"I don't know of anything on my side, either. Although I've never really thought to ask." But he should have. One more strike against him. Not that either of the women were looking at him strangely.

But Dr. Rachel did look down at her tablet. "I don't see you listed as the father." She gave him a direct look.

This time Rese answered. "We did a paternity test. I was engaged at the time, but he—"

"It's okay," Rachel said. "We're just going to take this as it comes. When do you find out who the father is?"

"Probably sometime this week."

Rachel looked at him again. "If you are named as the father, I would like to get some background on you as well. The more we know, the more we can prepare for."

"I understand. I'll try to get some of that." He and his mom had avoided talking about his father for a long time. And maybe they still didn't have to directly discuss him. Maybe he could just ask if she knew of anything in their family tree that could be of concern. Other than narcissistic personality disorder.

That's not what they're looking for here.

He hadn't told his mom about Rese's pregnancy. He figured there'd be plenty of time, once they knew more. But that time was starting to run out. She was going to be thrilled. Although she might not be as thrilled that they weren't getting married. Despite what she'd been through, she still carried that traditional idea of romance. And she'd remarried a couple of years ago to a really nice man who treated her the way she deserved to be treated. She'd said several times that she wanted that for Seth, too.

Little did she know that her relationship with his birth father had soured him on that idea.

"Well, let's get some baseline measurements, and then I'll want to do a preliminary ultrasound just to see where the baby implanted and make sure we're good there."

A niggle of some weird emotion went through him. He hadn't actually thought of the possibility that she might lose the baby or that there might be something seriously wrong. So now there were thoughts piling one on top of the other, all waving for his attention.

But like the doctor said. They were just getting baseline data. She didn't seem concerned at all, and she hadn't even mentioned Rese's age. Yet. Although it was inevitable that those discussions would happen. But today was not that day.

So maybe some of Seth and Rese's hard discussions didn't need to happen today either.

Rachel had her lie back and took a tiny measuring tape from the pocket of her tunic and felt Rese's belly, palpating it before carefully placing the tape. "I need to do an internal exam as well. Just to check your cervix."

She pressed a button on the wall, and a nurse came in and got things ready as the doctor continued to ask questions and chat as if they were old friends. When she heard that Rese played the banjo, she smiled. "That's awesome."

Fortunately, the way the chairs were placed gave Rese some privacy as they did the exam. It was quick, and the doctor snapped off her gloves before donning a fresh pair. She helped Rese take her feet out of the stirrups. "Everything looks good. The last thing I want to do is the ultrasound, and then you'll be good to go. You'll call to update your chart once you hear the results of the paternity test?"

"Yes," Rese said, glancing at him for confirmation, which he gave with a nod of his head.

"Perfect."

The nurse set up a portable ultrasound, giving the wand and a tube of lube to the doctor. She held it up with a rueful glance. "This will be chilly. But it'll be worth it."

Would it? Seth wasn't sure what that even meant. What would be worth it? A look at the baby? Going through pregnancy and labor?

"Here we go." She squirted the lubricating jelly on Rese's lower abdomen, and he felt frozen in place. They were about to see their baby in real time and he wasn't sure he was ready. But they hadn't asked him, and the time to have bowed out had long passed. So he sat there as the doctor slid the wand across the surface of Rese's stomach.

He could hear a kind of roaring sound as the instrument picked up various sounds on the monitor and once he could swear that he heard Rese's stomach growling. The doctor's face was a study in concentration, though, as she stared at the monitor. "Come out, come out wherever you are," she said.

Had this all been some kind of cosmic joke?

"There! Found you, now let's get a look at you." She adjusted the angle of the probe and then glanced at him. "Do you want to come over and see the baby?"

See the baby? Of course that was the expected thing. So he got up and moved over to stand beside Rese as they looked at the screen. He could make out the sac, which appeared as a kind of black nothingness. But off to the right, there was a tiny form inside the sac. "Is that her or him?"

"Yep. The implantation site couldn't be better. And from what I can see so far—" she smiled at them "—two arms and two legs and…" A sound came from the monitor, and it took Seth a moment to place what the "lug-lug…lug-lug…" was.

A lump came to his throat. It was the fetus's heartbeat. Strong and steady and surprisingly fast. But it was there.

"Oh Seth."

He took her hand and gripped it. "I know."

If he was moved by what he could see and hear, how much more amazed must Rese be, since this was happening inside her body.

"Everything looks great, Mom. I couldn't ask for anything more than this. At least not right now." She glanced at them. "Do you want a printout of the ultrasound?"

"Could I?" Rese smiled up at him. "Do you want one, too?"

To refuse was to step on her obvious joy, and there was no way he was doing that, so he said, "Yes."

The doctor printed two of them out, handing them both to Seth. "I'll let you have these so Therese can get dressed. That's all I have for you today, unless either of you has any questions."

"I can't think of any," Rese murmured.

Thank God neither of them asked him, because right now, the only question he could think of was how was he going to handle this. This baby would eventually be born, and everything would shift.

Not that he was going to back out of being in its life, but he was starting to get that strangling feeling that happened whenever someone wanted something of him that he couldn't give.

Except this time he was going to see this through, no matter how uncomfortable it might be. Because he cared about Rese. A lot. And the one person he didn't want to let down was her.

"Be thinking about how you want this pregnancy to go. Do you want a midwife to be the principle on the case and have me ready to step in if there's a complication? Do you want me to be the primary?"

"I haven't even thought about any of that. Can I get back to you?"

"Of course. It's a lot to take in. If you want a midwife, we actually have one practicing through this office. She can be at your next appointment."

"Do you have a doula in your practice?" Rese glanced down at her hands. "My mom asked about being my labor coach, but I think it might be too hard on her."

For some reason, Seth had assumed he would be her coach, but looking back on it, she had never even implied that she might want him to step into that role. While he should be relieved that he didn't have the responsibility that went with being a labor coach, he was experiencing something he didn't recognize.

The sensation of being left out of a part of Rese's life. Maybe even left behind. And he didn't like it. But this was her choice, and he needed to respect that.

But if she left him out of this part of her life—the most important part—what did that say for the rest of it?

Nothing. It said nothing. But one thing was for sure, if he was going to be a father in name only—like his dad had been by his own choice—if he wasn't going to play a real role in Rese's life anymore, then he wasn't sure if he could sit back and take an observer-only seat somewhere in the back of the plane.

He wanted to be with her. Through it all.

Like Rese had said, though, this was all new. All unfamiliar territory. She was trying to feel her way through things, just like he was. So maybe once the results came back on the paternity test, they could sit down and have a long chat. About a lot of things. And hopefully if they disagreed on some things, they could at least find some middle ground that worked for them both.

The printed images of that tiny being seemed to burn his hands as they went out to the car. And the same picture stared up at him from the console as they drove back to the hospital. And when he got home that night, he couldn't make himself toss it onto the pile of mail that sat on the edge of his kitchen table—that seemed like sacrilege. So instead, he went over to the side table where there was a framed print that Rese had given him as a birthday present almost ten years ago. It was them at Cajun Fest.

They looked young and innocent. Just friends on an outing. He'd almost forgotten the picture was there. But he took the ultrasound image and propped it up against the frame. Where he would see it each and every day. And maybe by some process of osmosis, he would begin to accept the reality that was coming. That he might very well be a dad.

CHAPTER NINE

THE SEALED ENVELOPE from the testing lab was sitting in her purse, ready to go with her to work this morning. Out of sight, but definitely not out of mind. It had come two days after their visit to the ob-gyn. She hadn't seen or heard from Seth since then, and it made her nervous. But then again, she hadn't contacted him either.

Maybe they'd both needed time to digest everything that had happened. She'd been slightly disappointed that he'd sat there silent when she asked about a doula to be her labor coach. There wasn't even the slightest hint that he wanted to be there for the birth of what might be his baby.

He can't read minds, Rese.

No, he couldn't. Just like she couldn't imagine what it must be like to be in his shoes. She should look at the test results to prepare herself one way or the other. But she was too afraid. She wanted Seth there. Wanted them to open those results together. Wanted to tackle this like a…couple?

How unrealistic is that?

Ha! Evidently her sarcastic side had to land at least one punch.

She wandered over to the refrigerator to get a drink,

and there was a face staring back at her from beneath a magnet affixing it to the surface of the appliance. Well, some semblance of a face. She'd used her little copier to enlarge the ultrasound. The features were blurred since they weren't super high resolution and the baby was still developing, but she could make out his or her eyes, nose and mouth.

And she already loved it, a warmth stealing over her heart whenever she looked at the image. This was their baby.

No. She didn't know that yet. Didn't know if it actually was Seth's, and yet she was already wondering which of his features the baby might have if it were.

His incredible brown eyes? That sexy mouth that could relay a thousand emotions with just a subtle tightening or a come-hither smile? And the things he said when he whispered in her ear.

The same warmth she'd felt a moment earlier filled her, as her mind drew up a picture of a shirtless Seth leaning against a doorframe smiling at her. Of a laughing Seth dumping her into her parents' pool when they were teenagers. Of a serious Seth running his index finger down her arm after they made love. The sensation expanded outward and reached to her very toes and infiltrated her soul.

Oh God. She swallowed once. Swallowed again.

She loved him. And not that platonic friendship kind of love they'd shared in earlier years. This was the kind of love that could make sweet memories well into old age, or it could break a heart. Her heart.

Seth had been so adamant that he wasn't the marrying kind. And she'd believed him. She still believed him.

She'd sifted through the evidence and accepted it as truth. Could that have shaped what she allowed herself to feel toward him and what she didn't? Could she have been so afraid of losing him that she turned away from the truth that had been staring her in the face?

She sat on the couch, suddenly terrified by the weight of the revelation. What did this mean for their friendship? For their co-parenting if the baby ended up being Seth's?

Okay, think rationally, Rese. Just because Seth claimed he wouldn't marry didn't mean he couldn't fall in love. People didn't always need the piece of paper in order to be together. Some of the things he'd said to her in the heat of the moment had driven her wild. And they'd been meant just for her.

Maybe he felt something for her and just hadn't realized it for what it was. After all, he had to be attracted to her or he wouldn't have slept with her, right?

One hurdle at a time, girl. They needed to get through the paternity test issue first. Then she—*they*—could tackle the emotional stuff. Right?

At some point during the pregnancy she could, in typical Rese fashion, ask him straight out if he cared about her in more than a friendship type of way.

And if he said no? She closed her eyes and blocked it from her mind. *Just take that first step.* If he wasn't the father, it was a moot point, because it was doubtful he'd want to shift his whole worldview for someone else's child.

Even though he said he wanted to be involved?

Well, if she stayed here moping and letting her anxiety get the best of her, she was going to be late for work. Really late. And she had Marinda's last PT session this afternoon. It would be bittersweet, but Rese was glad they could end things on a good note.

Ending things on a good note. Wasn't that always the goal? Maybe if things didn't go the way she wanted them to with the baby—or with Seth—she could still end things on a good note. There was no way their relationship could stay the same after realizing she loved him. To even try to go on as they were would just set her up for a heartbreak that she didn't think she would ever heal from. But what she could do was tell him honestly how she was feeling. And then if he didn't reciprocate, they would go their separate ways with a smile and a few well-wishes.

And that would be that. She'd have to find another place to live, or she'd have to go to her parents' house until she could.

And so, double-checking to make sure the envelope hadn't somehow fallen from her purse and giving a last glance at the ultrasound image on the fridge, she headed out the door and into whatever the future held. Good or bad.

A knock sounded at his door. Seth glanced up from some tricky MRI images he'd been studying and frowned. He wasn't expecting anyone that he knew of. Rather than inviting whoever it was into his office, he got up and went to the door. Opened it.

"Rese..." He studied her face. "Are you okay?"

"I am. I just...er, have the results from the lab."

He dragged a hand through his hair. Although he'd known this was coming, he still wasn't quite ready to face whatever it was. But he'd better figure it out and fast. Because time had just run out. "Come in."

She came into the office and sat in a chair, waiting as he tried to make his way back to his desk, slogging through a layer of emotional muck that grabbed at his shoes with each and every step. But he finally made it, gripping the wooden edge of it as he lowered himself into the chair.

She studied him. "I, um… I can come back if this is a bad time."

He wasn't sure there was a good time. But putting it off was just going to let his mind keep dreaming up scenarios that didn't end well for him.

"No. Sorry. I was just looking at MRIs for a tough case."

"Anything that I'll be involved in?"

He shrugged. "Maybe. It depends on how involved the defect is."

"What kind of defect?"

"It's an infant. Bilateral cleft lip and palate with some sinus involvement."

Her eyes widened. "Will you do the entire surgery?"

"Probably not. The palate and sinus issues are much worse than the lip. Doug…" Realizing she would have no idea who Doug was, he clarified, "He's one of our ENT surgeons. He'll do the repairs on the sinus and palate. I'll do the aesthetic portion of the surgery: reconstructing the nose and lips and making sure everything looks as natural as possible with maximum range of motion."

"You'll be able to do it. I know you will."

He couldn't do everything, and long ago he'd accepted the things he either couldn't do or didn't want to do. The second Doug had sent over these images, his thoughts had immediately gone to Rese's baby. Would he or she have problems because of Seth's age? Or Rese's? "Thanks for that vote of confidence, even if it isn't always warranted." He sighed. "I guess we should look at the results, shouldn't we? Do you want to go first?"

If she'd wanted to do that, she probably would have just told him what the test said.

She shook her head, a strange expression on her face. "I'd rather we do this together."

"Okay, let's get it done." The second he said the words, he regretted them. It made it sound like this was an onerous chore. One that he'd rather not be involved in.

And Rese's face registered her distress. "Maybe I should just—"

"No." He got up from his desk and came around to sit in the chair next to hers, then squeezed her hand. "That came out wrong. I meant it would be better to do this now than for both of us to sit here and worry about it. Like you've probably already been doing."

"Pretty much." She pulled out the envelope and toyed with the flap for a few seconds before closing her eyes.

"Here, Rese, let me." He took the envelope from her and slid his thumb under the glued section, loosening it and pulling out two folded sheets of paper. "Ready?"

She nodded.

He opened the pages and held them so they could both look at them. There was a lot of complex jargon about genetic markers and probabilities. His eyes skipped to the conclusion. *It is therefore postulated with 99.1% certainty that Seth Alexander Graham is the biological father of the child.*

He was the father. *He* was the father.

The world went dark for a few frightening seconds.

Neither of them said anything, and Seth felt like everything he saw or heard was coming through a black tunnel. One with no light at the end of it. His sudden inner turmoil made no sense. After all, he'd spent weeks mentally preparing himself for this possibility. But all the preparations in the world couldn't make someone fully ready for a life-changing event. This was one of those times, and the turmoil morphed into a wave of sheer panic. It crashed over him, knocking him flat, and he lay there flailing around unable to get back up.

There was no light at the end of that tunnel because this was *forever*.

He hadn't wanted this. Not as in this baby, but fatherhood itself. He'd done everything he could, in fact, to avoid it. And yet… It had found him.

Is this how his father had felt after finding out his mother was pregnant?

"What are you thinking?"

Her low question made him shake his head, still trying to grasp that this was really happening. He stalled by carefully folding the sheets of paper. Once that was done, he gripped them tight, unable to remember anything that had been written in the report other than the fact that he had fathered a child.

His actions had led to this moment. He'd traveled a path that couldn't be untraveled no matter how much he might want it to.

He closed his eyes, trying to think of something to say that would lighten the mood. There was nothing. No quip that could save the day or joke that could make everything all right. He desperately wanted to do right by Rese. By this child. He tried to power through, hoping the needed words would come.

"It's a lot. I just need a few minutes to process."

That sounded like something Rese's ex might have said. Or his dad. Evasive. Self-serving. Trying to buy some time before coming up with a response that wouldn't paint him in a terrible light.

She studied him, and something in her face cleared. As if she'd found the answer to her question without his help.

"It's okay, Seth. You can have all the time you want." She stood and turned toward the door, her steps sure and unhurried.

"Rese..." He got up in a rush. "Wait."

She stopped.

"No. I told you from the beginning that I don't expect anything from you. I still don't." He couldn't read her eyes as she turned to face him. "I want this baby with all my heart. I love it already. Do your thinking, Seth, but just know I don't want anyone in my child's life who doesn't feel the same way I do. Or in my life."

"I didn't say—"

"No. You're right. You didn't say the words." She turned back and gripped the doorknob, opening it. "But if you can't do this, don't worry. We'll be fine."

He stood there as if paralyzed, unable to think of anything he could say—anything that would be truthful, at least—to keep her from going through that door. And if she did, he knew in his heart she wouldn't be back, despite what she said about giving him time. He opened his mouth, but nothing came out as she opened the door and went through it. Then, as she closed it behind her, her hand lifted and he swore he saw her dash away something on her cheek.

He could rush after her and demand she listen to him, but he faced the same problem he had a moment earlier. Nothing he could say right now was going to help the situation. He didn't want to charm his way out of anything. Not this time. He'd told her the truth: he needed to sit down and digest the information and decide what he wanted to do—what he was mentally *able* to do.

Somehow Rese got through the rest of the day without falling apart, although she'd come pretty close to it in his office. If she hadn't left when she had, he would have seen a flood like he'd probably never seen before. She'd made it to the elevator—which thankfully had been empty—before breaking down completely. Then she made it through her last two patients before heading back to the RV park.

Once there, she parked her car and went inside, still feeling a numbness she wasn't sure would ever go away.

She'd warned herself this could happen, but somehow, she'd let herself believe a fairy tale. One where the hero would hear the news and kiss her, and then they would ride off into the sunset.

That wasn't fair to Seth.

Was she sorry he'd ended up being the baby's father? No. Because it meant she owed Bill nothing. No explanation, no anything.

What this did mean was that unless Seth had some sort of crazy revelation, she would be raising this child on her own. Wasn't that what she'd told herself she wanted at the beginning of this process?

Yes. But things had changed now. She'd realized she loved the man. And if he'd had that reaction to the paternity test, she could only imagine what a declaration of love would bring. She didn't even want to imagine that scene. Besides, it was a dead end.

As was this camper. There was no way she could stay here now.

She went through the space and collected her things—slowly, methodically—trying to do it in a way that wouldn't jostle her emotions and send her into another meltdown. Rese needed to be smart about this. Finding another place could wait for a few weeks. She called her mom, who immediately told her to come home. That they would always have a place for her. At least *someone* loved her.

That did it. She cried again, sitting on the edge of the couch until she had no tears left. Then she climbed to her feet. She was ready to face what needed to be done.

She took one last look around, making sure she

hadn't left anything behind. Then she stowed the last box in her car. It was crazy that she'd come to think of this place as "home." But she had, and leaving it was bittersweet. She was certain that Seth would tell her to stay as long as she needed. But what she needed was to leave. Because it held bits and pieces of him that, right now, were too painful.

She started to close the door and then stopped. Wait, she had forgotten something. She went up the steps and into the kitchen, lifted the magnet that held the image of her baby, and pressed the sheet of paper close to her heart.

"We'll be fine, sweetheart. We'll be just fine."

Then she made sure everything was off and the place was shut up. She turned to get in her car when one of the neighbors came out. "Are you leaving? You just got here."

Edna Baker, an elderly widow who lived full time in her small trailer with two cats, stood in her narrow driveway. She was a sweet soul who had grandchildren that visited on a regular basis.

How had she learned so much about her in such a short amount of time?

It didn't matter; she was leaving. She went forward and gave the woman a hug. "I am. I'm going back home to stay with my folks for a while."

"Won't you even visit?"

"Maybe. But not for a while, Miss Edna." She thought of something. "But could you do me a big favor?"

"Of course, what is it?"

She undid the key to the camper from the ring that

held her car's fob. "Could you give this to Seth next time you see him?"

The woman's eyes widened, and a sense of understanding seemed to pass across her face. "Oh, honey, are you sure you want to do this?"

She was sure. Rese had done a lot of thinking over the last couple of hours. She didn't blame Seth. She couldn't. He was a wonderful human being. This just seemed beyond the scope of what he could do. And in that light, it was beyond what she could do to just go on as if things were fine between them when they were actually messed up beyond repair. "I am."

Edna took the key. "Okay, well, if you change your mind, you can always stay with me. I have a pull-out couch that you could sleep on."

A wave of emotion went through her. She hugged Edna again. "Thank you. Take care. Give Tito and Max a hug for me."

With that, she got in the car and drove away, her rearview mirror showing Edna shaking her head as if she disapproved of what was happening, but was helpless to do anything to stop it.

"You're not the only one, Edna. You're not the only one."

CHAPTER TEN

A WEEK LATER, Friday found Seth tackling the surgery on the baby with the bilateral cleft lip and palate. He hadn't seen or heard from Rese in that time, and he had no reason to go down to the PT department, since he didn't have a patient in rehab right now. And he still hadn't come up with any kind of plan.

Was it even possible to plan for something like this? But he knew from the way Rese had left his office that their friendship was irrevocably broken. He'd been right all along. Sleeping together had destroyed everything they'd built over the years.

"Starting on cleft lip repair." He was on the home stretch of the surgery, and so far, everything had gone according to plan.

Well, at least something in his life had.

This baby was going to get a new lease on life. One that didn't involve the deficits he'd been born with following him into the future.

Something about that slid into his head and began processing in the background. But he couldn't bother with that right now. He had a surgery to complete. He eyed the amount of skin he'd prepared on either side of the baby's nostril and began stitching, keeping everything nice and even. He would need the lip margins to align perfectly—when he got there—and that meant slow and steady progress, and not trying to rush to the finish line. The preparation was as important as the execution. One without the other meant that things would not line up as they should, and it would affect the outcome.

There. He reached the upper edge of the lip line and found it had worked. Just as it always did when he took the time needed. He picked up the exact edge where skin met lip on either side and sutured it together.

He leaned back and studied it looking for puckers or anything else that didn't seem right. No. It was perfect. He finished the last few stitches and made sure the inner surface of the baby's lip was just as securely fastened as the visible parts. Then he tied everything off.

"Okay, that's a wrap." He dropped his needle into the tray with the rest of the instruments he'd used during this surgery with a sense of relief. "Let's wake this little guy up."

Seth liked silence while he worked, although he knew a lot of other surgeons preferred to have music playing. He just found he needed to concentrate on what he was doing. Anything that interfered with his thought process could be translated through his hands and ultimately through his needle. He couldn't risk it. Sutures inside a patient didn't have to be pretty, they just needed to do the job. But the ones on the surface had to be done in a way that distorted the skin as little as possible. His job was to smooth away the damage that had been created by nature or by trauma.

If only it was that easy in life. Some damage caused scarring that nothing could fix.

Or could it? There was such a thing as scar revision, in which various methods could be used to make a scar less visible. The most invasive technique was to cut the scar out completely and stitch the skin back together in layers, just like he'd done with this baby.

The process was the same. Advance preparation and then meticulous needlework could make things better. The scar would always be there in some shape or form, but its presence would be less damaging.

Had he ever attempted to address the scars formed by his parents' dysfunctional relationship and his dad's moral defects?

No, because it hadn't seemed necessary before.

The baby started moving as the reversal medication did its job. Seth watched the infant's lips as they moved with each grimace and reflexive smile. The stitches held. That meant, barring infection, this surgery was a success.

He touched the baby's cheek with a gloved finger, the warmth of his soft skin penetrating the rubber barrier and creeping through Seth's hand. This child was beautiful. Just as his own would be.

God. He'd allowed the mistakes his dad had made—and his own mistakes in shoving his feelings about them into a tiny corner of his brain—to affect his relationships. With his mom. With the women he'd been with.

With Rese, whom he loved more than anything.

Loved.

As a friend, right?

His brain lit up a flashing red "No."

And he knew it in a split second. Over the years, the line between friendship and love had blurred until he couldn't tell where one ended and the other started. And at some point, without realizing it, he'd crossed over that line. Looking back, he could see that he'd left the land of friendship and had entered a zone whose terrain was new and unfamiliar. And there was now a concrete barrier that prevented him from going back to where he'd once been.

So what did he do now? Did he walk away from the relationship completely?

Did he allow the damage caused by his own childhood to destroy something that could be beautiful? Or did he stop and attempt some emotional scar revision?

He wasn't sure he could do it on his own, but maybe with some professional help to guide him through...

What he did know was he did not want to lose Rese. He searched his soul for the answer to her question from a week ago. *What are you thinking?*

He was thinking that he wanted this baby. And he wanted Rese with a strength that he'd never felt for anyone before.

He didn't have all the answers. And he knew that, like with his current patient, he would need to lay the groundwork that would serve as scaffolding for a successful surgery. But he finally *wanted* the surgery. Finally wanted to work on becoming a better person. A better man. And a better friend, partner and lover for Rese. If she still even wanted that.

She'd seemed pretty firm about walking away from him that day in his office. But maybe she would change her mind if she knew he was serious.

If he told her he loved her.

And if she didn't love him? Hell, she'd just gotten out of a relationship two months ago. But he was convinced that what she'd once had with Bill was gone forever.

And what she'd had with him? Was that gone forever, too?

There was only one way to find out.

After going out to talk to his patient's parents, reassuring them that things had gone well, he did something he didn't normally do: He hugged each of them and told them how happy he was that they'd entrusted him with the surgery. Then he told them he'd check on them later that evening.

But first he had something to do.

He needed to go find Rese and talk to her. Get her to listen and hope he hadn't screwed things up permanently.

He made his way to the elevator and went to the first floor, walking down the corridor to where the large sign over the PT department made its presence known. But when he entered the door, he knew right away that she wasn't there. Not from the empty cubicle, but from way the space felt. Her vibrant, smiling presence was absent.

Luca, who was heading for the exit, nodded to him, but stopped when Seth motioned to him.

"Do you know if Therese has left for the day?"

"Not sure. I think I saw her leave the department a couple of hours ago."

A couple of hours ago. "Thanks. I'll catch her later."

It sounded like the repeat of a conversation he and Luca had had weeks ago, right after Rese had started this job. That now seemed like forever ago. And he hoped it wasn't the last time he'd come down here.

"Not a problem," Luca said. "Have a good night."

"You too." As he watched the PT leave, he wondered if the man's reserved nature might not house a few scars of his own. And he wished him the best, whatever his future might hold.

Turning back to glance at Rese's empty cubicle, he knew where he had to go: the camper. Hopefully he would find her there and could make her listen to what he had to say. No. Not *make* her listen. He would never do that. Instead, he would ask her to hear him out and pray that she would allow him to have his say.

Seth pulled into the lane of the RV resort that housed his travel trailer. The grounds were immaculate as always with their neatly manicured strips of grass and flower beds that encircled the trees. The only thing that was missing was Rese's car. He frowned. Maybe she'd had to go to the store before coming home.

Home. Was he already thinking of this as something permanent? Right now, there were no guarantees of anything. He knew he'd hurt her with his reaction to the paternity test. He hadn't meant to, but that part didn't matter. What did matter was that he make it right as best he could, whether or not she accepted the other stuff. Like the fact that he loved her.

But she wasn't here. Should he sit outside and wait?

Edna appeared at the front of her little camper and waved at him. His shoulders slumped. He wasn't really in the mood for small talk, but his elderly neighbor was sweet, and when she brought him baked goods he'd had no fear of ulterior motives. And maybe she needed his help with something.

He got out of the car and headed up her sidewalk, where she'd gotten special permission to plant a profusion of flowers that made her place look cared for and welcoming. The resort had been wise in that decision. The care she'd taken with her own little lot had enticed a couple of luxury rigs to land here, since their lane was on one of the main strips that led to the park office.

"Hi, Edna. Can I help you with something?" He reached her, and as always, she wrapped her arms around him in a warm hug. This time, he returned it.

"No, honey, I'm good. But if you're looking for Rese, she's not here."

Wow, she'd called her by her nickname, which few people besides Seth and her family did.

"I kind of gathered that, since her car isn't here. I was trying to decide whether to wait for her or not."

Edna held something out to him, and his heart squeezed in his chest when he realized it was a key. "You'd be waiting a long time. She's not coming back. She asked me to give you this."

Oh hell. That was it, then. She was either done with him, or she found an apartment. "Did she find a place, then?" He glanced at his trailer and noticed for the first time that the potted plants she'd bought for the little deck out front were gone.

"You don't know?"

As much as he hated to admit it, he shook his head and decided to own up to his part in her leaving. And he was pretty sure that was the only reason she'd left the trailer. "I reacted badly to something she told me."

"She told you she loved you?" The woman's voice was sharp, as if she, too, were upset with him.

"No." Wait. Rese loved him? "Did she tell *you* that she did?"

"No, but it was plain as day when she had to say your name when handing me the key. There was this hitch…"

"Hitch?"

The older woman nodded. "As if she was having to work hard to get it out in a normal tone without that quavery 'I'm about to cry' sound."

And it just got worse. He remembered his mom crying when she'd finally realized that his dad was never going to change and had kicked him to the curb. She'd truly loved him, but love had not been enough in that case.

And evidently Rese felt the same.

Except Seth did want to change. For the first time in his life, he wanted to open his heart and let a woman in. Really let her in. To see the scars and ugly parts that no amount of plastic surgery could fix. Or maybe she'd picked the lock and gotten in there on her own—which he was beginning to think was the case—and had looked around and decided it wasn't someplace she wanted to live. Or raise their baby.

Like she had decided with his travel trailer?

"She didn't tell me she loved me, but I hurt her without meaning to. And you know what, Edna?" He decided to go for broke and finally admit the truth to someone. "I love her."

"Oh, I can see that as clearly as I could see that she loved you. You were a fool to let her go."

He was. But he hoped he had learned from his mistakes in a way that his father never had. It hit him in a flash that left him reeling. The difference between him and his dad was that his dad hadn't cared about anyone but himself. And Seth did. Oh how he did.

"Do you think I still have a chance?"

Although he was asking Edna, it didn't really matter what she said. He would never forgive himself if he didn't at least go to Rese and tell her the truth. And the funny thing was, it had nothing to do with the pregnancy. He loved her, with or without the baby.

Edna pressed the key into his hand. "There's only one way to find out, Seth. And I sure would like to have you *both* as neighbors. Whether you live here full time or not."

"I can't imagine anything better. Wish me luck."

"You've had that, ever since that lovely girl moved in."

Rese spent the weekend getting settled in her childhood bedroom. How simple and easy life had been back then. She'd had wonderful parents—and was lucky enough to *still* have them—and a great childhood.

She sat on the bed and leaned against the wicker headboard—the one that had occupied that space ever since she could remember and was transported to the past and a thousand memories. Not everyone was as fortunate as she was.

Fortunate? She was pregnant and alone and no longer had a fiancé or her best friend. Okay, so life wasn't as certain now as it had seemed a few months ago. But she'd had a great foundation. She really would be okay, despite the heartache she was going through right now.

Seth, on the other hand, had had a childhood that wasn't anything like hers. She'd witnessed what his dad had put him through. Neglect would be one way to put it. Emotional blackmail and abuse would be a more accurate term.

It was no wonder he'd needed a while to process her pregnancy.

She sat up straighter. And she'd denied him that because of the hurt she'd felt over him not immediately declaring his eternal love for his child? And for her?

Why hadn't she seen it for what it was when he'd read that report? Fear.

She'd had a whole lifetime to prepare for—to *yearn* for—a baby. She'd wanted it with a strength that had defied reason.

And Seth? He hadn't had a lifetime to prepare. He'd had a couple of weeks at the most. And it wasn't something he'd hoped and planned for. Instead, she'd thrust him into a role that he'd neither wanted nor expected. How could she think he'd just get out of his chair and leap for joy when something he'd hoped to avoid had been plopped into his lap, with a "Here you go…now be happy or else"?

And when he'd wanted a few minutes to think about it, she'd basically thrown the request back in his face as if it were a personal affront.

She'd been so unfair to him. So very unfair.

Maybe it hadn't been rejection. Maybe it had been actual fear. Fear of not measuring up to a standard that he'd had no experience with.

But he hadn't once tried to get in contact with her since then.

So why did he have to make the first move? She'd told herself that she owed him the truth, and instead, she'd run out of his office and kept it to herself.

Because he'd already been freaking out and to add to that a declaration of love?

Well, freaking out or not, saying she loved him would be making a definitive break in their relationship if he didn't feel the same way. And she needed it to be one way—with him in her life—or she needed him out of it. This time there was no middle ground, and she needed to know.

She found her phone and found the speed dial icon that had their picture beside it. She stared at the tiny thumbnail of them at Cajun Fest a few years back when they'd asked someone to snap their picture at one of those silly poke-your-head-through cardboard cutouts. She was a shrimp and Seth was a gator.

And she couldn't imagine anyone better to accompany her on those crazy adventures of life. They'd had so many. So many that she wondered how they hadn't realized they were perfect for each other before now.

Because they'd been too afraid things would change.

Well, they had. And there was no going back. So she needed to call and meet him somewhere. Just as she was getting ready to push the button to dial his number, the doorbell rang. She froze before realizing it was probably a delivery person. Her mom had mentioned ordering something.

Only she and her dad weren't home. They'd gone shopping for a bassinet, despite the fact that she'd told them it was far too early to be doing any of that. But she couldn't spoil their excitement, so she'd let them go, waving away their invitation to join them. Right now, buying anything would just bring tears. Things were still too raw.

She sighed and got off her bed and went to the front door. She opened it and there stood the very person she was just thinking of.

"What are you doing here?"

She realized how churlish her tone was and gave her head a mental shake. So much for telling him how she felt. But she was just so shocked to find him standing on her doorstep. That could only mean that he'd gone to the RV resort and Edna had given him the key. Maybe she'd left something there and he was here to return it. Except his hands were empty.

"I came to find you." He looked at her face. "Can I come in, Rese? Or is there somewhere we can talk?"

"Of course." She opened the door wide enough to let him in, only wondering afterward if they should have spoken on the front porch instead. But the only seating out there was the hanging swing—where they'd sat so many times before in the past—but it was narrow enough that they'd be touching, and that would cloud her thinking as it seemed to always do nowadays.

She invited him to sit on the couch, while she sat in one of the side chairs that flanked a wide electric fireplace her parents had put in a couple of years ago. More for the ambiance than anything else.

They looked at each other for what seemed like ages before she opened her mouth and said, "I'm sorry."

Except he said the same thing at the same time, their words overlapping each other's.

She smiled. "Well, now that we've gotten that out of the way…"

Unlike her, though, Seth seemed deadly serious. "I really am sorry, Rese. You deserved more from me that day you came to the office."

"No. That is… I thought I did. But I shouldn't have expected to. I've wanted to be a mom for a very long time. But you… It's never been something that was on your radar. And yet I acted like you should be as happy as I was. But how could you be? I gave you no time. No time at all. And for that, I'm sorry. More than you'll ever know." She twisted her fingers together. "I didn't give you a chance to get past that moment. I just…well, I just let my own emotions whisper that you were rejecting me, and I ran away. I should have stayed."

"You might have been there a while. It took me a few days to work things out. But I have now." He scooted forward onto the edge of the couch cushion and held his hands out to her. She took them, barely able to reach across the coffee table. Then laughed at how ludicrous they probably looked.

This time he did grin and came around to crouch in front of her chair. Then he took her hands. "Promise you won't run this time. Not until you hear what I have to say. It won't take long."

Oh. She wasn't sure that sounded good. But why would he want to hold her hands to tell her something bad? So she nodded.

He put one set of their linked hands to his mouth and kissed the top of hers. His lips were warm and soft, and her heart started to pound. This did not sound like the beginning of a "see you later" speech.

Then he looked into her eyes. "I love you, Resie Cameron. I think I have for a long, long time. I just refused to believe I was capable of it. My dad…"

"You are not your father, Seth. You are warm and caring and have been a very good friend."

"Have been?"

The look in his eyes made her get out of her chair and kneel beside him. "Still are, Seth. I just hope we can be so much more than that, and I… Wait." Her mind replayed what he'd said before the mention of his father. "You love me?"

"Yes."

A thought morphed that she didn't like. "Are you saying that because of the baby?"

"I'm saying it because it's true. Baby or no baby. But, just so there's no mistake this time, I love this child, too. With all my heart. And I want it to carry my last name. I want *you* to carry my last name. If you feel the same way."

"Are you asking me to marry you?"

He chuckled. "Yes, in my messed-up, dysfunctional way."

"You are not dysfunctional. It's just so unexpected. So very unexpected."

"I know. And I'm sorry. I could have picked a more romantic place than your parents' living room." He glanced around. "Are they here, by the way?"

"No, they're out on a shopping trip and won't be back for hours. And I love you, too. I was going to tell you in your office that day, but then the moment went sideways—because I let myself think things that weren't true."

He grabbed her close and whispered in her hair, "Thank God. I was so afraid…because I, too, let myself think things that weren't true. Like how this would destroy our friendship. But it didn't, did it?"

"No. It only makes it that much sweeter. This isn't the order that I would have chosen to do things in—to get pregnant before the I-love-yous."

He leaned back to look at her. "Maybe this was the order in which they needed to happen to get us to the point where we could say the words and to recognize what was right in front of us."

She smiled. "Are you trying to say our baby played matchmaker?"

"Maybe. It worked, didn't it?"

"Yes, it did."

He pulled her in for a long kiss, his arms going around her to hold her close. Things quickly heated up as her hands slid beneath his shirt, kneading the incredible muscles of his back.

Taking her shoulders, he eased her back. "How long did you say your parents were going to be gone?"

"Hours and hours." God, she hoped she was right, because all she wanted to do right now was to be in his arms and get the order right this time: declaration of love followed by an explicit demonstration of that love. She wanted him so badly that her legs were shaking. Or maybe that was from kneeling for so long.

As if he knew what she was thinking, he drew her to her feet and swept her into his arms. "I'm pretty sure I remember where your bedroom is."

With that, he headed down the hallway and set her gently down on her bed. She reached for him and pulled him down on top of her. But when he settled his weight over her, the narrow bed suddenly gave way, and the mattress and box springs crashed onto the floor. They both froze, then she started laughing, tears springing to her eyes. When she finally got control of herself, she said, "Well, we'd better figure out how to fix that before my parents get home, or we'll have some explaining to do."

He started to get up, only to have her grab him again. "No. Didn't you hear the 'hours and hours' part? We have plenty of time to fix the bed. But since it's broken anyway, we can be as...er, energetic as we'd like."

Leaning on his elbows, he looked down at her with what looked like shock. "Is that a suggestion?"

"No, Seth. It's a promise. And one I'm going to hold you to."

With that, he kissed her again, and this time he didn't hold anything back, and she felt how much he loved her. And there was a freedom that hadn't existed there in their earlier lovemaking sessions. Because they were no longer afraid they were messing anything up. Instead, they were now completing a friendship that had begun a very long time ago. Taking it with them into a new future. One that held the bright hope of wonderful things to come.

* * * * *

Look out for the next story in the San Diego Surgeons duet Forbidden to the Millionaire Doc *by Juliette Hyland*

And if you enjoyed this story, check out these other great reads from Tina Beckett

**Las Vegas Night with Her Best Friend
Reunion with the ER Doctor
ER Doc's Miracle Triplets**

FORBIDDEN TO THE MILLIONAIRE DOC

JULIETTE HYLAND

MILLS & BOON

For Bianca…welcome to the world.

CHAPTER ONE

DR. WREN FRESON counted to ten to keep herself from bouncing with glee as she stood in the center of the San Diego Central Library. Growing up, libraries were her refuge. A place she didn't feel gawked at for reading well above her grade level. At five, she'd meticulously read her way through the fantasy section. Then the ocean life section, so she could impress her big brother. This marked sixty-seven on her ever-growing list of libraries she'd visited around the country.

It was a silly thing her brother, Ronan, used to make fun of her for. No matter the city, she always visited the library. Or libraries. It was a task made easier by seeing as many of her brother's minor league baseball games around the country as possible. She'd been in tiny libraries and palatial ones. But this nine-story beauty was the most breathtaking she'd visited yet.

Since Wren had accepted the position of plastic surgeon for the burn unit at Sunrise Medical, this was also now her library. She patted her purse where the shiny new library card sat. She always had at least three books on her bedside table, usually ones her current patients were interested in.

Today she was here for another purpose.

She pursed her lips and pulled a baseball card from her purse. Ronan's grin brought a smile to her face, but the ache of knowing she only saw him in photos never truly went away. Her brother had lived and breathed baseball. Or he had, before he'd died in a car accident.

Three days away from his dream. He'd just been traded to a team that planned to start him in the majors. An accident stole it all from him and two other players in the car with him. That night had also stolen away the only person who ever truly saw her.

Her brother hadn't cared about her IQ. Didn't lead off every introduction with, *This is my sister, the genius.* He'd talk about his fish, her current schoolwork and gripe with her about their overbearing parents.

Her eyes misted, but she was not giving into tears. This was a happy moment. She was finally here. Heading for the elevators, she stepped on and got off on the eighth floor. The Sullivan Baseball Research Center. The largest baseball history research collection in the United States. In the world.

It had opened just before her brother started high school. When Wren, a *happy accident* according to her parents, was five. Ronan had talked about it constantly. His favorite topic was how one day he'd be in the records here.

That day was never coming, but she owed it to him to let this moment be his.

Walking into the research center, she smiled at all the baseball references decorating the walls. This was not a memorabilia collection; it was a *research center* dedicated to the history of the game. It was where authors came to dive into the deep lore for their books. Something Ronan had told their father more than once. Not that the man was ever interested in their interests.

Her parents had looked at her love of oceanography as a hurdle to get over as she headed for med school. And baseball—that was not something they'd ever enjoyed. They went to Ronan's senior year games because he was a starter; the other years—the benchwarmer years—they'd ignored.

Her parents were impressed by accomplishments. If Ronan had debuted in the majors, they'd have gone to every game. Bragging to anyone who got close to them. But when you weren't at the top, they weren't interested.

And they got to determine what *the top* meant.

She held the baseball card against her heart as she walked through the area. Wren didn't care about baseball. But she'd loved Ronan more than anything.

"I made it," she whispered to her brother. Hopefully his spirit knew his minor league card was wandering the research center.

Turning down one stack, she saw a dark-haired white man sitting at a table by a window. Her breath caught, and Wren blinked.

Luca? Luca McDonnell?

Wren blinked several more times as the name reverberated in her brain. This was a mirage. A fantasy conjured by her brain while she was remembering her brother. There was no way. *No way.* Luca wasn't in San Diego.

He might be.

The last time she'd seen him, she was sixteen, in her first year of med school. At Ronan's funeral. She'd spent twenty minutes talking to him. About what, she couldn't remember. That sad day was the first time he'd returned home since he stood in the front of the small chapel and called off his wedding…which had been supposed to start ten minutes before.

Ten years. Ten years that had been more than kind to him. He was tan. Broad-shouldered. And the last bits of boyhood had dropped away to chiseled features. Damn. Time had been *good*.

"Luca?"

His head snapped up, and Wren realized she'd spoken. At least that confirmed it was really him.

His dark beard was new. So was the hard look in his eyes

as he tilted his head. The boy was cute. The man striking but not approachable. He waited a second, his gaze flicking across her. Did he recognize her?

"Do I know you?" He crossed his arms and leaned back in the chair.

Apparently not. That shouldn't sting. The last time he'd seen her she was sixteen with braces. A genius, according to all her professors and parents, but a girl lost in a world that only saw her for the mind she had. A child trapped in a world of adults. Not accepted by the children her age or the adults impressed by her brain.

Ronan and Luca spent nearly every moment together before going to separate colleges. And they'd let his little sister, who never fit in anywhere, tag along on some of their adventures.

"Are you Luca McDonnell?" It was him. She knew it in her gut. But there was an air to him. A hardness she didn't remember.

"You called my name. Now you're questioning who you're talking to? Listen, if this is the birthday song from the hospital crew, I'm good. You don't have to do your little song and dance routine. Tell the owner of A Cappella Ambush you got me." Luca gestured to the stacks. "This is a library. Not really a good place for a birthday sing-along anyway."

"Are you hiding in the research center to avoid a birthday sing-along?" Wren walked up to the table and looked at the books covering it. Medical journals. Not a baseball book in sight. "Luca, why don't you want to be sung to?"

"My reasons are my own." He closed the book he'd been looking at, reached into his back pocket and pulled out a wallet. Then a hundred dollar bill. "You can tell whoever paid you that you found me, sang to me, and I was thoroughly embarrassed. That is the point of those, right?" He pushed the bill toward her, his eyes clearly telling her to get lost.

"I always thought it was for people to show you how much they cared about you?" Not that Wren really knew. Her parents didn't celebrate birthdays—being born wasn't impressive. She hadn't gotten a birthday card or present since Ronan passed. "It's sweet that your friends want to celebrate you." Wren wasn't sure why she was arguing with him rather than telling him who she was. Maybe it was a futile hope that he'd realize she was not some singing telegram he was avoiding.

That he'd see her. Recognize her.

Luca rolled his bright green eyes to the ceiling. "Why are you just standing there? Do you want me to pay you more to go?" He pulled another hundred dollar bill from the wallet.

Holy hell!

If she was from the singing company, she'd have snatched the bills up and bid him goodbye. She'd done her fair share of odd jobs when her parents cut her off for daring to choose plastics instead of neurosurgery. The best discipline—the only one she was allowed if she wanted their praise and monetary support. She'd racked up monumental loans that she was only now getting a full grip on.

But that was not why she was here. It was almost like her brother had led her here. She grinned and laid Ronan's baseball card on the book in front of him.

Luca looked down and let out a breath. "How do you have—" His head snapped up. "Wren?"

"Don't need money." Not completely true, but that wasn't a topic for this interaction. "And not here to sing. Though, happy birthday." She frowned. "Wait, your birthday was two weeks ago."

Luca stood, and any hope she had that he'd reach out for a hug vanished as he crossed his arms. "It was. Why do you remember my birthday?"

There was a hint of anger in the question. A flash of something she didn't understand. They'd been close once. As close as the little sister of his best friend who was nearly a decade his junior could be.

When you put it that way, no wonder he's asking why you remember.

Words escaped her.

After a moment, he chuckled, a deep sound that carried in the quiet center. "Forgot." He tapped his head. "Your mind is basically a steel trap. Nothing gets out."

Wren rolled her eyes. She'd started kindergarten reading *Pride and Prejudice*. The teacher had marched her to the principal's office and demanded she test Wren to figure out where she belonged because it wasn't her room. It was an argument her parents had tried to make with the principal before she started. They'd not been pleased to hear the principal say she was sure her parents loved Wren and that she was bright, but every kid started in kindergarten.

Every kid in the town...except Wren.

She'd graduated high school at eleven. Started college at twelve and med school at sixteen. The steel trap mind. A gift...and a curse.

"Why would I forget your birthday? You're my friend." She paused. "Or you were. I guess we haven't seen each other in years."

Damn, this was awkward. Maybe she should have just walked past him, but she couldn't unring that bell.

Luca pulled at the back of his neck. "Your birthday is September 30." He grinned, his face finally relaxing. "I don't have a steel trap here—" he tapped his head again "—but I didn't forget. It's good to see you, Wren."

"It is nice of you to say that. Even if I'm not sure you really mean it." She laughed and held out her hand.

Luca looked at it, then shook his head. "Come on. We're old pals." He opened his arms, and she stepped into them.

Her body relaxed as he gripped her shoulders. She wrapped

her arms around him. Her grip was too tight, but this was the first time in forever that someone had hugged her. Really hugged her.

She was apart from so many things. An oddity in conversations, where people much older than her looked at her accomplishments with jealousy or like she was some sort of zoo animal. Luca was a piece of home.

She squeezed him once more, then forced herself to step back, aware of the heat in her cheeks. "Do you live in San Diego?" The city was about as far as you could get from the small town they'd grown up in in Rhode Island.

"Yes." Luca pushed his hands into his pockets, pulling into himself.

"Wow. Don't give too much detail, Luca." Wren bit her lip, then grabbed Ronan's card from the top of the book. "It was nice running into you."

"I feel like that's a lie." Luca looked at the books on the table, then at her.

She found a smile, trying to ignore the pinch of pain knowing it was clear he wasn't super excited to see her. "We're just a little rough around the edges discussion-wise. Ten years of lived experience between our younger selves and all." This wasn't a reunion any television show would emulate, but it was nice to know Luca was well. Even if he didn't want anyone to sing to him.

"Still the sunshiny optimist." Luca raised a brow. "The world hasn't sucked it out of you, yet?"

The world tried to steal her sunshine at least a few times a week. She simply refused to let it go. "I should get going."

"Bye, Wren." Luca nodded.

No way to stretch any conversation from that. Wren offered a final smile and tried to ignore the pain caused by the fact that he hadn't asked if she was just visiting or had moved here, or if she wanted to get together sometime soon.

He ran away from Lincoln and everyone in it. That includes me. What did I expect?

She turned on her heel, pitifully hoping he might call her back as she headed out of the stacks.

It wasn't until she was dropping the four fiction books the librarian recommended on her kitchen counter that she let the first tear fall. She was in a city where she knew exactly one person. And that man didn't want a connection with her.

Wren gave herself a little shake. She was starting at Sunshine Medical tomorrow. She'd meet people. Find friends. Build a life here.

The city was big enough. With any luck she'd never run into Luca again.

"If you want a pup cup before my shift starts, you need to get a move on, Hippo."

The beefy gray pittie mix tilted his head like he'd heard Luca, but then went right back to sniffing the spot on the sidewalk. The pup knew Luca wouldn't follow through with the threat.

Hippo might not know days of the week, but he knew that when Luca pulled the slip leash from the hook instead of the standard long blue leash, it meant it was treat day.

Luca waited a moment more, feeling a little bad that his best bud was going to be at day care for almost twelve hours today, then pulled on the leash and whistled.

Hippo snuffed, then moved beside Luca and started toward the coffee shop.

"I deserve that disgusted snuff, man." *Just not because I cut short your sniffing time.*

Luca had sat in his condo last night, Hippo in his lap, and thought of Wren.

Wren.

The girl he'd known had transformed into a stunning

woman. One he'd not-so-subtly checked out: her long hair pulled into a loose braid, her dark chocolate eyes, the button nose. It had taken him a moment to react, telling her to get lost; because he thought she was part of the sing-along crew the hospital peds unit hired. The one trying so hard to make sure he got the "gift" the peds department purchased.

Then he'd realized who she was. He'd been checking out his late best friend's little sister. Hell, he'd had to cross his arms to keep from reaching out to her. Then he'd hugged her anyway....and held on way too long. She'd been the one to end the hug. He'd made sure the conversation didn't drag on after that.

Rude. I was rude.

There was no sugarcoating it. Wren was Ronan's little sister; Luca owed it to him to find a way to make amends. So he'd spent far too long looking for her online last night.

He'd deleted all his social media apps from his phone a while ago. The only contacts who reached out were exes in search of money. Or family, also in search of money. A fact that was clear when he logged back in and found more than sixty direct messages from his mother and father. Both had his phone number. Both could call to check on him. Say hi.

He didn't know why social media was the one place the people who were supposed to love him reached out. Always with the same ask for more money.

If they acted like they cared about him at all, he'd cave and send what they asked. But they couldn't even ask basic *how are you* questions. Or tell him they missed him. Apologize for the giant fight they'd had the last time they'd talked.

Because they don't miss me.

That was a tough lesson to learn.

Still he'd logged back into all the apps last night to see if he could locate her. Then he'd created a few dummy accounts on apps he heard about at the hospital. Wren wasn't on the one most of the young nurses and doctors discussed, and she wasn't on the networking site the newest physical therapist, Therese Cameron, suggested he join if he wanted to advance his career.

No one believed him when he said he had no interest in making a career change. He'd worked at Sunrise Medical since graduating from physical therapy school. Still held the same position as staff doctor of physical therapy, DPT in medical jargon.

He never put in for a promotion. Never tried to move to another place.

After all, it wasn't like he needed the money. A fact none of his colleagues knew. After his ex-fiancée, Madeline, walked out on him, he'd made sure to never tell the women he dated about his financial situation.

Though they all eventually found out. Then the demands started. He had the same issue with friends.

Once upon a time he'd been the friend people called to tell good news and bad. The friend who took you to the bar when your significant other cheated. The friend who listened when the world was upside down and celebrated when you were on top of the world.

After people found out about his worth, he became the bank. No more silly texts with gifs and inside jokes. No more happy hour trips to share a bucket of beer. Nope.

Hell, when he'd told one of his friends about Madeline's confession that she didn't love him, the friend had joked that Luca could buy love. The man got upset when Luca said it wasn't funny. His friend made it clear that he thought it was dumb that Luca was so upset when he had enough money not to worry about anything. *Take yourself on vacation. Buy a new sports car.*

Like things could make up for finding out the woman you loved saw you as a checkbook.

He'd quickly figured out that no one thought he could have problems because he had money. It didn't take long for him to become the invisible friend...until someone needed a loan, or more accurately, a gift.

The only person who hadn't cared about his unexpected windfall was Ronan. His best friend. The brother of the woman he'd treated so poorly yesterday.

If his friend had seen him, Luca would have gotten a smack on the back of the head. And he'd have earned it.

He owed Wren an apology but had no idea how to find her. She'd been in her first year of med school at Ronan's funeral. Had she completed it? Of course she had. Probably with honors. Wren was a certified genius.

What was her specialty? Was she working at Sunrise? Or in town for a medical conference?

All questions I could, and should, have asked yesterday.

Hippo let out a squeal. The squat pittie mix hardly ever barked. He chirped. It was a weird, solely Hippo thing.

"Yes, we're almost there." Luca grinned as the dog started his happy dance, his routine every time they stepped onto the block for the Cupcake Café. In the morning, it had coffee and breakfast. At ten, it switched to coffee and cupcakes.

The door of the café opened, and Hippo let out a soft "ahroo!"

The woman holding the door turned, and Luca's breath caught. It was like he'd willed her into being. "Wren."

"Luca." Wren looked at the door and let go. Then reached for it again. "Did you need this? Wait—" Her eyes darted to Hippo, and she released the door again. His appearance clearly frazzled her. At least he wasn't the only one out of sorts. "And who is this?"

Hippo danced and nosed toward the door of the cafe. "Hippo. Who needs his pup cup. Although *need* is probably an overstatement."

He headed to the light pole where he always tied Hippo before he slipped into the bakery. He ordered online, so it never took more than a moment.

"I can hold him. If you want. And if you think he'll let me." Wren bent and rubbed Hippo's head.

A hint of chamomile wafted through Luca's senses, and he started to lean a little closer.

Ronan's sister. Ronan's sister.

The dog sighed and laid his head against her knee. For just an instant, Luca was jealous of his dog.

Ronan's sister.

He shouldn't need the reminder. The pink bandana he'd let the dog choose fell across Wren's knee. *Choose* was a relative statement with Hippo, but Luca always held up two bandannas for the chunkster to select from. The dog refused to go anywhere without one, and the collection he'd amassed was more than over the top.

Mentally, Luca shook himself. He needed to get moving, both because he had to get to work and because his brain was far too focused on the way Wren's pencil skirt hugged her hips. "The only thing he loves more than pup cups is attention. If you don't mind—"

"I don't." Wren held out her free hand for the leash. "I have to have the leash if I'm going to pet you."

Luca slipped the leash around her wrist, careful to make sure his fingers didn't brush her delicate-looking skin, then started for the door, very aware that neither Hippo or Wren were paying him any attention. At least he'd get a chance to apologize. He grabbed the order and headed right back out the door.

"See, no time at all." He bent and held out the pup cup.

And Hippo ignored him.

"Hippo?" Luca waved the whipped cream mini cup in front of the dog. Hippo had tippy-tapped down the sidewalk, knowing what was coming. And nothing! He just kept soaking in Wren's attention.

"Maybe if I stood, he might be more interested in what you got him." Wren kissed the top of Hippo's head and then stood. "It was nice to meet you, Hippo." She turned to Luca but didn't say anything.

Like I can blame her.

"Need to get him to day care before my shift," Luca began. That was not what he was supposed to say, but his brain seemed to give up its ability to make words around her. He felt his stomach drop as Wren simply nodded. She turned and started walking the opposite way he needed to go.

"Wren!" His call was too loud. It wasn't like she'd taken more than a step.

She lifted her coffee to her lips and looked at him over the lid.

"Sorry I wasn't more welcoming yesterday. I was rude. It was undeserved." Luca crumpled the very empty pup cup that Hippo had made quick work of and threw it in the trash can. "Just…sorry."

"I'm the one that sneaked up on you, Luca. No apology needed." She beamed.

Sunshine seemed to bend around her. Beauty and brains. The complete package. And his best friend's little sister.

Your dead best friend's little sister.

The definition of forbidden.

"It was good to see you. Not a lie." He paused as the next words he should utter stuck in his throat. *Ask why she's here. How long she's staying. Her phone number.*

But none of those questions made it from his brain to his lips. He'd cut off everyone from his hometown after Madeline's announcement in the bridal suite the day of their wedding. Only Ronan had been allowed to stay in his life.

And he was gone, too.

Wren was a tie to that old life. A link to the man Luca had been. The man he'd buried when he heard his fiancée confess to her maid of honor that she wasn't really in love with him. But she'd found out that he had inherited his aunt's estate… and the millions she'd hidden from his family.

His aunt's final letter to Luca had told him she thought the money was cursed and hoped it brought him more joy than it did her. He'd laughed at the line, half wondering if his aunt, so sharp, had lost it in her final days without him knowing. Then he heard Madeline explain her plan to stick it out, at least for a year or two…because there was no prenup.

The worst part was knowing he should have picked up on it. She was distant for weeks before the wedding. Excited at the idea of the party, the white dress, but not their life together. He'd chalked his concerns up to cold feet. Ignoring the tiny voice inside his head screaming *danger*.

Then there were the not-so-subtle hints that they needed to make the most out of their first years together. When he'd reminded her that he was finishing residency, she'd pointed out that she could find someone to travel with her. Not bummed at all that her future husband couldn't accompany her on the trips she planned.

She'd never pointed out that with all the money he had, they could both quit their jobs… Something she did the day after he told her about his inheritance.

The red flags were there. He just hadn't wanted to see them.
Curse: 1. Luca: 0.

That was not the only time the curse had crossed his path. Once Luca had learned he was only wanted for the funds he brought, he'd clammed up, just like his aunt. Still, you always remembered the one who hurt you first.

Wren waited a minute longer, the silence hovering loudly between them. Then she raised her coffee cup. "Have a good morning, Luca."

This time when she turned to walk away, he didn't try to stop her.

He watched her round the corner. Her pencil skirt, bright yellow button-down shirt and two-inch pumps hardly indicated she was heading to a hospital. Most likely in town for a conference.

He'd bought a condo near the San Diego Convention Center because it was available and the area was busy. Technically, he'd bought the building, but the location was the reason. The area was easy to get lost in. The rentals were mostly tech bros and tired medical professionals. On the streets, it was tourists he ran past most days.

Since he wasn't interested in networking, he never looked to see if there was anything of interest at the convention center. Maybe he'd check the schedule later. See what was in town. If there were any times in the schedule when Wren might be on a break.

To do what?

He'd been downright rude in the library. And awkward as hell this morning. A third meeting to make sure she knew he wasn't interested in rekindling any relationship from his past was hardly necessary.

Luca shook his head and whistled for Hippo to follow. "Time to get you to day care and me to the hospital."

Hippo snuffled and walked beside him.

"At least you never tire of me." He rubbed the dog's head and let out a sigh.

The millions his aunt left him were supposed to make his life easier. And, in many ways, they had. He'd graduated college and physical therapy school with no debt. A feat few of his classmates could boast of. He owned a building in a city most only dreamed of moving to.

But as soon as people found out, they looked at him different. Madeline had simply been the first.

There were three other partners who'd seen him as a ticket to freedom rather than a loved one, once they discovered his fortune. Three partners he'd nearly convinced himself would be different.

And they never were.

Then there was Ronan. The only one he'd had to pester into letting him help. Ronan's parents had refused to help him get a car. Refused to help him with anything. So Luca cosigned on the loan for the car Ronan bought. He'd have bought him a new car, but Ronan had barely wanted the signature.

If Luca had pushed him into a new car, would things have been different? A bigger vehicle, one that might have stood a chance when it was T-boned by a huge truck? He'd never know.

Curse: infinity. Luca: 0.

He had Hippo and the career he wanted. Luca didn't need anything else.

Most days he believed it.

CHAPTER TWO

Orientation day. Her least favorite day in a new hospital. Wren had hoped the hospital wouldn't make a big deal about her arrival. Yes, she was the youngest board-certified plastic surgeon in the country. And she had helped develop a new debridement technique that gave patients a better chance of full recovery of movement in their limbs following a third degree burn. But she was also just another new hire starting this month.

Except, unlike others starting today, she was currently being shown around the facility not by human resources, like the rest of the new hires, but by Dr. Seth Graham, one of the top plastic surgeons in the city, who she was certain had other things to do.

"This is maternity." Dr. Graham pointed to a wing with pastel colors and a locked entrance. "You have to scan to get in, and all the babies have coded bands around their ankles to make sure they don't leave."

Wren nodded. It was a security measure most hospitals had in place to prevent kidnapping. Not something parents wanted to think about, but there had been cases.

"And this…" Seth beamed as they rounded a corner "…is physical therapy."

"You spend a lot of time in physio?" Many physio patients would rotate down here following their surgeries, but there wasn't much need for their surgeon to check in on them beyond the notes in their chart. Though she had made it a habit to stop in at least a few times when her patients were transitioning to PT.

"Seth." A white woman grinned at the surgeon as they stepped into the surprisingly quiet physio room.

"Dr. Freson, this is my fiancée, Therese. Dr. Freson is the new plastics specialist everyone has been so excited to meet."

Wren held out a hand. "Please call me Wren. It's nice to meet you, Therese."

"Nice to meet you, too. I bet you're loving this walk around, right?" The woman smiled. "I started not that long ago. First days are nerve-racking."

"Yes. Yes, they are."

Seth looked around the room, raising an eyebrow. "No patients?"

"Nope." Therese blew out a breath. "Both my morning patients refused to come to therapy today." She looked at the empty stations. "Frustrating. This is why I prefer working with peds. The kids always want to give it a go."

Adults had the right to say no to treatment. The right to ignore the doctor's orders, even though it would set their progress back. It was a frustrating but not infrequent occurrence.

"Physical therapy is hard." Wren had heard more than one patient refer to physio as torture. It wasn't, but often the road to health was paved with pain.

Therese nodded. "Where are you heading to next?"

"You are our last stop." Seth smiled warmly at Therese. "Saved the best for last. And we got lucky because McSteamy isn't here."

"McSteamy?" Wren repeated. She watched the hint of color rise on Seth's neck.

"I shouldn't call him that," he said.

Therese shrugged. "She's going to hear his nickname soon anyway."

"Is there a hot doc I'm supposed to be warned off?" Wren had never had any interest in dating her colleagues. Besides, when you were so much younger than your colleagues and classmates, it didn't allow for much romantic socializing. Though she was twenty-six now, so opportunities might arise.

Not that I'd have any idea what to do with a hot doc.

She'd gone on exactly three dates—ever. Each a spectacular failure. So she was a twenty-six old virgin with no dating experience. What a catch.

"He is conventionally attractive, but that's not the reason for the nickname. He's—"

"A hothead. Annoying. And short with everyone." Luca's words filled the space behind her as he stepped into the physio room.

No. No. There was no way he was here. Yet, "McSteamy" fit the man she'd met in the library…and this morning. Hot. Man of few words.

She watched him walk past her, his gaze firmly planted on the tablet chart in his hands. "Mr. McDaniels had therapy in his room. He promises to come here tomorrow."

Luca walked over to the computer station and started typing notes—presumably into a chart. No hello, no surprise that she was the new surgeon on staff…which if she was fair was probably because he hadn't bothered to look at her at all.

"He promised me the same yesterday." Therese shook her head. "On good days, this place is loud and noisy. And some days…" She gestured to the room. "Hopefully the afternoon cases will be better."

Luca made a short sound under his breath but didn't add any commentary.

"Luca." Seth's voice was level, but she heard the stern surgeon voice used to get attention. "I apologize for discussing your nickname with the new surgeon."

"Everyone knows it. Not a secret." He still didn't look up from the monitor.

"This is the new burn specialist. I was tasked to show her around." Seth waited a minute, but when Luca didn't respond, he turned to Wren. "Dr. Freson, are you—"

"Freson?" Now Luca's head popped up.

If Seth was surprised by the reaction, he didn't show it.

Luca's gaze met hers, his eyes wide. He didn't say anything for several seconds. Finally, he cleared his throat. "Freson like the Link-Freson technique?"

He was covering. Using her achievement to push away any chance to show they knew each other.

Fine. Two could play that game.

"Yes, I am Dr. Freson from that technique." Her face heated. Why did she always have that reaction when someone brought up her greatest achievement? She and Dr. Sonja Link had spent more than one late night studying in the library as interns. Going over burn images, horrid images, and spitballing new ideas. Not that they'd expected it to become more than shop talk. Until one night they struck gold.

Her male colleagues would never blush over such a discovery. It made her seem young and inexperienced. She was young...but not inexperienced.

"Sonja, Dr. Link, is still at the hospital in New York where we developed it."

"Why are you here? A big hospital in New York is most people's dream." Luca tilted his head, his jade gaze pinning her down.

He still hadn't acknowledged that he knew her. That she'd spent a few minutes holding his dog for him this morning. He was gruff and unapproachable. The exact opposite of the young man she'd known.

"Memorial General in New York City, like this one, is a

teaching hospital. Sonja stayed there, and I came here. We can teach more plastics and burn specialists the technique. Aid in healing." Wren shrugged. "I am here because we drew straws."

"Was Sunrise the short-end straw?" Therese wasn't frowning, but there was tension in her shoulders.

"No." Wren turned her attention to Therese. "I drew the long straw, which meant I got to choose. I was ready to leave New York City."

She'd started at Memorial as a resident. A very young, inexperienced resident. She was at the top of her field. But there were some there who would only ever see the resident who was too young to drink on their first day in scrubs. A genius physician, with very little life experience.

Wren wanted, needed, a new start. Somewhere people had a chance to see her for her. That didn't mean it was easy to leave Sonja behind.

"Sonja will be the head of plastics at Memorial in a few years, I have no doubt. Plus, her girlfriend and family are in the area. I was probably always the one coming out here, but no, Sunrise was my choice. Doesn't mean starting here isn't nerve-racking. Hope that's okay." She glanced at Therese, hoping the physical therapist knew she was where she wanted to be.

"One can be thrilled and terrified at the same time." Therese's gaze shot to Seth. His look was so full of love that Wren felt like she'd stepped into a private conversation.

She looked toward Luca; his gaze was rooted to hers. But the friendly face she'd hoped to find was absent.

It was fine.

He didn't want a connection to his past. In many ways she didn't, either. They were strangers. A decade between them and their younger selves.

Fine!

* * *

"I wasn't going to come." Patrick McDaniels gripped the railing and started to slowly climb the four steps the physical therapy room had to simulate climbing much larger stairs.

Luca nodded. The man was only sixty-five. If he worked hard, there was no reason he couldn't return to the life he'd had before the car accident that broke his left leg and fractured his pelvis last month. The road was long, and he probably hadn't undergone his last surgery, but pushing through physical therapy was the only way to get back to that—no matter how much it hurt.

"Wasn't gonna come." Patrick puffed as he made it up the third step.

If that was the mantra he needed to push himself through, fine. Therese was the nice physio—or at least nicer than Luca. The woman still very much pushed her patients. He was the one who firm. Never mean but straightforward. Some patients needed that.

Patrick started making his way down the stairs and let out a breath. "I blame Dr. Freson." He glared at the stairs as he hit the bottom step.

"You need to go up again." Luca wasn't sure why a patient who should have no interaction with Wren was blaming her for coming to physical therapy.

"I know!" He let more than one curse word out under his breath, then pushed himself up the first step. "Dr. Freson said she'd get me an ice cream if I came down here. This is not worth ice cream." He glared at Luca.

Luca had spent the last two days hearing all about Dr. Freson. Wren had started her shift the day after the horrid introduction in this room. Not that they'd needed an introduction. Though no one would have known it from his reaction.

He'd been focused on three patients who'd refused treatment, pissed and glaring at their charts on the tablet looking for some reason the entire morning group would tell him to pound sand. Luca convinced two of three to do a few workouts in their rooms, but both had given up after less than five minutes.

He hadn't even realized there was anyone with Seth and Therese. Ever since those two had gotten engaged, it wasn't surprising to find Seth spending his limited free time saying hi to Therese. He'd heard them jabbering about the nickname a nurse gave him years ago. It didn't bother him. Luca was a loner.

By the time he'd realized that Wren was there and connected her to the debridement technique, his brain had lost most of its ability to think clearly.

The Link-Freson technique had revolutionized burn care. And yet she'd blushed when he mentioned it.

If almost anyone else had codeveloped that, it would be off their tongue immediately after saying their name. As it should be, honestly. But Wren would not have brought it up if he hadn't.

More than one exhausted resident had boasted how nice it was to have her at the hospital while waiting in line at the cafeteria. How caring and approachable she was.

It was not making it easy to drive her from his mind.

"Let her talk me into this for ice cream." Patrick made it to the top step again and started his descent. "Not even my doctor."

"Then how did she convince you to come to physical therapy?" Patrick McDaniel was the first person he'd heard complain about Wren. Everyone was quick to talk about how sunny she was. How happy. Quick to smile. A good listener. And so down to earth.

In other words, perfect.

Patrick hit the bottom step and started back up without Luca having to goad him. A good sign.

"My roommate needs reconstructive work on his hand. I was grumbling that he got ice cream, and Micah said I didn't deserve any since I was just loafing." Patrick rolled his eyes, but there was color along his neck that indicated he was embarrassed by the assessment.

Maybe that would motivate him.

"Dr. Freson said she'd get me ice cream if you said I'd come to the room and done all my exercises."

"All your exercises?"

His patient hit the top step and looked back at him. "Yes. But this is the last of the exercises you listed when I got here. I expect you to tell Dr. Freson I earned that ice cream."

A deal was a deal. "I will relay the message in the chart." Luca doubted he'd see Wren. The woman had no reason to be in the physical therapy room. No reason to seek him out. He'd made sure of that.

Patrick finished up his exercise and accepted the water cup Luca offered.

"You did good work here today."

"I know." Patrick raised his arms. "All for a cup of vanilla ice cream."

There was something in the way he said it. "You don't like vanilla?" Weird to work for something you didn't want, but Luca would take it.

Patrick finished his water and passed it back. "It's fine. I mean vanilla is vanilla, and it's not like I can get cherry chip in the hospital." He closed his eyes. "I am tired."

Luca nodded. "You worked hard, and your stamina is not what it was. You have to work back up to it. I know it hurts to come here, but it's the only way you'll get to feel like yourself again."

"I hate you. And I hate this." Patrick swallowed as he pinched his eyes closed. The man was close to tears, and

Luca knew he wanted to be alone while he went through the emotions racing through him.

"Let's get you back to your room." As a physical therapist, he was used to being his patients' least favorite person. He saw them at their lowest, weakest point. He'd accept the hate if it made them better.

After dropping Patrick off, Luca headed to the nurses' station to give a short report and find out if they knew where he might find a pint of cherry chip ice cream. Patrick had earned it.

As soon as he headed toward the elevator, he got a tingle on the back of his neck. He looked back at the nurses' station. One of them was on the phone and had too big a smile.

Luca waited for the elevator to open and stepped inside. But he didn't hit the button for the second floor where the physical therapy suite was. He smiled as the elevator started heading up instead of down. He was not going to get caught by the singing telegram. Not today.

The door opened on the sixth floor. Luca stepped out and headed for the stairwell. He raced down the steps and nearly ran into Wren on her way up.

"Dr. McDonnell." Wren put her hand on his shoulder to steady herself and lightning shot through his body.

A silly schoolboy reaction to a gorgeous woman. A woman completely off-limits to him, even if he was interested in dating.

"I thought you were on a first-name basis with everyone." Luca pulled back, far too aware of the chamomile scent wafting from her hair and the tilt of her lips as she frowned.

Wren stepped around him. "You are clearly in a rush."

"Not really. Just avoiding a singing telegram. It was clear when I dropped Patrick McDaniel off the nurses were giving a heads-up to someone that I was heading down. They aren't allowed in patient spaces. I'll slip into the back of the physio room and wait them out."

Wren rolled her eyes. "You'd think people who call you McSteamy would figure out you don't want this."

Luca leaned against the stairwell wall. "This is the first year they've tried to get me. I guess one of the nurses said it wasn't fair that I was left out." This would be the last year they attempted it, he was certain of that. "No doubt they regret it now. McSteamy is no fun after all."

He started to move around her, but she put her hand on his shoulder. The touch lasted less than a second, but it was enough to send his heart rate up.

"You may have them fooled, but I know the truth. You're still just a giant softie."

Once upon a time, a gorgeous, intelligent woman putting her hands on him and looking at him with soft brown eyes would have brought him to his knees.

Who was he kidding? Wren was causing that exact reaction.

"The nickname is dumb, but don't romanticize me. I do not make friends. I do not date." He leaned a little closer, to make a point, not because he was drawn to her. "And I am a grade A asshole."

"A grade A asshole with a chunky dog named Hippo. Nope."

Luca crossed his arms and forced himself to retreat. "Lots of assholes have dogs."

"Sure. But true assholes don't have bandanna-wearing, pup-cup-craving, tippy-toe-dancing babies." She started up the steps but turned on the next landing. "Don't worry, McSteamy, I won't spill your secret." She gave a quick wink and was off.

CHAPTER THREE

LUCA ROLLED HIS SHOULDERS, trying to loosen the pinch between his shoulder blades. He'd slept wrong. Or, more accurate, hadn't been able to sleep given the constant tossing and turning he'd done while trying to drive thoughts of Wren from his mind. Since running into each other at the library, she stormed into his dreams every time he'd drifted off.

Stormed.

Luca laughed at the thought. Wren didn't storm anywhere. She entered, gracefully, fully in control of every room. And in his dreams, she was entering wearing far less clothing.

Ronan's little sister.

Why was the one person on this planet who was firmly off-limits the one he couldn't drive from his thoughts? Ronan was his best friend. The only person from his old life who'd only wanted just his friendship. The only one who'd kept their relationship exactly the same after his aunt's legacy. Lucas owed it to him to find a way to banish the thoughts.

"You're frowning so hard the whole coffee shop is afraid to step over here." Wren grinned as she hit her hip against his. "Smile."

"Very cute, Wren." He looked over the crowd, and a tingle shot down his back. He needed his coffee…and the orders were moving slowly. Too slowly. The Sunrise to Sunset Café catered to the hospital staff and visitors who wanted to be with their loved ones. They were efficient. This was unusual.

Something he might have noticed, if he hadn't been thinking about the beauty before him now.

"I am very cute." She tilted her head. "Smile. You remember how, right?"

Luca furrowed his brow and looked toward the area where the baristas were dropping orders. "I don't need to smile."

Wren looked at her feet, then back at him, her dark gaze mesmerizing. "You're right. You don't need to. It was rude of me to tell you to."

"Wren."

"Are you okay?" She put a hand on his arm.

The connection burned. Where was his damn coffee? He'd already paid, so there was no reason to just walk away.

"I'm fine." He looked around her. Was she trying to keep him here? It had taken her exactly twenty-four hours to make everyone in the hospital her friend. At this rate, most of the facility would do anything she asked. At least that was the way it seemed.

The woman was the talk of the hospital. And not because she was a legit genius. Everyone was talking about how personable she was. How kind. How good with patients.

"Ronan used to joke that when his girlfriend said she was fine, it meant danger. I wonder if it means the same for you?"

Ronan. Girlfriend.

The connection to his past. Wren was that connection. She was a colleague. But rather than making sure a singing telegram didn't go to waste, she was checking on him.

When was the last time that happened?

"I'm just anxious because my coffee is delayed. Considering it's just a basic coffee, I wouldn't have thought it would take this much time, but..." He looked at the counter and closed his eyes. "I'm being trapped."

He moved to step around her, but Wren held up her hand. "Wait."

He opened his mouth, but before any words came out, the song started. "Happy birthday to you…"

The singing group was all smiles. The people around the coffee corner were clapping and singing along. If it wasn't for Wren, he'd have darted out before it started. He'd been so absorbed by her that he missed all the signs gathering around him. Too late to do anything about it now.

He waited for them to finish, nodded his head to the group who looked more than a little relieved to have gotten the job done, then looked at the barista. "My coffee finally done?"

"Oh, I have to get it made. Sorry. We just—"

Luca waved them off. "Just forget it. Nice job trapping me, Wren. No doubt that will be the talk of at least a few nurses' stations today. You accomplished what they couldn't." *Because I let you.*

There was no point waiting for her response. He had patients and needed to get going. He raised a hand to the singers and headed for the physical therapy room.

They had gotten him. Fair and square. *All because I can't get my best friend's little sister out of my head.* That ended now.

"Luca! Luca!" The call followed him down the hall.

"You won, Wren. Nice job." He spun and nearly knocked the two coffees out of her hands.

"Yours." She pressed it toward him. "You already paid for it, and the barista was in tears. I told her I was the one who called the peds floor to let them know where you were, so she didn't need to feel bad for letting them know, too."

"So you *did* rat me out?" He'd suspected that. Hated that he'd missed the warning signals, but somehow it still hurt to know that she'd helped with something he so clearly didn't want.

Not like it's the first time I didn't pick up clear signals.

"No. I didn't actually call peds." She shook her head. "But Maggie was so upset, and this way she doesn't have to worry over it."

Luca took a sip of his coffee. "It wasn't you?" His stomach unclenched, and his soul felt like it took a breath. He hadn't misread Wren.

"No. Though I still don't understand the reason you hate the birthday sing-along." Wren rolled her eyes before looking over her shoulder. "They did it because they thought it was nice, and despite the aura you put off, you are good with patients. Peds didn't want you left out."

The lid of his coffee cup popped. Clearly, he'd squeezed more than a little too hard. He bent down, grabbed it and blew out a breath as he looked at Wren. "You were probably too young to remember, but my parents announced their divorce on my tenth birthday." He shook his head. "It did not make me a huge fan of celebrating it."

After that nightmare, every birthday was a one-upmanship contest, his parents only caring about him when they could use him to hurt the other. His parents were takers, two people unable to see other people for anything more than what they could gain from them. A lesson it had taken him far too long to learn.

Wren's face lost all its color. "I was a newborn at that party, assuming my parents even brought me. I didn't know."

"Yeah, well, the only other person that would remember was Ronan, and he…" Luca was done with this conversation. "Thanks for the coffee. I have patients to see, and I'm sure you do, too."

"Do you want me to let them know? Or are you counting on this display of aggressive avoidance getting you out of celebrating next year?"

He didn't have time for this discussion. "There is no way they will get me a birthday song next year. Please. I know they tried to get a refund, but the owner of the company stood his ground. Said that he'd never not provided a perfect service." It was ridiculous. Jessica, one of the charge nurses working on the peds floor, had apologized repeatedly. They'd already found another company for the next go-round.

Wren looked at her watch. This conversation was drawing to an end. Something he was now loath to have happen. He needed to get himself in check.

"They won't do the song, but if you are anti-celebration, letting them know so there isn't a birthday cake or something small to recognize you next year isn't a terrible idea." Wren shrugged. "Anyway, if you want me quietly let them know, you know where I work. Always happy to help."

"How the hell do you do this?" The words escaped, and he wanted to scream at himself. *McSteamy never talks* was a complaint he'd heard more than once from one colleague to another. Yet somehow his tongue loosened around Wren without fail. And not in a good way.

"Do what?"

"Act all bubbly? Put out this vibe of sunshine when you know the world is horrid."

Wren straightened her shoulders. "It is hardly horrid."

"Your brother died right as his dreams were coming true." He pulled a hand across his face. "That was over the line."

"Saying it was over the line is not an apology." Wren raised her chin. The look in her eyes touched his core. It was pure strength.

This was a woman who'd graduated high school, college and med school with people ten years her senior. The woman who'd created a new technique to change lives and moved across the country on her own.

"I apologize."

She nodded, and this time it was Wren turning on her heel and walking away.

"I hate this." Lena Stevens looked away as Wren pulled the dressings from her hand. The burns were healing nicely. That did not mean her hand looked anything like it had before her ex-boyfriend doused her arm in lighter fluid and lit a match.

"It's looking good, Lena." Wren looked at the damaged fingers. "I know it hurts, but have you met with the physical therapists?"

It was a question Wren knew the answer to. Lena had refused to meet with Therese yesterday and Luca the day before. According to the nurses, she'd gotten out of bed to use the facilities but nothing else. Mental health had done an evaluation and added antidepressants to the medicinal cocktail she received. But it would be weeks before the SSRIs took full effect.

Lena let out a puff of air. Not much of an answer.

"It's important to start doing small movements to get your range of motion back. The wound—"

"Looks good. I know. Everyone says it's healing. It looks so much better than we thought. Oh, Lena, don't you know how lucky you are." Lena pinched her eyes closed, but it didn't stop the tears leaking down her face. "Lucky. Lucky. I hate that stupid word. I hate it."

Well, she was talking, and Wren was going to take every advantage. Anger was a fantastic motivator.

"None of this is lucky. And my hand does not look good. It looks monstrous. But hey, Donald only destroyed my hand. The fire could have been so much worse."

Her tone let Wren know she was mimicking someone. Whether it was a nurse or family, Wren didn't know.

There was truth in the statement, though. The incident occurred two weeks before Wren started at Sunrise. From what she'd heard, if Lena hadn't had a fire blanket nearby because of her artwork, it would have been much worse. That did not mean it was helpful information right now.

"My hand. My art." She bit her lip so hard Wren worried she was tasting blood.

Wren sat on the edge of the bed. "I am not going to lie to

you, your hand will never look the same." She gently lifted Lena's injured hand. "The skin graft is adjusting well. I fully believe that you will get full range of motion back in your fingers and hand."

"He took the thing I loved most. He stole my primary means of making money. My way of making joy." Lena moved her hand, slowly, but she was looking at it. This was her body; the body part that was the driving force of her livelihood.

Wren had heard so many platitudes growing up.

They're just jealous of you.

You'll make friends when you're older.

Your mind is a gift, don't waste it.

Not a single one made the situation better. She was a genius. That was what people saw. What people cared about. That life experience meant she never sugarcoated the news she had to deliver to her patients. "I mean it, Lena. Your fingers will regain the same range of motion in time. It won't be easy, but it can be accomplished."

"So my art will be the same." Lena looked at her with a flicker of hope.

"I doubt it." Wren let out a sigh. "You've gone through a life-changing event. It changed you. And I suspect your art will change because of that. But your hand will accomplish what you want it to."

"I didn't want the change." More tears streamed down Lena's cheeks.

Wren understood that. Her life had a few breaking points but nothing as sizable as the chasm that opened at Ronan's funeral. Before that fateful day, her mind had protected her.

Despite knowing what had happened, part of Wren believed she'd wake from the nightmare. Ronan would send a silly meme when she texted him the horrid dream. But seeing his urn at the funeral home was the second it became truly real, and she changed. Not intentionally. And not because she wanted to.

There was a before. And there was after. A person was not the same when they stepped into the after.

"I know you didn't want this. It is not fair. In fact, it is downright shitty."

Lena's mouth widened at the curse, but her eyes brightened. "Yes. It is."

Naming it, calling the change out helped Wren. She'd stood in the cemetery when everyone was gone and screamed at the stone. Cursed the world, the fates, the universe. All of it. Grief stayed with you. A constant that never really faded. Your life grew bigger around it but never vanquished it. However, you couldn't let it rule you.

"You can't let him win, Lena. You have a gift. He only steals that gift from you if *you* let him."

Lena looked at her arm, but she didn't cringe this time. "You think I can get the full range of motion back? That I will be able to hold a fine tip paintbrush and create the softest strokes?"

"I do." Wren stated it firmly. There was a long road ahead, but Lena's injuries would not stop her from creating. "It won't be tomorrow. Or even next week, but with time and physical therapy, you will get everything back."

"Did someone say physical therapy?" Luca stepped into the room. His gaze went directly to Wren, and she suspected he'd heard at least part of the conversation.

Lena was still looking at her hand. "Full range of motion." She smiled and looked at Luca. "I want my full range of motion. I want to paint. I need to paint. Yeah. I'm ready for physical therapy."

There was a small twitch in his jaw, but he smiled at Lena. "Music to my ears." Luca nodded to Wren. "Why don't you stay a moment, Dr. Freson? We're going to start with some exercises here. Things you can do on your own without me," he told Lena.

Wren stepped around Luca. She wasn't sure why he wanted her in the room, and after their argument this morning, she'd plotted different pathways to limit her chances of seeing him.

"Please stay a minute, Dr. Freson. Please." Wren had not considered leaving, but Lena's plea would have stalled her feet if she had.

"Of course."

Luca pulled a soft ball from the small container all the physios carried around with them. Little tools they could use in the rooms and leave behind for patients.

"Step one is squeezing this ball." He passed the ball to Lena. She looked at it. "This shouldn't be hard."

Luca didn't correct her. This was a humbling lesson many patients had to learn. You started at least two steps behind where you thought you would.

Lena started squeeze it, and though she was trying to keep her face clear, it was obvious this was rougher than she expected.

"It's a squishy ball." She made the comment to herself, but Luca nodded.

"It is. And if you're in here watching TV or reading or just lying here, squeeze it several times until you're sore but not hurting. Hurting will not do you any good. In fact, it will set you back. Once you are able to do it for three minutes, I'll shift you to this." He pulled another ball from his container.

"Doesn't look much different." Lena glared at the ball in her hand, but she forced her hand to close around it two more times. "Full range of motion. Full range of motion."

If that was the mantra that kept her going, Wren was fine with it. But the look in Luca's eyes made her uneasy.

"I am going to see another patient. Good work, Lena." She ducked out before Luca or Lena could say anything else.

CHAPTER FOUR

WREN'S FEET POUNDED on the treadmill. She'd planned to do at least five miles outside, but the rain and not really knowing her surroundings had forced her to the gym in the basement of her new building.

The building catered to young tech bros and a couple of tired surgeons. The manager had insisted on showing her a massive apartment on an upper floor that was empty. The rent for the year would have run her close to a million dollars. As if she could afford that.

She was in a one-bedroom. The manager had not hidden her frustration at her inability to upsell Wren to a two-bedroom. But what did she need two bedrooms for? Plus, she was still making payments on student loans that would stay with her for at least another ten years. Med school was not cheap. And she'd even had a few scholarships and help from her parents—at least for the first year.

Wren spent the first weekend unpacking and trying to figure out the decorating scheme she wanted. She'd chosen this apartment because the lease agreement stated that as long as she didn't change the structure, she could do whatever she wanted. As soon as she figured out what that was. Today, though, she was checking out the gym.

At least the tech bros the manager had bragged about weren't around. Likely they had expensive gym equipment in the four bedroom apartments they rented or memberships to an upscale gym.

Wren started running in college. Though considering she'd started at twelve, one could consider it a childhood activity. It was freeing. Headphones, trails, nothing and nobody to compare herself to.

That was not true of all runners. She'd quit two running groups because they were competing for most miles or some other metric. This was the one thing she never measured.

The gym door opened, but she didn't turn around. She was here to work out. There were three treadmills, and she saw the man start the one next to her. Wren rolled her eyes but didn't turn her head.

Luckily, despite choosing the machine next to her, the man never initiated conversation. He'd sped up his machine and kept a solid pace beside her. That might be intentional, but she still had at least two miles to go, and if he insisted on running the same speed as her, she might go for a solid thirteen miles. She'd never competed in a marathon, but she'd run many on her own.

Usually after a difficult case.

"Damn, Wren. How long are you gonna keep this pace up?" Luca sounded winded.

She didn't dare turn her head to look at him. She did not live in the same apartment complex as Luca. She didn't. She didn't. "I plan to go until I am tired. What are you doing here?"

"Running. I thought that was obvious." He let out a pant but didn't slow his machine down. "You've already done eight miles. How are you not tired?"

Wren shrugged. She was exactly two weeks into her twelve-month lease. Maybe he was closer to his renewal date. With any luck, he'd choose some other place. "When is your lease up?"

She had not meant to ask that.

"I own my apartment. On the top floor." Luca pressed the button to slow his treadmill down as she sped hers up.

Own. *Own. How?*

He was a physical therapist. A darn good one, but he wasn't head of the department. And even if he was, that would still be a hefty mortgage. Though she'd heard about more than one doctor purchasing expensive property and then having basically no furniture while they tried to make payments.

But Luca didn't strike her as the type to make that mistake.

"You shouldn't have told Lena that she could get full range of motion back. She's counting on that."

"Good." Counting on it would make it more likely to happen. Lena needed that mantra because there were going to be days when she wouldn't think it was possible. Days she'd want to give up.

"Damn it, Wren. You can't know that."

"I can." Her feet hit the treadmill one after the other, and she focused on the burn in her limbs to keep her frustration in check. "It is in fact what I was trained to know. And I am very good at my job."

"Her road to recovery—"

"Is going to suck, Luca. I am aware of that. And I made sure she was, too." She blew out a breath. "I am young. I am new to the hospital. But I know a patient capable of full recovery. I will *never* lie to a patient just to make them feel better."

"Wren."

"She can make the recovery, Luca. She believes it, *and* you need to believe it. Period." She sucked in air. It was time to slow down, but her brain refused to lower the speed. "If you can't do it, then I will talk to Therese to ensure she is the only one working with Lena."

"There is no need for that, but absolutes—"

"The world needs some absolutes. Some I am not negotiating." Her heart was pounding in her ears.

The room was silent except for the pounding of their feet against the treads for several minutes.

"I will make sure Lena pushes on the days she wants to give up. And…" the pause hung in the air for a moment "… I owe you an apology. A real one. A heartfelt one. I'm not always a jerk." He huffed out the words as his feet moved forward. "Seriously, I run three miles most days, and my legs are burning."

Wren slowed her machine to a gentle jog and finally turned to look at him. "Why are you so angry at the world?"

Luca blinked several times, and for a moment she feared he was going to slip. "How are you not?"

Wren shrugged. "Ronan would never forgive me if I spent my days wallowing in the unfairness of it all. My parents are living their best life, getting to tell people who I will never meet that they are the sires of a genius. Never mind that they never see me and cut me off when I didn't choose to follow their life plan exactly. Focusing on unhappy memories will not make the world better."

Luca blew out a breath and stopped his treadmill. "I make the world better."

"You do." She slowed the machine down to a brisk walk and took a sip from her water bottle. "But you aren't letting it make you happy."

If he had words for that, he didn't share them. He swiped a towel across his face and stepped off the machine.

By the time she turned off her machine, he was gone.

Wren was making popcorn and dancing to a pop song when a knock on her door echoed through her place.

There was exactly one person who'd be knocking. Apparently, their discussion in the gym an hour ago wasn't enough. She looked at the closed door and weighed leaving it be.

Ronan wouldn't leave it closed.

That was what made her turn the music off and open the door.

Luca stood there, loose blue jeans and soft-looking green T-shirt. It was the half dozen cupcakes in his hands that took her completely off guard.

"Cupcakes?"

He passed them to her. "I said I owed you an apology. Can I come in?"

She stepped back, not sure what to make of the gesture.

"Guess you already have your evening treat. Popcorn. What are you getting ready to watch?"

Wren swallowed. "An animated movie with a singing mermaid."

Her parents had never allowed cartoons for her. Ronan had grown up on the animated movies from the major studios. Wren discovered them two years ago when her roommate pointed out that she wondered if Wren knew what she liked. She'd put the cartoon on to prove a point that Wren couldn't remember now. She'd instantly fallen in love with the music, the cartoons. The documentaries she'd grown up on were fine, but sometimes the brain needed something else.

"Are you purposefully not naming it so I might not recognize that you like a kids movie?"

"There are plenty of adults who like these films. In fact, there are entire online groups." She pursed her lips. This was not something that needed defending. It was a habit she'd gotten into with her parents. They never understood why she'd want to do something "normal," whatever that meant. "I didn't get a lot of kid activities growing up; had to be the genius and all." She let out an uncomfortable laugh. "I never saw the movie, not until I was out of the house. But I wanted the original Princess Ariel mermaid stuffie. Found it online in some resell shop. I have no idea why it called to me, even though I never saw the movie it was based on. But I wanted it so bad. I was getting ready to head to college."

"Which means you were what, ten?" The tone of his voice was harsh.

"Eleven. Almost twelve." She smiled, but he didn't return the look. "Anyway I begged my parents for it as a graduation gift. Silly."

He let out a scoff. "And you didn't get it."

There was no indication he was doing anything other stating a fact. "It wasn't educational." She wasn't sure why she was word vomiting about a mermaid stuffed toy. It wasn't that big of a deal.

The stuffed toy was a symbol. A part of childhood she'd never gotten. A fixture in her mind of the moment she realized her parents cared more for her brain than for her. At least, *academically* she'd understood that. It had taken far longer for her heart to accept that they didn't love her like other parents loved their kids. Even longer to stop trying to earn what wasn't freely given.

Moving to San Diego was the first major step she'd taken since going no contact with them a few years ago. She liked the movie. It was a comfort watch, and she planned to watch it tonight.

Luca took a step closer, a look in his eyes she couldn't quite decipher. "I haven't seen it in ages, but I remember little girls playing mermaid at the public pool with Ronan and me. Though the play mostly revolved around who could hold their breath their longest."

"And you always won." Back on a neutral topic. That was a blessing.

"How on earth do you remember that? You were still in the toddler pool when Ronan and I were there."

"No. I wasn't there at all. I started reading at two, at an alarming rate, and from that point forward, my free time was dedicated to mental growth. But come on, Luca. You sped up your treadmill to match my speed without any warm-up. And physical therapy school is notoriously difficult to get into. Doesn't take a genius to guess you're competitive."

He chuckled, a deep sound that echoed in the apartment and sent shock waves down her body. The man was stunning. He was also the only person she knew in this city, so having a small crush on the familiarity wasn't surprising.

"I am competitive. But I have also been less than welcoming." He looked at the cupcakes she'd set on her counter. "I'm sorry about that, Wren. Do-over?"

He held his hand out, and she took it without hesitating. "Of course. Want to stay and help me eat all this popcorn?"

She saw him hesitate. The man was on his own. Whether because he liked it that way or for some other reason, she didn't know.

She went to the microwave and grabbed the popcorn. Holding the bag up, she waved it front of him, "Do I put this in a bowl so we can share, or do my hands get to be the only ones in the bag?"

"Put it in a bowl." He swallowed, like the words had cost him something.

But it was just popcorn and a silly movie with an old friend.

Wren had quietly hummed each of the movie's songs. He was pretty sure if he'd turned down the invitation to stay and watch it with her that she would have belted out the lines from her couch.

She was in his building.

His.

He'd bought the property when an investment company put it up for sale a few years ago. Luca hired a management company to run the daily issues and never kept track of who

from the peds unit. We had a blast. Though the carrot one of the patients borrowed from the cafeteria was a little mushy, pretty sure it was a cooked carrot. Not ideal for a snowman, but it worked in a pinch."

He could see her standing in the hospital courtyard, a heavy coat covering scrubs and snow boots. Laughing with kids. Helping roll the snow for them. A bright snowcap covering her head. The image was cute and fun, and he suddenly wished there was a reason to build a snowman with her.

"I should get going." He was having too much of a good time. Wren was fun, brilliant and gorgeous. In another time or place, he'd transition this discussion to something far more flirtatious.

Wren's dark hair bounced as she pulled back. "Right, of course."

It felt like an awkward cutoff, but he needed to put distance between them now. His thoughts had slipped past friendly long ago.

Standing, he headed for the door, hearing Wren's soft footsteps behind him. "Thanks for the invitation, Wren." He pulled the door open and stepped out but then turned to lean against the doorjamb. Why was it so difficult to walk away from her?

"Technically you invited yourself. You showed up unannounced *with cupcakes*." She held the door, leaning against it as well.

At least I'm not the only one putting off goodbye. Not that that thought was helpful.

"I said I owed you an apology. And cupcakes are always a good way to say sorry." He playfully rolled his eyes. "*You* invited me to watch the movie."

Wren held up her hands. "Fine. Let's call this one a tie."

He nodded.

"But one more thing." She let out a breath. "Can you recommend a running path? I'm not a huge fan of treadmills, but I don't know the paths around here."

Her free hand was swinging loosely, and his hand itched to reach for it.

"I go for a run before most shifts. I start at five, do three miles in one of the local parks. I know that isn't a half marathon, but—"

"You going tomorrow morning?"

"Meet you here?" He should have said he'd meet her in the lobby. Set some form of boundary. But no. The words were out, and there was no reason to withdraw them. Even if he wanted to...which he very much did not.

"I will be ready at five till five." She pursed her lips. "This is turning into a Midwestern goodbye."

He raised a brow.

"One of my roommates in New York, Rebecca, she was from Ohio. I used to joke that it took her thirty minutes to tell everyone she was leaving and another twenty to actually walk out the door." She gestured between the two of them. "Like we're doing. She swore it was a thing, even an expectation where she was from."

Luca grinned. "Good night, Wren." The words were hard to say, but it was time to step away.

"Good night, Luca."

CHAPTER FIVE

WREN STRETCHED AND waited for the knock on the door as she replayed the evening. They'd started off uncomfortable. Her calling him out in the gym. That had somehow turned into him bringing her cupcakes and watching a kids movie with her.

Parts of the night had felt like flirting. Right? She didn't have much experience with that, so maybe she was reading into the long goodbye. The subtle leans toward her.

Ugh. Overthinking it wasn't going to help anything. And neither was waiting by the door. She stepped out of her apartment, locked the door, then hooked her keys on her hydration belt.

Luca was already walking down the hallway. The man was punctual, she'd give him that.

"A hydration belt with multiple water bottles? I thought we were going for a short jog?"

Wren stepped beside him as they started down the stairs to the first floor. "I need it for long runs, and it seemed silly to buy more than one running belt, so I use it for all runs." That wasn't the whole truth, but it wasn't a lie, either. "Good news is, it makes me feel weird if I leave one empty. Your lucky day. If you get thirsty, I have an extra filled and ready to go."

"Makes you feel weird to leave one empty or at home?"

They stepped into the crisp morning air, and Wren grinned. He wasn't wrong about the nice weather.

"Yeah. I always fill both. Habit, but once I form one, I

have a hard time breaking it." Wren pulled her hands over her head, then gestured to the street. "Which way we off to?"

Luca tilted his head, then set off at a steady pace. "Park trail is this way. Why do you have a hard time breaking a habit?"

She fell into pace beside him. "What?" She'd heard the question but needed a moment to think of an answer. Because this wasn't really about habits.

"Why do you have a hard time breaking habits? I mean, other than the fact that habits, by their nature, are difficult to break. Thus the reason they are called habits." He turned his head and grinned, but there was a look in his eye that made her glance away.

"As you said, habits by their nature are difficult to break." If only she'd just stated that fact.

"Come on, Wren," Luca pressed as their feet hit the pavement.

"Ronan always had to do things certain ways. Remember?" She wasn't sure Luca would recall the issue. Her brother probably had a form of obsessive-compulsive disorder. Not that their parents ever had him checked. He was *normal*— their word—and therefore boring.

Her brother was anything but boring. And if he'd gotten his chance, she was sure he'd have gotten at least a few seasons in the majors. Whether he could have made the hall of fame or not, who knew? But until he did something extraordinary, their parents largely ignored him.

"Yeah." Luca huffed out a breath as his feet fell into the same rhythm as hers. "He had some things that, if they got messed up, sent him into a spiral. He was working with a therapist on it."

"He was?" Ronan had never shared that with her. Though, when he'd passed, she was sixteen. That wasn't necessarily something one shared with such a little sister.

"Yeah. His team found a therapist, and they were hav-

the renters were. But after seeing her in the gym, he'd called the manager to find out Wren's apartment number, so he hadn't had to figure out which was hers.

The credits started rolling, and Wren leaned across him to grab the remote he'd absentmindedly picked up. Her body brushed his for milliseconds, and his heart jumped. This was why he should have told her he had plans when she asked him to stay.

Though she would have known he was lying. The only plans Luca ever had were meetings with his investment advisor every quarter and shifts at the hospital.

And he'd wanted to stay. Wanted to sit closer to her on the couch than he had. Their hands had touched in the popcorn bowl four times. He'd counted.

Ronan's little sister. Not for you.

"Thanks for watching with me." Wren stretched her arms overhead, showing off a thin line of skin as her shirt lifted.

He was thirty-eight years old. He did not need to react to half an inch of skin like a teenage boy.

"Of course." His voice sounded stilted, but if she noticed, Wren didn't say anything. "Next movie night should be at my place."

Why had he said that?

Wren sat up on the couch, grinning from ear to ear. She was so cute. So sweet.

Focus.

"What kind of movies do you like? I'm willing to bet they aren't cartoons?" She pulled her bottom lip through her teeth and let out a sigh.

His mouth was dry. Focusing on anything other than the thump, thump, thump of his heart pounding in his ears was taking all of his strength.

"Or maybe it is? Anime?" She tapped her head, the grin never faltering.

Of course not, she doesn't have any reason to suspect that I'm sitting here getting turned on by just her existence.

"No." He shook his head. "Honestly, I like horror movies. Psychological thrillers. Stuff that makes you jump in a dark room."

Wren giggled. "Ronan used to say he took first dates to horror flicks hoping they'd hop into his arms when they got scared." She pushed his shoulder, then stood. "You aren't trying to get me to jump into your arms, right? Slide from Dr. McSteamy to *Doctor McSteamy.*"

The adjustment in tone from playful anger to sultry vixen set his skin ablaze.

"Take a breath, Luca, I'm playing with you." Wren leaned over and grabbed the popcorn bowl before heading to the kitchen.

He took a few deep breaths, not that they steadied him much, then stood. "I knew that."

Wren didn't call him on the lie.

"You talk about Ronan." He barely got his friend's name out. They'd joked about buying houses next to each other. Raising kids together. Brothers from a different mother.

And then he was just gone.

"He's my brother." Wren shrugged. "His life was short. In a couple of years, I will have spent more time without him than I spent with him. Talking about him keeps him alive. Keeps him real."

"I have never had another friend like him." Luca had had no secrets from Ronan. Hell, the man had been with him when the lawyer explained that Aunt Maude had left everything to him. And that *everything* included quite a bit more than the old house the rest of the family grumbled was too big for her, too old, too much.

In other words, they'd wanted her to sell it, so there might be some profit when she was gone.

Ronan understood that Luca would have given it all back if it meant Maude was still there.

The woman made sure he was taken care of. Treated him as more of a son than his parents had. Loved him just for himself. The only family who ever had. And when she'd gotten too fragile to take care of herself, he'd stepped in.

"He was great." Wren stepped into the kitchen. "I'm getting a drink, you want one?"

"What do you have?" He took a few steps, following her. Another moment when he could have stepped away. Another chance to offer an excuse. His colleagues and the half dozen or so women he'd dated for more than two dates complained he was a one-word answer man. Yet around Wren—

"Water, pop, a bottle of wine that I'm saving, so water and pop." She looked at him. "Sorry. I don't do much hosting."

He put an arm around her shoulder, squeezing before his brain had time to think it through. "It's your place. Water is fine. What are you saving the wine for?"

"I don't know." She laughed as she stepped out of his arm. She poured the water and handed him his glass before heading back to the living room with hers.

Color was cresting on her cheeks. Maybe Wren knew the plan for the wine. And whatever it was just didn't include him.

That shouldn't sting. But he wanted to know what she wanted. Wanted to know the joy she was looking forward to. Given how he'd acted, there was no reason for her to share that with him.

"So why San Diego?" She lifted the glass to her lips.

"What?"

Wren shook her head. "Why San Diego? This is literally across the country from where we grew up. And you own your apartment, so obviously you're staying. So why San Diego?"

"Tell you what, you ask me that again in January." He leaned a little closer, then forced himself to pull back. Why was he so drawn to her?

"January? That's nearly six months away." Wren shook her head as she giggled. "Is it that hard of an answer?"

"No." Luca took a sip of water, then set his glass on the coaster. "But you're from Rhode Island, studied and earned your degree from Johns Hopkins in Baltimore and worked in New York City for the last several years. Go through a winter here, then ask me why I stayed."

"You don't miss the snow?" Her eyes widened as she laid her hand on his knee.

Fire. That was the only word to describe the sensation running through his body. The lightning bolt created by her touch. Rather than pull back, he laid his hand on hers and lowered his voice. "You tell me if you miss the snow, the ice, the bone-chilling wind, when you've spent a winter in paradise."

"Paradise." Her mouth slowly formed the word. "That is an awfully big description."

Luca ran his thumb over the soft skin on the back of her hand. "It is. Doesn't make it untrue."

Wren lifted her chin as she pulled away from him. "All right, fine, I will ask you again in January. But then I want a real answer."

There was so much he held back. Truths he spoke to no one. But this one wasn't deep. "I swear, when you get to January, you'll understand."

Wren gave him a playful look. "But that means the two of us will never get to build a snowman. I mean, come on, you have to miss building snowmen."

"When was the last time you built a snowman?"

"Last year!" She put her hands on her hips, a little awkwardly given her position on the couch. "With a few kids

ing success overcoming what was habit and what was compulsive." He looked at her again, and this time the look was very brotherly. "Do you struggle with compulsive thoughts?"

"No." She didn't like that look. Didn't appreciate the tone change, either. "But this is Ronan's belt. He's the one I started running with. And he always, always had to have both bottles full. So." She shrugged.

They ran in silence for a few minutes before he turned onto a smaller path. "Come on, I want to show you something."

They ran until they were on a clearing overlooking the San Diego Bay. The sun was starting to rise, causing glittery beams across the water.

"The sunset is prettier. After all, it sets right over the bay, but I like the shine it gives as it starts to rise."

"It is gorgeous." Wren wrapped her arms around herself, very aware of the man standing next to her. Aware that she wanted more of the flirtatious tone from last night. And none of the protective tone he'd slipped into. "Thanks for bringing me. We'll have to come back at sunset."

"Sure." Luca looked at her and took a deep breath and leaned toward her.

He's about to kiss me.

She hadn't misread the signs last night.

"Luca." She leaned toward him, putting her hand on his chest. How did he kiss? Soft and slow? Passionate and demanding?

"I know Ronan isn't around, and your parents are your parents, so if you need someone…"

She dropped her hand and pulled back. How had she misread this so badly? Her mouth was dry, and if the earth opened beneath her right now, she'd gladly step into the hole to get away.

"I mean, I owe Ronan to look after you."

Owe Ronan. Not for her. Not really.

"Stop." She backed away as the word fell from her lips.

Misreading the signs about what he wanted was bad enough, but San Diego was supposed to be a fresh start. A place where she wasn't seen as the naive genius. Despite all her accomplishments, people still saw the scared nineteen-year-old resident standing next to the men and women who'd started med school at the traditional age.

It was nice that Luca was here. More than nice, but if he saw her as a duty...a person needing protection... Her stomach rolled. She'd thought maybe—

No. She wasn't traveling down that road.

She loved her brother and hated how his name had disappeared from everyone's lips weeks after his funeral. A ghost no one wanted to bring up.

She'd thought the two of them were reminiscing. It was refreshing that Luca spoke of him. But she wanted to be Wren to Luca. Her own person with a shared history and exciting future.

Such a lovely thought but apparently not reality. To him, she was Ronan's little sister. A debt he owed a friend. A burden. Though she knew he'd never use those words. But it wasn't possible to pay off a debt to a ghost.

"Wren."

She shook her head, pushing off whatever he planned to say. "I wanted a friend, not a brotherly protector. So uh, yeah. I'm going to head back now. Thanks for showing me where to come to watch the sunrise and sunset on my runs. I'll see you around the hospital."

Then she turned on her heel and headed back down the trail.

Luca had gone all day without seeing Wren. And he'd looked for her.

His offer this morning had been stupid. He'd never replace

her brother. And he damn well didn't want the position. He'd done it to remind himself who she was.

Because the sunbeams hitting her cheeks this morning had sent a wave of longing through him. He dreamed of kissing her, every night. Dreamed of sliding his lips down that soft neck. Then she'd put her hand on his chest. He'd had to remind himself somehow.

He cleared his throat as he climbed the stairs. He was checking in on Lena. She'd proudly showed him she was ready for a new ball this morning. A shock considering she'd had that one for less than twenty-four hours. But she was determined.

Wren had done that.

He knocked, then entered Lena's room, tossing the ball up in the air. "Here it is. I want to make sure you know that it may take you several days or even a week to level up from this ball. This is a marathon, not a sprint."

Lena took the ball, a frown crossing her lips.

"You all right?" The woman was never perky with him. Most of his patients rolled their eyes when he pushed them to do one more exercise. Physical therapy was tough, physically and mentally. He never took it personally. But there was something about her expression.

"Dr. Freson was just in here."

He waited a minute, but when she didn't elaborate, he pushed, "Did Dr. Freson have concerns about your wound?" He'd checked the notes before coming up here—if Wren was worried she'd not said anything in the notes. Though if she just left, she wouldn't have had a chance to update them.

Lena rolled the ball around her palm. "She was kind and said my hand looked good, no sign of infection."

All of that was good news. "That is what you should expect to hear. Burns are notorious for infections. It's what Dr. Freson will focus on most."

He understood that not every day netted fresh news. That was rough, but it was to be expected.

"It's not that." Lena squeezed the ball and didn't hide the wince. "She wasn't her sunshiny self."

Their talk this morning was certainly rough. He hadn't meant to upset her. A routine he was breaking with her *now*. "I'll check on her." He'd planned to give her space today. Give himself space to acknowledge the desire she raised in him. But if she was upset, he wasn't waiting.

"Thanks. Her happiness is infectious. I don't think she realizes that. Plus, she's my favorite doctor. I don't want her sad."

Luca laid a hand across his heart and gave a playful wounded sound. "*She* is your favorite? What about me?"

"You're nice, but it's no competition." Lena squeezed the ball again and huffed as she released it. "You're kind of a torture artist."

"Kinda. But it gets results." He winked, then headed out of the room.

"Luca." Therese was marching up the hallway. "You should head back to the physio room using that stairwell." She pointed to the door she'd probably exited from.

"Why?"

"Call it a feeling." She nodded and walked away, never looking back.

He looked at the stairs and headed for them. Pushing the door open, he headed down the first flight and saw Wren looking out the window. That particular window showcased the parking lot, so it certainly wasn't for the view.

"You all right?"

"No." Wren shook her head but didn't elaborate.

"Is it about this morning?" A dumb question. One he regretted as soon as her eyes turned toward him.

The tears hadn't fallen, but they were clear in her dark eyes.

"Luca, this morning was uncomfortable and awkward,

nothing more." Even with tears in her eyes, it was said with a kindness he didn't deserve.

"Fair." He moved to stare out the same window. "Not the hospital's best view."

"No. But it works in a pinch." She let out a sigh. "Difficult patient. A surgery didn't go as planned. It happens." She blinked a few times, then took a deep breath. So much unsaid but communicated in those words. "Have a good day, Doctor." She started for the stairs, but he couldn't let her go. Not yet.

He grabbed her hand, as stunned by the action as her wide eyes indicated she was. "I like spending time with you."

She nodded but didn't add anything to the conversation.

"Not because of Ronan. I like just hanging out with you. It's easy." He was rambling. "What I mean is that I said a dumb thing. I want to be friends."

It would be easy to want more with Wren. But he wasn't going to focus on that.

She looked at his hand holding hers. "Actual friends?" She hesitated a minute before adding, "Not stepping into a position I don't need filled?" Wren arched her brow, but she didn't pull away.

"Yeah. In fact, why don't we do movie night again? My place this time. I think I promised you a horror movie. Though if your day's been bad—"

"Sounds great. What time?" Wren finally pulled her hand from his.

He looked at their separated hands, instantly missing the connection. "Seven? I'll order dinner delivery." That made it sound almost like a date.

Because part of me wishes it was.

"Okay. I'm not a picky eater, so whatever you want is fine. I'll cash you some funds."

She was obviously not thinking it was anything but two awkward friends hanging out. "You are my guest, Wren."

"All right."

"Before you go…" He was seeing her in a few hours. There was no reason to slow her down. "I gave Lena a new workout ball. She's made excellent progress in just a day. You were right. She is going to get full range of motion back. Fast, too, if she puts as much effort into it as she did yesterday."

Wren bit her lip rather than smiling. That meant she was probably thinking the same thing he was. It was fast, but plateaus happened. "She's going to hit at least one wall. And when she does, maybe Therese can play good physical therapist and you play bad guy. Let Therese be her outlet to complain to, while you keep pushing her to get where she wants."

It was a good idea. A great one. "I don't think Therese knows any other role but good guy. And I am the resident grump, so it makes sense."

Wren tilted her head, a tiny frown appearing. "You aren't a grump. Or rather you are."

He playfully hit his chest again, this time pretending that Wren was the one wounding him. "The sunshiny surgeon thinks I'm a grump."

"You just called yourself a grump." She wagged a finger at him. "But you aren't really. You just don't like to show this side of you to everyone else. Maybe you should."

He almost wanted to give a little salute at the request. Instead, Luca shrugged. "I am who I am."

"I think you have layers." Wren looked at her watch and headed for the door. "I want popcorn if you're going to make me watch a horror flick. Only fair."

Only fair indeed.

CHAPTER SIX

You sure you don't want to cancel? I know the surgery took more than five hours. You must be exhausted.

L*UCA LOOKED THE* text over and then forced himself to hit Send. He should have sent it before he left the hospital. The last thing Wren probably wanted was a movie night after today.

That afternoon, a car caught fire on Interstate 15, and Wren and two other surgeons had treated the trapped patient. He'd heard through the hospital grapevine that it was touch-and-go, but touch-and-go meant still alive. After the rough surgery at the start of her shift, a movie night was probably the last thing she wanted.

Headed up now. Unless you and Hippo need a night off.

Nope.

He looked over at the dog snoring—loudly—on the giant bed Luca purchased for him last year. He'd bounce up when Wren got here and then sleep through their movie.

Movie. Wren.

All right, he grabbed the popcorn kernels and threw them in the fancy maker he'd bought himself last Christmas so he could start them as soon as they were ready for the flick.

There was exactly no reason for him to have a movie theater-grade machine in the theater room. Particularly since, after Wren's arrival, he'd have hosted exactly one person in it.

But as a kid he'd always joked that one day he'd make movie theater buttered popcorn any time he wanted. A joke that made Maude laugh until she started coughing. She'd told him that she believed he'd have it one day. The only hint he'd had about the wealth she was hiding.

He'd put off the purchase. But then, on the anniversary of her death a few years ago, he'd given into the whim, promptly made six batches of popcorn, then let it largely collect dust. A problem he'd fixed as soon as he got home today.

It was shiny and ready now.

The doorbell rang, and Luca headed to pick up his guest, Hippo catching up to him before he opened the door.

Her stomach said hello before Wren could get a word out. "Don't suppose you ordered food already? Guess I was hungrier than expected."

Hippo pressed against her legs. Wren dropped down and gave him attention. Then her stomach let out another gurgle.

"Bed, Hippo."

The dog gave him pouty eyes, but he followed the command and headed back to his bed, looking over his shoulder at Wren the whole time.

Luca stepped back to let her in. "I've got sushi and fried rice. You said you weren't picky."

"Poor Hippo."

"Poor Hippo, nothing. He's already had his dinner and a treat. You're the one who needs to eat. So, is what I ordered okay?"

"Sounds perfect." Her stomach grumbled again.

"Pretty sure you'd say it was perfect no matter what I had, given what your stomach is saying." Luca chuckled and led her to the kitchen.

He turned, surprised to find her still standing several feet behind him.

"You own the whole floor." Her eyes roamed the entry and living room with its huge windows overlooking the San Diego Bay.

"Come on, you're starving. We can talk real estate while you eat." He reached for her hand and pulled her along.

"Yeah, but this is the whole floor!" Wren's voice was soft, and she was staring out the window as he led the way. "I mean I only saw one door, but somehow it didn't register until just now."

The view was why he'd purchased the building. It was one of his favorite places. There was a little pit in his stomach as he watched her. Was Wren piecing together what it meant that he owned the floor?

She stopped in front of the window for just a minute. "Man, I was excited I paid my med school loans down enough to afford to rent my place. This is so impressive."

Med school loans.

Something most physicians carried well into their late thirties. Though he would have expected a genius to get most of her bills paid for by scholarships. Or her parents, they could certainly have afforded it.

A chill went down his spine. Would she become someone different, someone who only looked at him for his wallet, like everyone else when she figured it out?

I don't want to lose her.

He wasn't sure how to process that thought, so he let go of her hand and pointed toward the dining room. "Come on, let's get you fed. I got a whole selection of sushi. And the fried rice." He set the bowl out, then placed the sushi board to her across the table.

Wren looked from the sushi to the fried rice, then to him.

"Selection is certainly the word." She grabbed a pair of chopsticks and dug in.

For several minutes, they sat in silence, munching on food.

But far too soon, she leaned back and gestured to the apartment. "How? I mean, physical therapy pays, but I mean—" Wren opened her arms wider. "How?"

"An investment hit big." Heat was in his cheeks. Not a complete lie. He'd made some very good decisions with Maude's inheritance. But it wasn't exactly the truth. Was this the moment? The transition? The change?

"I'd say so." She looked toward the window.

He held his breath. He'd gone through this countless times. If it happened again, he'd figure it out.

Somehow.

"Not sure I'd ever leave the view." Wren put her head on her hands, gazing out at the bay. Then she looked back at him, her dark gorgeous gaze holding him tight. "How much do you want me to send you? What cash app do you use?"

For a second, he wasn't sure he'd heard the question right. He might not have hosted anyone in the theater room, but many dates and a few men he thought might be friends had made it to this table. And each one saw the view and pieced together what it meant. No one who crossed his threshold ever offered to pay for anything.

A couple of fingers snapped in front of him. "Earth to Luca."

"Sorry, you're good. I told you. You're my guest."

"I know you said that, but you must have bought the entire sushi menu." She waved at the still very full plate of food. "I can pony up some coin to cover it."

Her grin struck his heart. "Nope. I got this. You had two long surgeries." He never minded paying; it was the audacity to assume that it was his only role in any relationship that had him cut everyone out.

"Fine. But…" she stood, grabbing her plate "…my treat next time."

Her hip brushed his as she stepped around him, a lightning bolt of desire streaking across his skin.

"So, where in this cavernous place are we watching a horror movie?"

"I have a theater room."

Wren giggled as she rinsed her plate and put it in the dishwasher. "*Of course* you have a theater room! As long as there's popcorn."

"I promised." He started to reach for her hand to lead her toward the theater room but caught himself. Barely. He'd already held it once. He did not need to do so. Not again.

Wren looked at his hand but didn't reach for him.

"This way." They entered the theater, and he immediately walked over to the popcorn machine and flipped it on.

"Get out! I always wanted one of these. Always. I mean, how are you not eating popcorn ALL THE TIME?" She clapped her hands and bounced as the corns started popping out of the oil.

"Who says I'm not eating it all the time?" There was no way to stop the grin on his face. Wren's brightness was infectious.

"Fair."

He pushed a few buttons, and the screen rolled down.

"You might get sick of me. Because anytime I want to see a movie, I am knocking on your door. No more microwave popcorn for me." She reached for the salt shaker by the machine, then hesitated, "Can I?"

"Why not?"

"Perfect answer." She salted the popcorn, filled the bowl he'd left by the machine, then turned to him, popping a piece through her perfect lips immediately. "Showtime."

He only had a small couch in the center of the room. He'd planned to put in theater chairs, but the realization that others wouldn't sit in them had stopped the acquisition. A sad little fact he wasn't upset about now.

Wren sat on the couch, and he slid in next to her.

"You are in charge of popcorn." She pressed the bowl into his hands. The brush of her fingers against his drove his pulse up.

"Don't trust yourself with it?" He looked at the bowl, then back at her. Not that he'd minded, but she'd gripped her bowl so tightly the other night he assumed she'd want full control of it.

Last night. He was at her place last night.

Time moved swiftly and also, somehow, slowed when Wren was with him.

"I get jumpy in these types of movies. There's a good chance we'll end up with more popcorn on the floor than in our bellies." She chuckled and looked away, color staining her cheeks.

Luca put his hand on her chin, turning her to look at him. "We can pick any other movie. This—"

"Does the killer get what's coming to him in this?" She didn't pull away from his touch.

Luca's thumb traced the edge of her jaw. What would happen if he replaced it with his mouth? *Focus.* "Spoiler, but yes. It's a very campy movie, but there's blood, gore and jump scares."

"Perfect. I want an outlet for my feelings. A justified ending. I can handle it." She put her hand on his knee. "But I am staying right next to you during this flick. And not just because you have the smallest couch ever in here."

Luca put his arm around her shoulder. "That is perfectly fine."

"Eeek!" Wren pinched her eyes closed as she leaned her head against Luca's shoulder—again. She'd spent more time in this position than any other.

Maybe this movie hadn't been such a good choice. She'd wanted something different. Something to take her mind off the day. A different reason for her dreams to have a haunting quality to them than the day she'd had.

Her first surgery was for a skin graft failure. The infection spread was more than she'd anticipated, so amputation was the only option. Her role in the second was more as an aid to the general surgeon. The patient wasn't stable enough to worry about plastics, but the surgeon had wanted her expertise for the burns that covered more than forty percent of his body.

A young man. Newly engaged. Life forever changed. His fiancée had not taken the news well. In fact, Wren watched her slip the ring off her finger as she walked out of the room where they'd gone over the surgery details with her.

The patient wasn't even awake, and the woman he planned to spend the rest of his life wasn't going to meet him at the altar. The life he'd planned was over.

She'd learned long ago that life wasn't fair. She didn't let the fact steal her joy. That didn't mean tough cases didn't puncture the happy bubble she kept around her.

Luca squeezed her shoulder. "The killer is about to get their due, if you want to watch?"

She turned her head but didn't lift it. She peeked through her eyes and watched the final battle come to a satisfying end. "Sorry I spent most of the time burying my head. I admit that was scarier than I anticipated."

"We watched an animated film yesterday. I should have started with something lighter." He chuckled but didn't pull away from her.

She let out a breath. "I pushed it. I mean, you offered, and I was all like…" Wren lifted her head and pointed to herself as she mimicked the tone she'd used earlier, "…*I can handle it*. The one thing I will never understand is why every horror flick starts with an easy out. I mean all the hero had to do was *not* say the cursed words. He knew he was cursed, but *no*—"

"Humans are selfish at their core. He knew he was cursed, but he didn't really believe it. He thought he'd be different. He'd be the one to make the change. That the rules didn't apply to him."

The words were sharp. Pointed. A full-on critique she'd not expected. "I don't think that's fair. I mean, curses aren't real—"

"Oh, I disagree there."

She laid her hand over his chest. "You are not cursed." Wren wasn't sure why she said the words. They sounded silly, but he didn't laugh or give her any indication that he agreed with her statement.

He started to shrug, then must have realized her head was still on his shoulder.

She needed to move. *Why is it so hard to pull away?* Waiting wasn't going to make it easier, so Wren forced herself to pull back.

Did he frown?

His shoulder is probably sore from hosting my head.

Don't read into things, Wren.

He wanted friendship. He'd made that clear. Just because her heart danced around him didn't mean he felt the same. "Sorry. Movie over, no reason to crowd your space."

"You can bury your head in my shoulder anytime, Wren." Luca leaned toward her.

Her skin burned as her gaze focused on his full lips.

He pushed a loose hair behind her ear. A *very* friendly gesture.

"I should get going." The words tasted like ash, but she forced them out. There was no reason to think Luca had any interest in kissing her. She'd practically forced her way into his life.

There is no "practically" to it.

The man was hot. He was smart. He was kind—when he let people in. The perfect crush candidate.

He stood, and she followed suit. She had said she needed to go. No sense dragging it out.

Still, she wandered over to Hippo. The dog had slept through the whole movie and only opened one eye as she rubbed his head. But his tail happily whapped against the bed.

"Does he have a fancy bed in every room?" She rubbed his head once more, then stood. She'd seen a bed in the living room, the dining room and a small one in the corner of the kitchen that she couldn't imagine the goober ever curling up in.

"Yes. Oh no. The guest bathroom is bed-free. But no one ever uses it, so not sure that counts." Luca winked and put his hands in his pockets. He didn't head for the door, and she didn't move, either.

"Thank you for hosting me. I meant it… My treat next time. You can even bring Hippo for dinner. Though you will have to bring a bed. I don't have one."

"You ever wanted a dog?" His gaze darted to Hippo, then back to her.

"You offering this sweet boy?" she playfully teased as she stepped closer to Luca and put her hands in her pockets, mimicking him. It also meant she couldn't easily touch him.

Luca opened his mouth, making a horrified face she knew was all for show. "Of course not. He's my baby."

Loves dogs.

Another mental box checked on the crush list.

"My parents never let us have an animal. They promised Ronan once that if he got a perfect score card, he could get a cat."

"I remember that." Luca let out a sigh. "He had it, too. Except he forgot a math assignment on the last day of the quarter."

"He didn't forget it." The old anger surged in her chest. Her parents had casually let the secret out of the bag after he passed. "Mom took it out of his backpack while he was making his lunch."

"What!" Luca swallowed as the word echoed around him.

"Yeah. They didn't want a cat. So Mom sabotaged him." She pulled her hands from her pockets and wrapped her arms around herself. "She told me about it a few years ago. Last time I talked to them. All they ever cared about was achievement, but when he was on the cusp of a truly impressive feat, they swiped it away from him."

She took a deep breath, shocked at the words spilling from her. But the dam was broken, and more flowed forth. "It was one thing to say stuffed animals for a genius were unnecessary or to never celebrate birthdays or—"

"Never celebrate birthdays?"

"Yeah, well. They only ever saw my mind." Wren shrugged. "I spent all night with my head buried in your shoulder. Now I'm spilling my guts in your theater room." She looked around the room. "This really is impressive, Luca."

He shifted his feet, color rising in his cheeks. "Thanks."

"I should get going."

"You already said that." He took a step toward her but didn't lead the way to the front door.

"I did." There was so little distance between them. The room was suddenly hot. She watched his eyes lower, looking at her lips. Wren wanted far too badly to believe he was thinking of kissing her.

She'd kissed a few men. Brief kisses ending a second date. Awkward moments that always ended her desire to have a third.

Wren's body ached with need as he shifted. If he lowered his head, their lips would touch.

Or if I lift myself up.

"Luca—"

"Wren?"

He had not been called, but Hippo let out his own bray at the moment, and both of them jumped back. The dog wagged his tail, and he pushed himself between them.

That was probably for the best. She'd never had a second kiss. And she wanted Luca in her life now that she'd found him again.

But part of her wished Hippo had waited a second before making his presence known. At least then she'd know if Luca had wanted to kiss her. Or if it was just in her mind.

"That is my cue." She smiled down at Hippo, then nodded to Luca. "Thanks again for tonight."

"Any time." This time he stepped around her and led her out of the room and right to the front door. No hesitation. No stretching things out this time. "Sweet dreams, Wren."

She stepped out, and the door closed behind her.

Wren stood there for a moment, a finger to her lips. Then she shook her head. With any luck, her dreams would be filled with Luca instead of the horror movie or today's highlights from the hospital.

CHAPTER SEVEN

Luca looked toward the door of the therapy room, very aware that Wren had not stopped in.

"When is Wren coming by?"

It was like Therese had read his mind. Which meant he was obvious enough about who he was hoping might pay a visit.

"No idea." He looked back at the file on the tablet. He had three more patients this afternoon. "Why are you asking?"

"Because you keep looking at that door. Plus, she usually stops by around now. Wren is fun. And I enjoy her company." Therese went to grab a bench for her next patient.

"Wren is fun." Luca moved without thinking. Therese was pregnant, and she did not need to move all the heavy equipment on her own.

"I could have done that on my own." Therese shook her head as he grabbed the other end of the bench. "But thank you."

Luca nodded.

"Any chance I can get the chatty version that appears with Wren?" Therese chuckled, but it sounded forced.

"What?"

They set the bench down, and she crossed her arms. "Come on. You really don't see it, McSteamy?"

He looked to the door…again. No Wren. Damn. He didn't

realize how much he missed the bright ray of sunshine she brought when she entered the room. "No."

"That." Therese pointed at him. "That right there."

"What?"

Therese pinched the bridge of her nose. "Seriously. She is the only one who can get more than a few words out of you. I take it as a personal win if I manage more than three words at a time."

Luca crossed his arms, not enjoying the statement. He chatted. Sort of. "I speak with my patients all the time."

"Yes. It's the reason so many people like you. But none of us can get close to you. The best we can do is know that you live on coffee. Which almost everyone in this place does, so that isn't exactly personal insight. No one knows where you live, if you're married or seeing someone."

"I'm not." He hadn't meant to comment. His love life was a dismal record.

One broken engagement—on his wedding day. A handful of uneventful dates. One of whom became interested in him only after she'd done some digging on him. Luca still wasn't sure how the woman found out his exact net worth, but it was clear that she'd changed her tune when the dollar signs appeared. He'd had to hire security for the apartment building because she kept finding ways into it.

No one had gotten close in years. That was easier than losing people when they discovered the truth.

"So you aren't dating Wren?" Therese raised her brow.

Dating Wren?

His body heated as his tongue tried to force out the word *no*. They were friends. Only friends.

Though over the last two weeks, they'd spent nearly every minute outside the hospital together. She'd "repaid" the sushi by cooking him pasta. He'd asked her to come on evening walks with Hippo. Last night, she'd even showed off the dog bed she purchased for Hippo, so Luca didn't have to keep bringing one down. Hippo had certainly approved.

"No." The word burned. "We are simply friends." *Simply.*

He cared about her. She was hot. And funny, sweet. *And my dead best friend's sister.* That was against the code. You didn't date little sisters. At least not without asking. And there was no way to find out if Ronan was okay with the idea.

Therese let out a laugh. "Yeah. I used to say the same about Seth." She rubbed her belly to emphasize how much that relationship had shifted. "Now we're expecting and trying to figure out where we're going to put the crib in Seth's cramped apartment."

"Well, Wren and I are just friends." The words nearly stuck in his throat, but he got them out.

His dreams were haunted by her. There was nothing friendly about those, and he relished the night knowing for a few hours his mind could hold what his soul wouldn't.

"Great." Therese smirked. "So you don't mind if Seth and I set her up with a friend of his?"

His soul screamed no. But that wasn't fair to Wren. She was wonderful. She deserved a partner who worshipped her.

I could do that.

"Which friend?" Like he'd know whoever the answer was. Luca knew his colleagues...as colleagues.

"Dr. Griffen."

He knew that one. "The playboy in peds. Absolutely not." Luca was shocked that Therese would even suggest such a thing.

Matt Griffen was nice and a great pediatrician. He was also known for having dated the most nurses, doctors and other staff in the hospital. Luca had even heard that HR had a discussion with him following the rumor he'd dated the entire phlebotomy staff. He'd politely told them that he had in fact only dated three fourths of the staff. And to the best of his knowledge, there were no complaints.

That was the thing. No one ever said anything untoward went down. Just that the man was *never* settling. Wren did not deserve to be another notch in his bedpost.

"Dr. Reeves is single."

"He's been divorced less than a month." Luca was incensed on Wren's behalf. She was not rebound material.

"I wasn't aware you followed hospital gossip so closely."

He raised a brow. "I hear things."

"Mm-hmm. What about Scott Rogers?"

Luca opened his mouth, then shut it. The emergency room nurse was great. He'd heard nothing but nice things about him. *Damn it*.

"Anyone want a coffee?" Wren walked in, coffee carrier in hand. "Oh. Sorry. I clearly caught you two deep in conversation."

"You didn't." Luca rushed the words out as his shoulders relaxed seeing her smile.

"I was talking to Luca about setting you up with one of Seth's friends." Therese smiled at him, a dare clear in her eyes.

Wren's eyes shifted to Therese, then to him. There was something unsaid in those eyes. Something that made his stomach drop.

"You were talking about setting me up?" The question was aimed at him.

"Therese was discussing it."

"And Luca was shooting down everyone I suggested." The physical therapist stepped toward Wren.

"Shooting them down?" Wren looked at him, swallowing.

"None of them are good enough for you. As I was explaining to Therese." This was a minefield.

Wren opened her mouth, then closed it.

He was pretty sure that he'd just stepped on a pin.

"I'm sorry, Wren. Seth and I were talking, and we thought maybe…but…" Therese sucked in a deep breath, her cheeks darkening. "I see three cups. Any chance one of those is decaf?"

Wren nodded as she handed Therese her coffee, but she still didn't say anything.

Therese hesitated for a second. "I'm sorry. I overstepped. I appreciate the coffee, and I hope our new friendship is okay."

Wren's dark gaze held his. "I don't date." She swallowed and turned her sunshine toward Therese.

"Oh." Therese shook her head. "Got it."

Don't date? What the hell did she mean by that?

"But you didn't know that. And of course we're fine." Wren reached her hand out and squeezed Therese's arms, "I heard Becky in radiology complaining that all her matches on a dating app were coming up duds. I bet she would love a setup. But not with Dr. Griffen. Apparently, she is well aware of his reputation." Wren smiled at Therese. A genuine smile that Luca suspected she didn't plan to direct toward him.

"His reputation does precede him." Therese looked at her watch and cleared her throat. "Speaking of peds, I need to see a patient up there now. You might want to call the floor, Luca. I would have thought your patient would be down by now." Therese used the excuse to make a quick escape.

Luca walked over to the terminal to give the third floor nurses station a ring. Therese was right. His patient should be here by now. If Mrs. Johnson had a holdup, he needed to know.

"Here's your coffee." Wren set it on the terminal, then turned to go.

He reached for her free hand, gripping it tight. "Wait a minute, please." He held his breath as Wren looked at the door, clearly weighing heading out.

When she turned to face him, Luca sighed into the phone.

"Quite the sigh, Dr. McDonnell," the voice on the other end said. "We are still bringing Mrs. Johnson, but the porter is running behind." The nurse didn't offer a goodbye after imparting the information. Fair. They were more than busy.

He put the phone down, then turned all his focus to Wren. But before he could get any words out, she started in on him.

"You want to explain why you shot everyone down?" Her chin was raised, daggers shooting directly at him. Not the sunshiny reaction he enjoyed getting from her.

"What does it matter? You don't date. Why?"

"I told you I wanted a friend. Not a protector. I don't need protecting. I don't need you vetting my dating life." She bit her lip and looked at the door but still didn't start for it. "I am in charge of my life."

"I wasn't protecting you. I mean. I was. Dr. Griffen has dated most of the eligible members of the hospital. Which you clearly know, and Dr. Reeves is looking for a rebound after his wife left him." He had no answer for Scott in ER, so he left him out. Luca took advantage of Wren not adding to the conversation to press her again. "Why don't you date?"

"Because." She shrugged but didn't add anything else. "I stopped by Lena's room. They're prepping her for discharge, but she'll still come here for therapy, right?"

Luca didn't enjoy the shift of topic, but he let it go for the minute. They were supposed to have dinner tonight. Her place again. She'd promised him pho and chocolate cake.

Tonight he'd figure out the answer behind that because...
Why?

He didn't want to press too much at that mental question.

"Yes. I think it would be helpful if we can schedule her at a time when you can see the progress. She's concerned the scar tissue is limiting her movement."

Wren's brows furrowed. "Scar tissue moves differently. You know that."

"I know. And I have told her that more than once, but hearing it from the expert..." He gestured to her and gave a little bow. Usually, it made her smile, but today her lips didn't crack at all.

"Wren—"

"Dr. McDonnell." Mrs. Johnson clapped to get his attention. She'd finally arrived. "Watch." It took the elderly Black woman a moment, but she pushed herself into a standing position with no help from the porter.

Wren clapped. "Way to go. I can see how hard you worked on that." Then without telling Luca goodbye, she headed out.

"What a nice woman," Mrs. Johnson remarked.

"That is Dr. Freson. One of the plastic surgeons here." Luca stepped up to his patient.

"Well, nice, beautiful and smart. Sounds like the whole package."

She is.

Luca looked at the distance between himself and Mrs. Johnson. "I am here to catch you, but can you take two steps for me?"

"I can tell a subject change when I hear one, young man." Mrs. Johnson let out a chuckle as she resolutely took one slow step forward.

Wren rolled her head on her shoulders, trying to relieve the knot so that maybe she could focus on the scans in front of her. Charlie Simpson's body was rejecting the skin graft her plastic surgeon had done three years ago following a skin cancer diagnosis.

The plastic surgeon had used Charlie's skin. So it should have healed quicker. The body rejecting its own skin was rare, though it happened.

This felt off. The rejection should have happened sooner, and part of the skin looked like it wasn't rejected. It was a puzzle, and she couldn't figure out what she was missing.

The door opened, but she didn't turn.

"Sorry, I didn't realize anyone was in here." Seth Graham started to close the door, then stepped back in. He stood quietly looking at the scans. "Rejection issue?"

"Yes." It was good he was here. Maybe another pair of eyes could see what she kept missing. Wren pointed to the left side of the graft. "But here the tissue looks fine. I've never seen it reject like this."

Seth tilted his head, his eyes roaming the image. "Each rejection is different."

That was true, but she could usually spot the pattern. Figure it out instantly. A gift and a curse. Today the image was stumping Wren. Her head was almost stuffy. Like the neurons wouldn't quite fire.

Because I burned too many out focusing on Luca's conversation with Therese.

"The blood flow is off here."

As soon as Seth said it, her eyes snapped to the location. That was it. That was what was keeping her rooted in this spot. "Not by much." She looked at the tiny vessels in Charlie's cheeks. They were delivering blood flow but not enough. "Impressive catch."

"You'd have figured it out." Seth stepped up and pointed at the area on the left of the graft. "I bet one of the vessels hooked up here failed."

Wren knew she'd have eventually caught it, but the pros of having another pair of eyes take a look could not be overstated.

"There are so many tiny vessels there. Usually the body would compensate, but in this instance it didn't happen."

Which meant it was possible it might happen again. "What would you do to ensure blood flow next time?"

"You're the plastics genius."

She mentally bristled at the word. *Genius.* The tag assigned to her before she understood its full meaning. The tag that still kept her as an other.

Wren refused to refer to herself as a genius. Her mind was a steel trap, but there were so many things she didn't know. Other experts she deferred to. That tag interfered with everything from friends to her nonexistent dating life.

"Humor me, Dr. Graham. You are hardly a junior plastics resident."

Seth sighed, a sound she knew was a precursor to an uncomfortable truth. "I don't know, honestly. The graft looks like it was well done. Sometimes these things just don't work."

Such an unsatisfying truth. People expected doctors to have all the answers. She had a lot of answers but not all of them.

"You all right?" Seth was still looking at the images on the screen, but she felt him shift beside her.

"Fine. I just…" She hesitated and then figured his fiancée was likely to fill him in on everything anyway. "Therese told me about your plan to set me up with Dr. Griffen."

"What?" Seth's voice echoed in the small room before he cleared his throat. "Sorry, I mean, what are you talking about? I would never suggest Griffen! Great pediatrician, but not partner material." He pursed his lips, then crossed his arms. "I bet she was messing with McSteamy and—" The words died as he looked at Wren.

"And?"

Color was rushing up Seth's neck. There was so much hanging on that cutoff sentence. "Nothing." The word sounded like it caught in Seth's throat on the way out.

"Why would she mess with Luca?" Wren crossed her arms, suddenly very defensive of the man she was still annoyed with.

Seth took a deep breath. "Because he is finally talking."

Wren raised an eyebrow.

"To you, at least. You're the first person I've seen get more than a handful of words out of him. He's great with patients, talkative with them, caring, but with colleagues?" Seth shrugged. "The man is a black box."

Wren didn't know what to say to that. "We're old friends."

"Yeah. I've said that before." Seth chuckled. "Now Therese is pregnant, and we're living in my tiny apartment. The little family I wasn't even able to dream of."

"Tiny apartment?" Wren didn't want to explore the happily-ever-after Therese and Seth had found. She was glad the two seemed so happy. But Luca didn't have any interest in following that same path.

And I do.

Another certainty she didn't want to address right now.

"Oh, yeah. She couldn't find a place when she moved here and then…" his cheeks darkened "…with the baby, it makes sense for us to be together. Plus, I want her with me, always."

It was cute. The man was so in love. "My building has some two bedrooms available. I know because the manager tried very hard to get me to sign a lease for one of them. I'll send you and Therese the information."

"Thanks."

Wren clicked the images off the screen. "All yours, Dr. Graham. Thanks for pointing out the issue. Saved me time." Then she walked out before he could say anything else.

She had the information she needed for Charlie's consult. Not the best news. They'd need to do another surgery. Something no patient enjoyed hearing.

"I said get the hell out!" The clattering sound of something hitting the wall came from Eddie Jenkin's room, and Wren took off without thinking.

Eddie's life was the definition of hell right now. A car accident two weeks ago had destroyed everything he thought he had. He was the patient who had burns over forty percent of his body and the fiancée who'd informed him the moment he'd woken from surgery that she didn't want to stand by him in the situation. The man's long road to recovery was getting no help from his attitude.

Luca was in the corner, his hands up. "Don't throw anything else." The words came up as he saw her walk in, and a frown immediately crossed his lips.

Protection mode.

It seemed that was the role Luca was most prone to stepping into. She replayed those moments she'd thought they might kiss, and he—well, that was not the problem for right now.

"Eddie." Wren kept her voice low but made sure it was clear she expected him to listen.

"I don't want to hear it, Doc. I don't care if I will get *mostly* better." Eddie glared at his chest, still covered with bandages to help with the infection he'd gotten. "Will the scars disappear? Will it bring Beth back? Will my life be exactly like it was?"

"No." She always made sure she was honest with her patients. Eddie's life was forever changed. Though she personally thought he was better off without Beth. If the woman bailed before she ever took her vows, then that meant she wasn't cut out to spend the rest of her life abiding by the *in sickness and health* part.

Eddie closed his eyes, water leaking from them.

"But you will have a life," Luca added from the corner.

"Some life."

"It is what you make of it. Do you know how many families wish they had the chance to bring a loved one back? How many people would beg for a do-over for someone who left this mortal plane?" Luca's voice cracked.

Wren looked at him. The emotion in his face broke her heart. Who was he speaking of? Ronan? A person who'd entered his life in the decade they'd lost touch?

"I would take their place in a heartbeat."

"No, you wouldn't, Eddie." Luca walked over to the bed and sat on the edge of it. "You didn't deserve this. And you certainly have the right to be angry, scared and hurt. But if you only let yourself feel those emotions, you will miss out on the hope, joy and love that life has to offer."

Eddie opened his eyes and shook his head. "Who is going to love this?"

"Someone worthy," Wren offered. "You have an entire life left to live. The answer is someone worthy."

"Exactly as Dr. Freson says. Now let her take a look at the wounds because the simple stretch I was showing you should not hurt as much as it did." Luca crossed his arms and nodded to Eddie. "I suspect you're in more pain than you're telling anyone."

Wren stepped to the bed. "Is that true?" She looked at the wet bandages.

Eddie bit his lip. "My body was literally roasted in the car accident. I am always in pain. My dad was an opioid addict. Started after he broke a leg." He started to cross his arms and flinched.

"I understand your concern about addiction issues." It was actually a good sign. A man intent on not caring about himself didn't worry about such things. "But we have to let your body heal. I am going to take the wet bandages off."

His patient record indicated that he didn't always let the nurses do their checks. He was just skirting the line of asking to leave against medical advice.

And Wren suspected that, if he could take care of himself, he would do exactly that.

He didn't fight her, whether because he wanted help or because he was too mentally exhausted, she wasn't sure. And it didn't matter.

It took all her years of training not to gasp at the red streaks snaking up his chest. She saw Luca's eyes widen out of the corner of her eye, but he held his tongue.

This was a moment she hated having with patients. There was no sugarcoating this. No sunshiny way to make it better. He was killing himself by not letting the staff help him.

"I need you to make a choice, Eddie." Her voice was firm, and his gaze was rooted on hers. "You've told more than one nurse here to leave when they needed to change your dressing. Thrown things to make them leave."

His eyes filled with tears, but he didn't interrupt.

"You are an adult. Mentally competent. Which means they have to abide by your wishes. So you need to choose. Are you going to fight for the life you can live? A beautiful life story that you can write however you want."

"Or?" The squeaked-out word was barely audible.

"Or the infection crawling up your chest will almost certainly go to your heart. Weaken it and shorten that life story. You get to decide. But the moment to decide is now. Because I need to start an aggressive form of treatment in the next hour."

It was not hyperbole. He needed intravenous antibiotics stat. And she'd make sure to alert cardio that their expertise might be needed. If the infection hit his heart—

That was a problem for the future. One they could hopefully avoid.

Eddie looked at his chest for several beats, clearly weighing his options. "Antibiotics. I don't want to die."

"I am glad to hear that. We are going to start now. But from this moment on, every nurse that walks in here, you let them do the work they need to do. You do not have to do it with a smile, but you will let them do it and be polite."

Luca shifted beside her but didn't add anything to the commentary. This was her show. Her patient.

"I am putting in the orders now. If you refuse again, I will instruct the nurses to give you the Against Medical Advice paperwork." She clicked a few buttons on the tablet, making sure it was notified as stat. And a note to cardio to make sure they understood Eddie might need their services. "I will check on you tomorrow. And I will stop to get a report from the nurses station first." Wren waited a minute, but it was clear that Eddie had exhausted his word bank for now. She'd make sure the staff psychologist saw him, and maybe the chaplain.

He needed to find someone to talk to about the anger clawing through him.

She stepped out and knew Luca was behind her. A nurse was headed toward the room, a bag of antibiotics in her hand.

"If he gives you trouble, give him AMA paperwork." The nurse's eyes widened at Wren's words. "But I think he's pretty docile right now."

The nurse took a deep breath, then headed into the room.

Luca tilted his head and, after a moment, smiled. "I don't hear anything crashing."

Wren nodded, exhaustion hitting her hard. "Thank you for talking him down."

"I never thought I'd play good cop while you, the sunniest person in this hospital, played the bad guy."

It wasn't a role she liked, but there were times it was necessary. "He needed to know."

"And you handled it brilliantly, Wren."

"Thank you. If you don't mind, I'm going to call a rain check on pho." She needed a night to figure out what she wanted to do. A night to plan out a way to make sure the crush she'd developed on the man before her stayed controlled in its little box.

He pushed a hand through his dark hair. "Listen, about Therese—"

"I have a patient. I am running behind. Thanks for your help, Luca." She started down the hall and made sure she didn't look back. The encounter with Eddie had stolen all the air from her.

She needed time. And maybe to put some distance between the friendship that had developed so easily between her and Luca.

CHAPTER EIGHT

WREN STOOD IN the kitchen trying to force herself to make dinner. Or use her phone to order delivery. It was such a simple choice.

And I am frozen.

She wrapped her arms around herself and tried to take deep breaths like her therapist in college had instructed. *Executive freeze* was the term he'd used over and over again.

Wren didn't have attention deficit disorder, which was where the term was most often used. Still, her therapist insisted that her occasional inability to make decisions after rough days and high stress was the same. It was her always-on brain finally shutting itself off for a change.

Her parents had insisted that she was being dramatic.

It's just dinner.

Tears flooded her eyes. This wasn't worth crying over. But she couldn't stop them.

Her stomach grumbled, adding its voice to the conversation but no helpful notes for her brain. If she hadn't canceled her dinner date with Luca, she'd have at least had pho and chocolate cake ready to go.

It wasn't a date. And that was why she'd canceled. Because her brain couldn't make her heart understand that. And now she was frozen over a dumb food decision.

Pick something. Pick something. Pick something.

The repetitive mental scream did nothing but send more tears racing down her face. She'd burned all her energy giving Eddie his options and avoiding Therese and Luca for the rest of her shift.

Avoiding them hadn't made her mind stop twisting through scenarios where she mentally replayed ways to tell Therese she actually was interested in dating. None of them worked.

Why did I say I don't date?

Those words had just popped out. Not a complete lie but not helpful, either. Walking them back would be embarrassing. Particularly because she was interested in dating...just not any of Therese's selectees. And then add all that to what Seth said about Therese ribbing Luca.

Luca.

Wren's head overflowed with of thoughts of him. An acknowledgment that the friendly nights they'd spent together meant far more to her than to him. So many thoughts that her brain refused to process one more.

A knock at the door.

Wren spun, well aware there was only one person who could be standing on the other side of that barrier.

Now there were three options flooding her brain. Dinner. Leaving the knock unanswered. Letting Luca in. Her feet didn't move. If she stayed frozen, option two was going to win by default.

"I know you're in there, Wren. I have a surprise."

She brushed the tears off her cheeks, fully aware there was no hiding the fact that she'd spent far too long crying. Over something she'd heard time and time again growing up was "no big deal."

Another knock, then her phone buzzed.

You out? I have a surprise.

She swallowed and stepped to the door. The look on his face as he met her gaze was confirmation enough that she looked terrible.

The stuffed mermaid doll in his hands fell to the floor. "What's wrong?"

"Nothing. Everything's fine." She ran a hand along her neck, very aware that the squeak in her voice made it clear that everything was, in fact, not fine.

"Wren." Luca bent down to grab the surprise, then stepped into the apartment. "You're crying."

She stepped back to let him close the door.

The tears were still coming. "I never cry." She gestured to the offending wet streaks. "Because when I do, I can't turn them off. Not great company tonight, Luca."

"You don't need to be great company. Why are you sobbing?"

She laughed, but the sound held no mirth. "I can't figure out what I want for dinner."

"Dinner?"

"Yep." She shrugged and barely caught the second laugh bubbling in her throat. She was dangerously close to losing it even more. "My parents used to call this my crazy brain. Not a nice term."

"I'd say it's pretty freaking derogatory." His hand found hers, and she didn't like the way her heart sighed and her brain calmed just a bit.

"Executive freeze. I guess I overdid it today and—" Her mind had no follow-up, so the *and* just dangled in the air, waiting for a completion her brain had no ability to offer.

"I want pizza," Luca said suddenly. "I was actually getting ready to order a pie. How about I order us a large pepperoni with pineapple and black olives?"

Not her first choice of pizza, but if he was taking the lead, she could pick the pineapple off. "Sounds good."

"No. It doesn't." He squeezed her hand, a reminder that she hadn't pulled away.

Neither has he.

Luca pulled her into a hug, and her body ached to collapse into him. "Okay. That was my bad. I figured the combination would get a laugh. So this is more serious than I imagined. I will order pepperoni with black olives unless you nod to tell me you want the pineapple, which I will get, but I will be putting all the pineapple on your pieces."

"No!" She shook her head against his shoulder. "No pineapple."

His hand ran down her back. "All right. And ice cream. We are ordering ice cream. I want strawberry. I will get a tub of chocolate, vanilla, and rocky road."

"I can't eat all that. Just chocolate. Dark chocolate if they have it." The words came easier this time.

He laid his head against hers. For a moment, she thought his lips had brushed her hair.

They didn't. Right?

"You okay for me to step away and order?"

"Oh." She started to pull back, but his arms didn't release her.

"I asked a question, Wren. Oh is not an answer; it is a response—one that seems like you might be thinking you did something wrong. I will stand here holding you all night if you want."

She wouldn't mind that, but not in the way he meant.

"I am all right." She stepped back. "Thank you."

"Of course." He grinned, his jeweled gaze holding her so close. After a minute, he held up his phone. "Ordering time." His fingers flew across the screen.

Her brain was silent. So calm. She took the first breath that didn't feel like knives running to her lungs in hours.

Luca put his phone away and held up the mermaid stuffed toy

he'd laid on the counter by the door. "This is why I'm actually here." He pushed the stuffie toward her. "Is it the right one?"

She looked at it, not wanting to hurt his feelings. "It's nice. How sweet. Thank you."

"It's not the right one. I can tell." He glared at the stuffed toy. "You'll have to show me a picture."

She pressed her hand against his shoulder and started to lean toward him before she caught herself. She was not kissing his cheek. "That movie was more than twenty years old when I saw that stuffed animal. Assuming there are any left, they are with collectors and far too expensive to fulfill a childhood want. This one is perfect."

"Except it isn't the right one."

"Luca." She put her hand on his chest. He leaned toward her, and even after forcing herself to pull back seconds ago, she leaned in and kissed his cheek. The platonic kiss was over in milliseconds, but that didn't stop her lips from burning. "Thank you."

Her brain was quiet. Her heart rate level. Because Luca was here. She didn't feel like investigating that too closely right now.

He frowned. "I got the wrong one. The online shop said it was an original."

He'd gone looking for her. A present just for her. It didn't matter if it was "wrong." It was the best gift she'd ever gotten. She pressed the stuffed toy to her chest. "You searched for something for me. Just me. I can't explain how much that means."

His phone dinged. "Delivery's here. I am going to run grab it."

"And get Hippo, too. Don't want the poor boy to get lonely."

"I'm getting another piece, you want one?" Wren popped off the couch, a lot happier than she'd been when he arrived.

His sunshiny Wren was wrecked, and he'd nearly panicked when she answered the door. The tears, the frustration—he'd wanted to wipe away whatever caused the issue.

She's not mine.

It was getting harder and harder to remember that. This was friendship. It was easy. She was a person who only saw him for himself.

Because she doesn't know about the money.

The inside of his cheek stung as he forced his teeth to unlock. Wren wouldn't care.

Probably.

That was the problem. He'd hadn't expected Madeline to care. Or his parents. Or his friends.

And each one had lost sight of Luca and focused on the wallet they coveted. He never got to go back to the Luca they cared about once people knew. He couldn't lose Wren. He just couldn't.

"Earth to Luca! Do you want me to bring another piece?"

"I am quite full." His cheeks heated as he rubbed his belly. Hippo let out a sound that indicated he'd be more than happy if a piece landed on the bed Wren bought, and Luca laughed.

Maybe that was a warning sign that he and Hippo were here too often, but it wasn't one he planned to listen to. At least not tonight.

"You had *a* piece, Luca. One small piece. You don't really expect me to believe you are full. Pu—leee—ase!"

He held up a hand, grinning. Might as well let the cat out of the bag. "Don't get mad."

She tilted her head. "I am making no promises." But the grin on her face relaxed him.

"I ate before I stopped down. I had some leftovers and chowed down on them in my kitchen."

"Over the sink?" She giggled and slid two more slices onto her plate.

"I could lie." He'd made a joke about his eating habit last week. That if no one was around he ate in the kitchen, usually over the sink.

She'd "lovingly" reminded him that he was always alone—at least until she forced her way into his life. A truth he didn't care to look at too closely.

"Why don't you date?" The question was out, and sirens were echoing in his head. He wanted to know. Hell, he'd planned to ask, though every script he'd started was more like the monologue of a bad made-for-TV movie than the last.

Each of those would still have been better than blurting the question out into the open.

Wren took two bites of her pizza, then set the plate in her lap. "Why are you asking?"

Her dark gaze glittered as she stared at him across the couch. Less than two feet separated them. Two feet and a gulf of indecision. The answer to this question meant something. But he had no idea what.

"You said it almost in a hurt way today. Like a wound."

She frowned but didn't say anything.

"I don't want you alone, if that isn't what you want." Almost the truth.

"Right. Protecting me. I don't need you doing that, Luca."

His responses to Therese today had everything to do with jealousy. The idea of Wren with someone else burned. It wasn't fair to her, but it didn't change his reaction.

"I do date. Sort of." She pushed the plate off her lap, putting it on the coffee table.

Hippo opened an eye, raised his snout and let out a huff as Luca motioned for him to stay on the bed.

"Sort of? What does that mean?" He started to reach for her hand but pulled back.

Her dark gaze floated to his hand. "I am the odd gal out. I had friends in New York, but while they were falling in love and juggling med school, relationships, sometimes new babies, I was celebrating my sweet sixteen. Or my twenty-first birthday after they'd been legal drinkers for years."

"Always a little apart." That was a feeling Luca understood. One he hated that they had in common.

"Right."

"Okay, but now you're twenty-six. So the age barrier—"

"Twenty-six, and I've kissed exactly three people in my life." Her hand flew over her mouth, her eyes wide as the secret hovered in the short distance between them.

"So inexperienced?" Luca knew he wasn't hiding the shock on his face. She was perfection. Wren should be beating would-be-suitors away.

"Virginal. Happy? There, I said it." Her bottom lip popped out as she pointed at him. "That face. That face right there is why I don't tell anyone. Particularly men."

Luca held up a hand. "Sorry. I'm just stunned."

"Yeah, well, twelve-year-old college student, sixteen-year-old med student and plastics resident at nineteen meant the only people interested in me were criminals and creeps. And now—"

She took a deep breath, crossed her legs and wrapped her arms tightly around herself. Pulling herself together. Protecting herself.

He'd answered wrong. The gulf widened, and he wasn't sure how to string a rope across the roaring tides. The sunny demeanor was something people might think was a weakness. But there was steel coursing through Wren's veins.

"And now?" he pressed as he mentally tried to figure out how to dig out of the hole he'd dug. Something he always seemed to do with this incredible woman.

"And now…" Wren looked over his shoulder, out the window. "I am either seen as too much work or a prize to be won. A coveted object."

Object.

Luca didn't have any words for that horrific revelation.

"Why are you so concerned with it?" Wren lifted her chin. "I was very specific that I didn't want you stepping into a brotherly role."

"That is *very* much not the role I am trying to claim." The husky words poured forth, and he watched Wren's eyes widen.

Before he could process what was happening, she was in his lap, lips against his, arms around his neck.

Luca's arms wrapped around her waist, pulling her closer. Whatever this was, he wasn't thinking. Wasn't second-guessing. There was no one in the world but him and Wren; nothing but this moment.

Her hands slid down his cheeks as she pulled back. "Luca—"

He leaned forward, capturing whatever words were destined to flow from her sweet lips. Her mouth opened, and he took full advantage. She tasted warm and spicy.

His hands wrapped through her dark hair, pulling her closer—though that shouldn't be possible.

"Luca." This time his name sounded like a prayer on her soft lips.

Wren's hands went to the edge of his shirt, hesitating for only a moment before slipping under. The subtle touch of her fingers on his belly was fire, a flame darting under each movement.

His lips trailed along her chin, reining in his own desire. Tonight was Wren's. Only Wren's. Wrapping his arms tightly around her waist, he flipped them. Now it was her leaning against the back of the couch cushion.

Her bright eyes held his as his fingers trailed up her toned legs, slowing on her inner thigh. Wren's breath caught and her head fell back.

He took complete advantage of her exposed neck, nipping kisses along it until he got to the top of her collarbone. Her pert nipples were straining against the light pink tank top, confirming what he'd suspected. That cotton top was the only thing between him and her perky breasts.

Letting his thumb wander to the top of the loose black running shorts she wore, he stared at her. Wren's dark gaze glittered with need—for him.

Wren's hips pressed against his, and he watched the awareness of his need register in her eyes. Her hand started to slip between them, but he grabbed it, kissing the tip of each finger before placing it over her head. His erection pressed against his pants, demanding in a way he'd never known.

Wren's hips molded against him as she pulled his shirt over his head.

"You are so beautiful." Her fingers danced across his shoulders.

"That is supposed to be my line." Luca let his hand roam the edge of her tank top, need coursing through his body. "Can I take your top off?"

Heat coated her cheeks, but she nodded and adjusted her position, just a little, to make it easier for him. *Damn*.

He placed the shirt on the back of the couch within easy reach, if she wanted it.

Running a thumb along the edge of one perky nipple, Luca bent his head, feathering kisses along her lips. Slowly, he slid his mouth down her throat and chest before finally capturing one nipple. He stroked it with his tongue, enjoying each tiny moan slipping from Wren's lips.

"Luca." The pant coming after his name sent shivers down his spine.

"Wren," he breathed as he slid his mouth across her chest and started worshiping her other nipple.

"I burn."

"Mmm." No woman had ever said such a thing in his arms. He slid a free hand up her thigh. "Where do you burn, Wren?"

He lifted his head, watching color crest from her perfect breasts to her cheeks. She writhed under him, forcing his hand farther up her thigh.

"Where, honey?" Luca wanted her to say it. Wanted to hear the words from her sweet lips.

"Between my legs." She didn't look away as she said it. "I ache."

"That is a problem I can fix." He returned his lips to her chest as the hand on her thigh flew higher, darting to the inside of her shorts. Cotton panties greeted him. Letting his thumb sweep against her mound, he lifted his head.

By her own admission, no man had ever touched her this way. He was going to watch the orgasm crest across her features.

"Luca, mmm." Her hips undulated against the caress. "It's…it's…not enough."

Each caught breath anchored him.

Pulling her panties to the side, he pressed his thumb to her nub and grinned as her back arched. "That's right, Wren." Keeping the pressure on her, he slipped a finger into her heat.

She bit her lip, surging against him, need clearly driving her. Luca didn't change anything, he let her control her body, using him as the tool to get what she craved.

Perfection. That was what this moment was.

"Luca."

His name echoing around them as she orgasmed was spellbinding. As her body relaxed, he pulled his finger from her and slid it across his lips. "You taste magnificent."

Wren's glazed gaze captured him as she pressed on his shoulders, sliding into his lap. "I think it's your turn."

"No." He caught the argument he knew was brewing. "Tonight…" he kissed her "…was just about…" his lips dragged across her, as her hips danced on his erection "…you."

"Tomorrow?" Her finger floated along the edge of his pants zipper. His pants were already damp with precum, and the feel of her hand through the denim was nearly enough to bring him to completion.

"Tomorrow." He brushed his lips against her. "Tomorrow."

CHAPTER NINE

Wren looked over the notes in Eddie's chart. He'd let the nursing staff change his bandages. He'd refused pain meds but was taking the antibiotic treatment. A win.

"Morning, sunshine." Luca grinned as he stepped next to her.

Her body heated with the memories of his lips on hers. His fingers. His touch. She'd acted rashly. He'd nearly growled that his interest wasn't brotherly, and after the long day her impulse control was apparently shot.

Thank goodness.

"McSteamy." She raised her chin and winked at him.

He leaned a little closer, not touching, but his breath was warm on her ear. "I've never minded the nickname, but I might actually like it from your lips."

Any words she had were stuck in the back of her throat.

"I am headed in to see Eddie." Luca tilted his head toward the door as he raised his hand in a wave. "Multiple nurses are staring."

"Well, you *are* hovering." Wren tucked the tablet under her arm. She didn't turn to look at the nurses station, knowing her cheeks were already stained with heat.

Tonight. The promised word. She had to get through today, and then tonight.

Focus.

"I need to see to Eddie, too. Why are you headed that

way?" Eddie needed physical therapy. A lot of it. But right now, the infection was the top priority.

"He is so angry." Luca let out a sigh, the playboy attitude disappearing as he shifted to physical therapist mode.

"His fiancée left him because he was in an accident. Even if his road to recovery was easier, that would send most people for a loop." She'd watched the woman take the ring off, and fury had rippled through her. And Eddie was a stranger. The man had a right to be angry. But it could also destroy him. A delicate balance.

"I know. But I have been there."

Madeline. How had Wren forgotten her? She'd sat in the front row, making faces at her brother from the groom's side until Luca had raced out and pulled him to the side. It was Ronan who announced the groom was leaving.

"I thought you left her at the altar." The words slid out. If there weren't people in the hallway passing by, she'd let out a curse. "Sorry."

"Water under the bridge." His shoulders were tight, but his jaw was relaxed. "I did. Sort of. I overheard her talking in the bridal suite. Came to surprise her, and well, let's just say I heard more than she intended."

Maybe it didn't matter what he'd heard more than a decade ago, but Wren's brain was running through a list of possible reasons anyway, given that he didn't seem interested in elaborating.

"I was angry for a long time. Furious." He let out a breath that she was pretty sure he didn't realize he'd held onto.

"How long?" Was the aborted wedding the reason his colleagues didn't know him? The reason that, until she came along, he ate over the sink in his supersized apartment?

"What?" Luca looked at her.

He'd heard her. But if he didn't want to answer, she wasn't

going to push. Particularly because they'd reached the door of Eddie's room.

"Doc." Eddie nodded to Wren. "Torture artist." He didn't offer a smile to Luca, but he looked more relaxed than he had yesterday.

"I can see you've accepted all the treatments from the nurses. With grace even." Wren set the tablet on the counter. "How are you feeling?"

"Like burned meat. But the pain is less." Eddie caught himself as he started to shrug. "I still don't feel like myself."

"That makes sense." Wren had requested a counselor appointment for him, but that request was still pending. Hopefully this afternoon, someone would be here.

"I used to be happy. All the time. People used to joke that a party never really started until I got there. The life of the party." Eddie rolled his eyes. "I hate this version of myself."

Wren laid a hand on the tiny unburned portion of his shoulder. "You can get that person back."

"Why is the torture artist here?" Eddie glared at Luca, and Wren thought there was a decent chance the glare was serious. Shifting topics was fine, but she'd make sure to elevate the request for a counselor.

"Because you need to do some stretches. Little ones. And to talk." Luca sidled up to the other side of the bed.

"What do you want to talk about?" Eddie narrowed his eyes. "New ways to make my burned body scream?"

"No, but if you do the stretches I recommended, your healing will speed up. I…" Luca took a deep breath, his gaze shifting to Wren for just a second before focusing on Eddie. "My fiancée told her maid of honor she couldn't imagine spending forever with me. But she planned to hang out for a few years. Get some advantages of married life, then leave me in the dust." Luca crossed his arms.

At least Luca was too focused on Eddie to realize what

that revelation was doing to Wren. She'd met Madeline a few times, never gotten on with her. Which was expected. After all, they were nearly a decade apart in age. But now she wanted to throttle the woman.

Eddie raised his arms to let Wren look at the wet bandages, but his gaze didn't leave Luca. The wounds were less angry today. He'd set his healing back at least two weeks, but hopefully they'd turned a corner.

"Beth left me because of an accident. Why did yours leave you?"

"Same reason yours left you." Luca pulled a stress ball from the bag he carried to all the rooms he visited. "She didn't love me. Just the idea of me. Or the idea of a wedding."

Wren risked a look at Luca; his gaze was rooted on Eddie. Either Eddie didn't realize Luca hadn't given an answer, not really, or he didn't want to push. It made sense. Luca was helping, but he didn't really know Eddie.

But will he give me the full answer? Wren wasn't sure.

"Either way, you got lucky." Luca looked at Wren, the easiness in his gaze halting her worry. "She outed herself before you put in all the down payments on venues. Before the divorce attorney had to get involved."

"Doesn't feel very lucky." Eddie turned his attention to Wren. "Am I looking better, Doc?"

"You've had twelve hours of intravenous antibiotics. That is not a lot of time, but I am no longer as concerned about the infection getting to your heart."

Luca offered a grin. "That is doctor speak for better but still a long way to go."

Eddie chuckled, then paused, like he was shocked the sound had come from him. "I didn't realize torture artists were also doctor translators."

"They serve many roles." Wren put the wet bandage back

over the wound. "Ideally, we'd be getting you ready for skin grafts, but with the infection, surgery will need to be pushed."

Again. *Ideally*, they'd have done grafts last week. But the uncooperative patient had made that impossible. Eddie looked away, color creeping along his neck. Hopefully he was turning a corner in accepting care.

"I'll be back to check on you tomorrow."

"And I am going to go over some stretches you can do in this bed," Luca said. "And we can talk, if you want."

"I don't." Eddie pinched his eyes closed as she headed for the door. "How long until you found someone to spend your life with after your fiancée destroyed everything?"

Wren's hand stilled on the room's door, her ears pricking to hear the answer.

"Still working on that. But let's just say there are some glimmers on the horizon."

Glimmers on the horizon. Tonight. The promise burned in her belly.

Stepping into the hall, she saw Therese coming out of one of the other rooms. "Therese."

The woman's cheeks filled with pink as she stepped toward Wren. "Wren. I want to apologize again. Seth told me how uncomfortable I made you. Not that I hadn't picked that up on my own. I was giving Luca a hard time and—"

"Thank you." Wren hadn't gotten Therese's attention to talk about Luca, but she was sure that without being at her wit's end, she would never have jumped into his arms last night. And if she hadn't done that, she doubted she'd be spending today looking forward to tonight's encore.

Therese's eyes widened. "Oh my gosh." She clapped her hands. "I knew it. I am going to make sure Seth knows that forcing the issue didn't completely blow up in my face." She let out a sigh.

"I didn't call you over for that revelation." Wren pulled

a brochure out of the deep pocket of her doctor's coat. "I checked, and one of the two-bedroom apartments I told Seth about is still available. If you mention that you know me and Luca, the approval process should speed up quickly."

Therese looked at the brochure.

"Seth mentioned the tiny apartment, and with the little one coming—" Wren waited a second, concern building as Therese's eyes looked like they were filling with tears. "I hope I didn't overstep."

Therese waved a hand. "Hormones. I cry at the drop of a hat these days. And, I mean, I overstepped yesterday. Just because it worked out doesn't change that truth. So I know what overstepping is, and this is not it. The building looks nice, I'll have Seth make the call. I suspect hearing from a well-established plastic surgeon will hold a little more weight than me and my less than stellar credit. I couldn't find a single place when I first moved here. Though, that ended up working out." She grinned as she ran a hand over her little baby bump.

It had indeed.

"Let me know if you need a reference. Though Luca is probably the better reference. I have almost a month under my rent belt, but he owns his apartment."

Therese's eyes widened. So it wasn't just Wren that thought that was beyond impressive. "Wow."

"Yeah. Maybe Seth should mention Luca." Wren grinned. "I need to finish rounds. But thank you, Therese."

"You're welcome."

Luca started to light the candles on the dining room table, then held off as he looked at his watch. Wren was always punctual. There were still three minutes before she was due up here.

Three minutes that feels like three hours.

If she wasn't hungry for dinner, he didn't want to have to come back here to blow out candles when he could be spending important time exploring her body.

Luca rocked back on his heels and did not check his watch again. Time was moving but not fast enough. The whole day had seemed that way.

He'd checked back in on Eddie just before leaving. He was doing his exercises. Grumpy but moving. Luca was taking the win.

But the words he'd uttered this morning had struck Luca's soul. *I hate this version of myself.*

Luca had encased himself in an armor he'd never intended to wear. Formed the day Madeline said she was only marrying him for money, hardened by his parents that only called when they needed a favor and sealed when his best friend passed away in the car he'd help secure for him.

Wren had loosened the steel around his heart. Made him feel like himself, feel whole. A man he hadn't realized he was missing until she'd beamed into his orbit. He hoped Ronan's spirit didn't mind. The idea that he'd never get to ask bothered him, but it was a tiny squeak in the back of his mind now rather than a bleating alarm.

Hippo started for the door, his little toe dance making it obvious he'd picked up on Wren's footsteps before she reached the door.

Luca followed, not dancing, but his soul was certainly celebrating. He ripped the door open, grinning as Wren's hand, poised for knocking, stilled.

"Were you staring out the peephole waiting for me?"

Luca grabbed her hand, pulling her in. She wore a black lacy sheath dress that made his mouth water. The freedom to touch her…to drop a light kiss on her lips… He finally understood the definition of exhilarating.

"I have my own alarm system." Luca nodded to Hippo.

"I mean, he's actually a terrible alarm system." The dog thought everyone in the world was a friend. "But his hearing is excellent."

Wren bent down and gave the gray pittie a pat. She didn't release Luca's hand, though.

"I've got pasta and a cookie cake." Luca grinned. "Hungry?"

Wren bit her lip. "I might have had a snack before coming up. But if you're hungry."

Luca snapped his fingers three times, and Hippo started for his bed. He didn't want the dog underfoot for this next part. "I am starving." He lifted her off her feet, enjoying her squeal and the feel of her arms wrapping around his neck. "But dinner can certainly wait."

"Luca." Wren's lips pressed against his neck, light kisses that sent bolts of desire flowing through him.

"I do like the way you say my name." He kicked the bedroom door shut as he took her to the bed.

"I say it normal." Wren popped up on her knees and lifted his shirt with ease.

There was a frenzied energy about her. That was not what tonight was about. "Wren."

"Don't look at me like that."

He lifted her chin, making sure she was looking at him. "I am a drowning man, honey. I have never needed someone as much as I need you." He grabbed her hand before it could reach the button of his slacks. "But we are not rushing this. Anticipation has coated my skin all day. And I plan to make you beg with need." His fingers danced along the edge of the lacy dress. "You should wear this out sometime. It is absolutely gorgeous." He slipped his hand underneath her, cupping her tight ass, enjoying the hitch in her breath as she pulled closer to him.

"I'm glad you like it." Color shot up her neck, and he dropped his head, dragging his lips along her neck.

"I loved the tank top and shorts last night, and this outfit is mouthwatering. But my favorite is…" he slid his hand up her thigh "…nothing at all." He lifted the dress over her hips. "Raise your hands, honey."

She did as he instructed, and he stripped it from her lithe body.

Tonight she wore a black thong, a matching piece to the slinky dress. Gorgeous, and another night, he'd beg her to wear this combo and spend hours out on the town with him, knowing the perfection waiting for him when they got back home. But tonight, he needed her naked, beneath him, panting his name.

Hooking his fingers through the material, he pulled the thong down her thighs and threw it on the floor. "Naked," he breathed and captured her mouth. His thumb danced along one breast and then the other.

Wren's hand ran through his hair as he lowered his attentions to her breasts. Suckling each as his fingers skimmed her upper thigh.

Slowly, ever so slowly, his mouth moved lower. He felt her still, and then gasp as his tongue darted along her bud.

"Luca." Wren gripped the bedsheets as his tongue darted across her slit.

"You taste magnificent. I got a taste last night but…" He drove his tongue into her heat, loving the moans echoing above him.

"Luca…" This time his name was a pant on her lips. "Luca, please."

The plea nearly broke him, but he wasn't joining them until she'd come for him at least once.

Replacing his tongue with a finger, he returned his mouth's attention to her breasts. She was spiraling, so close to the edge.

When the moment came, it was his name on her lips.

"Wren." His mouth captured hers as he quickly undid his pants and kicked them and his boxers off.

Her hand darted to his length, and her long fingers stroking him was maddening. Luca grabbed a condom from his nightstand, sheathed himself, then pressed against her core.

Wren's dark gaze held his, and he heard the gasp as he joined them together. His lips were on hers, as he held himself, letting her adjust to his length.

"Luca?" This time his name was much less certain on her sweet lips.

"Yes?"

Her hips shifted a little, the motion screaming through his body.

"I don't have any experience, but…is this all?" She bit her lip.

His Wren.

"Not at all." He slipped a hand between them, rubbing her swollen nub as he moved. Her motions were uncertain at first, but then her rhythm matched his.

"Luca." Her arms were wrapped around his shoulders, her feet interlocked on his back, driving him ever closer to the edge.

When he finally crested, she held him, kissing his cheek. Their hearts beating seemingly in time.

CHAPTER TEN

Wren ran her hand along Luca's chest, enjoying the quiet blend of his breaths with Hippo's snores. She'd never slept in anyone's arms. Never felt the heat of another's body next to her. It was oddly satisfying.

Her hand dipped lower, and his manhood jolted. She grinned. The idea that so little from her turned him on was quite thrilling. She was still sore from last night, but also wildly curious. He'd been in control.

A fact she didn't mind, but she'd touched him so little compared to the bliss he'd given her.

Her fingers wrapped around the hard length, and she knew from the change in his breathing that Luca was very much awake. "Do you want me to stop?"

He shook his head against the pillow, his eyes flying open to look at her. "Wren."

She could see why he liked how she said his name when he was tormenting her with pleasure. Such a satisfying sound.

Wren dropped a light kiss on his lips as she continued her slow strokes along his length. The man was literal putty in her hands. Intoxicating.

Moving along his body, she pressed kisses to his chest, his abs, his hips and then just above his manhood. One of his hands trailed along her thigh, the other ran through her hair. No pressure, no demands.

Her core ignited as she took him in her mouth. Licking

the tip of his erection, she enjoyed the shift in his position as she pleasured him.

"Wren." His hips bucked, and he pulled her head off him just before he came. "You are going to be the end of me." His mouth covered hers before she could think of anything to say.

"What do you say we grab a shower and then figure out a plan for the day?" he asked.

"Plan?"

His jade gaze rooted to hers, a look there she wasn't able to decipher. "We have the day off. I assumed you'd want to spend it together."

"Yeah. I need to get clothes and eat and—"

"Shower with me, Wren. We will plan all of it out after a shower, breakfast and coffee." Luca grabbed her hand, slid off the bed and moved them swiftly to the bathroom.

Wren smiled as she headed back up to Luca's apartment. They were heading to the aquarium after taking Hippo for a walk. The entire day. Just the two of them.

Her phone buzzed, and she pulled it out of her pocket.

Talked to the apartment complex.

Told them we knew Luca. It got a little weird.

Weird? What could that mean?

Weird how?

It was standard to list tenants you knew. There was space on the form she'd filled out. Of course, Wren had left hers blank.

Wren pinched the bridge of her nose. Of course. Luca wasn't a tenant. The idea of him owning his whole floor seemed so out of place she hadn't thought of it when suggesting Therese and Seth list him. He had lived here longer, but the rental agency didn't deal with him.

Ugh. It's because Luca owns his place. I shouldn't have recommended putting him down. I didn't really think about it.

The elevator opened, and she stepped onto his floor but didn't move toward his door. She hesitated over the call button, then pressed it. Better to figure this out through actually talking than back-and-forth texts.

Therese answered on the first ring. "Hey, Wren. I was trying to figure out how to answer the weird question. Glad you called."

"Guess owning the apartment means he isn't a tenant. Duh. The idea is just so foreign to me."

Therese laughed. "Fair. I mean who owns an apartment in this city? Seth is one of the top plastic surgeons in San Diego, well established in his career, and even he is renting. Man. Good for Luca, but yeah, we should have considered he wasn't a tenant, too."

The laugh was happy but the words after it sent a tiny warning bubble through her belly. It was odd. And he didn't own an apartment. He owned the penthouse floor. The entire top of the building was his.

An investment hit. That made sense, but it also wasn't an in-depth answer. And she hadn't dug any further.

Just like she hadn't dug any further on the reasons Madeline had wanted to stick around for a while but not forever.

"The renting agent asked how I knew Dr. McDonnell. Pressed pretty hard actually. I don't know. We just listed his name. And Luca mentioned the place to Seth, so I thought... I don't know. Ugh. I keep saying that. It was a vibe thing. I know that sounds dumb."

A vibe thing. There was no answer in that.

"It seemed like they were asking if we were looking for a discount because we knew him." Therese's sigh was heavy on the other side of the phone. "I mean, usually it's the tenant making money from the referral, not the renter, right?"

"Right." The rental form had indicated that if she referred a tenant who signed a one-year lease she got two hundred dollars off a month's rent. Not much, but it was fairly standard in the city.

"Seth is wondering if he should check with Luca or if we should just look elsewhere."

"I'm actually a few feet from his apartment. I'll check and text, okay?" Wren looked toward Luca's door and bit her lip. This wasn't a big deal. But there was that bubble in her stomach again.

"I really want to know more about that." Therese said something to Seth that Wren couldn't make out, then came back to the conversation. "I appreciate you asking about the apartment. And seriously, I want to know more about you being outside his place."

Wren said goodbye and grinned at the phone. It was nice to have a friend that wanted information for fun's sake. Not intelligence questions or medical facts. Just a friend.

Luca's door opened, and he brought Hippo out, already in his harness. "Any reason you're just hanging out in my hall? Hippo has been going nuts for the last few minutes waiting for you to wander down this way."

Wren walked up, kissed his cheek, then bent to pat Hippo on the head. The giant potato didn't seem too bothered by anything. "Was Hippo missing me or was it you?"

Luca pulled her to his side. "Maybe a little of both." His lips pressed against hers. "But also, *why* were you just hanging out here?"

"Talking to Therese. They ran into a little trouble when

they put your name on the rental form. Said the rental manager made it seem like they were asking for a discount."

"Were they?"

Wren stepped out of Luca's arms, shocked by the statement. "They listed your name on the rental agreement as a tenant."

"I'm not a tenant." Luca pressed the button on the elevator. The words were almost cold.

What was happening here? "I know. I told Therese that I forgot what you owning your apartment really means."

"You forgot?" Luca stepped into the elevator, and she followed. His gaze held some emotion she couldn't place.

"Your housing is hardly the most interesting thing about you, Luca." She wasn't sure where this conversation had taken such a turn. But discomfort was pouring from him.

"Even the view from the living room?" He raised an eyebrow.

Was he joking? "It's a nice view. Still, not that interesting of a thing. At the end of the day, it's just an apartment." She placed her hand on his chest. Why on earth would his apartment matter to her?

"Right." He shook his head, like he was clearing brain fog or something. "I had someone a few years ago who found out I owned the top floor. They tried to tell the manager they knew me personally and that they were supposed to get an apartment for well below market value."

"Oh. Okay. I'm sure that was frustrating, but Therese said you talked to Seth about this place."

His eyes widened. "I did do that." He slapped his head with a free hand as the door of the elevator opened on the first floor. "And then forgot to tell the rental office. Good grief."

So it had all been a misunderstanding. But it felt like there was more to the story. A bigger reason for the overreaction.

He pulled his phone from his back pocket and swiped his

fingers across the screen. "I sent Seth a text. Apologizing and telling him I'd let the front office know."

Wren pulled his free hand into hers. "Why don't we stop by the office, let them know and then take this guy for a pup cup? And get me a…" She put her finger on her lips. "Do I want a cupcake or a fancy coffee?"

Luca beamed, the fog of whatever this conversation was vanishing. "Why not both?"

"Here we are." Luca threw open his car door and ran around to Wren's so he could open it for her.

Wren's hand was warm in his palm.

He'd dated. Not a lot since his aunt's estate closed, but he'd dated. And he'd never felt as excited as he did with Wren. He wasn't sure why the rush felt greater, but he wasn't planning to delve too far into it today. Hearing her say that his apartment wasn't the most interesting thing about him had nearly brought him to his knees before her.

"So the aquarium?" Wren began as they started for the entrance. "I don't know why, but I would never have thought you'd suggest this."

Luca chuckled. "I am a patron of the Birch Aquarium."

"A member. Wow. That I really didn't expect." Wren reached for a map.

"You don't need that." He tapped his head. "I know this place from top to bottom."

Luca had used the right word. He wasn't a member but a patron of the aquarium. He, and some other wealthy families had donated recently to the Living Seas exhibit. It was set to open in just a few weeks. He was on the invite list to the private viewing party just before the public ribbon cutting. He hadn't planned to go, but Wren might enjoy the private exhibit.

"Why do you know the aquarium so well?" Her nose was wrinkled, and her eyes crinkled in surprise.

"Because there are octopuses here. They're off display right now because of the construction, but I have an inside source so we can see if we can get a peek."

He was fascinated by the creatures. They had no bones. No skeleton. His world revolved around muscles, bones and movement. These creatures had structures completely different from humans and moved majestically.

"Octopus. The eight-legged creatures that are the basis for the mythology of sea monsters?" Wren giggled as he stuck his tongue out.

"It's not their fault that humans saw their magnificence and corrupted it." He let out a playful huff. "Plus, I want to point out that the kraken is most likely based on a giant squid, not an octopus."

Wren squeezed his hand. "My apologies."

He flashed his patron card at the entrance, and the ticket taker let them both through.

"Whoa. You're a member, but I am not. I need to pay—"

The fact that she fully expected to pay her way, with no assumption that he would cover it, was sexy as hell.

Provided he didn't remind himself that she didn't know the depths of his wallet.

"I told you. I'm a patron. Now, you want to see the octopus or the rest of the aquarium first?"

"You are seriously excited to be here." Wren pulled him to a stop at the sea horse exhibit. "Oh my gosh. Look!"

He leaned close to her ear. "I thought you were judging me about my love of octopuses. Did I just discover you love sea horses?"

Wren rolled her eyes. "I don't love them. I like them a lot, though. They are fascinating. I read through a whole set of books on them when I was little." She stepped a little closer to the tank. "I actually thought about going into marine biology. Joked about it several times. My bachelor's degree in microbiology could have led me to multiple graduate programs."

There was a wistfulness to her words. Life was a set of paths taken and missed. It wasn't a bad thing to think about the roads you missed. But there was something in her tone that made him think there was more to it.

"You went to college at eleven. How could you joke about it?" There was something in her tone. A sad acceptance that her life had been scripted?

"Technically, I didn't start until I was twelve." Those words sounded like they should be the punchline of a joke, but there was nothing funny about them.

It took him a minute to finally ask, "So why was marine biology a joke?"

Her parents had been blissfully absent from his and Ronan's lives. At the time, it seemed like he and Ronan could do whatever. Looking back, his parents had just never been interested in him, and Ronan's had felt the same. Through adult eyes, he was able to tell just how messed up that was.

She didn't take her gaze away from the tank. "I mean, it was just accepted that I would go into medicine. And it worked out. The human body is fascinating."

"But you wouldn't have chosen it?"

"I don't know." She shrugged as she watched a sea dragon move in front of them. "I can't imagine being anything other than what I am now. But we are who our parents made us."

The words made him bristle. His parents had all but abandoned him except when they wanted to punish the other. One Christmas he'd gotten the exact same gifts from his mother as he received from his father. All because his father had wanted to upstage his mother by giving him the gifts first.

It was never about Luca.

The only thing he'd gotten from them was Aunt Maude.

The woman had loved and cared for him. No questions asked. And made him promise that his parents got nothing.

It wasn't a promise he'd kept at first. He'd tried. Wanted to believe that they wanted time with him. Wanted to make up for never being there in his childhood, for using him as a weapon against each other in their nasty divorce proceedings. All the signs were there, screaming in his face. The red flags that they were never going to care for him the way other parents cared for their children. And he'd ignored them, until they'd made it impossible to look away.

"I didn't take anything from my parents. I am nothing like them." He hadn't meant to speak the words out loud, but there was no rewinding the tape.

Wren looked away from the tank, her dark gaze holding him in place. "Then what you got from them was choosing to act nothing like them."

His parents were a thing he'd locked away. A piece of his past that got no place in his future.

The last day he'd spoken to his father and mother, they'd all blown up at the other. His father had called him a loser, a piece of crap son. His mother, siding with his father for the first time in at least a decade, had agreed. In that moment, Luca matched his parents' outsize emotions. Screaming all his hurt, his worries… It hadn't made him feel as good as he thought it would.

They still reached out sometimes, text messages, the odd birthday card, always delivered at least a month late. Luca never answered.

"And you?" Luca pushed away the memories, the hurt that still rose too close to the surface if he thought about it too long. "Are you a doctor because of your parents?"

"Yes. But not the right kind of doctor. Plastics was not the specialty they wanted for me. I racked up quite a bit of debt when they cut me off over my choice."

Debt. The word chilled his bones. Every friend who'd ever asked for money started with a soft pitch. A quick word about their debt, their misfortune. Laying the groundwork. But Wren was discussing her parents cutting her off because she'd dared to carve her own path. It was wicked. "They cut you off?"

"Yeah, they wanted me in neurology." She held up her finger, clearly mimicking a parent. "We did not put all this work into you for you to do something other than neurology."

"It's your life." Why did she seem so nonchalant about it?

"Sure." There was no anger in her voice. "I did my rotation in plastics, and there was no other specialty that held as much interest."

How far does she bury the hurt? It had to be there. Even sunny Wren couldn't just accept this, could she?

He'd heard people talk about finding their specialty as a magic moment. The realization that they were in the exact right space. Sure, there were physicians that went into specific specialties for the money attached to them, but those individuals were few and far between.

Wren was describing the defining moment of her career without any passion. Plastics was one of the hardest specialties to get into. Everything about her was impressive. But if it wasn't what she wanted... "You wanted marine biology."

Wren let out a little puff of air. "I loved the thought of it, but as you pointed out, I was sixteen when I was ready for grad school. Most of my life was lived in the library getting ready for the next test or quiz. Reading knowledge, absorbing it, but not really living it. That section just interested me more than others when I was twelve. Though Ronan also loved fish. He had a tank in his room, if you remember. So it was a bonding thing. Who knows? Maybe it was just because Ronan loved them. I was basically a kid. Not exactly ready for permanent life decisions."

Luca swallowed the angry words that he couldn't say to her parents. The words had no place to land. She'd been a kid. And they'd pressured her then, cut her off for making the "wrong" choice. And here she was nonchalantly discussing it.

Lifting her hand to his lips, he pressed a kiss to her palm. "I have seen more than one coffee mug that says something like a reader lives a thousand lives." At least she had books.

Wren rolled her eyes and turned back to the tank. "Yeah, I am pretty sure that's attributed to a fantasy author. Did you know that male sea horses are the ones who carry the eggs until they hatch? The female lays the eggs in his brood pouch—think of it as kinda like an underwater kangaroo pouch." She watched another swim by, then looked over her shoulder at him.

"There are thirty-six species of sea horses."

Wren's eyes lit up. "Oh. You know about them, too."

He pressed his lips to her cheek. "I have been here a lot." He pointed to the sign in front of the tank. "Not as impressive as it seems."

"Yes." Wren laid her head on his shoulder. "It is. But you are here for the octopuses, if I recall."

That was his original thought, the animal he most wanted to show off. But now he had a different idea. "We can come back for that another time. What if we do the behind-the-scenes tour for sea horses? They have a world-renowned breeding program."

"Baby sea horses. We can see baby sea horses?" Her eyes were bright, and he was pretty sure she was trying not to do a happy dance. He could give Wren this experience…and so many others she'd missed out on.

"We absolutely can."

CHAPTER ELEVEN

Luca pursed his lips waiting for Lena to at least try the new exercise he'd given her. The woman had made so much progress. Her hand was functioning better than he'd thought it would at this stage. That didn't mean it would ever be exactly like it was.

"I shouldn't have come today." Lena brushed a tear away and then let the others just fall.

"Lena—"

"I know, Dr. McDonnell, I have to practice. I have to do the exercises. I have to work at it. But why bother?" She looked at the door, and he wondered if she was about to call their session off.

Lena was an adult. He couldn't order her to stay.

Therese walked in, and Wren followed behind her. The two women had formed a fast friendship. Luca had caught himself wondering over the last week about how much he was going to have to share Wren when Therese and Seth moved into the apartment complex.

A selfish thought indeed. But he enjoyed who he was around Wren. The man she brought out in him.

"Lena!" Wren grinned, walked over and bent down so she was eye level with Lena.

Therese gave him a short nod. So Wren being here at the same time as Lena wasn't a coincidence. He mouthed *thank you* over Lena and Wren's heads.

"Dr. Freson." Lena tried a smile, but it was clearly faked. "If you're coming to check up on me, I am failing."

"Why?" Wren's gaze was soft, but there was a firmness in her tone. A deliberate one-word question.

"My art is messed up." Lena ran a hand along the skin graft that Wren had overseen. "No matter what I do, it's wrong."

Luca looked at her fingers. They didn't have all their strength back. That would take time, but they were significantly more functional than they were before. She should be able to hold a paintbrush and maneuver it however she wanted. At least for a while. Stamina would come with time.

"How?" Wren still hadn't broken eye contact with Lena.

"It's dark." Lena shook her head. "Everyone always chatted up the brightness. I'm an expert on light. And now it's vanished."

Luca could not pretend to know what that meant.

"Shadows are light."

Lena rolled her eyes. "Shadows are areas without light."

"Shadows answer to light. They are the absence." Wren pulled a pencil from her coat pocket. "How well are you holding things like this?"

Her dark gaze floated to him, and he nodded. Lena's hands were tight. Because she hadn't done the exercises at home he'd recommended? This would let him see exactly how she was handling it, without it coming directly from the physical therapist.

Lena moved the pencil through her fingers, grimacing as she clutched it. But she didn't let go. Didn't drop or throw it. Progress. "It's uncomfortable. But I can hold it like this for an hour before the pain is too much."

"An hour?" Luca snapped his mouth shut. The issue wasn't underuse. Lena was pushing herself. Hurting herself. Because she needed to feel like herself. A person she no longer knew.

"Yes. An hour. I used to stand in my studio with my hands moving for hours! And my hands cramped then but not like this. Not making it impossible. And the colors won't come." Now she was gripping the pencil like she was going to throw the offending object.

"Lena, take a deep breath." Luca's words were firm. Throwing the pencil might feel good for a moment. But she'd feel guilty later. And that guilt would slow her down.

Lena followed the order and then passed the pencil back to Wren.

"Reinventing yourself isn't easy," Wren said. "I know."

Was Wren reinventing herself? *Yes.* That was part of the reason she was in San Diego.

Lena looked skeptical. "You ever reinvented yourself after your world was destroyed?"

"Yes." Wren took a deep breath. "My brother was killed in a car accident. I lost the person I could lean on. The one who would always answer the phone." She hesitated for a moment. Weighing her next words? Her gaze darted to Luca. Words she didn't want him hearing?

"I had planned to be a marine biologist. I was enrolled in a masters program for it."

Whoa. That was more information than she'd given him before. It wasn't a path she'd looked at. It was a path she planned to follow.

"My brother was my biggest cheerleader and a barrier between my parents who had other ideas. When I lost him, I lost the ability to fight. For years. Ended up in med school, and I would have ended up a neurologist if my parents had their way. I fought back before residency. It cost me."

The sea horses. It was more than just a passing fancy, but she hadn't shared that with him. He wasn't sure why that stung so much. But he knew the cost. The debt. The thing her parents intentionally burdened her with.

"Now I'm a plastic surgeon specializing in burn care. I make the difference I want. However, it is a different dream."

"Do you miss that first dream?"

"Sometimes." Wren tilted her head, then pointed to the skin graft. "But it passes quickly. You are still the woman that painted light into every corner. She will always be a part of you. Now she has expanded."

"I didn't want to expand." Lena looked at the pencil Wren had left on the small table she was working on.

"I know. I didn't, either."

Luca had to swallow to make his tongue function. There were so many statements in this short conversation. Insights to help Lena but revelations about the woman he'd woken beside this morning, too. Revelations she hadn't shared with him. Even when he was with her behind the scenes at the aquarium.

"The next steps will be hard, but there is beauty and growth that comes with the hard steps." Wren's voice wobbled just a little but Luca doubted Lena noticed. Then Wren looked at him and grinned.

How was the woman able to smile after just admitting that her life wasn't her choice? That what she'd wanted wasn't considered?

It was one thing to not buy a stuffed toy or celebrate her birthday. Her parents had changed the course of her life. Forced her into a career path. Then gotten angry when she'd finally charted her own course.

"And I bet those paintings you are so angry at are gorgeous." Luca kept his gaze firmly rooted on Lena as he offered the advice. If he looked at Wren, he was terrified a wave of words would flood out. Demands. Worries. Hurt.

"Do you have any pictures of them?" Therese asked.

Lena had mentioned, when she was focused on her therapy a few weeks ago, that she took photos of every canvas at all the stages. Just so she could see the painting come to life. He was willing to bet her phone had at least one image of the creations she claimed to hate.

Lena shrugged and pulled her phone out. It was an angry sea. Dark waters competing with a dark sky, the moon barely adding its graceful light to the dance.

"It's breathtaking." Therese's voice was quiet, her hand over her heart. "What's it called?"

He was glad Therese was able to comment because the image had stolen all thoughts from him. It was captivating. If this was what Lena considered failure, then what was her definition of success?

"It doesn't have one. Not yet. My agent keeps trying to get me to name it. Wants it up on my website. Says it will bring in at least a quarter of a million dollars."

If it went for auction, Luca suspected it would fetch quite a bit more. Hell, he'd reach out to the agent and see what the price was. He could put it in his living room. The evening sun hitting the shadows... It would be perfect.

"Shadow storms." Wren's hand flew to her lips. "Sorry, as we can tell, I'm not great at creative things."

Lena's head shifted as she tilted the picture back and forth, her gaze rooted to the screen. "No. That actually makes sense. I might steal it."

Wren beamed. "It's yours if you want it." She looked at her watch. "I need to get to rounds, but as I know Dr. McDonnell is going to tell you, you're pushing yourself too much. Your hand needs time to recover. You shouldn't have any pain." She started to stand, then took one more look at the image. "This is a masterpiece. Maybe it doesn't feel that way right now. Doesn't make it untrue. Let me know which museum purchases it. I want to know where to visit it in all its glory." Wren offered Lena one more smile and then a quick one for him, and she was off.

"Dr. Freson is right."

"About this being a masterpiece?" Lena was still focused on the painting. So much of physical therapy wasn't about the exercises but the life the person wanted, needed to live. Lena had hit a plateau. Not because of therapy but because of life outside of therapy.

"Yes. But also about you needing to not overdo it." He held up a hand, forestalling the fight he could see building in Lena's eyes. Good. Fighting was good. He could work with fighting. "Next week, I want you to bring your largest and smallest brushes." He held up the stress ball they'd been using for weeks. "I think it's time we transitioned to a new tool."

Wren blinked and tried to fully relax her shoulders but her body was tighter than ever. Why on earth had she let so many things out with Lena?

Yes, the woman was struggling. And yes, Wren understood the feeling of losing yourself. It was easier to comply when Ronan was gone than to fight. And she loved the work she did. That didn't mean there weren't times, like behind the scenes at the aquarium, that she didn't wonder what might have been if her parents had seen past the genius and just loved her.

But everyone had what-ifs in life.

If she hadn't chosen this field, the Link-Freson technique might not exist. That procedure changed lives. It made a difference. This was why she didn't look back at the possibilities. Why she buried it in sunshine.

"Dr. Freson!" The nurse running toward her was pale.

Wren didn't know what had happened, but today's plans had just shifted exponentially. She ran to the nurse, who turned and started back toward the ER. Wren matched her pace. "Details." The more she had now, the quicker she could react.

"Kitchen worker. Twenty-three. Pressure cooker was making weird noises, and they leaned over just as the lid popped off. Steam burn. Full face. You're needed in the ER."

Her stomach sank. Pressure cookers were excellent and saved time. But when they malfunctioned, the devastation could be extensive.

"Why didn't you page me?"

"System down. Guess those budget cuts from last year are coming home to roost." The nurse pushed open the door of the ER, and the screams coming from the bed down the hall were clear.

"Why the hell isn't he sedated?" Or at least under extensive pain meds. Though the fact that he still had feeling was in some ways a good thing. It meant the nerves were intact.

"The pain meds were pushed. But..."

But they weren't working.

Wren walked into the room, the horror show clear around her. The man was burned from the face down across his chest. There were also cuts, and he'd need extensive reconstruction.

Dr. Michaels, a trauma surgeon, didn't turn as he barked out orders to get the man under and get a surgical suite ready.

Wren washed her hands, gloved up and moved over to take a look. The burns were extensive. The skin was already pulling away.

A person Wren didn't recognize stepped to the door, and Scott, an ER nurse, stepped away from the bed. "I do not care if you need a report. I do not care if you want to cover your ass."

"Scott!" One of the other nurses was already trying to get the angry nurse under control.

"Get your company ready, because they will answer—"

"Scott!" Wren's shout seemed to catch the nurse off guard. "Now is not the time."

"They want him to check some box and sign away his

worker's compensation." Scott stepped into the hall, and less than a second later, security was carting away whoever had decided it was a good idea to reach their employee when they were in a literal medical crisis.

"All right, everyone!" Dr. Michaels called over the chaos. "We are heading to surgical. Now!"

Wren stretched her arm over her head as she waited for the water to boil. She'd planned a more extensive dinner than buttered noodles and garlic bread, but surgery had taken it out of her.

That did not mean she wasn't looking forward to dinner with Luca and snuggling Hippo. He still didn't let the poor guy up on his couch, but in *this* apartment the dog was her snuggle companion. Though Luca was right when he pointed out that Wren snuggled Luca, and Hippo flopped on the other side of the couch, more hanging on than snuggling. She still thought it counted.

A knock came at the door, and Wren called for the two of them to enter.

"Hi, honey." Luca walked in, kissed her cheek, then pulled out a giant bouquet of flowers. Reds, yellows and a smattering of blue.

"Oh my gosh." She couldn't take her eyes off them. "This is so sweet." Wren started to reach for them and then paused, her hands hanging in thin air as she spun around her kitchen. What was she supposed to put them in?

A vase. Duh.

An easy answer. Assuming one had a vase. "I don't think I have a vase." She turned back to look at the bunch of stems… Perhaps a really large cup?

"Don't think? You aren't sure whether you have a vase? Are these your first flowers?" Scarlet invaded Luca's cheeks as soon as the question was out. "They are, aren't they?"

Wren shrugged. She'd had a lot of experiences in her life as a child prodigy, but that cocoon didn't let in a whole host of experiences most people got in their teen and early twenties.

"You're my first boyfriend, so it makes some sense that these are my first flowers." *Boyfriend.* The title was out, hanging in the open. They'd technically never addressed their status. They were together nearly every night. They planned days off together. Drove to the hospital together when they were on the same shifts. A little over a month of being nearly inseparable.

But the words boyfriend and girlfriend were left completely out of the discussion. It had simply rolled off her tongue. A poetic declaration just waiting for confirmation.

"I know I'm your first." Was there a tiny edge on the word *first*?

Wren reached for the flowers to give her hands something to do. She'd had a long day. Looking for pinpoint signs was how she'd lived with her parents. An attempt to stay ahead of their ever-shifting moods. She hadn't lived that way in years, and there was no reason to start now.

"But flowers, Wren? You've graduated college—"

"At sixteen." She gave him a wink, hoping to loosen whatever had tensed his shoulders.

The quip clearly didn't help. "And med school at nineteen. People bring flowers to both those events. Your family didn't even bother?"

What was there to say? She'd asked for a toy when she was eleven. Begged for it. It was the first thing she remember truly craving. And they'd told her no. Expecting something like flowers for achieving what they expected of her was hardly something she'd consider.

"I like that there aren't roses. The hibiscus reds with the dark center are fantastic. And the lilies! I have never seen a yellow so deep. But I don't know what these are." Her finger touched the tiny blue flowers.

"You know hibiscus and lilies but not forget-me-nots?" Luca's smile eased the tension away from his eyes—almost all the way.

"I guess so." She started looking through her cabinet as the timer over the oven went off. "Grab the noodles and toss them in the drainer please." Why were all of her cups regular size? "Hope you don't mind buttered noodles. After the surgery, I didn't have time to make the planned meal." Maybe she could put the flowers in a giant bowl?

Luca turned the timer off, dumped the water from the pot and then wrapped his arms around her waist. "I don't mind at all—also, I have a vase upstairs. I'll grab it while you put the finishing touches on this."

Wren leaned her head against his shoulder and pressed her lips to his. "My hero."

"Uh-huh." He gave her derrière a quick tap, then headed out the door.

Wren waited for a moment, then looked at Hippo. "Do you think he didn't register that I called him my boyfriend or was he ignoring it?"

The giant head tilted one way and then the other.

"Not a lot of help, buddy. At least you're cute."

CHAPTER TWELVE

HE WAS THE first to bring her flowers. That thought had kept him up far too long last night. Wren lay in his arms, her nude body snuggled so close. His hand traced up her hip, so slowly, careful not to wake the beauty next to him.

There were far better thoughts he could pass the time with, but it was that one that kept running through his mind.

First boyfriend, too.

Luca had known that. But somehow hearing it from her sweet lips last night brought that truth to the forefront of his mind.

Firsts were important. Milestones. Wren had had so few experiences. She deserved the world. And any choice she wanted.

His heart clenched as the sun started pouring through her window. They slept at his place most nights. He wasn't sure why she'd asked to stay here.

Keeping some of herself apart?

He didn't think that was what was happening. But if it was, that was her right.

He was falling for her. Who was he trying to convince when there was no one with him but his thoughts? He'd fallen for her. Hard.

Love.

Luca's gaze roamed her face. Even in sleep, there was a

soft lift to the ends of her lips. Wren smiled even when she was asleep. His little ray of sunshine. He loved her.

And if she fell for him, it would be another first. His heartbeat pounded in his ears. Wren loving him. Holding him. He craved it.

But she deserved everything. Her parents stole her childhood, and then the career she wanted. The universe, in its cruelty, stole Ronan. She'd never dated before Luca. Never lain with another.

First loves were sweet. But there was a reason people called them *first* loves. More tended to follow.

Luca pressed his lips to her head. He would love Wren for however long she wanted. And if she decided she wanted more adventures, he'd find a way to step aside.

Wren let out a little sigh and rolled over. Her sunshine blasting his soul.

"You look like rough thoughts are traveling through your mind?" Her fingers pressed lightly against his temples. "Should I kiss the thoughts away?"

He dropped a kiss on her nose. "I won't say no to kisses, but this is just my face before I've had coffee."

Wren raised an eyebrow, but she didn't call out the lie. Her hand slipped down his thigh, her fingernails grazing his skin. His manhood rose to the occasion instantly.

"I like being able to turn you on so easily." Her dark gaze held his as she cupped him.

"Wren—"

"Mm-hmm, when you say my name like that."

He reached his hand up to skim her nipples, but she pulled away.

"You said you needed coffee, but I think there's another way to force whatever you don't want to tell me out of your brain." Her lips traveled down his body, kissing him nearly up to his manhood, then easing away.

"Tease!" His hands ran over her head, the only part he could touch in this moment. When her tongue swept his shaft, he let out a groan. Her mouth captured him. Luca resisted the primal urge to buck as her tongue swirled the tip of his erection.

He craved this. Craved her, but it wasn't enough. "Wren." Placing his hand beneath her chin, Luca pressed up until she was looking at him. He grabbed a condom from the side table and couldn't contain his smile as she ripped the package open.

Wren's hands wrapped around his length as she leisurely unrolled the condom down his length.

"Tease."

She threw a leg over him and pressed her opening to the tip of him but no farther. "You've already called me a tease. Now I feel honor bound to make sure I've earned the title." Wren lowered herself just a hair.

His finger ran along her nipple, twirling until it was perky and hard. She wasn't the only one who knew exactly how to drive the other mad.

Gripping his free hand, she guided it to her center. Forcing it exactly where she needed it. Damn. This woman would be his undoing.

Luca knew the exact pressure, the exact movements to bring her to oblivion. Part of him ached to rush through them. Make sure she was panting as she fully took him.

But this was her morning. She was in charge. Demanding what she wanted.

It was the hottest thing ever.

She squeezed him with her core and glided down him. Her head fell back as he filled her completely.

"Lean back." Luca let the words out between his teeth. He needed to come, but that was not happening until Wren tripped over the edge.

She didn't ask questions, didn't resist. She simply laid

her hands on thighs and leaned back. She was fully open to him now. His thumb stroked her as she moved against him.

As soon as he felt her clinch, he sat up a little, pulled her to him and drove himself into her until he'd claimed her completely.

Wren slid off him but didn't move from his chest. "That has to be the best way to start a morning."

If there was something better, he had no interest in searching it out.

"You got your place packed up?" Wren sipped her coffee as she added in her notes regarding a patient she'd seen in the ER. The actress had demanded a plastic surgeon to make sure she had as little scarring as possible.

The ER doc had been less than impressed with Wren when she commented that it shouldn't only be people in the public sphere who got the option. Most people didn't realize that plastics was able to stitch up any skin, not just surgeries, to ensure the best scar outcome. It should be offered to everyone, particularly if the scar was on the face.

"Nearly." Seth tapped in his notes. "I hate putting these in."

"Certainly not what we went to med school for." Wren laughed. "I've joked with Luca that maybe we should find a way to hire assistants to do our charting for us. He was fully onboard."

"He could afford that." Seth continued typing away. "Wonder if he's ever floated it by HR? They won't provide the service, but if he contracted out, they'd probably let it slide."

"I mean, I doubt he could actually afford it. But it is a nice dream." Wren wasn't sure why the joke she'd made suddenly felt like it was far more serious.

Seth looked up from his terminal. "Wren, he owns the building. I am sure from the rent alone he could hire three assistants. In fact, if he decides that, tell him I claim the third."

She laughed. "Oh no. He owns his apartment. It's the entire top floor." The words poured out, and the truth started to register. No. He couldn't. "Owning your penthouse suite is wildly impressive. But he doesn't own the building."

Seth pursed his lips, with a look she worried was pity carried in his bright gaze.

"No. He'd have told me." Even as she said the words, Wren wasn't sure they were the full truth. "Are you sure?"

"Yeah. I was curious about the place after the rental agent got weird with us. I mean, she acted like we were trying to pull a fast one on the rent." Seth shrugged. "It made sense once I realized. I mean, claiming to know the owner of the building is what a scam artist would do. Though I will admit I was tempted to ask if he could use his ownership connections to let us move in tomorrow so we have a full three days to get settled before shifts start again."

Seth's chuckle wasn't full. The joke was a halfhearted attempt to rectify an uncomfortable situation.

Her notes were done. She needed to leave. Take a few minutes to gather her thoughts.

"Why didn't he tell me?" The question was out before she knew it. "Sorry, inside head thought."

"Understood. I, um, actually wanted to ask you if you and McSteamy might want to help us move in this weekend. Therese swears she can lift the boxes, but with the baby and all, but I um—"

"It's fine, Seth. I am sure that we can be there. Just have Therese text me the details." She headed out. She needed a moment, more than a moment to work through all the tumbling thoughts in her head.

They'd lain in bed this morning, every morning over the last month. They'd gone to the aquarium and had so many movie nights.

But when I mentioned the situation with Therese, he seemed short.

"Hi there, sunshine." Luca popped beside her, a cup of coffee in his hands. "You look pensive."

"Do you own our building?" The question was out, and she crossed her arms. "No. Don't answer that. This isn't the place for this discussion. Actually, maybe it is. Do you?"

There were too many thoughts racing through her mind. He owned the building. And hadn't told her.

"Does it matter?"

"My boyfriend can buy whatever he wants, including buildings, and doesn't tell me. Yes, it matters." Wren crossed her arms. How could it not matter?

"Why? You looking for a huge payout?" The playful look in his eyes vanished. His chin raised slightly. This was McSteamy standing before her. Not Luca.

So, the answer was yes, he owned the building. And he didn't want her knowing. That stung.

"Because." Not a great answer, but she wasn't sure why it bothered her so much that he'd kept it from her. It felt purposeful. And there had seemed like times when he was holding back.

He said an investment hit big. There was an investment hitting big, and there was owning prime real estate in the most expensive city in the whole country.

"Why does it actually matter, Wren?"

Wren looked at her feet, tears threatening to push their way out. "Why not tell me? Why are you hiding it?"

"I wasn't."

When she met his gaze, she saw him flinch. "Come on, Luca." She couldn't do this. Not here. Not now. She wanted, needed, more information. But in a place where they could actually discuss it.

"I need to see a patient." Wren stepped around him, her

body tight as she tried to figure out why he wouldn't want her to know. It didn't matter.

Maybe it does?

Turning the corner, she waited a minute. Hoping that he might chase her down. Might come clean. Might say something that didn't mean she'd asked a question and opened a gulf between them.

The gulf was always there. He just didn't want me to know.

Wren got to the door of the patient's room and mentally shook herself. She was here to check in on Cristan Bell, the man who'd taken a steam bath straight to the face. He was wrapped in gauze and medicated to make him as comfortable as possible.

"Good morning, Cristan," Wren said, entering the room. There was a woman sitting on the couch, a big pillow next to her. "I'm Dr. Freson, the plastic surgeon."

"Nadia, Cristan's wife."

The man turned toward their voices, "Is it morning?" His eyes were bandaged tightly. The burns over his eyelids were horrific. He'd need at least half a dozen facial reconstruction surgeries, if not more.

"It is. A bright sunny morning."

Cristan's head tilted a little. "Not sure San Diego knows how to create any other weather."

Wren nodded, then caught herself. Cristan couldn't pick up on nonverbal cues right now. "It is certainly nice. I lived on the east coast before heading here. I don't miss the winter and chilly rain."

"You will." Cristan turned his head toward the window, though he couldn't see the sun. "Or maybe not, Nadia has never missed the snow."

Nadia pushed a tear away from her cheek. "We used to live in northern Ohio. Lake effect snow, meant we got three to four feet of the white stuff at a time. I like the sun, but I do miss the seasons." Her gaze traveled over her husband as more silent tears fell.

"How are you feeling today?" Wren looked at the chart. The man never requested pain meds. Never complained. He was the perfect patient according to the nursing staff.

That did not align with his injuries.

"Fine."

She was certain that was a lie. "How are you actually feeling?"

"Fine." There was no emotion in the word. No hint that he was anything other than fine. She wanted to believe him. Maybe she would if the night nurse hadn't noted that his fingers tapped when he was in pain—at least she thought they did.

Right now, the fingers of his right hand were bouncing off his thigh in a rhythmic fashion. If the nurse was right, and Wren saw no reason to doubt her, then Cristan was hiding a decent amount of discomfort.

"I am going to get a drink. Do you want me to bring you back a smoothie?" Nadia laid a hand against his knee.

"Mango, if they have it."

"You know they only have banana and strawberry." Nadia kissed the top of his head, the only place on his face not covered with white gauze.

"I know. But if you keep asking, they might realize what a mistake they've made in not having the best flavor."

"Not sure that's how it works, but I will be back in a little while." Nadia looked back at Wren as she reached for the door and mouthed a sentence. *Ask him how he feels when I'm gone.* Then she went out the door and pulled it closed, firmly enough to make sure that it was clear she had left.

"Do you want to tell me how you feel now?" Wren moved toward Cristan. She needed to get a look at the wounds and see if they were on track to schedule his next surgery.

"I'm sore. But handling it." Cristan let out a sigh. "Nadia is worried I'll hold this against her."

Wren started gently pulling back on the gauze. "Was she at the plant kitchen when the accident happened?"

"No." Cristan flinched but didn't let out a noise as a piece of gauze caught on his cheek. Wren used a bit of gel to wet the gauze down, then started to pull it back slowly. "We moved here for her job. She's the main manager at the biggest hotel in the city. A real big promotion from the place she managed in Cleveland." The pride in his voice was palpable.

"But my job didn't transfer. I've worked odd jobs here and there. The plant kitchen doesn't pay well, and it's dangerous. Obviously." He gestured to his face. "She thinks that it's her fault. If she'd turned down the job offer, then we'd still be in Cleveland." He shrugged as the final piece of gauze came away. "She deserved the promotion. And this is the company's fault."

His burns had to hurt. His face must ache.

"You're hiding the pain to make sure she doesn't feel worse." Wren made a note in the chart. They needed to make sure that Nadia was out of the room to get the proper answer. Protecting each other was sweet, but it might hurt Cristan's recovery in the long run. "I know you don't want her to know. But she knows. Maybe not all of it but enough. Let her in. Let her help you through all of this, Cristan."

The man nodded, but Wren wasn't sure he planned to follow through with any of it.

Would Luca ever let her in? She didn't know…and that terrified her.

CHAPTER THIRTEEN

Wren exited the elevator but hesitated as she started toward Luca's door. The plan was to come here. At least it had been before she confronted him at the hospital. Not her smoothest moment.

It was just so shocking. He owned the building.

She waited another minute, then purposefully made herself move forward. They needed to discuss this. She had to understand why he hadn't told her.

Her knuckles rapped on the door, and Hippo's excited bark echoed into the hallway. Luca opened the door, but he didn't step back to let her in. The distant look in his eyes made her throat seize.

She waited a moment, hoping he'd laugh or step back or say something! Anything.

Instead it was her putting out the first words. "Are you going to let me in, or do I stand out here to have the conversation?"

"If you are here to talk about the building, then there is nothing to discuss." Luca shrugged.

"Like hell there isn't." Wren crossed her arms over herself to keep from pushing past him. This was his home. She wouldn't invade it. At least with him owning the floor, it meant there were no nosy neighbors seeking reasons to walk down the hall for a better look at the drama.

"Why didn't you tell me?" She'd told him so many things.

Opened up and shared secrets no one knew. And he'd never done the same. A fact she'd realized this afternoon.

"Why does it matter?" Luca leaned an arm on the doorway. If they weren't arguing, it'd be sexy.

It was like they were repeating the script from this afternoon. Not getting anywhere. Wren shook her head. When she was growing up, the adults around her, fellow students and colleagues had done the same. Shielding her from bad news. Protecting her. It all boiled down to the same thing, keeping secrets from her instead of treating her as an equal.

"You told me you owned the apartment. Why not say you owned the building? That is more than an investment hitting big."

"It is." Two words. No inflection to them.

He owed her the truth.

"What is it you want, Wren? Might as well let it out."

"I want the truth, Luca." She waited a second, but he didn't respond. "You don't trust me with the answer." She said the words more to herself. A person wasn't an equal to someone they couldn't trust. The walls of the hallway felt like they were closing in. This wasn't happening. It wasn't.

His mouth opened, but he didn't say anything.

"Okay. Yeah." Filler words. Words her brain spat out while it was still reeling with the information forcing its way through. He didn't trust her. Didn't want her to know. If Seth hadn't let the information out…

Her chest ached, and blood rushed to her face. Without trust what was this?

Nothing. Such a simple, painful word.

"Fine, Luca. You don't need to tell me. If you'll just pack my clothes up and send them to my place." She had months left on her rental agreement. And then there were the hospital run-ins—at least that was something she could avoid.

Mostly.

A tear slipped down her cheek, and she headed for the stairwell. There was no way she was waiting for the elevator when they were the only people on the floor.

"You want your stuff?"

The words hit her back, but she didn't have the strength to turn around. "Yes, please."

"Wait, you really want your stuff? *That* is what you want? All you want?"

Was this some kind of joke? Whatever it was, her heart was too broken to play along. "Luca, I am tired, and honestly broken by this."

That was probably too honest, but she didn't have it in her to cover the truth. She'd fallen for him. Hard. And yet, she didn't know him. Not this part of him, the McSteamy persona he wore so well for others. He was different with her. That was true. She'd thought that meant more than it did apparently.

"Yes, I want my stuff. I will keep my distance at the hospital until we're more comfortable." Who was she kidding? She wasn't going to be comfortable around him. Ever.

Wren hit the stairwell, grateful to get away. She was halfway down the stairwell when she heard her name. Her feet paused, despite her brain ordering them to run on.

"What!" She rounded on him, tears streaking down her face. What could he possibly want?

"You don't want anything?" He reached for her, but she stepped back.

"I told you, I want my stuff. You don't trust me. You don't want me knowing your secrets. Fine. I shared so much with you, and you've shared nothing. I get it." She didn't get it. Not really, but she was not going to puzzle it out here. With him.

The tears were truly streaming now. But now most of them were from anger. How dare he draw this out?

"I meant, you don't want me to pay for your apartment? Or go on some fancy trip? Pay off your student loan. Or—"

"No, Luca. I don't want anything from you other than the stuff I left at your place. I don't know what sick game you're playing, but I am done with it."

"Wren." He started for her again, and this time she took two steps down. "I'm confused."

He was confused? He was the one who started all of this. The one who hadn't trusted. The one keeping secrets. "Then let me make it really clear. Whatever this was, is over. You don't trust me, and I shared all my secrets with you. Told you—" She'd confessed that she'd wanted another job. That she'd never gotten a birthday present. Her desire for a kid's stuffed toy. That she felt alone and othered. Personal stuff. Deep. Hard.

Instead of sharing with her, he'd hidden something. That might have been okay, if he wasn't so defensive when she found out. It was so clear that he didn't want her knowing.

"I thought you'd want something. Want me to buy something for you."

Wren let out a shrill laugh. "Sure. I find out my boyfriend owns a building, so he must be my bank now. Wow. I really did make a bad impression." They'd spent nearly every night together, and he could jump to such a stupid conclusion.

"Everyone else does." Luca pushed his hands through his hair and sighed.

Those were tragic words hinting at betrayal that unfortunately she knew nothing about. Because he'd shared none of it with her. And, even if that were the case, she'd never given him any reason to expect she'd follow that same path.

"I wouldn't have thought I'd be lumped into 'everyone else.'" She used her fingers for air quotes. "Which is also absolutely false because Seth and Therese know. And have known for at least a week. And unless I am mistaken, the only help they've requested is with moving in."

His eyes widened. Maybe with understanding, but probably because she hadn't told him yet that they'd asked for help with the move.

"Or is it just the women you sleep with who you think look at you like a cash withdrawal machine?" The words turned her stomach. To be reduced to such a level.

"Wren—"

"Everything okay up there, Dr. McDonnell?" The security guard's words floated up the stairwell, cutting off whatever Luca planned to say.

"Fine," Luca called down.

She shook her head. Wren had no words left. She was empty. So she turned on her heel and fled before he could say anything else.

Not that he'd said much anyway.

Luca stood in the stairwell not sure how he'd screwed up so badly. No, that wasn't true. He knew exactly how.

He'd seen Wren's look in the hallway at the hospital. Heard the words, *my boyfriend can buy whatever he wants*, and decided the moment he'd feared was upon him. Rather than acknowledge the fact that he hadn't told her, his walls had slammed down. He'd accused her of wanting something.

And instead of apologizing for it tonight, he'd waited for the hammer that always fell to drop. He was prepped to hear it. Shield at the ready and heart closed off.

Those words never materialized, though.

Her accusations were fair. She'd accused him of not trusting her. Of not telling her anything. Not sharing.

The worst part was she wasn't wrong. He'd listened to her hidden truths. Kissed the tears off her cheeks. Each time she'd asked anything about his past, about anything deeper than his day-to-day activities, he'd pulled back. Retreated.

He'd worried that when she found out, he'd lose her.

I did.

But this time it was because he'd trashed everything. Wren had wanted his truths, not his wallet. Rather than accept that incredible gift, he'd tossed it away. Thrown it away.

His feet were moving. Heading to her floor. There might not be a way to repair this, but she was owed the answers he'd kept from her.

Stepping onto her floor, his feet were suddenly boulders. It felt like hours passed as he walked to her door. She might not answer.

He deserved that.

Standing before her door, he wished he had something to apologize with. Then he shook his head. He'd brought cupcakes before; this time he brought truths.

He raised his fist and wasn't surprised to hear her yell to go away.

"Wren, please. I need to say something. Then I'll go if you want." He raised his voice to make sure she heard him. He wasn't surprised when one of the neighbors opened her door and peeked out.

One nice thing about having it out on his floor was that no one had been there to watch.

Wren's door opened, just a crack. She didn't open it any wider. He waited a moment, then stepped in.

She was already back in the kitchen. The bottle of wine she'd said she was saving was open on the counter.

He didn't know what she was saving it for, but he was certain it wasn't a massive fight with her boyfriend.

She lifted the glass to her lips and stared at him.

"You opened the wine?" It wasn't what he meant to say. Not what was important.

"Yeah, well, I am nowhere near paying off my student loans, so I figure I can get another when that day finally comes." She took a deep sip. "And no, that is *not* a request for you to pay anything off."

He deserved that. Luca waited a minute, then pushed his hands into his pockets. "I am worth over six hundred million dollars."

Wren took another sip of her drink. As if the bombshell he'd held so tight meant nothing.

"I haven't met with my investment advisor this quarter, so it is probably safe to say it's a decent amount more given the state of the real estate market. This isn't the only rental complex I own."

She let out a huff. "I don't care how much you're worth. If that's what you came to tell me, you can leave."

She didn't care. Words he'd longed to hear. Words she meant. He was a damn fool.

"I told Madeline about inheriting Maude's estate two months before we were supposed to wed. The estate was large, and the investments have made it larger over the last ten years."

Wren drained the last of her glass and poured another healthy amount. "I cannot emphasize enough how much I do not care about your investments and the amount they are worth."

"I know."

"Do you?" She raised her glass and tilted her head. The sunshine soul was a storm cloud.

He'd done that. Stolen the beams.

He sucked in a breath. "I walked into the bridal suite on our wedding day and heard her telling her maid of honor about the inheritance. They were laughing because she'd planned to end the engagement the night I told her about the money. She was seeing someone on the side, but she cut it off as soon as she knew she was marrying into a sum greater than she had ever imagined."

Wren sipped her drink but didn't say anything.

Luca took a deep breath. "She was joking that she could

spend a few years with me to get half, since I didn't ask for a prenup. Maybe even have a kid or two, so she'd get child support."

Wren's eyes widened. "That is evil."

"Yeah." Evil was a solid word for it. He'd been an unwanted kid. To joke about doing the same for child support... He couldn't even imagine.

"After I ended things, she made sure pretty much everyone in our hometown knew, even though I'd asked her not to say anything." He scoffed. "A final revenge. My friends suddenly saw me differently. All except Ronan. He only ever asked me to cosign a loan."

"It doesn't surprise me that he didn't change." Wren shifted. "So your big secret is that you're worth more money than anyone else I know, and you thought I would hear that and demand a healthy slice." She shook her head. "I made quite the negative impression then."

"Wren." He took a step toward her. "You didn't. This was my fault. All my fault. Everyone always changes when they know."

"Everyone but Ronan. And Seth. And Therese. And me." She let out a breath. "Actually, that isn't true. I have changed. I am furious and heartbroken. Most people see me as a genius. A prodigy. Naive little Wren. You're the first to see me as a gold digger."

He deserved that.

"Is there any way for me to make this up?" He'd grovel. Do anything. But if she wanted him to leave, he'd do it. Accept the fact that he'd destroyed the thing that brought him peace. The woman who made him feel whole.

"What if I say pay off my student loan?" Her voice shook.

His eyes shot wide. This was a test, and he needed to pass it. Wren wasn't interested in his money. She'd made that very clear.

"I don't think that is what you really want." He took a step toward her.

Her bottom lip was trembling, but she wasn't telling him to get out. "What do I want, Luca?" She raised her chin, her dark gaze holding him.

He had one chance to bridge the chasm he'd created. What she wanted—needed was the truth.

"The truth."

She raised a brow. "Which is?"

He took another step toward her. Close enough to touch her but not reaching for her. "I panicked today because I love you. And the thought of losing you to what I've lost everyone to sent me into a spiral. It is not fair, and it's not right, but I wanted that distance, so when you came to the door to ask the favor everyone else seemed to want from me, it wouldn't hurt as bad."

"Did that work?" She set down the still mostly full wineglass.

He tilted his head. "I think we both know this is a textbook definition of something very much *not* working. I royally screwed up. In fact, if someone wants to put my picture next the words *screw up* in an online dictionary, I could not blame them."

"Screw up is two words. I don't think it's in the dictionary."

He chuckled. "It's acknowledged slang. I am pretty sure it's in there. But we can look it up? Set that part of the argument aside."

"Luca."

He held his breath. His life revolved around this moment. Whatever she decided, he'd find a way to deal with it.

"I don't—" Her voice caught, and the world around him darkened.

Breathe.

"I don't want your money. I wanted you."

Past tense. Damn it.

She looked at him. "Do you trust me?" She held up a hand before he could say anything, "I mean really trust me? If I make a joke about you paying for something, are you going to see that as me stepping into the role you've assigned everyone else?"

It was the easiest answer he'd ever had. "Completely. I trust you completely, Wren." He was stunned by how true that was.

Stepping up to her, Luca hesitated for only a second before reaching for her. As her hand wrapped through his, he finally felt like he could breathe again. "I love you, Wren. I trust you."

She laid her head against his shoulder, letting out a soft sigh. Wren didn't say anything, but that was okay. She was in his arms. He had another chance. One he did not plan on screwing up again.

CHAPTER FOURTEEN

HE LOVED HER. Wren rolled over, her gaze falling on Luca's still slumbering face. They'd come back to his place last night. Talked more.

He'd opened up about his parents demanding money. Calling him all sorts of names when he reminded them that they'd ignored him until it benefited them. How lost and alone it made him feel. And telling her how Maude said the money was cursed.

Wren bit her lip. He believed that. At least to some extent. He'd opened up—fully. Answered any question she asked. Held her hand and kissed her lips.

And she still hadn't been able to say the words back. She loved him. It was the only reason she'd let him into her place last night, her heart so broken, hoping for a miracle.

One Luca delivered.

So why was the truth still buried deep in her chest?

Because for a moment, he'd seen her as something she'd never been. *Gold digger*.

Not that he'd used that word. But there was no other term. The man who'd never treated her as an outcast or called her a genius had picked something different.

He'd also apologized. Something no one else did.

Apologized, then told her he loved her.

But what if he still didn't really see her?

It was an unfair question.

Is it?

He stirred, and she forced the worry to the back of her head. Today was a new day. Wren was an expert at finding bright spots and marching on. Luca loved her. He loved her.

From this moment on, she was looking forward. Period.

"Wren?" Luca said her name like he was a little surprised to still find her in his bed.

"Expect me to vanish?" She ran her hand down his cheek. The stubble of his beard was rough under her hands.

Luca grabbed her free hand, pulling it to his lips. "Maybe."

She grinned. "Well, I am still here, but I forgot with everything going on yesterday. Seth made a joke, but I think we can probably make good on it anyway. Provided you are willing to use a little of your leverage as owner of the building."

Luca kissed her fingers again. "What joke?"

Not an immediate yes. But not an unqualified no, either. That was progress. "Given that Seth, Therese and both of us are off until Monday—"

"Three-day weekend!" Luca grinned, a full smile. One free of worry.

"Yes, well, they aren't supposed to get the keys to their place until tomorrow, but he joked about asking you to see if he could get them today to give them an extra day." Wren rubbed his cheek. "He doesn't know I'm asking. I think he used it to try to lighten the mood after he let out your secret. But I mean—"

Luca laid a finger against her lips. "I'll make the call now." He reached for his phone, placed the call and made sure they'd reach out to Seth as quickly as possible.

So easy. No hesitation. No worry that someone was taking advantage of him.

As soon as he hung up, her lips were on his.

His hands slipped down her back as he pulled her on top

of him. They'd slept in clothes for the first time in weeks last night.

Luca's fingers traced along her back but didn't slide up her shirt.

She laid her forehead against his, breathing in his soft scent. There was no agenda here. No move to make love. Just two people holding each other in the morning light. Reminding the other that they were still here. Somehow it felt more intimate than anything they'd ever done.

"Wanna get breakfast and walk the dog before we have to go unload boxes?" She rubbed her nose against his.

Luca's lips brushed hers. "Sounds like a great plan."

"I am more than capable of lifting boxes." Therese crossed her arms and put a playful pout on her lips.

"I know, Rese." Seth gave her a wink as he and Luca started back out the door with two moving dollies.

Wren looked at the first box, labeled baby's bedroom, picked it up and passed it to Therese.

"You giving me this one because it isn't too heavy?" Therese hefted the box and started toward the bedroom as Wren grabbed another.

"No. Just grabbing the first one." It was mostly true. The box wasn't heavy, but it wasn't light, either. They set them down in what would be the nursery. "Do you want to start unpacking some things or wait until everything is up here?"

The men were bringing up the stuff, but there was no reason Wren couldn't do more than just put boxes in rooms. Assuming that was what Therese wanted.

Therese looked at the room. "It is probably a good idea to get Seth's and my room set up first. Given that this little bit won't be here for months. Still…" she looked around the room "…we aren't moving our bed over until tomorrow. Not like we're sleeping here tonight."

"So..." Wren could see the hint in Therese's gaze. She wanted to unpack the baby's room.

"The baby's stuff has been in boxes all this time." Therese looked at the corner where the crib was. "Wanna help me put it together?"

"Sure." Wren headed over to the crib box and took a look at the side. "Says we need a screwdriver." Before the frown she saw materializing on Therese's face could form, Wren popped up. "I'll grab my toolbox. Give me just a second."

Therese clapped. "I'll get the rest of the baby's boxes ready."

Wren ran up to her place and headed back down with the whole box. Never knew what you might need in a pinch.

"Glad you have that. Ever put together a crib?" Therese had used scissors to open the box and had the pieces out on the floor.

"Nope. I'm not really maternal." Wren shrugged; kids were nice. But she'd never really gotten to be one. What did she know about raising children? Nothing.

"You don't have to want kids." Therese pulled the crib rails up. "It says we start with these."

"I didn't say I don't want them. I just..." Wren blew out a breath. "I wasn't really a kid."

"Geniuses are kids, too." Therese winked. "So you were, by definition, a child."

There was something in the way Therese emphasized the last few words. Something Wren couldn't quite place.

"Not really." Wren looked over the instructions and grabbed the pieces for the next step. "I mean, I didn't play. Or have toys or picture books. Never did the macaroni art or any art for that matter."

"Did you want to?"

"Want to what?" Wren stuck her tongue out while she slid

piece four into piece five. Sticking her tongue out wasn't strictly necessary, but it felt right.

"Play, Wren? Run your fingers through finger paint? Play make-believe or with dolls or with medical sets? You know, prep for the big role you'd take on. I played doctor, though honestly it was mostly just giving pretend shots to my parents."

That must have been nice. Wren could not even imagine asking her parents to play pretend.

"Well, I never planned to be a doctor. At least not as a little kid. So playing doctor wouldn't have really made sense." She slid the next pieces together. "I told Luca that a while ago."

"Most kids play doctor and never become one. Wait." Therese's gaze was rooted to Wren. "Never planned. What did you want to be?"

"Marine biologist was the dream. I mean as much of a dream as a sixteen-year-old college graduate can have."

"Why didn't you do that?" Therese's hand lay on top of her barely showing baby bump. The protective mother.

"My brother died. Life got unsettled after that." Wren slid another piece together. "It was easier to follow my parents' path. Took a while for me to figure out that I was not going into neuro. They were not pleased." Wren let out a laugh. That was an understatement but still the truth. "But plastics is the best medical place for me. Things change, and I am pretty good at finding the bright side." She looked up, stunned to see Therese's frown. "You okay?"

Her hand was running over her belly, her eyes wide. She nodded. "Yeah, I'm fine. Just stunned that your parents didn't let you play or even choose your own path. Did you get the boxes unloaded, Luca?"

Wren turned and beamed at Luca, who also looked like he had a frog stuck in his throat.

He shook his head. "There are few more to go. I was just checking on you two. You disappeared."

"Therese wanted help setting up the crib." Wren pointed to the partially done crib. "Once it's done, decor time? Maybe?"

"For someone who is not maternal, I appreciate your willingness to help with the nursery." Therese swallowed.

"Always happy to help." Wren grinned, not quite sure why Luca and Therese looked like she'd said something so off.

She hadn't said she loved him. Three days. Three days of perfection. Except…

Luca mentally shook himself. He needed to focus on the chart in front of him. Lena was making amazing progress. She was brighter today. Almost bubbly as she showed off her newest art to Therese.

Like Wren. Finding the bright spot.

Luca still couldn't shake the words she'd said so unconsciously to Therese. *Plastics is the best medical place.*

Not the place she was meant to be. But the best medical place.

If Ronan hadn't died. If he hadn't cosigned the loan. There was no way to know what would have been. So he had to find the bright spot. That was what Wren found. Always.

Was that why she'd let him back in after he'd been a right ass? He was grateful for the second chance, but he didn't want to be another bright spot she forced herself to find. Another path she accepted.

"Luca." Therese's voice pulled him from his unsettling woolgathering. "You have to see this painting."

Luca walked over, happy for the distraction. It was the piece Lena had shown Wren a few weeks ago. But now it was hanging in a proper gallery.

"My agent got it listed. I stole Wren's name for it. *Shadowed Storms.*" Lena looked at the image on her screen.

"There have been several offers on it so far. Might even go up for auction. That'll be a first in my career."

"That is wonderful, Lena."

"A bright spot in the storm, as Wren is so fond of saying." Lena beamed. "Well, she doesn't say exactly that, but it is the general feeling."

It was. Wren pushed past the negative. Looked for the glimmer of good. But was it what she really wanted? He wasn't sure.

And worse, he wasn't sure she knew. She'd done it for so long it was simply second nature.

But that was a problem for another time. "In more wonderful news, I am not sure there is much left for you here. I think this is your last session with us."

"Yeah." Lena looked at her hand. "I figured this day was coming. Any chance you know if Dr. Freson is around? I wanted to show her the picture hanging for people to see."

She would love that. "She's in her office. I'll call to let the office assistant know you're heading that way."

"Thanks." Lena signed the final discharge papers on the tablet, then headed out.

"Wren is going to love seeing that canvas hanging." Therese ran a hand over her growing belly.

"Yeah. Do you think Wren is happy?" The question was out, and he wasn't sure what to do with it. He also didn't like the look on Therese's face or the fact that she hadn't immediately said, *Of course she's happy.*

"Why are you asking?" Therese let out a heavy breath.

"We haven't had a fight. Or rather we did, all my fault, but she said something while helping with your crib—"

"About not knowing if she could raise a child because she'd never been one?"

Luca blinked. "No. Though there is a more than enough to unpack in that statement."

"Genius sounds great, on paper." Once more Therese's hands ran along her belly. "But I think in reality..." Her words died away, and there was sadness there.

The same ache had hit his chest when he'd heard Wren's statement.

"If your child had that label, you and Seth would treat them very differently than Wren's parents treated her. I know you had a loving family, though Seth's indicated his was less than perfect. Neither Wren nor I had parents that put us first." Luca waited a second, but Therese didn't say anything else. "You didn't answer my question. Think she's happy?"

"I don't know the answer." Therese offered him a kind smile. "I like Wren. A lot. But I have never heard someone say something so tragic, so easily, then just mention that she looks on the bright side. I am not saying she is unhappy."

"Just that she doesn't know what she missed out on?" Luca knew what she'd missed. Playing mermaid at the pool. Cuddling stuffed animals. First crushes. Sleepovers.

Therese shrugged. "Yeah."

"Did you see Lena's picture?" Wren was bright as she walked into the therapy room. "I mean, wow! Should I call it a picture? Painting on canvas? I never did much art stuff."

Therese's eyes hit his.

Had she wanted to do art stuff? There were tons of places around San Diego. He could see about an outing. Would see.

"I think artwork, painting or picture work." Luca kissed her cheek. "Though I admit that I don't have a lot of experience with what Lena does."

"She is magnificent." Wren grinned. "I am tempted to go to the auction. Run the price up. Though I would probably have to force you to come, my checkbook is not going to get me past the entrance." She held up a hand. "Only joking, of course."

It was a joke. One he easily recognized. But her dark gaze

held just a hint of uncertainty. An uncertainty that he'd put there. Mentally kicking himself wouldn't do any good, but his brain was adept at self-flagellation.

"We could go." Luca shrugged. "I mean there is a place for it in the living room."

He heard Therese gasp.

"And art appreciates." It was a good investment.

Wren's eyes were huge. "We can't do that."

"We could, actually." Luca raised his brows. "Easily."

She waved away the words. "I *mean,* it belongs in a museum, Luca." She looked at her watch. "I have a few minutes and was going to grab coffee. Want one?"

Luca had a few minutes, plus he wanted to run the date idea by her. "Sure."

"I really was just kidding about the painting, Luca." Wren's words struck his heart.

"I know. And I know that it's going to take time, but seriously, honey, I know you aren't thinking like that. But I still think we should bid on it because it does belong in a museum, and maybe one day it can be loaned there, but no museum is buying her work. Not yet." Though given Lena's ability, he didn't doubt that the day was coming when that happened.

"You." Wren hit his hip.

"What?"

"You should bid on it. If you want to. Not we. I wasn't kidding when I said there was no way they'd let me in." She stepped into line at the coffee shop.

He was going to find a way to make sure she understood it was *we*. From now on, for as long as she wanted, they were a pair.

"Shifting the topic, want to go on a date?"

Wren crossed her arms. "Of course, but why do I feel like this is not our standard make dinner or order it in and watch a movie? With your popcorn machine."

He put an arm around her shoulder. "You really love that machine."

She didn't even try to hide the glee in her eyes. "It is one of your best qualities." She stepped up to the counter and ordered her coffee and his and quickly paid for both.

He wanted to argue that she didn't need to do it. Didn't need to prove anything to him, but he wasn't shifting the conversation there. "So, is that a yes? A date that doesn't involve my popcorn machine?"

She giggled. "All right." Her pager went off, and she lifted her coffee. "Tonight?"

"Might take me a few days to get the idea together." He wasn't sure where the creative shops were. He'd find them, but it might take a little time.

"So, what I am hearing is tonight we *can* have popcorn."

He playfully rolled his eyes to the ceiling. "Yes, tonight we can have popcorn."

CHAPTER FIFTEEN

"Not sure where we're going, but I love the dress code." Wren was wearing a pair of loose shorts and an old tank top. "I think this might be the most comfortable I've ever been on a date." She laughed. "I guess there isn't much to judge that on."

Luca's shoulders tensed, just a bit.

"Seriously." She leaned over the car's console and kissed his cheek. "Where are we going?"

"I told you." He took her hand, kissing her fingers. "It's a surprise."

Wren looked around. "Sometime we should do a date where you show me around the city. And we have to go to a ball game."

"That can be arranged. I haven't been to a Padres game in years. Want to sit in a box?"

Wren shook her head, uncomfortable with the ease he now discussed his ability to buy what he wanted. He said he trusted her. She wanted to believe him.

There is no reason not to.

But there was something holding her back. A hesitation. Fear that it was a trick? Her parents had tricked her brother and manipulated her, but that wasn't what was happening. Still, the shift seemed so quick.

Too quick.

She wanted him to be open, but she'd meant it when she said she didn't care about his money.

"No. I want to sit in the nosebleeds. I never got to do that with Ronan. He used to talk about sitting at the top of stadium in New York. The very last row. He claimed they were the best seats."

Luca chuckled. "I promise you they are not the best seats to see the game. But they are the best to have a good time in. We can always do both."

"True." They pulled into the parking lot for a small building that just said Pottery.

"Ta-da." Luca put the car in Park.

Wren looked at the nondescript building, then back at Luca. "Are we doing pottery?"

"Yeah. I thought it would be fun. Try something new."

Wren shrugged. "All right." She had no interest in messing with clay, but if he wanted to, then she'd happily follow along.

He opened his door, then ran around and got hers, too.

"It makes me feel fancy when you do that," she said, "though I am not dressed fancy."

"When we head to the Patron Banquet at the aquarium, you will be fancy." He kissed her cheek. "But you are always fancy to me, love."

He'd not put any pressure on her saying the words. He still told her loved her, and each time she wanted to say it back. Wanted to jump into his arms, pull him tight and whisper it in his ear.

So why don't I?

"Wait until you see the dress I got." It was a mermaid dress that hugged her in all the right places. Started off pink at the top and blended into a blue green at the bottom. She'd found it at a consignment store and nearly cried when it was her size.

"I look forward to it." He gripped her hand, and they walked into the pottery studio.

"Dr. McDonnell?" An older Black woman stepped around the corner.

"Yes, but please call me Luca. Are you Libby?"

"That is me." She held out her hand, and Luca took it quickly. Then Wren did the same. "And you must be Dr. Freson."

"Just Wren is fine."

The woman was beaming at her. Wren wasn't sure why the excitement in Libby's eyes sent a shiver down her back. They were here for Luca.

"I hear that you've never done art."

Wren looked at Luca, her heart sinking. So this was a setup. It was true, she hadn't, but she also didn't have any interest in pottery. Or painting. She was fascinated with cake decorating, her social media feed was full of it. But fascinated and wanting to replicate were two different things.

Luca's grin was so big. "She hasn't. That's why I set up this treat."

Treat.

Wren looked to Luca, then at Libby. What was happening?

Libby nodded, but there was something in her gaze as she looked at Wren.

"I'm sure this will be fun." Wren wasn't sure why Luca thought this was the perfect date idea. Had she mentioned pottery? No. She was positive that wasn't something she'd discussed.

"This way." Libby led them to the back of the studio where three wheels were set up with huge blocks of clay next them. "Take a position. Today we learn to throw a pot."

Luca sat at the wheel beside her, so pleased.

Wren grabbed her clay and did her best to follow the gentle instructions Libby gave them.

"I don't think there is any salvaging this pot." Wren scrunched her nose as her pot collapsed for at least the twentieth time. "I am an unmitigated disaster for this block of clay, Libby."

"It's fine, Wren. Pottery is a skill that takes years to truly master." Libby turned her attention to Luca. "You, however, picked this up very quickly."

Luca grinned at the pot sitting on his wheel. It was a real pot. The right size and thickness. His pot had only collapsed twice. And the happiness in his face was infectious. "This is surprisingly calming."

Wren had to hold back a gasp. That was the exact opposite of the description she'd give to this activity. Her blood pressure must have risen several points over the last two hours.

"We have classes." Libby started to reach for a flyer, but Luca held up his hand.

"With my role at the hospital, it's hard to make regular classes work."

Wren bit her tongue to keep from interrupting. Saturday classes might not always work. There were hours on the weekend, and he did some shifts on Sundays, but as a physical therapist, his hours rarely went past six. He could do this, if he wanted.

"I also offer private lessons." Libby pointed to the pot. "If you work at this, I have no doubt that you would pick it up really fast."

"I appreciate the vote of confidence but…" Luca's gaze hit Libby's. "What do I do with the pot now?"

"That is up to you. I can set it outside and let it dry, then put it in the kiln for the bisque firing. Or we can wrap it in plastic, and it will stay wet for a while so you can do more work on it."

"More work on it?" Luca looked at the pot, a gleam in his eye.

He had enjoyed this. Wren would need to reach out to Libby to find out more about private lessons. Maybe if she gifted him some lessons, he'd come back to enjoy himself.

"Sure." Libby pointed to a wall of tools that looked terrifying to Wren but must create the beautiful designs on the pieces she'd seen lining the front of Libby's studio. "You can add designs or any number of things. Or we fire this one, and then you put a glaze on it."

"Oh, like those paint-a-pottery places?" Wren put her hand on Luca. "A friend in New York did one of those places for her bridal shower. It's fun."

Luca looked at her hand. "Do you want to glaze it?"

Taking a deep breath before she answered was the only to keep her voice level. "No. It is *your* pot. Your art."

"Sure, but we came for you."

Her gaze flicked to Libby. This was not a discussion she wanted an audience for, but here they were. "I know, but you are the one who enjoyed this activity." She squeezed his arm. "And I loved watching you enjoy it, even as I crashed my pot, over and over."

Luca looked at the busted clay on her wheel. "Well, you don't have much to work with there."

She giggled. "I do not."

He stared at his pot for a minute, then looked at Libby. "I think it's done. That sounded weird. I mean, I would know if it was done. It's a pot. It's done."

Libby waited a moment, probably trying to make sure the words he'd slipped out actually meant what he wanted them to. "You are the artist. If it feels done to you, then it is done."

Luca gave the pot one more stare. "Done."

"Perfect. I will let you know when it is ready for glazing." Libby gave Luca a bit more information, and Wren hated how he kept sending glances back at her.

It was fine that he loved this, and she'd found it frustrating as hell. She just hoped he'd realized that.

Pottery had been a huge fail. Wren had done her best, but it was clear she hadn't enjoyed it. So what was next?

"You look pensive?" Wren leaned over and kissed his cheek. A cake-decorating video was running on her phone.

"Do you want to try cake decorating?" There were classes on that. Right?

She let out a sigh and purposefully shut off her phone's screen. "That was not an answer to my question."

Luca couldn't argue that point. "You didn't enjoy pottery the other day."

A little puff of air broke through her lips.

"You don't have to lie. It was easy to see." He'd been so proud of that idea. Something fun and different. "Should we have started with painting?"

"Why are we doing art stuff? Because I liked Lena's masterpiece?" Her dark eyes were wide. Confused.

"Because you didn't get to do any of this." He let out a huff. He had all the resources he could imagine. Wren could do anything she wanted. Anything. She only had to ask.

"What?"

"You told Therese that you didn't do art or play make-believe." She'd also said that she didn't play doctor…and that it wasn't the plan. Silence hung in the air, so he pressed on, "Any interest in going back to school?" Maybe it was a weird question, but the woman loved the library. She stopped by at least once a week. If she had headphones on during a run, it was an audiobook piping through them.

Her eyes shifted, just a hair. With excitement? He thought so. All right, that made sense. She was a genius. There had to be tons of stuff she'd wanted to study that had been deemed off-limits.

Luca thought back through the books he'd seen on the floor. The fiction novels were all thrillers this week. The nonfiction books… He tried to think. What was in the stack?

She'd gone directly to the non-fiction section while he slowly roamed the stacks, trying to find anything that might call to him. He enjoyed reading, but in the week it took him to finish a book, Wren dropped through six or seven. So what was the focus this week?

Dark covers. Crowns.

"The Tudors!" He snapped his fingers.

Wren giggled. "Not sure why you're so excited about the Tudors. Suddenly have an interest in King Henry the Eighth or Elizabeth the First? Those two are the ones people are most interested in."

"Not bloody Mary?"

Wren stuck out her tongue. "I guess there is a lot of interest in her as well. Why are you asking?"

He wasn't actually interested in the Tudor Queen. "I only know her from the mirror game."

The playful look in Wren's eyes disappeared. "Mirror game?"

And the reality of why she looked confused hit his gut. "Yeah. You go into a dark bathroom with a flashlight or a candle and chant Bloody Mary." Luca put a finger on his chin. "Three times, four? I didn't play at many sleepovers, but then her ghost is supposed to come haunt you."

"Children were playing with candles in the bathroom?" The horror on her features might have been cute if it wasn't another reminder that her childhood was spent in auditoriums and classrooms, listening to lectures.

"That is what you took away from this conversation? Candles in the bathroom?"

She pulled back a little. "I mean, I never slept over. Not like the high school girls wanted the random eleven-year-old from the back of class, who always broke the curve, at their sleepover gatherings. Was it supposed to be scary? I mean, it's not like the ghost would appear."

Luca shrugged. "You so sure of that?"

"Of course."

"Come on, then." He gripped her hand, pulling her off the couch.

"Where are we going?"

"To get a candle. I have some in the closet in case of power outages." It was a silly game, but spooky stories were rites of passage.

She raised a brow. "I thought you also did this with flashlights."

"Yes." He leaned over, his lips just above hers. "But we are adults. I think we can be trusted with candles." He brushed her lips. Then pulled a candle down from the shelf, along with the matches he kept next to them.

He opened the guest bathroom door, lit the candle and handed it to her.

Wren hesitated. "I just go in and say, Bloody Mary, three or four times…" she grinned, mimicking his uncertainty "…and come back out. Really?"

"Why the hesitation?" He raised both his eyebrows. "You scared?" He made sure to keep his voice playful, far from the accusatory tones he remembered growing up.

She took the candle and looked at the door. "In the dark?"

"Yep, oh, and you put the light just below your face. If it was a flashlight, it went under your chin, but with the candle, I don't recommend it." He kissed the top of her forehead, then gestured to the bathroom. "You going?"

Wren rolled her eyes to the ceiling, then stepped into the bathroom. He closed the door and stepped back. This was ridiculous.

It took just a moment before she swung the door open, a little faster than he'd expected.

"All right. Fine. I can see why that might be scary for kids." She blew out the candle. "The face in the mirror is yours, but it's creepy. No ghost but unsettling."

"Exactly!" Luca's fingers brushed hers as he took the candle. "But hey, now you know what a lot of American preteens did at sleepovers. We could always walk down to Seth and Therese's place and see if they want to play light as a feather, stiff as a board. Get the full experience."

"I am not even going to ask what that is." Then her lips were on his, arms wrapped around his neck. When she pulled back, there was a look in her gaze that sent a shiver down his spine.

"That was fun. Creepy but fun. However…" she tapped her temple "…steel trap here, so why were you looking so pensive?"

Luca squeezed her tightly. "I hate how much you missed." He laid a finger over her lips to stop the argument he suspected was coming. "There are adventures and activities that you should have had. So I tried the pottery, which I loved and you hated."

"I didn't hate it."

Luca raised a brow.

"I liked watching you do it, but the clay got under my nails, and it just felt icky." She looked over her shoulder at the mirror. "I have no interest in arts and crafts. I mean, I love watching cake-decorating videos but I don't want to do that. And to head off your other questions, my student loans keep the very idea of going back to school off the table."

Maybe the dream of marine biology hadn't died. Not completely at least. Wren was only twenty-six. Sure, she had med school and residency behind her, but lots of people walked away from careers for another life.

The loan was something he could take care of. Wipe it out of existence and let her chase whatever she wanted. Have the life she wanted. The life she deserved.

CHAPTER SIXTEEN

EDDIE LET OUT a wheeze as he stepped off the bottom step of the stair simulator they kept in the physio room.

"All right, let's go up again." The man was making good progress, but good progress when you'd been nearly burned to a crisp still left a lot of room between now and whatever his final new normal was.

"You suck, Doc. You know that."

"I've heard it a time or two. Now come on."

Eddie threw him a glare, then started up the steps. Glares were motivators. Luca could work with glares.

"I saw Dr. Freson today." Eddie went up another step.

"I'm sure she's happy with the progress of your burns." He'd heard from Wren that Eddie needed another surgery. Already scheduled for next week. From what she'd said, Eddie had not taken the news well.

"Sure, my skin is ready for the next round of plastic surgery to make it less hideous, maybe." Eddie reached the top step and turned to head down the stairs. "But she wasn't in my room to talk about the upcoming surgery."

Luca watched the steady but trembling steps Eddie took. *Can he go one more round on the stairs or is it time to shift to hand workouts?*

"What did you two discuss?" If Luca kept him talking, Eddie might turn around on the bottom step and head back up. Probably not. But it happened.

"Tudor England." Eddie let out a wince as he hit the bottom step. "One more, I assume?"

Luca nodded. If Eddie felt like it was possible, then it was. But he took a step closer just in case. "Why Tudor England?"

"Oh, I wrote my PhD on Mary the First and Elizabeth the First's relationship. Dr. Freson is shockingly knowledgeable on the topic."

The books on her floor this week. All Tudor dynasty books. Suddenly the image of his patient, Mrs. Demer, holding a thriller novel while waiting for her session flashed in his brain. Wren had headed straight to the librarian's desk and asked for thriller titles. He'd assumed she wanted something new. She did…because of Mrs. Demer.

A few weeks ago, the books were all art history. Which was certainly for Lena.

And her sudden interest in the Tudors… Eddie.

"Yeah, she is a font of information on many topics." Luca crossed his arms as Eddie hit the top step. But what did she like?

Did she even know?

No.

His stomach sank as the truth pushed into him. Wren spent her life making others happy. The genius people pleaser. The ray of sunshine who hid her emotions behind a brilliant smile.

"She was talking to me about the Bloody Mary mirror game." The words brought a grin to Eddie's tired features.

"I informed her of the game. Last night actually." And she hadn't mentioned this week's books were for Eddie. That she was reading to benefit her patients and other long-term residents; Mrs. Demer was here for a broken hip.

"Yeah. She told me. I guess she wasn't allowed to sleep over as a kid." Eddie hit the bottom step.

That wasn't quite the truth, but Luca wasn't going to add to anything that Wren hadn't shared.

"It was nice to have someone to talk to about it. My ex—" Eddie let out a breath. "She wasn't interested in my work. I think she thought marrying a college professor without tenure was beneath her."

Luca didn't know what to say to that.

"It's wild how easy that is to see now that we aren't engaged." Eddie looked at his scarred hand. "The red flags were there."

Luca nodded. He'd missed a lot of red flags with Madeline. Things that were very obvious once she wasn't in the picture. It lessened the hurt, though it did not remove it entirely. Only time healed that wound.

Eddie stepped to the ground and looked back at the steps. "I can't do it again, man."

Luca didn't try to hide his grin. "You did it two times more than I wanted you to. I think that progress is fantastic."

Eddie rolled his eyes, but there was no anger in his expression. "I feel like I got had."

"Nope. You were just very involved in the discussion and working on yourself. And you stopped when your body was ready. That is exactly what you should do." The door to the room opened, and the porter and Wren walked in together.

"Looks like my ride is here." Eddie gave Wren a quick grin, then settled into the chair. "One day soon, I am going to walk next to the porter back to my room."

Wren gave Eddie one of her brilliant smiles. "One day, you are going to walk into this room from outside the hospital."

"One day." Eddie nodded, but the grin faltered just a bit.

Wren clearly clocked it. "What if I stop by before my shift ends and we talk the odds of Elizabeth's involvement in Wyatt's Rebellion?"

"Oh, that discussion will take at least half an hour. And that is just for the overview." The historian's face was brighter than Luca had seen it in the weeks he'd known him.

"I will make the time." Wren gave a quick goodbye, then turned her attention to Luca. "I got you a coffee." She passed him the cup. "Decaf since it's already past three."

"Decaf?" He looked at the cup in horror.

She giggled. "Of course not."

Luca let out a playful sigh as he brought the lid to his lips. "Thank you. And was Elizabeth involved in the rebellion?" He didn't really care, but he was curious what her response might be.

"No one knows for sure. She was found innocent but…" Wren shrugged "…who knows? The books I read on the subject were rather dry."

There it was. The admission and his entry point. "So why read them?"

The pure shock on her face was enough for him to register that she truly didn't understand the reason for the question. "Eddie is a Tudor historian. I mentioned that last night. Oh, actually, I think you started ghost talk, and that distracted me."

"And the thrillers?"

"Mrs. Demer reads two to three a day. Claims that there is only so much television one can watch, and she refuses to keep it on all the time. I wish I had more patients that felt that way. The faster they're up and moving, the faster they can leave." She sipped her drink. "Why are you asking about Mrs. Demer's reading habits?"

Did she really not understand what she was doing? Was it so ingrained in her to follow through with what made others happy that she didn't recognize what her decisions meant?

"I am not questioning Mrs. Demer's reading choices. I am questioning yours."

"Mine."

"Yours." Luca lifted the coffee to his lips. "What does my love enjoy reading?"

"Are you looking for a book to get me?" She tapped his shoulders, but there was color rising in her cheeks. This struck an uncomfortable nerve.

Which meant he was on the right path.

"Come on, Wren, you've spent more time in libraries than anyone I know. What section is your favorite? What is your favorite genre? What authors do you have to read the second their books are released?"

"I don't know." The words slipped from her perfect lips, and her eyes widened. "I mean, of course I know. I love books."

He didn't doubt that. Luca also knew she looked for ways to please others. She'd claimed she'd chosen San Diego. But also mentioned that Dr. Link's family was fully settled in New York. Wren would never have made the choice to make her colleague leave the city. So she was here. And he was grateful for it.

But it wasn't a true choice.

She took a deep breath. "I don't know what my favorite is. What I know is that I love books, and I love you."

Words he'd ached to hear drop from her tongue. Words his heart broke to hear right now. But it felt like she was shifting the subject. And giving another person what they wanted instead of answering what she needed.

"Wren."

Therese walked in, a patient walking with a cane beside her. A very proud patient.

Wren looked at Luca, but all his words were stuck. Why had she said it? Did she really mean it?

"Enjoy the coffee." Wren held hers up and waved at Therese as she headed out.

Luca gave a thumbs-up to the patient, but his eyes darted back to the door. He'd missed so many red flags with Madeline. What if he was overlooking a few now?

No. That couldn't be true.

So why couldn't he stop the panic settling in his stomach? Why was it so hard for her to identify what she liked for herself?

And is she saying I love you because it's what I want to hear?

There was no way to ignore the somersaults Wren's stomach kept doing as she stood in her apartment. The executive freeze was dropping—again. She was mentally pushing it back, but it was going to fail.

It always failed.

She'd told Luca she loved him. It was true. She did. But the declaration seemed so anticlimactic. No grand gesture. No giant meaning. In the moment, her brain and heart just had to have it in the world. The conversation on books was ridiculous. And sweet. And so Luca, trying to guide her to an answer about herself.

The words she'd feared releasing flowed so seamlessly into the conversation.

And he didn't look thrilled.

Nope. He'd had the same look on his face that he'd had at Therese and Seth's apartment. The same look when pottery hadn't held any appeal for her. Disappointment.

She'd seen it in so many faces over the course of her life. The teens mad that the kid who belonged in elementary school was killing the curve in honors high school classes. The overachievers in college frustrated that she was stealing the attention because of her genius. The med school colleagues that didn't know what to do with her.

And her parents when she refused to do what they wanted and go into neurology, even after she'd done everything else asked of her. Followed their path so closely. It wasn't like she'd dropped out of med school.

She smiled and went along with what people wanted. And it was never enough. Never.

Now it was Luca. Looking at her, his jeweled gaze filled with disappointment.

He's trying to fix me.
He hasn't said that.
Does he need to?
Wren!

The mental screams seemed to echo through the apartment as she wrapped her arms around herself. He knew she didn't care about his money. It seemed to free him, which was good. But…

Now he's using it to give me experiences I missed. Poor little genius!

Her brain hammered away, chipping at her heart.

A knock at the door. Luca.

She swallowed and turned. He'd come in. He had a key. She wanted him here.

And I want him gone.

Why would her brain not shut the hell up?

"Hey. I've got news." Luca held up a bottle of wine. The same bottle she'd opened the night they had their fight.

Why was it the same bottle?

He walked over, kissed her cheek. No words of love. No discussion of the announcement she'd made this afternoon. Was that a good thing?

No.

But he has wine.

Luca grabbed two wineglasses and got the bottle opener from her top drawer.

"Why do you have the wine I had in my refrigerator?" It was a coincidence. It was. Please.

Luca grinned as he poured two glasses and passed her one. The wine was chilled. So whatever this was, was planned. "I know you followed your parents' ideas. Med school instead of marine biology."

This again? She liked sea horses. Enjoyed reading about the ocean. The depths of it were still fully unexplored. "I was sixteen, Luca. Yes, marine biology was interesting, but I followed my own path. I have the student loans to prove it."

Would she have ended up a marine biologist if Ronan hadn't passed? Maybe. But it was just as likely that she'd have found her way to plastics. He'd pushed back on her parents, but it hardly ever worked. She wasn't sure she'd have had the strength to walk away completely.

"Sixteen." Luca chuckled. "At sixteen I was learning to drive and spending as much time away from home as possible. I was sneaking into movies with friends and going to school dances, and you were in med school."

She shrugged and looked at the wineglass. "Life of a genius."

"That is the first time I've heard you call yourself that." Luca took a step toward her.

The tag defined her. She didn't want it, but that didn't mean it wasn't true.

"Why the wine?" She took a deep breath. "Did a patient graduate physical therapy that I am not tracking?"

"The wine is for you."

She raised a brow as her stomach dived. She hadn't accomplished anything. Not recently at least. "For me?" What on earth did that mean?

"You are wrong." Luca raised his glass. "You don't have the student loans to show for med school. You are free. And I found the right bottle to celebrate. This is the one, right?"

"You paid off my student loans?" The words were barely a whisper.

"I did." He was so happy.

And she couldn't match the energy. Not yet. "Why?"

Everything hung on this answer. The world stopped as she looked from his raised glass to the subtle frown settling into his features.

"Why?" Luca shook his head. "What do you mean why?"

"I mean why did you pay them off?" *Because you love me. Say because you love me. Let that be the reason. Not because of how I was raised or what I missed or didn't get.*

Because I love you.

She tried to will those words to come from his lips. Just those words.

"You didn't get to decide what to do. You followed your parents' outlined path." Luca set his glass down.

She hadn't, though. Not completely. Why couldn't he see that?

"Wren, you're free to do—"

She held up her hand. "No. No. No." She set her glass next to his. "No."

An uncomfortable laugh erupted from her throat. This was not happening. She'd told him she loved him this afternoon. Unceremoniously but still. That should be what they were talking about. Instead, he was wiping away hundreds of thousands of dollars of medical school debt without even talking to her.

"How did you even get the information?"

His cheeks colored. "Made a few calls. That isn't what's important right now."

"I disagree."

Luca took a step toward her, "Wren, that debt is keeping you from going back to school."

Back to school? She blinked as the words she'd planned to say evaporated from her mind. "Luca."

"It is not off the table now. It is squarely on the table." He lifted his glass. "To new beginnings."

"I told you, I don't need protecting. I don't need to be fixed. I didn't ask you to pay off my student loans."

He'd lost his mind just two weeks ago about money and people demanding it from him. Now—without asking her—he'd wiped away over two hundred thousand dollars' worth of debt.

"I am not protecting you. I am not fixing things. I mean, I am, but damn it, Wren, you've earned it."

"Why?" It felt like that word was constantly on her lips right now. "Because the poor little genius didn't get the perfect childhood? Please. You didn't get it, either. Far too many kids don't get it."

"You didn't get to find yourself." The words were out, and he snapped his lips together.

"You think I don't know myself." Wren wrapped her arms around herself. "I love you, Luca."

"Are you sure? Or are you just trying to make me happy?" He set the wineglass down. No toasts were happening tonight. "Because you are so sunny, so bright, but how much of it is what you want and how much is you pleasing everyone around you without asking for what you need? You aren't a ray of sunshine. You're a woman who marches past her pain to help others. Which is fine—if you acknowledge it. But you are burying it."

That arrow landed a direct hit.

"You used your money to push people away. And now you're using it to try to make me happy. What makes you happy, Luca? What brings joy to your life? Because you are hiding behind the wealth someone left you. Using it as an excuse to avoid people."

He flinched as her words found their mark.

"And you are hiding behind the title genius." Another direct shot. "You expect everyone to look at you that way, and you hold yourself apart."

Their last fight was loud. The people across her hall had checked on her after. This one was nearly silent. Two adults pointing out the pain they'd seen in the other but not reaching for them.

"I don't need to be fixed. And I will pay you back the loan." She hadn't wanted his money. She'd made that clear. If only he'd paid it off just because he loved her.

"Wren."

"Goodbye, Luca."

He didn't argue. Didn't hesitate to walk around her. Didn't say anything else on his march out the door.

When it was closed, she let the first tear fall.

CHAPTER SEVENTEEN

"You scowl any deeper, and even the patients won't be able to pretend to ignore it, McSteamy." Therese didn't laugh as she said the words. Some of the first she'd said to him all day.

Luca shrugged and walked over to the computer to look at the notes for his next patient.

"So we are back to the no-word responses. Wow." Therese crossed her arms.

Luca pulled up the chart but didn't feel like engaging with any of this. Not today. Three days since he'd walked out of Wren's apartment. Two days since he'd found a box of his clothes by his door. He hadn't packed her stuff yet.

And she hasn't asked. He swallowed the lump in his throat.

"She get tired of you playing master of ceremony for her life?"

"Excuse me." Luca looked at her. "What the hell is that supposed to mean?"

Therese raised her chin as she met his gaze. "You asked if she was happy."

"And you told me that you didn't know." Luca's voice was too loud. He took a deep breath. "Sorry." He turned back to the computer.

"It is not my job to know." Therese took another step toward him. "But it is yours."

"Was." Luca keyed in a few notes and pulled up Eddie's

chart. The man had therapy in an hour. There were notes from Wren. Short. To the point.

The kind of notes doctors routinely left. But not Wren. She'd always expanded. Given hints on the patients' day. Any knowledge she'd learned that might help motivate them for physical therapy.

"Luca, I am not going to push this, but…" Therese ran her hand over the ever-growing baby bump. "But when we found out that Seth was the baby's father…" she let out a deep breath "… I expected a reaction from him. I didn't give him time to accept the giant life change. I put my expectations on him. It wasn't fair." She waited for a moment, but what was he to say to that? "It nearly cost us everything." Therese stood there for a second, then turned and walked away.

Luca stared at Eddie's notes for another moment. So short. No extras. Nothing that had come to define Wren.

I wasn't playing master of ceremony.

Except he had.

He bit the inside of his cheek. Therese was right. He'd seen a lack, and rather than have a discussion about it, talk with Wren about her wants, he'd just started planning.

Because she didn't tell me what she wanted.

Why would she?

That truth hit him squarely in the chest. He'd made a huge show of not telling anyone about his money. Then flipped the switch when she didn't care about it. Trying desperately to earn what he feared wasn't freely given.

Hell, he'd planned to step away as soon as she decided she was done. Planned to be an adventure she enjoyed and then step back so she could do whatever she wanted. She'd said goodbye, and he'd followed the plan to a T.

Luca pulled at the back of his neck.

"Hey, doc." Eddie's voice hit his back. "I am not really in the mood for stairs today. In a funk."

Funks happened. And since Luca was in the deep depths of one, he could hardly fault Eddie for this one.

Pushing his own emotions away, Luca offered what he hoped was a convincing smile. "Why are you in a funk?" He waved to the porter as Eddie stood and moved to the sitting bicycle that Luca pointed to.

"Beth stopped by." Eddie sat down. "Said she was sorry."

Luca crossed his arms as he gestured for Eddie to start the bike. Madeline had never apologized. It probably never crossed her mind. He wasn't sure what he would have done had his ex-fiancée tried to walk back into his life.

"I think she expected me to be happy she came back." Eddie shifted on the seat and started pedaling. "If you and Dr. Freson hadn't talked with me over the last month, I might have been. But…"

Luca didn't interrupt. He'd heard a lot in this room. People told physical therapists all sorts of things. Some because they wanted to pass the time, some because it took their mind off the hard work, and some because they were talking to a person they knew wouldn't tell anyone.

It took a moment, but Eddie continued, "But I realize I spent all of our relationship trying to make myself worthy of her." Eddie laughed, no happiness behind it. "Which might be fine, if she didn't expect it?"

"What do you mean?" The question slipped out.

"She expected it. I wasn't good enough for her, I never would have been. But if she didn't expect it, if I was pushing myself to be worthy of her because I was worried that I wasn't good enough, it might have been all right. I think."

"No." Luca pushed the word out. "No. That wouldn't work, either. You have to know you're good enough on your own." The words were for Eddie but mostly for himself.

He'd spent his childhood trying to be enough for his parents. Only when Maude's inheritance come through had they wanted him. Then he'd used the inheritance as an excuse to hide away after Madeline's betrayal. If he didn't give anyone a chance, they'd never realize he wasn't worth it.

Wren loved him. And rather than accept the words, he'd wondered if she was saying them to make him happy.

If she'd planned to do that, she'd have said it the moment he said it to her. Instead, she'd offered the words in a moment when she felt them.

He'd paid off her loans, granting her a freedom she'd never asked for. His soul clenched. He'd stopped by with wine. With an expectation that she'd be happy—and that he'd been worthy of her in that moment.

No one ever saw him for himself…because he didn't give them the option to.

He looked at the clock. Six hours left on this shift. Six hours until he could find her. Apologize, tell her he loved her and ask to walk beside her. Not as a master of ceremony giving her whatever he felt she missed out on. But as a partner who loved the other.

Six hours.

A lifetime away.

Wren stared at the dress in the closet. The mermaid gown she'd planned to wear to the ball. The ball taking place tomorrow night. She should be planning her hair and makeup for the evening she'd looked forward to for months.

Instead she was fingering the delicate beading. She loved the dress. Not because it was aquarium themed, though that was a nice touch. She felt perfect in it. And the second it was on, all she could think was about how Luca would love it.

And she wasn't going to get to wear it because she got mad her insanely wealthy boyfriend paid off her student loans.

Wren turned away from the dress. Maybe she should see

if the consignment shop would take it back. Surely it would sell again. But she didn't want to give it up.

She looked at the stack of books on her nightstand. Three thrillers she'd promised to talk to Mrs. Demer about and another book on the Tudor dynasty. None of which held any interest for her.

Wren crossed her arms as she looked at the books. The titles screaming at her.

Who was her favorite author?

Her favorite genre?

She pulled up the app she used to track the books she read, even though Wren knew what she was going to find. A list of books she'd read to talk to others about. Even the digital shelves she'd created were named after patients or colleagues. It was like she'd gotten out of school and continued studying. Except instead of coursework, it was books to please her patients.

"What do I like?"

This was not a hard question. Wren put her phone in her pocket and bit her lip. Luca was right. She hated the title genius. Never used it, but it was her identity. The thing that kept her separate.

Because she let it.

Luca should have talked to her. But he was right, she put others first—always. Even in her reading preferences.

She knew what she wanted. Who she wanted.

She needed to make a quick stop, then she needed to see Luca.

Wren held the books to her chest. Once she'd walked in the stacks for herself, the answer had become so obvious. She had six in her arms right now.

Stepping out of the elevator, she took a deep breath as she turned to look at his door at the end of the hall.

Take the first step, Wren.

She was meant to be in San Diego. Meant to be a plastic surgeon. Meant to help people. But there were things she'd missed. Experiences she wanted.

And she wanted them with Luca. She just had to hope he still wanted them with her. She started toward his place—only one way to find out.

The door to his apartment opened as she was halfway there, and Luca stepped out.

"Are you going someplace?" She had a plan. Sort of.

"No." Luca put his hands in his pockets and nodded toward the door. "Hippo started his tippy-tap dance. He only does that when you're on the floor."

Now or never.

"Fantasy." She stated the genre as she stepped up to him.

"What?"

"Fantasy. Epic fantasy. High fantasy. Urban fantasy. Romantasy. Low fantasy."

"What is low fantasy?"

"A story that takes place in the normal world with a few fantasy elements." She grinned and pulled a book from the bottom of her stack. "Like this one."

Luca smiled. "And the reason you have five fantasy books in your arms right now?"

"Six. I have six fantasy books in my arms right now." She pursed her lips. The conversation had already gone off the path she'd meant for it.

"Sorry, six."

"Not important. You were right, I put others first to a fault. And I did miss out on things. A lot of things. But I know myself. I am Dr. Wren Freson. A plastic surgeon who cocreated a radical new procedure that changed the treatment for burn patients. I love animated movies and fantasy novels. And I love you." There were tears coating her eyes.

"Wren."

Why had she thought it was a good idea to bring so many books? She could have made the point with one or two and easily thrown her arms around him. Instead, the stack was clumsily in her hands right now.

"I should have talked to you about what you wanted," he began. "You were right, not that I was trying to fix you, but that I hide behind my wealth. First using it to keep people away and then trying to use it to make all your dreams come true, so I was worthy of you."

"Worthy?"

Luca held up a hand. "I spent my childhood, like you, trying to prove myself. I tried everything to earn my parents' love. Madeline's. I never felt good enough. Then I fell in love with you. You are kind, intelligent, quick-witted and able to eat way more popcorn than anyone I know."

"Hey!" She sniffed as a happy tear slipped down her cheek.

"All true." He closed the small distance between them, taking the books out her hands. "I want to give you everything, Wren. Not because you missed out, though I will never forgive your parents for that, but because I love you."

"I love you, too."

EPILOGUE

"I like that dress, Dr. Freson-McDonnell." Luca ran his hand over her back, kissing the top of her exposed shoulder.

Wren brushed her lips against his. She'd never get tired of hearing him call her Dr. Freson-McDonnell. "It's the same dress I wore last year." The mermaid dress was quite the statement piece.

"I know." Luca's hand traced her bare back. "I remember what happened after this event last year. I am still as excited by it as I was then. If I recall, we left the Aquarium Patron Banquet early last time."

Wren leaned her head against his shoulder. "This time we can't. We have to wait until Lena's masterpiece is revealed."

Luca shook his head. "I still think that piece looks best in our living room."

Wren hit her hip against his. "It is only on loan here for a year."

"This is so exciting." Therese walked up, Seth right behind her, head bent over his phone.

"It is." Wren looked at Seth. "He all right?"

"It's our first date night away from the baby. The sitters—"

"Are not answering their texts." Seth let out a tiny huff.

Therese playfully rolled her eyes. "I was going to say the sitters are probably enjoying playing grandma and grandpa."

Luca pressed his lips to the top of Wren's head, but she could feel the laughter he was trying very hard to hide.

"Seth is a wonderful dad." Wren didn't hold in her giggle as she watched Seth send another text to his in-laws.

Therese's gaze shifted as she starred at her husband. "Yes. He is."

"Oh!" Luca pointed to the stage. "I think it's showtime."

Lena's gaze was searching the crowd, and when it settled on them, she seemed to let out a sigh.

What a difference a year made.

Wren looked at her husband, then at Seth and Therese. From all alone, to a family of her own creating. She couldn't imagine finding a better life path.

* * * * *

If you missed the previous story in the San Diego Surgeons duet, then check out Expecting Her Best Friend's Baby *by Tina Beckett*

And if you enjoyed this story, check out these other great reads from Juliette Hyland

Fake Dating the Vet
One-Night Baby with Her Best Friend
Dating His Irresistible Rival

All available now!

MILLS & BOON®

Coming next month

SINGLE DAD'S CHRISTMAS WISH
Alison Roberts

'I want to buy new decorations for the house this year. I'm thinking of doing it online and having them delivered but I might need a bit of help choosing them.'

That glow that had been missing from Eva's face today had already returned – probably during that ride on the carousel. But it had just gone up a notch or two and she looked genuinely joyous, her eyes shining and her lips curving into the happiest smile ever.

'I can help.' Her words were an excited whisper. 'I *love* Christmas.'

Noa was smiling back at her, watching as she caught her bottom lip between her teeth. As if he didn't know that already.

And then it happened.

He was caught.

He couldn't look away from Eva's mouth. He didn't dare raise his gaze to her eyes because he might see what he'd thought he'd seen in the on-call room the other day – that she might be seeing him as something other than a colleague or the parent of one of her patients.

That she might have been aware of what he'd been thinking. Or rather, feeling. That *attraction*.

The desire to touch her. To hold Eva in his arms. To *kiss* her…

Continue reading

SINGLE DAD'S CHRISTMAS WISH
Alison Roberts

Available next month
millsandboon.co.uk

Copyright © 2025 Alison Roberts

COMING SOON!

We really hope you enjoyed reading this book.
If you're looking for more romance
be sure to head to the shops when
new books are available on

Thursday 23rd October

To see which titles are coming soon, please visit
millsandboon.co.uk/nextmonth

MILLS & BOON

MILLS & BOON TRUE LOVE IS HAVING A MAKEOVER!

Introducing

Love Always

Swoon-worthy romances, where love takes centre stage. Same heartwarming stories, stylish new look!

Look out for our brand new look

OUT NOW

MILLS & BOON

FOUR BRAND NEW BOOKS FROM
MILLS & BOON MODERN

Indulge in desire, drama, and breathtaking romance – where passion knows no bounds!

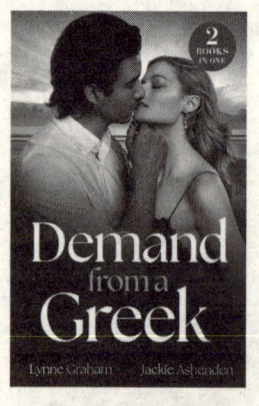

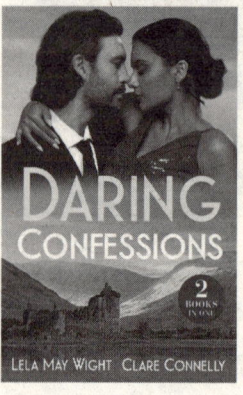

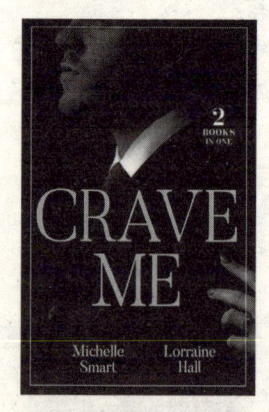

Demand from a Greek — Lynne Graham & Jackie Ashenden

Crave Me — Michelle Smart & Lorraine Hall

Daring Confessions — Lela May Wight & Clare Connelly

With his Ring... — Lucy King & Millie Adams

OUT NOW

Eight Modern stories published every month, find them all at:

millsandboon.co.uk

OUT NOW!

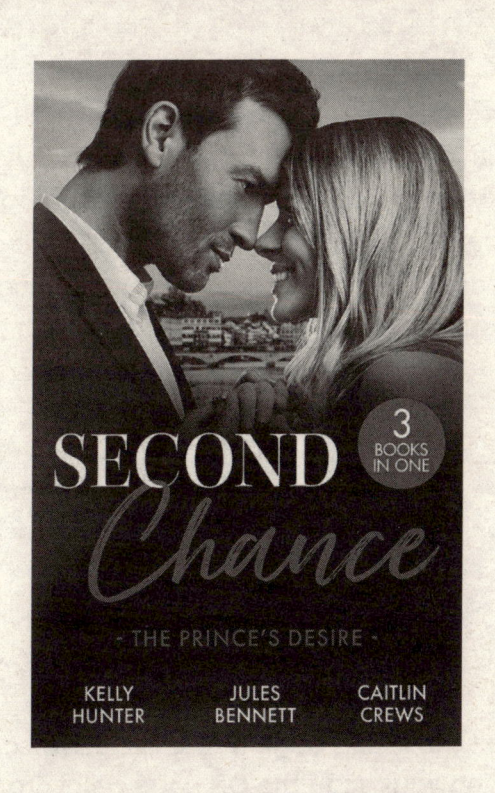

Second Chance

- THE PRINCE'S DESIRE -

KELLY HUNTER · JULES BENNETT · CAITLIN CREWS

3 BOOKS IN ONE

Available at
millsandboon.co.uk

MILLS & BOON

afterglow BOOKS

Afterglow Books is a trend-led, trope-filled list of books with diverse, authentic and relatable characters, a wide array of voices and representations, plus real world trials and tribulations. Featuring all the tropes you could possibly want (think small-town settings, fake relationships, grumpy vs sunshine, enemies to lovers) and all with a generous dose of spice in every story.

@millsandboonuk
@millsandboonuk
afterglowbooks.co.uk
#AfterglowBooks

For all the latest book news, exclusive content and giveaways scan the QR code below to sign up to the Afterglow newsletter:

SCAN ME

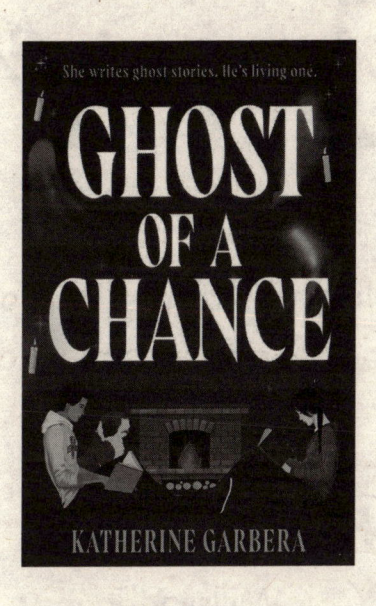

afterglow BOOKS

GHOST OF A CHANCE

She writes ghost stories. He's living one.

KATHERINE GARBERA

- 🛏 One night
- 💕 Second chance
- 🎭 Secret identity

OUT NOW

To discover more visit:
Afterglowbooks.co.uk

LET'S TALK
Romance

For exclusive extracts, competitions and special offers, find us online:

- **f** MillsandBoon
- **X** @MillsandBoon
- **O** @MillsandBoonUK
- **d** @MillsandBoonUK

Get in touch on 01413 063 232

For all the latest titles coming soon, visit millsandboon.co.uk/nextmonth